CW00816393

THE SOLDIER

THE PREACHER SERIES
BOOK 3

NATHAN BURROWS

First printing, 2023.

Nathan Burrows
Unit 130535
PO Box 6945
London W1A 6US

www.nathanburrows.com

CHAPTER 1

Caleb watched through half-closed eyes as fluorescent lights on the ceiling flashed past him. He was flat on his back, both arms clutching his abdomen where white-hot jolts of pain shot through him every time the gurney he was lying on went over a bump in the rough floor. His head lolled to one side and he saw the concerned face of one of the people pushing the gurney. It was a woman, her face half covered by a hospital mask. If it weren't for the concern in her eyes, they would have been beautiful. The woman said something, but Caleb couldn't understand what she said.

There was another jolt as the gurney was pushed against a door. Caleb bit down on his lip to stop a cry escaping, but all this did was turn it into a moan. He sensed the air changing, and tried to look around. All he could see were green canvas walls. They were moving as if they were being buffeted by the wind outside and the fluorescent tubes strung from the ceiling rocked in tandem. Caleb managed to raise his head a couple of inches to see an operating table a few feet away from him. It had two extensions on either side. The woman said something else, but again, Caleb couldn't understand.

A few seconds later, he felt a strong pair of hands in his armpits, followed by another pair around his ankles.

"*Azim,*" a male voice said. "*Dwa. Tree.*" As the voice said *Tree*, Caleb felt himself being lifted onto the operating table as a fresh wave of pain swept through his midriff. Another pair of hands, feminine from the feel of them, took one of his wrists and gently pulled it away from his abdomen. Caleb was naked, the material of the table cool against his skin. He heard a woman's voice shushing him, trying to reassure him as his arm was strapped to one of the extensions. A moment after that, his other arm was similarly secured. Caleb closed his eyes against the pain in his abdomen. A bizarre thought came into his head of executions back in his home state of Texas.

Two men spoke to each other, the language they were speaking full of consonants and unfamiliar sounds. Caleb couldn't even differentiate the individual words, but every few seconds he heard something that sounded familiar. As he felt the sharp prick of a needle in his arm, he realized the two men were listing pharmaceuticals. Anesthetic drugs. Would they make the pain go away? Caleb sure hoped so. He'd been injured before, but never like this.

Caleb raised his head again to try to see what was going on. At the foot of the operating table was a stocky man, his arms almost too large for the surgical scrubs he was wearing. The man lifted one of Caleb's legs, causing him to cry out.

"Please," Caleb said, feeling a tear pricking at the corner of his eye. "Please, stop." The man paused before lifting his leg a couple of inches further. Then a woman started wrapping some sort of felt material around his legs. There was another scratch, this one in his other arm, and Caleb saw a bottle of intravenous fluids being raised. A hand reached up to open the valve, letting the fluid rush into Caleb's body. Caleb closed his eyes as he saw a syringe being prepared from the corner of his eye and listened to the unfamiliar language the medical team was speaking. Although he couldn't understand the words, the urgency in the way they spoke was obvious.

The voices faded away as Caleb felt a breeze across his face. He opened his eyes to see a man standing in front of him. Like the others, he was wearing green scrubs a few shades lighter than the canvas walls of the operating theatre. A matching cloth cap covered his hair, and half of his face was obscured by a surgical mask.

"English?" the new arrival said, his voice heavily accented.

"American," Caleb replied. His mouth was as dry as Texas sand and he struggled to get the word out.

"But you speak English, yes?" Caleb just nodded in reply. "I am Vitali, the head surgeon. You have pain?" Caleb nodded his head again and the man barked something in his mother tongue. A few seconds later, Caleb could see one of the medics preparing another syringe. Some sort of Velcro strap was being wrapped around his thigh and the female member of the team covered his dignity with a towel. Caleb felt for the medical team having to deal with him. He hadn't washed in days. It might even have been weeks. He couldn't remember.

Caleb felt a hand resting on his forearm and looked to see the contents of the syringe being pushed through the cannula in his arm. A few seconds later, a warm feeling started to spread through his body.

"Morphine," Vitali said. "You will be asleep soon. No more pain."

Vitali said something to the rest of the team and they all fell silent. When they started speaking again, it was in unison and Caleb realized they were reciting something. He waited until they had finished before speaking again.

"What were you saying?" he asked Vitali as one of the team approached with a black rubber mask in his hand.

"We were praying for you," Vitali replied as the mask came toward Caleb's face. "Praying for your soul."

CHAPTER 2

THREE WEEKS EARLIER

Natasha leaned her head against the glass of the train window, gazing at the somber looking buildings that were flashing past outside. She glanced at her watch. Only a few minutes to go, and they would be in the center of London.

The train she was sitting in was much more modern than the trains in her native Belarus. It was comfortable, fast, and clean. There were wide windows, not obscured by graffiti. Like the windows, the seats were also wide and comfortable, although every one in Natasha's carriage was full. Several seats had more than one occupant as mothers nestled their children on their laps. There was a constant human noise in the carriage as people snored, took part in muted conversations, or children cried,

The train was also very unlikely to be blown off the tracks by an artillery shell or strafed by an aircraft. Natasha thought back over the previous twenty-four hours since she had left her home and most of her family behind. She knew she had been lucky to get a ticket so fast. The ballot that allocated them was supposed to be tightly controlled, but she knew that many of the other women on the train had paid someone for their tickets to get away from the war that was raging across the country. Even if she'd had the money to buy a ticket, she would not have known who to approach. Natasha had tried, and failed, to exchange her ballot ticket so that her son could escape in her place, but hadn't been able to.

Above her head, a loudspeaker crackled to life. A female voice spoke in English. Natasha listened carefully, keen to understand the message even if she couldn't recognize every word.

"Ladies, gentlemen. We are now approaching King's Cross Station in central London. On behalf of all the staff at Eurostar, welcome to England." A smile crept across Natasha's face as the message was repeated by another female voice, this time speaking Russian. As soon as she finished speaking, a ragged cheer went up through the train. It was high-pitched which, given that all the passengers were either female or children, was no surprise.

Around her, people started getting to their feet to gather their belongings. All Natasha had was a single small suitcase, hurriedly packed the previous evening under the tearful gaze of her fourteen year old son, Mikhail.

"I'll see you in London," Natasha had said, trying to keep her voice light so Mikhail couldn't see how upset she was. But she knew she hadn't fooled him for a second. "As soon as you get your ticket."

The government in Belarus, or what was left of it, was trying to evacuate as many people as possible from the war-torn country. All along the country's western flank, thousands and thousands of refugees were waiting for their names to come up in the ballot. Natasha's journey had started in her home town of Hrodna, not far from the Polish border in the West. Under cover of darkness, a bus had taken her to the border with Lithuania in the North. It was one of a line of them, every one full of terrified people waiting to see if their bus was going to be attacked on the way. It had happened before, and would no doubt happen again.

The most stressful part of the journey had been at the border, where grim-faced men in uniform had examined every passport and ballot ticket to ensure that only those who were entitled were able to leave the country. When they had finally crossed the heavily-guarded border into Lithuania, a cheer like the one that had just followed the announcement on the train had sounded. They were safe.

Natasha looked out of the window again at the buildings, worrying at her wedding ring. She had spun it round so many times in the last few hours there was a red welt underneath the gold metal. When the Eurostar train had emerged from the Channel Tunnel, it had been into rolling green countryside. Natasha had pressed her face to the glass, keen to see the country where her mother had grown up. But as the green countryside gradually gave way to buildings, the gray uniformity of them reminded her of the country she had left behind. Even the graffiti that lined the railway looked the same.

A few moments later, the drab buildings disappeared as the train entered a tunnel. It slowed down as around her, the excitement of the other passengers started to increase. There was another, muted, cheer as the train stopped and a few people started clapping. On the platform outside, Natasha could see several people in orange bibs waiting for them.

Natasha pulled her coat around her, trying to ignore her racing heartbeat. She took a deep breath in through her nose before exhaling through her mouth. She was safe. Soon, Mikhail would be safe as well.

She took another deep breath, trying to fight the rising panic. She'd come so far, been through so much. So why was she starting to panic now?

CHAPTER 3

Caleb put his hands on the railing and leaned forward to look down at the seething mass of people on the concourse below. He'd found an ideal spot on a raised balustrade to watch the activity beneath him. He was looking at the Eurostar arrivals hall, part of King's Cross Station in central London, where an area had been roped off for the arrival of this particular train.

Below him, within the cordoned off area, were several hundred people, almost all of them women, some with children. They were milling about, some of them looking for people, some of them just taking in their surroundings. As he watched, several families were reunited. Some of them screamed in joy when they saw their loved ones. Most of them just cried. Amongst the crowd were people wearing orange bibs, most of them clutching clipboards. Some of the logos on the back, Caleb recognized. The Red Cross's emblem was instantly recognizable. Other bibs carried just letters, most of which Caleb didn't understand. UNHCR.

FCDO. MSF. DFID. A veritable alphabet soup of humanitarian organizations.

Not everyone appeared to be meeting someone. Caleb saw one of the orange-bibbed people belonging to the Red Cross, a lady with a shock of gray hair, approaching a young woman who was looking lost. The gray-haired woman checked her clipboard, shuffling through several sheets of paper. Then she said something to the new arrival and the two of them made their way through the crowd to a desk where a man in a similar outfit greeted them.

Caleb spent a few moments surveying the crowd below him. He had heard about the train's arrival from a waitress in a small cafe he'd had a coffee in just round the corner and thought he would come and watch the refugees arriving. He looked around the impressive building which was a collision of the old and the new. The station's original red brick building, built in the mid-nineteenth century according to a plaque he had read as he entered the station, contrasted against the vast glass modern roof that covered the concourse. Caleb closed his eyes to soak up the atmosphere in the building. It was one of excitement, but just underneath the excitement he could sense something far darker. Fear. Naked fear.

Along with everyone else in Europe, Caleb had been watching the events unfolding in Belarus over the last few months with concern. What had started out as protests against the government's involvement in the Russian invasion of Ukraine some months earlier had rapidly deteriorated. First the police cracked down on the protests, which only served to fuel them. Scenes of rioters, tear gas, and burning vehicles in the streets had become an almost nightly event. Then the military had been brought in to restore law and order. The first thing they did was impose a curfew. The next thing they did was start shooting people who broke it.

What happened after that took the world by surprise. Within weeks, a massive uprising took place in the country. Far from cowering to the military, the local population rose up as if they were an army themselves. The government appealed to its neighbor to the east who didn't send troops. They sent mercenaries. Being Russians, not Belarusians, the local population saw them as legitimate targets and a vicious game of tit for tat had ensued with deadly consequences.

Caleb had watched some horrendous footage on the television which reminded him of the black and white imagery from the second world war. The government closed its borders to all men of fighting age, on the basis that they would almost certainly be part of the revolution. There was footage of terrified young men being herded into trucks, their destination and fate unknown to all but the heavily armed mercenaries. Caleb had prayed for the civilian population. The world had prayed for them, or at least those who partook in that particular activity. But God didn't seem to be listening.

Moving his eyes slowly, Caleb looked at the perimeter of the crowd below. There were a few police officers dotted about, quite a few people who from their equipment had to be from the press, and others like him who appeared to be just watching. But not everyone who was watching was there to help. Caleb could see a small group of men, in their early twenties perhaps, who were deep in conversation just beyond the perimeter of the crowd. Caleb watched them closely, studying their body language. If the crowd was prey, here were the predators.

Caleb saw a woman standing alone towards the edge of

the crowd. She was perhaps in her late twenties or early thirties and had one hand pressed to her sternum. He saw her taking a deep breath as he had just done, then another, and another. She was standing next to a small suitcase and wearing a long brown coat, her long black hair cascading over her shoulders. As Caleb watched, he saw her take a few faltering steps toward the perimeter of the crowd. His gaze flicked to the group of young men he had seen a few seconds before. They were also watching the woman, their heads down to make it less obvious. Moving slowly, they started walking in the same direction as she was.

Caleb eased himself away from the railing and straightened the cloth bag he had slung across his chest. He adjusted the shoulder of the gray robe he was wearing, and made his way toward a staircase that led down to the concourse. As he walked down the stairs, he murmured under his breath, earning him some curious looks which he ignored. Caleb was used to curious looks, and he paid them no mind.

There were more important things on his mind.

CHAPTER 4

Stepan looked at the three men in front of him. All of them were kneeling, facing away from him and toward a shallow trench they had just dug. Their hands were in the air and the shovels they had used to dig lay discarded by the trench. He could tell from the way their shoulders were shaking that two of them were crying. The third man was not, but was staring in front of him as if he was resigned to his fate.

The men disgusted Stepan. They were traitors to their country and therefore, although Belarus and Russia shared a difficult history, traitors to Russia herself. His namesake, the Soviet commander of the 1st Battalion in the Second World War who had fought to free the country from the grip of the Nazis, would be turning in his grave.

"Who are you?" one of the men said, his voice breaking as he spoke. Stepan glanced at the man with him who was holding a Kalashnikov AK-74 trained on the three men, and nodded for him to respond. Both of them were wearing black uniforms with no ranks or insignia.

"We are the People's Army," Stepan said, his voice graveled. "We are Belarus."

"But you are not Belarusian," the kneeling man replied. "Why are you doing this?" As he spoke, his voice seemed to gain confidence and he half turned his head to look at the man holding the gun on him. The man's response was to jab him between the shoulders with the weapon.

"You renounced your citizenship when you rose up against the country," Stepan said. "You are nothing more than traitors."

Stepan looked over at the village around a hundred yards away from their wooded location. It was a small one, perhaps only five or six houses. Only one had been occupied when he and the rest of his squad had arrived. Its occupants were the men kneeling in front of them. Brothers, perhaps. Stepan didn't know and didn't care.

The sound of a woman's scream echoed across the ground from the houses. Stepan grinned as the man in the center of the trio stiffened and he saw his colleague's grip on the wooden buttstock of the AK tighten in response. Another scream rang out, but it was cut short by a loud slap.

"She sounds like she's having fun," Stepan said. "Who is she?" he asked, directing his question at the man who had just moved, even though the man couldn't see Stepan's face. "Your wife?"

"My sister," the man replied, the tension in his voice obvious.

"I heard they're the same thing round these parts," Stepan replied, sharing a grin with the other soldier. "Is that right?"

The kneeling man said nothing. Stepan regarded him for a moment as the sound of male voices echoed across the forest from the houses. He could hear cheering, and at the sound, the man's fists clenched. The other soldier looked at Stepan and raised his eyebrows.

"Don't worry," Stepan said to the men kneeling in front of him. "We'll let her live. Someone has to fill in this hole."

Then he nodded at the other soldier.

CHAPTER 5

Mikhail looked up at the ancient clock on the wall of his classroom. The school day was almost done. At the front of the room, Mrs. Ananič, their math teacher, was trying to explain fractions to the class. She was a short woman, almost as wide as she was tall, and was widely derided by most of her pupils for her cantankerous nature. Mikhail, who along with most of the other members of his class, had little, if any interest in the subject she was trying to teach them, stifled a yawn behind his text book so his teacher wouldn't see.

"I'm so bored," he whispered to the boy sitting next to him. His classmate was called Felix, and was probably the closest thing to a best friend that Mikhail had. They lived a few streets from each other in Hrodna.

"Me too," Felix replied, his hand over his mouth. "Just imagine her naked."

"Imagine who naked?"

"Mrs. Ananič."

"Ugh, no, that's gross, Felix."

"Well, she's married," Mikhail's friend continued, "so at

least one man's seen her naked. Just imagine her naked and bent over. Maybe her husband's behind her, whipping her?" Felix started laughing and it was all Mikhail could do to not join in.

"What, with his white stick?"

Felix spluttered a short, sharp laugh through his fingers, causing Mrs Ananič to turn on the spot.

"Who is that?" she barked. "Who is laughing?" Seconds later, she was striding down the space between the desks with a furious expression on her face. Mikhail stared at the chalk board where an almost indecipherable formula was half finished, keeping his face as deadpan as he could. In contrast, he could see Felix's shoulders shaking out of the corner of his eye.

"Felix! Get to your feet!" Mrs. Ananič shouted, her voice shrill.

The rest of the class, no doubt pleased to have something more entertaining to watch than the lesson, turned to watch what happened next. Mikhail caught the eye of Alevtina, a girl he had been friends with for a long time. He winked slowly, causing her to blush and turn away, but he caught the smile on her face as she did so. Alevtina only lived a few houses away from him and they had played together on occasion as children. He had watched with fascination as she had turned from a child to a young woman, realizing that her transformation was also changing how he felt about her. Mikhail wasn't sure as he had no frame of reference for such things, but he thought that perhaps she might feel the same way about him. But with his father away fighting for his homeland somewhere in Belarus, he had no one to discuss this with. Not that Mikhail would be comfortable discussing it with his father anyway.

Maybe Mikhail should ask Alevtina if she wanted to go

to the end of term party with him. It was only a few months away, and marked the end of their school years. He had heard from older boys that many things happened at the party. Things that he could only imagine. There were many stories of sexual encounters, some of which he believed but most of which he didn't. Mikhail knew all about sex, and what was supposed to happen. Some of it he had learned in the classroom, but most of it he had learned on the internet. But he hoped it was different in real life. The women on the internet didn't always look as if they were enjoying it, and while he tried to not imagine Alevtina in that way, on occasion he couldn't help himself.

As Mrs. Ananič berated Felix for his laughter, Mikhail continued to study Alevtina, knowing that she wouldn't turn back to look at him for some moments. He looked at the way her fine brown hair was tied into a complicated-looking French braid that ran all the way down her back, secured with a small yellow and green ribbon at her waist. The hairstyle exposed the nape of her neck and he wondered what it would be like to touch the soft skin there. What would she do if he did? What would it be like to wrap his arms around her slim stomach and move his hands over her, up to her breasts or down to her thighs? To his embarrassment, he felt himself stirring and he forced himself to look away. The last thing he wanted was for anyone in the classroom to see him with a tent pole in his trousers.

Mrs. Ananič was building to a crescendo with Felix, and Mikhail knew that a detention was imminent for his friend. Their teacher had a way of building up to it that was instantly recognizable. He watched, the ache between his legs receding, as Mrs. Ananič paused for breath, closing her eyes as she did so. Mikhail suppressed the grin he could feel building. Mrs Ananič was about to open her eyes, point to Felix, and shout the word *detention* at the top of her voice.

But Mrs. Ananič never got the chance to shout the word. Just as she opened her eyes and started raising her hand, an ear-splitting shriek sounded from the speakers in the corridor. Mikhail and Felix had noticed them being installed a few weeks previously, but they had never heard them sound before. Along with the rest of the class, the two boys jumped at the sudden interruption.

None of them had ever heard an air raid siren before.

CHAPTER 6

The pressure from the tight band around Natasha's chest increased. She had a hand on her chest to try to quell the panic she could feel rising, but it wasn't having any effect. Neither were the deep breathing exercises she was doing. Underneath the band, it was if her heart was fluttering instead of beating.

Natasha had never been very good with crowds. Her anxiety had started at school when she was perhaps twelve or thirteen. There had been a school assembly that they had all been told to attend. Natasha couldn't remember the subject, but she remembered being led from the auditorium by a friend in the throes of what turned out to be a full-blown panic attack. She also remembered how she felt just before it began, which was exactly how she was feeling now.

Trying not to gasp for air, Natasha looked around the concourse. The noise levels had increased in the last few moments, and every scream of joy or shout of recognition was ear-piercing. She had to get some fresh air, away from the crowd. Although the concourse was light and airy, she needed proper fresh air and to be able to see the sky.

Her legs trembling, Natasha started to make her way toward what she thought was an exit on the other side of the concourse. As she walked, her pace increased along with her desperation. She was sure she was about to faint, which only served to compound the panic. It was a vicious cycle, although she had never actually passed out before. Her suitcase knocked into one or two of her fellow passengers, but Natasha didn't stop to apologize. Her focus was on getting away from the concourse and into the open air. Somewhere quiet where she could be alone to wait for her symptoms to pass.

As she approached the edge of the crowd, Natasha saw a small green box fixed to the wall. It had a graphic of a stick man running and an arrow pointing down, with the words *FIRE EXIT* next to the running figure. With a sigh of relief, Natasha forced her shaking legs to head for the sign.

A few yards from the sign were two police officers, one male, one female. They looked nothing like the Militsiya, or police, back in Belarus. The police officers she was looking at were wearing a much more civilian styled uniform than the combat fatigues Belarusian police wore, and were unarmed. Instead of a black beret, the male officer was wearing a tall, black hat that made him look much taller than he actually was. They were both wearing bright yellow jackets, festooned with various bits of equipment. Handcuffs. Retractable batons. Equipment pouches. The male officer was looking at Natasha with a curious expression. Then he nudged his colleague and nodded at Natasha. The female police officer took a couple of steps forward.

"Are you okay?" the officer said, in English. She looked sympathetic, an unusual trait for a police officer in Natasha's experience.

"I am fine," Natasha replied, speaking English to an

English person for the first time in her life. Although her father had been born in England, not far from London in a town called Reading, his family had moved back to Belarus when he was a teenager. The only part of his British childhood he had retained was the language, which he had subsequently insisted that all his children learn to speak. "I just need some fresh air." Natasha waved her arms at the crowd. "Too many people." The police officer nodded and took a step back, watching Natasha as she made her way toward the fire exit.

Natasha could feel the woman's eyes on her as she walked to the exit from the concourse. As she reached the opening that led outside, she turned and gave what she hoped was a reassuring wave at the police officers. Then she stepped out into the fresh air, taking a deep breath as she did so.

The air in the alleyway outside the station couldn't really be described as fresh, Natasha realized as she smelled the faint odor of trash. But it was a lot fresher than the cloying atmosphere inside the concourse. Natasha looked around her. She was in some sort of service alley with large, industrial dumpsters lining one side. Above them were metal fire escapes that served the tall buildings that formed either side of the alley and she saw blue sky above the buildings. It was a one way street, inclined toward a busy road where Natasha could see bright red London buses flashing past the entrance. From Natasha's perspective, the most important thing about the run down alley was that it was empty of people.

Natasha took a couple of steps toward the blind end of the alley, looking for somewhere to sit down and gather herself. Seeing an upturned crate a few yards away, she walked over to it and sat down gratefully, pulling her cell phone from her back pocket as she did so. There were a couple of text messages from her cell provider which she ignored. Natasha pulled up her messaging app and composed a message to her sister, Iĺja.

I've arrived. All good. Have you heard from Anton? How is Mikhail?

She watched as the gray tick turned to two gray ticks, then saw them both turn blue. A few seconds later, Iĺja replied.

Nothing from Anton, but that's to be expected. Mikhail's fine and at school. He misses you. We all miss you.

Natasha swallowed to limit the lump that Iĺja's words had caused. She was just in process of replying to her sister when Natasha heard a male voice. She looked up to see four men standing between her and the exit to the alleyway. They were young and insolent-looking, no different in their demeanor to the young men that hung around in groups back at home, looking for trouble and usually finding it. The one who had spoken was a yard in front of the others. He was perhaps in his late teens to early twenties, and wearing low-slung jeans and a hoodie, as were the others. A uniform of sorts.

"Nice phone," the man had said. She watched as he nodded toward her suitcase. "What's in the case?"

CHAPTER 7

Caleb slowed his pace as he reached the concourse. The woman he had been watching had been approached by a couple of police officers but, as he watched, she waved them away. He saw her disappear through an exit, and a few seconds later, the four men he was also tracking did the same, taking a more circuitous route that led them behind the police officers. Caleb picked up his pace.

When he reached the station exit, Caleb slowed down to take in his surroundings. He stopped just before the exit and peered around a wall. Through the exit was a service alleyway, littered with large trash cans. Caleb could smell the odor of trash, along with other, more subtle odors. Urine, both human and rat. A fainter musty smell of unwashed human habitation. But apart from the woman and the four men, the alley was empty. It was a good spot for an ambush, both armed and unarmed.

The woman was at the far end, sitting on an overturned crate, staring up at one of the four men who had followed her into the alley. She was effectively cornered. One of the men was standing close to her, another a yard behind him. The final two were closest to Caleb, standing next to each other. A bunch of thugs, in Caleb's opinion, all four of them.

Caleb took a few steps toward the group, keeping his weight on the balls of his feet. He saw the woman reach forward and pick up her suitcase, holding it to her stomach as if it were a child.

"There's nothing in the suitcase," Caleb heard her say in clipped English, the emphasis on the consonants. She was holding the suitcase with one hand and trying to get her cell phone into her rear pocket with the other.

"Give me the phone," one of the men said, holding his hand out toward the woman. She shook her head, shoving the phone farther into her pocket.

"No," she replied, looking at the man with an expression somewhere between defiance and fear. The woman hadn't yet noticed Caleb, neither had the four men.

His mind working fast, Caleb assessed the situation. He had three courses of action, possibly more.

He could do nothing. He could just walk away. This wasn't his problem. But Caleb rarely did nothing, and he never walked away.

He could take the middle ground and return to the concourse to get the police officers. They were less than a hundred yards away. The only problem with that course of action was that by the time he returned with the police, the woman could have been robbed. The four men would have plenty of time to grab the phone and the suitcase, and disappear up the alleyway, never to be seen again.

Or he could take the third course of action, which was the one he was leaning toward. It was perhaps the most drastic, but it would be the most effective and just. One thing Caleb didn't like about the third course of action was that he was still wearing his robe, and he hated fighting in his robe. It was unbecoming of a man of the cloth. The other thing he didn't like about it was the odds. With four against one, they weren't in his favor. But the thing about odds was they could always be shortened.

Caleb took a couple of swift steps forward, raising his arms out at head height as he did so. His hands were vertical, his palms facing inward. When he reached the two men standing closest to him, he brought his hands inward, placing them on the mens' ears before smashing their heads together. The sound when their skulls collided was a satisfying crump, like a watermelon being split, but Caleb knew he'd not put enough power into the move to do them any serious damage. A side-on blow to the head rattled the brain from side to side as if it was in jello, but rarely did any lasting damage with the amount of force Caleb had just used. There was plenty of soft tissue that could be sheared, bruised, or torn, which he accounted for. Caleb wanted them down but not out completely. As the two men slumped to the ground, the man now standing closest to Caleb whipped around, much faster than Caleb had anticipated. His arm lashed out, and Caleb felt a red-hot line being drawn across his abdomen.

Most men would have taken a step back. But Caleb wasn't most men. His assailant should have stabbed, not swiped. A slash like that wouldn't be deep enough to reach any of the major organs in Caleb's abdomen, so he jumped forward, grabbing the man's knife arm by the elbow. Caleb spun him round, using the momentum from the arc to turn him round completely so he had his back to Caleb. Then, with his free hand, he drove it hard into the man's left kidney. Caleb knew it was petty, but he repeated the punch, this time to his other kidney. The man dropped to his knees, then onto his side where he flapped around like a fish on dry land.

Caleb looked at the last man standing, who was regarding him with a look of utter shock.

"Shit," he said, glancing at his three fallen co-conspirators. The last man Caleb had put down was trying to reach his hands behind his back, but failing.

"Shit out of luck," Caleb said. "Looks like you've drawn the best bull, though."

"What?" the man said.

"You're still standing. Now, phone and wallet." Caleb held his hand out in front of him. The man looked at him for a few seconds and Caleb took a half step forward. In response, the man reached into his pocket and pulled out a phone. A few seconds later, a wallet followed. He handed them over to Caleb, flinching as Caleb's hand took the items from him.

"Don't hurt me, man," the man said, his voice higher that it had been a moment previously. Caleb looked at him, tempted for a few seconds to punch him in the face anyway, but he thought better of it. He was already regretting that second kidney punch, but it was what it was. He couldn't take it back.

"Do you read scripture, my friend?" Caleb asked the young man. The look on his face told Caleb the answer. "I thought not. Genesis, chapter one, verse twenty-eight. You know it?"

"No," the man replied, shaking his head in response. Caleb nodded his own head toward the entrance to the alleyway.

"Go forth and multiply."

CHAPTER 8

Natasha stared, open mouthed, as the man who had threatened her a moment earlier ran up the alleyway, not once looking back. Of the other three men, only one was conscious but appeared incapacitated. The man who had taken them out turned to her and smiled, his icy gray eyes boring into her. He took a step forward, his hand extended.

"My name is Caleb," he said as he took her hand. The touch of his hand on hers sent a strange feeling through her entire body, as if she was being infused with something. She allowed him to pull her to her feet and then he shook her hand, turning the assistance into a much more formal gesture.

"Natasha," she replied. "I'm Natasha." He nodded once, and knelt down. Natasha watched as he rifled through the pockets of the men on the ground, taking their wallets and phones. The wallets he emptied of cash before throwing them in one of the dumpsters, and he placed their phones on the ground before bringing a sandaled foot down hard, sending slivers of glass and plastic across the alleyway. As he did so, his gray robe billowed out around his hips and she looked away, not wanting to embarrass him if he was not wearing any undergarments. But Caleb didn't look embarrassed.

As Caleb used his foot to nudge the phones around the ground, she looked at him properly. He was taller than her. Five foot nine, perhaps. He was slim, not overly muscular but obviously in good shape. His head was shaved so closely she couldn't tell what color his hair was, and he had a small cloth bag slung over his chest. When she ran her eyes over his torso, Natasha saw a flash of red on his abdomen. It was blood.

"You're hurt," she said, stepping forward and instinctively reaching out her hand. There was a slit in the material of the robe, perhaps six inches across. "Are you okay?" Had he been stabbed? The whole encounter had been over so quickly that Natasha had struggled to see exactly what had happened.

"It's nothing," Caleb replied, glancing down at the cut in his garment. He folded the paper bills he had taken from the men who had tried to rob her and placed them carefully in his bag. "Come on, let's go." He nodded back toward the station concourse. "We should probably tell the police about these three jackasses."

"You need to get yourself looked at," Natasha said, looking again at the cut in his robe.

"Let me find a bathroom and assess the damage," Caleb replied. "It sure doesn't feel like much."

"You're American?" Natasha asked, following Caleb as he walked toward the station entrance.

"Yes, from Texas," Caleb replied, "and you're from Belarus?"

"Yes."

"Your English is very good."

"Thank you. My father was from here." Caleb didn't reply, but just nodded.

Natasha paused at the entrance to the station. Caleb, as if sensing her reticence at returning to the crowded concourse, reached out and lightly touched her arm.

"It'll be fine," he said, looking at her. Natasha nodded. He was right, it would be fine.

They walked over to where the two police officers were still standing, watching people milling about the station. There were fewer than there had been when Natasha had left, but she held back as Caleb talked to the officers. A few seconds later, the officers were both striding with purpose toward the station exit, the male speaking into his radio microphone as he walked.

"I told them there'd been a fight in the alleyway," Caleb said as he returned to Natasha's side. He had an easy grin on his face. "Kinda true."

"Caleb?"

"Yes?"

"Thank you." Natasha sighed before continuing. "For what you did back there."

"It was nothing."

"Not to me, it wasn't." Natasha looked down again at the cut in his robe to see if the blood was spreading. It looked as if it could be.

A woman in an orange bib was just about to walk past them, so Natasha put her hand out to stop her.

"Excuse me," Natasha asked the woman. "Is there a medical facility here?" She stopped and looked at Natasha with concern.

"There is, yes. Are you sick?"

"No, my, er, my friend has hurt himself." The woman

turned her attention to Caleb. If she was surprised at his attire, it didn't show on her face.

"It's over there," the woman replied, pointing at the opposite end of the station. "Just past the news stand on the left. You'll see a red cross on the wall."

"Thank you," Natasha said. She took a few steps in the direction the woman had pointed before she realized Caleb was just standing there. "Come on, let's go."

Caleb laughed at her, but not unkindly. She watched as he put his hand to his abdomen before taking it away and examining it.

"The bleeding's stopped already," he said.

"You might have internal injuries."

"I haven't, but if it makes you happy, we can go to see the medics."

For the first time since she had arrived in England, Natasha smiled.

CHAPTER 9

"Doctor Sokolova?"

Phoebe turned at the sound of her name being called out. It was Jade, one of the nurses who had been volunteering with her for the last few weeks. She'd only been qualified for a few months, but seemed to be one of the more capable nursing volunteers they had in their small reception center. They were both wearing green scrubs, but Phoebe had a white coat over hers and a stethoscope draped around her neck.

"Jade, how can I help?" Phoebe replied, turning to smile at the nurse.

"I think we've got a mother and daughter with tuberculosis in cubicle three."

Phoebe groaned quietly. "What makes you think that?"

"The mother's been coughing for a month, maybe more." Phoebe watched as Jade checked her notes. "Weight loss, loss of appetite, loss of energy."

"And the child? How old is she?"

"She's only four, and not got any symptoms, but they've been living in a single room for the last few months."

"Does the mother have any other medical history?" Phoebe asked.

"Not as far as the interpreter was able to work out."

"Okay, I'll pop in and have a chat with her. In the meantime, see if you can get a sputum sample from the mother. I'll line up a chest x-ray." Phoebe tapped her pen on her lips, thinking for a moment. "We'll need to get an interferon gamma release assay test, or a tuberculin skin test, from the child to see if she's carrying it. But we can't do any of that here, so can you refer them to the integrated care board at their final destination?"

"Do you want a chest x-ray for the child as well?"

"Not if she's four, no. The pediatric team will get that if it's needed." Phoebe looked at Jade who was scribbling furiously in her notebook. "Happy?" The nurse looked up at her with a broad smile.

"Yep, no problem."

Phoebe turned and walked across the impromptu clinical room which, until the refugee trains had started, had been one of many disused retail units in the station. On the walls were still large posters showing the various sandwiches and drinks that used to be available. The sight of a larger than life baguette, filled with Philadelphia steak and Monterey Jack cheese made her stomach rumble and she realized she'd not eaten since breakfast. One more patient and she would take a break.

She picked up a medical form from the top of a pile in a plastic tray, the order of which was tightly controlled by the triage nurse who prioritized the patients. To Phoebe's surprise, there was only a first name on the form. According to the paperwork, he was presenting with a laceration. Phoebe walked to what passed for the waiting room where there were only five or six people waiting.

"Caleb?" Phoebe called out. She watched as a man wearing a robe and sandals got to his feet. He approached her, glancing apologetically down at his abdomen where Phoebe could see a blood stained cut in the fabric.

"Привет Калеб, меня зовут Фиби, и я врач," Phoebe said, switching to Russian. *Hello, Caleb. My name is Phoebe and I am a doctor.* He just looked at her blankly before replying.

"I'm better speaking English, to be honest," he said in a strong American accent. From the way he drawled the words, he had to be from the Deep South somewhere.

"Are you a refugee?" Phoebe asked him, reverting to English. "Only this medical facility is for refugees."

"I'm sorry, ma'am," he replied, looking back at the woman who he had been sitting next to. She made a pushing motion with her hands. "I'm here under duress."

Phoebe regarded him. He was looking at her with the grayest eyes she'd ever seen. They were almost luminescent and when he smiled, it seemed to intensify the effect.

"I tell you what," Phoebe said a few seconds later. "Let me have a quick look at you to make sure you're not about to bleed to death and we'll take it from there." She nodded toward a cubicle, in reality just a patch of floor against a wall that was surrounded by screens. "In there, top off."

"I'm, er, not wearing much underneath," he replied, his smile broadening. Phoebe was tempted to make a joke about how, as a doctor, she'd seen plenty of naked men before but she stopped herself at the last moment. From the robe and sandals, he looked to be some sort of man of the cloth and he might not find it funny.

"Well, top down then," Phoebe said, pointing at the cubicle with the paperwork in her hand. "I'll be in shortly."

Phoebe waited outside the cubicle for a moment to

allow him time to undress with privacy. She used the time to annotate his notes with the fact he wasn't a refugee. After an appropriate amount of time, she slipped between the screens and into the makeshift cubicle. Her patient was sitting on the couch, his robe wrapped around his waist.

"Right then," Phoebe said, her tone of voice switching to a more professional one. "Let's see what we've got, shall we?"

CHAPTER 10

Mikhail closed his eyes and tried to think about anything other than the young woman he had his arm around. Alevtina had at least stopped crying, and was now much calmer than she had been a few moments previously. Apart from the occasional sniff, she seemed content to just be sitting next to him and it had been her who had wrapped his arm over her shoulders, not Mikhail.

They were sitting on hard wooden benches in what had originally been an underground storeroom for gymnasium equipment but had been repurposed as an air raid shelter. Mikhail thought back to the moment the sirens had gone off for the first time, their tone rising and falling in an awful cacophony. The panic in the classroom had been palpable, despite Mrs. Ananič's attempts to maintain order. He remembered the look on Alevtina's face when he had turned to look at her.

"What's happening?" she had asked him, the tone of her voice mirroring her desperate expression. Mikhail saw tears welling up in her eyes. "Is this a drill?"

"I don't know," Mikhail had replied. Then he had reached out his hand to take Alevtina's. "Stay with me. I'll keep you safe." The moment he said the words, he regretted them for sounding lame, but it was too late. Along with the rest of the class, they had hurried down the corridor and toward the stairs that led down to the storeroom. As they got closer, the corridor got busier as other classrooms emptied, but Alevtina held onto his hand as they made their way into the makeshift bunker. Then, when they had found space to sit on the benches, she had finally let go before draping his arm around her shoulder.

"Mikhail?" Alevtina had asked him, her eyes full of tears. "Would you hold me?" Mikhail had said nothing at first, but ignoring the curious looks of a couple of other pupils, had leaned down and kissed her forehead.

"Of course," he had said a moment later, earning a hopeful smile in return.

If Mikhail had been asked to describe the atmosphere in the room, he didn't think he would have been able to. It was somewhere between excitement and fear, the latter gradually being replaced by the former as their sense of safety grew. There was a low murmur of voices as hushed conversations took place and he could see Mrs. Ananič and the Deputy Head having a furtive discussion close to the stairs that led back up to the school proper.

"Alevtina," Mikhail said a few minutes later. "Can I ask you something?"

"Sure," Alevtina replied, shifting her position slightly so she could look up at him. "What is it?"

"Are you going to the end of term party?"

"Of course," she replied with a faint smile. "I wouldn't miss it for the world."

"Only, I was wondering, maybe you'd like to go with me?

If you've not, I mean, if no one..." He let his voice trail away, suddenly feeling foolish.

"Oh," Alevtina said, her smile fading. "Andrei has already asked me to be his date."

Mikhail tried to keep his expression neutral at the news, but felt himself scowling anyway. Andrei was one of the more popular boys in the school, amongst the girls at least. Most of the other boys had little time for him for exactly that reason.

"Okay," Mikhail said. "No problem." Alevtina said something else, but he didn't catch it. "Sorry?" he asked her. "I missed that." When he looked at Alevtina, he saw her smile had returned.

"I said, I said no to Andrei," she whispered. "He's slimy. Did you hear what he made Katsiaryna do to him in the bottom field?" Alevtina giggled and started to blush. Mikhail had heard rumors about it from some of the other boys, but hadn't believed them.

"Is that true? She really did that?"

"I think so," Alevtina replied. "I overheard her telling some of her friends about it in the locker room." Mikhail saw her screw her face up. "Ew, gross."

Mikhail was thinking about the best way to reply when the sirens burst back into life. This time, instead of rising and falling, it was a single tone.

"All clear," Mrs. Ananič shouted from the entrance to the storeroom. "Back to class, all of you."

Mikhail and Alevtina stayed where they were for a few moments as the other pupils all stirred into life. A few moments later, there was only the two of them and a few stragglers left.

"We should go," Mikhail heard Alevtina say. He tightened his grip around her shoulder.

"Wait," he replied. A moment after that, they were alone. "Can I ask you something else?"

"Of course."

Mikhail looked down at Alevtina, wondering if she could feel how hard his heart was beating in his chest. Her cheeks were pink, and her pupils so dilated he could barely make out the pigment of her irises.

"Can I kiss you?" he asked after taking a deep breath. He watched as her mouth fell open into a perfect O. Then she closed it and pressed her lips together briefly.

"Have you ever kissed anyone before?" she asked him. Her voice was so low he could barely hear her. Mikhail thought about lying, saying he'd kissed loads of girls.

"No," he said.

"Neither have I. Not properly."

Mikhail paused, not sure what kissing someone properly meant. He adjusted his position so that they were facing each other.

"Is that a yes?" he asked, his heart hammering. Was this really about to happen?

"Mikhail," Alevtina said, a smile spreading on her face. "Of course it's a yes. But quickly, before someone comes."

CHAPTER 11

Caleb watched as the doctor's brow furrowed as she took in his injuries, both the most current one and the scars from the others. While her attention was focused on his abdomen, he took the time to study her in more detail. He knew she was a kind woman. He had recognized that in her eyes the moment he had seen her.

Doctor Sokolova, according to her name badge, was perhaps in her late twenties to early thirties. She was slim, slightly shorter than he was at around five feet five or six, and had dark, almost black, hair cut into a functional bob that showed off her high cheekbones to very good effect in his opinion. While the white coat she wore hid most of her figure, Caleb could tell she was toned just from the way she carried herself.

"Hmmm," the doctor said, pressing her fingers into his abdomen. "What happened?"

"I cut myself," Caleb replied. She looked at him with a flicker of annoyance on her face, and he saw that her green eyes were flecked with gold.

"Obviously." She took her hand away from his stomach

and crossed her arms over her chest. "Or, more likely, someone cut you. It looks like a knife wound to me."

Caleb shrugged his shoulders and smiled in response. He didn't mean to be rude, but he couldn't see how what had caused the wound to be relevant.

"Okay, if that's how you want to play it, that's fine by me," she said. "It'll need some sutures."

He watched her cross to a cupboard on the wall of the cubicle and open it, pulling out a tray wrapped in plastic. She placed it on a stainless steel trolley with a clang before returning her attention to the cupboard.

"Where is your name from?" Caleb asked as she rummaged through a box on one of the shelves.

"It's from my father," the doctor replied. "He had it first, and then he gave it to me." Caleb was about to apologize when she looked over her shoulder at him with a wry smile on her face.

"Very good," Caleb said, also smiling. "Is it Russian?"

"Yes, it is."

"But you don't have a Russian accent when you speak English?"

"That's because I am English," she replied, her smile broadening as twin dimples appeared in both cheeks like punctuation marks. "I went to medical school in Moscow after studying there for a year. It's much cheaper there than it is here."

"Ah, got it. So are you just Doctor Sokolova, or do you have another name?"

"Phoebe, but you can call me Doctor Sokolova." As she said this, she was still smiling at him. "Where are you from, Caleb?"

"Texas," Caleb replied.

"Where in Texas?"

"A one horse town you've probably never heard of."

"Try me."

"You heard of a place called Post Oak Bend City?"

"Nope." Phoebe turned back to the cupboard and pulled out some more items. Caleb watched as she opened the plastic wrapping around the tray. A few moments later, she had arranged her equipment how she wanted it and wheeled the trolley over to where Caleb was sitting. "Lie down on the couch for me, please," Phoebe said, her voice business-like. "I'll just put some local anesthetic in and then we're good to go."

"Okay," Caleb replied, putting his hands behind his head. On the tray, he could see the suture set, some saline, and a sterile pair of scissors.

"This might sting a bit."

"No problem." Caleb closed his eyes, knowing this was the worst part. As Phoebe slid the needle into the wound, he couldn't help but wince. He started reading a poster on the cubicle wall that asked for donations to a medical convoy planning to go to Poland to take his mind off what she was doing.

"Sorry, this won't take long," Phoebe said, as if she was talking to a child. "How come you wear a robe? It it a religious thing?"

"It's faith based, but not necessarily religious," Caleb replied, recognizing the distraction technique.

"Are you a monk?"

"No. I'm a preacher."

"What brings you to London?"

"A bus," Caleb replied. He saw Phoebe looking at him with a smile. Those dimples really were something, in Caleb's opinion. "Sorry, I couldn't resist. I don't really have any reason to be here. But I have to be somewhere."

"You're not involved with the refugees, then?" Phoebe returned to her task, her smile slipping.

"Kind of," Caleb replied. "I was helping one of them out when I, uh, when I cut myself."

"I see," Phoebe said. "Nearly done."

A few moments later, just as Phoebe put the syringe with the anesthetic back on the tray, Caleb heard a woman's voice calling out in the main department.

"Can I have a hand out here?" the woman shouted, and Caleb could sense the urgency in her voice. "Now, please?" Caleb smiled. Even when there was an emergency of some sort, the Brits still said please and thank you.

"I need to go," Phoebe said, snapping off her latex gloves and draping some sort of sterile paper over Caleb's abdomen. "I'll be back as soon as I can to stitch you up. The anesthetic will last for ages."

"No problem, thank you," Caleb replied, but he was already talking to Phoebe's back.

CHAPTER 12

Vincuk drummed his fingers on the steering wheel of the truck as it bounced along the forest road. Yuri, his second in command, sat in the passenger seat. His AK-74 was balanced between his knees, and he was smoking a cigarette. From the rear of the truck, Vincuk heard the rest of the small group talking and laughing. They had done well during the training session considering their age. It couldn't replicate combat, but would serve to toughen them up.

It was Vincuk's last day with this group. Tomorrow, he would be handing them over to another part of the resistance and he might never see them again. It would be a shame as he had enjoyed their company over the previous few days, but there were plenty more where they came from.

He wished he was the same age as the young men in the back. Vincuk was in his mid-fifties, overweight by thirty pounds, much of which was around his middle, and he had separate glasses for everyday use and reading. He was old enough to remember life in Belarus before the Budapest Memorandum in the mid-nineties which freed them from the Soviet Union. It was a freedom of sorts in which one authoritarian regime had been replaced by another, but the young men in the back knew no other way of life. For that, he envied them. He also envied them for their youth.

The resistance, formed of men like Vincuk, Yuri, and the recruits he trained, was gradually gaining pace across the country. It was a loose network, with regional commanders such as him but no clear leader. There was a man, his true identity unknown even to the regional commanders, who purported to speak for them. Vincuk paid him little heed as long as he said the right things to the media, which he usually did. Vincuk personally thought that by appearing on the television screens, balaclava or no balaclava, the man was living on borrowed time.

Vincuk drove on in silence, lost in his own thoughts. Perhaps, in time, their movement would rival the resistance during the Second World War? That was what he aspired to, but he knew they were a long way from that. Vincuk remembered in school, all those years ago, being transfixed by stories of the so-called Osipowicze diversion where a well-organized group of Belarusian nationals had destroyed four German trains and many Tiger tanks. The resistance in Minsk had been so tenacious that the city was awarded the Soviet title *Hero City* after the war. A grin spread across Vincuk's face as he imagined being awarded the same honor as Minsk had, even though he knew it was nothing more than a daydream.

"Vincuk, slow down," Yuri said, putting his hand on the dashboard. "Stop the truck." Vincuk started braking as Yuri banged on the panel separating the front from the rear of the vehicle. "Quiet in there!" he barked.

"What is it?" Vincuk asked his colleague. Yuri just pointed through the trees, to the left and in front of the truck. Vincuk looked where he was pointing, but saw nothing. "What?" he said. "I don't see anything." Just as he said this, he saw a flash of movement. It was subtle and could have been a large animal of some sort. Deer were common in the forest, but from the look of concern on Yuri's face, whatever Vincuk had just seen wasn't a deer.

"Turn around," Yuri said, "but slowly. As quietly as you can."

Vincuk did as Yuri said, performing a three point turn on the narrow road. When the vehicle was pointing in the direction they had come from, he started moving forward, keeping one eye on the rear view mirror. A few hundred yards ahead was a sharp turn, but up until that point the forest road was dead straight.

They were almost at the bend in the road when Vincuk saw activity behind him in the mirror. There was a group of men, all clad in black uniforms, doing something in the middle of the road. He couldn't watch them for long enough to work out what they were doing, but a few seconds later, he knew exactly what it was.

"Put your foot down!" Yuri shouted, just before the first burst of machine gun fire rang out.

CHAPTER 13

Natasha watched as two young men, both wearing orange bibs, half carried and half dragged an elderly woman into the medical center. She got to her feet to help them, but was brushed aside by a woman wearing green scrubs.

"What's happened?" Natasha heard the woman ask.

"She collapsed on the concourse," one of the young men replied. Natasha could see the fear on his face as they lifted her toward a gurney.

"Hello?" the medic asked the elderly woman. "My name's Jade, I'm one of the nurses. Can you hear me?" Natasha saw the nurse rubbing the elderly woman's sternum, but she didn't respond. Her face was a deathly ashen color, and for a horrific moment, Natasha thought she was dead. From the look of relief on the young men's faces when the woman groaned, they had thought the same thing. "Let's get her into the treatment room," the nurse said. Then she raised her voice. "Can I have a hand out here? Now, please?"

Natasha saw the door to the cubicle Caleb was in open and the doctor rushed out, her white coat billowing behind her. The two young men looked at each other nervously before leaving. Natasha was alone in the waiting area. She glanced over at Caleb's cubicle. Was she allowed in there? Natasha sat on the edge of her seat, not sure what to do.

Five, perhaps ten minutes later, Jade came out of the cubicle where she and the doctor were treating the elderly woman. She looked flustered.

"Excuse me," Natasha said to the nurse. "Can I go in and sit with my friend?"

"Of course," Jade said, her attention obviously elsewhere.

"Thank you."

Natasha got to her feet and walked toward the treatment room. She paused, knocking on the door a couple of times. When she heard Caleb calling out, she opened the door and peeped in.

"Hi," Natasha said. She could see Caleb sitting on the edge of his gurney. Next to him was a small trolley with medical equipment, including several blood stained swabs. Natasha ran her eyes over his torso, taking in the various scars. There was a round one in his shoulder that looked puckered, and several other, older, wounds that she could see. "How are you doing?" she asked, frowning. She wanted to ask him about them, but didn't feel comfortable doing so.

"Nearly done," Caleb replied, gesturing toward his abdomen. "I just need a dressing and I'm good to go."

"The medics are with a woman who's quite poorly from the look of her," Natasha said. "Will I have a look through the cupboards? They might be a while."

"Sure," Caleb replied.

Natasha walked over to the gurney and glanced down at the wound on Caleb's stomach. It had been sutured with small, neat stitches. Twelve of them altogether, spaced out evenly along the length of the cut.

"That looks very neat," she said.

"Thank you," Caleb replied. Natasha frowned, not sure what he meant by that. She walked over to the cupboard and opened it, returning a moment later with an adhesive dressing that looked large enough to cover the wound. But when she held it up to Caleb's abdomen, she realized it was too small. Natasha looked at Caleb who had closed his eyes and was moving his lips silently, as if he was in prayer. Natasha waited, not wanting to disturb him. When he had finished saying whatever he was saying, he got to his feet and crossed to a small window in the cubicle wall, opening it as far as it would go.

"Are you okay?" Natasha asked him. Caleb nodded in response, but said nothing. "The dressing's too small. We'll have to wait for the medics." He nodded again and returned to the gurney.

Around five minutes later, the cubicle door opened and the doctor walked in. She had a distracted expression on her face.

"Phoebe, this is Natasha," Caleb said. The doctor glanced at Natasha and nodded before returning her attention to Caleb.

"Sorry about that," she said. "I got caught up." When she looked down at Caleb's abdomen, she gasped. "Who did that?" Then she looked at Natasha with an accusatory expression. "Was that you? You shouldn't have done that."

"It was me, Phoebe," Caleb said.

"You sutured yourself?"

"I've done it before." Caleb raised his gown to bare his thigh. There was a jagged scar around four inches long with indentations along both sides. "At least this time I had some anesthetic."

Natasha watched as Phoebe inspected the freshly stitched wound, nodding as she did so. "That's not bad. Have you had medical training?"

"A bit, a long time ago," he replied.

"I'll send Jade in with a dressing. Have them taken out in seven to ten days," Phoebe said.

"Can I take a stitch cutter?" Caleb asked. "That way, I wouldn't need to bother anyone with it." Natasha saw the doctor smile, dimples appearing in both cheeks as she did so.

"I'm sure we can arrange that, yes," Phoebe replied. She turned and started making her way toward the door.

"Doctor?" Natasha called after her. Phoebe stopped and turned.

"Yes?"

"How is the elderly lady?" She saw a frown appear on Phoebe's face.

"She didn't make it, I'm afraid." Phoebe looked down at her hands. "She was very sick."

"At least she died peacefully with people who cared for her," Natasha heard Caleb say. She looked at him, but there was no surprise on his face. It was if he had known the woman had passed. "Thank you, Phoebe, for all that you do. Your reward will be in heaven."

Phoebe looked at Caleb with a wistful expression.

"I was hoping I might not have to wait that long."

CHAPTER 14

Stepan cursed as the white truck veered around the corner, disappearing from sight. They had certainly hit it—he had seen the sparks from the impacts—but they hadn't disabled it.

"Quick, quick," he shouted to his men. "Get to the wagon."

He ran over to their own vehicle, a four by four that was the same color as their uniforms. The driver, a young man whose original calling had been as a getaway driver for a gang of armed robbers, was sitting behind the wheel, revving the engine in preparation. It took the soldiers who had been manning the machine gun several seconds to disassemble their equipment and climb into the truck. Seconds that would cost them, of that Stepan was sure. He slammed his hand on the dashboard.

"Go!" he shouted. The soldier behind the wheel needed no further encouragement and the truck lurched into life, sending a shower of grit and dust into the air from its tires.

. . .

TEN MINUTES LATER, Stepan realized they had lost the white truck. He swore in frustration. All he could hope for was that the rounds that had landed had hit some of the resistance fighters. And the truck definitely had resistance fighters in it. Why else would they have turned and fled? There were numerous paths and rough roads leading into the forest from the main track. They could have taken any one of them. The peasants knew the land like the back of their hands, an advantage that the People's Army didn't have.

"Where to, sir?" the driver asked.

"Back to base," Stepan replied, sighing in frustration. Sooner or later they would catch up with these so called resistance fighters. Then they would hang them from the trees they hid in.

As they drove, Stepan reflected on the successful mission at the village. The next time they carried out one of these missions, Stepan intended to get any recruits he had with him more involved in the business side than the pleasure side. They needed to get their hands dirty, not just have some fun with the locals. But truth be told, Stepan hadn't really cared for the woman back at the houses, which is why he'd let the recruits have some fun with her instead of him. She was too old and too much like farming stock for his taste.

Stepan thought back to the scene as they left the village. Thick plumes of black smoke billowed up from the roofs. It would serve as a warning to the other locals that the resistance was not to be helped in any way. Stepan had made that very clear to the woman as they had left her behind, battered and bruised, but alive to spread the word.

He reached into his pocket for his cell phone to call in to what passed for his higher command. The incident with the white truck would not be mentioned. There was no glory in highlighting failure, only success. A few moments later, he had his new instructions. Stepan was to meet a team arriving over the border from the northeast and accompany them to their destination in the east of Belarus. He wasn't thrilled about the babysitting mission, but as the group were bringing some of the Nona-S self-propelled artillery systems, at least it would be an interesting trip. Perhaps he would stay with them for a couple of days to see how their weapons operated, although he was more interested in the effect they had. His higher command had hinted at a new strategy intended to send a message to the Belarusian peasants.

In Stepan's opinion, it was about time. If they couldn't catch the resistance fighters, then they needed a new way to subdue the locals.

CHAPTER 15

Caleb adjusted his robe and picked up his small cloth bag. After thanking and saying goodbye to Phoebe, he and Natasha left the medical center and returned to the station concourse. In contrast to earlier, the area was now almost empty. They stopped, Natasha looking around with a nervous expression.

"What are your plans now, Natasha?" he asked her.

"I'm supposed to register with the immigration desk," she replied, pulling a crumpled piece of paper from her pocket and scanning it. Caleb glanced at the paper but couldn't decipher the Cyrillic letters. "The Home Office has a desk somewhere. Once I've registered, then they have buses to the accommodation."

"It looks like they might have packed up. Let's ask someone."

A moment later, they found a young man wearing an orange bib packing some documents away into a box. On the rear of the tabard were the letters FCDO. When the man turned to face them, Caleb could see from his name badge that he worked for the Foreign, Commonwealth and Development Office.

"Excuse me," Caleb said. "My friend here needs to register with the Home Office. Do you know where their desk is?"

"That shower?" the man replied with a lop-sided grin at Natasha. "They've all done one."

"Sorry, they've what?" Caleb said, not understanding what he had just said.

"They've all gone home. The minute they've processed everyone, they disappear. Bloody jobsworths, the lot of them." He was talking to Caleb but looking at Natasha, still grinning. "You'll have to come back tomorrow when the next train gets in." He closed the box after placing the last of his documents into it, and picked it up. "They're normally here about half an hour before the train, so if you get here about half one, you can speak to them then. You want to translate that for your fit friend here?"

"I can speak English," Natasha replied, fixing the young man with a cold stare. "But I don't understand what you mean by fit? What does this mean?"

Caleb hid a smile of his own as the young man's disappeared, his cheeks coloring as it did so.

"Ah, it means like, athletic. Now, if you'll excuse me? I got stuff to do."

Caleb waited until the young man was out of earshot before turning to Natasha.

"Did I miss something there?" he asked her.

"Fit doesn't mean athletic in this country. It means attractive. Not just pretty, but in shape."

"That would explain his blushes, then," Caleb replied. He looked at Natasha who smiled briefly.

"What am I going to do now?" she asked him, sitting down on her suitcase and putting her head in her hands.

Caleb thought for a moment, looking around the concourse as he did so. Natasha had just under twenty-four hours before the Home Office returned, but surely they had some sort of out of hours service? He looked down at her and when she returned his gaze, he could see the exhaustion in her face.

"How about we get a hotel room and some food?" he said. Her expression turned to one of horror and he put his hands out, realizing what he'd just said. "No, not like that. A hotel room each. We can come back tomorrow when the Home Office people come back."

"I don't have enough money for a hotel room, Caleb," Natasha replied with a sigh. "Not one in central London, anyway."

Caleb opened his bag and looked inside.

"Yes, you do," he said, pulling out the bills he had taken from the men in the alleyway. There had to be several hundred pounds in total. More than enough for a hotel room for each of them.

CHAPTER 16

Mikhail closed his schoolbooks as he heard the sound of the front door closing. He was sitting in his aunt's kitchen, a half-eaten sandwich next to his homework. A moment later, Iĺja appeared at the kitchen door. She looked tired but as always she gave him a broad smile.

"Hey, Mikhail," Iĺja said. "Sorry I'm late. I went to see a friend down in Podlipki today." Mikhail looked at her curiously. Iĺja had been spending a lot of time with her friend in the small town to the south east of Hrodna lately. Although it was none of his business, he was about to say something when she continued. "Your mother got to London okay. She texted me to say everything was fine." She was a couple of years older than her sister, but the similarities were obvious. "Did you have a good day at school?"

"Not too bad," Mikhail replied, feeling his cheeks starting to burn as he thought about him and Alevtina in the storeroom. It had only been a kiss, and a very clumsy one at first. It hadn't taken them long to work out how to stop their teeth clashing and Mikhail remembered his surprise at the unfamiliar sensation. Her lips were much softer than he'd thought they would be. Then Alevtina's tongue had slipped inside his mouth, and he had realized that they were kissing properly for the first time.

"Really?" Ilja said with a smirk. "Only you look like the cat that got the cream. Did something happen?"

"No," Mikhail replied quickly, causing Ilja's smirk to broaden. "No, nothing." He could feel himself blushing under her gaze and he wanted her to look away. To his relief, a few seconds later she did just that.

"Okay, whatever," Ilja said, emphasizing the second word to let him know she didn't believe him. "What do you want for supper?"

AN HOUR LATER, Mikhail was sitting in Ilja's lounge, his stomach full. She had prepared one of his favorite dishes for them both. Draniki, or shallow-fried pancakes made from ground potato and grated garlic, was something that Ilja made several times a week. He would never say anything to his mother, but his aunt was a far better cook than she was. The small television in the corner of the room was showing an old episode of *Friends*, and Mikhail watched idly as the characters goofed around to the sound of canned laughter.

Mikhail picked up the remote control and was flicking through the channels to see if there was anything on. As he did so, Ilja entered the lounge and sat in one of the armchairs with a deep sigh. She had a large glass of wine in her hand, just as she did at this time every evening.

"Do you mind if we catch the news headlines?" Ilja asked. "They'll be on in a few moments." Reluctantly, Mikhail stabbed at the remote to find Belarus24, the state-run news channel, and they watched the screen in silence while they waited for the headlines to cycle back round. A few moments later, the familiar face of Irina Kozlovskaya appeared on the screen. Behind her was a photograph of a man dressed in combat fatigues.

"The leader of the mercenaries who are attempting to suppress the local insurgency, Vladislav Vostovski, is coming under increasing pressure to account for the actions of his soldiers," the newsreader said as the image behind her changed to a video clip of a burning house. "Belarus24 has credible evidence to suggest that his forces are engaging in war crimes, punishing local civilians who they think are sympathetic to the insurgents."

"Desperate," Iĺja said as she took a large sip from her glass. "The sooner your ballot ticket comes through, the better."

"I'm going to bed," Mikhail said, getting to his feet. He had no interest in what the anchor was talking about. After crossing the room to give his aunt a goodnight hug, he made his way to his bedroom, pausing at the bathroom to clean his teeth.

As he lay in bed, sleep seemed to be a long way off. Mikhail closed his eyes but a series of images kept flashing across his eyelids, mostly from the news. The war seemed a long way away from where he currently was. The majority of the fighting was in the east of the country, and they were in the west. Surely if it got bad enough, Poland and the other neighboring countries would just open their borders for civilians. But Mikhail knew it wasn't the other countries letting them in that was the problem. It was the Belarusian authorities letting them out. One of the first things they had done when the fighting had started was stop people leaving.

Mikhail had mixed feelings about going to England, if that was indeed where he ended up going, especially after what had happened between him and Alevtina earlier that day. But she was also waiting for a ballot place to leave. He let a smile play across his face as he imagined a future for them both together in a new country. It had only been a kiss, but it had been his first, and hers. Plus she was going to be his date for the end of term party.

He was still smiling when he finally fell asleep.

CHAPTER 17

P hoebe paused with the key to her apartment almost in the lock. She took a deep breath before inserting it, wondering what sort of mood her mother, Teresa, would be in. Hopefully it was a good one. All Phoebe wanted to do was to pour a glass of wine and lie in the bath as long as she could before eating and going to bed. What she didn't want to walk into was an argument.

The apartment was a two bedroom on the third story of a drab building on the Waterloo Road in southeast London. Phoebe had bought it when her father had died a couple of years previously, using the inheritance she received from him to almost but not quite buy it outright. It was a functional place for her to live rather than a proper home, but Phoebe wasn't planning on spending the rest of her life in London. The city was too busy, too noisy, and had far too many people jostling for space. And since her mother had moved in a few weeks earlier, so was Phoebe's apartment. It was supposed to be a temporary arrangement. Phoebe's mother had been in the hospital having surgery on her hip. With the pressure on the National Health Service, Phoebe had offered to let her mother convalesce at her apartment for a while. She had initially been glad of the company, but the apartment was too small and her mother was seemingly unable to step outside it more than once every few days.

When Phoebe opened the door, a glorious smell wafted out. She smiled at the familiar scent of casserole, and the knowledge that if her mother had cooked, it meant she was in a good mood.

"Hi, Mum," Phoebe called out, shrugging her coat off her shoulders and hanging it by the door. "That smells good." She made her way to the kitchen where her mother was sitting at the table, a mug of tea in front of her. When Phoebe walked in, her mother smiled.

"Hey, love," Teresa said, scraping the chair back and getting to her feet. "Did you have a good day?"

Phoebe let her mother hug her, surprised when she planted a kiss on the top of her head. "Not too bad," she replied, pausing as she remembered the elderly lady who had passed away. Teresa didn't need to know about that, especially if she was in a good mood. "How about you?"

"I went to the supermarket for us," Teresa replied, her smile broadening. "I got a taxi there and back, but I've stocked up on a few essentials, including wine, and plenty of it."

Phoebe laughed at her mother. She rarely drank alcohol, and when she did, it was never more than a single glass. "Thank you. Have I got time for a bath?"

"Of course," Teresa replied. "It's a casserole, so it'll keep. We just need twenty minutes for the potatoes."

Phoebe poured herself a generous glass of wine and went to the bathroom, fetching her pajamas and a robe from her bedroom on the way. As she waited for the bath to fill, complete with a bright pink bath bomb that smelled heavenly, she examined herself in the mirror. Phoebe looked as tired as she felt. She had dark bags under both eyes, and the fine lines next to her eyes seemed to be deeper than usual. Laughter lines, Teresa would call them, but Phoebe knew they would turn into crow's feet before too long. She raised one hand to her head and plucked out a single white hair, examining it carefully before putting it in the waste basket with a sigh.

NINETY MINUTES LATER, Phoebe was curled up on her sofa, watching the television. As usual, her mother's casserole had been amazing and they had chatted as they had eaten. Phoebe had told her about the strange man in a robe who had sutured his own abdomen, and Teresa had thought this hysterical. As her mother had laughed, Phoebe had thought about the man, realizing something she'd not noticed at the time. On his paperwork, there had only been a single name. Caleb. No last name. Phoebe had made a mental note to mention it to Jade tomorrow to stop it happening again.

"Do you want the news?" Teresa asked as on the television, a game show host with a bright orange face was just congratulating a very excited man who had won something. Phoebe realized she had been almost asleep, and had no idea what the man had won.

"Yep, that'd be good," Phoebe replied, shuffling on the sofa so she was sitting more upright. "Can you turn it up a bit?"

On the television, after the introductory music, a grave-faced man looked intently at the camera.

"In today's news, the conflict in Belarus is intensifying, with the so-called People's Army claiming to have driven insurgents out of Gomel, a key strategic town in the southeast of the country," the anchor said, his tone matching his expression. His face disappeared although he continued speaking as the television showed a group of armed men running. A few seconds later, they disappeared in a cloud of smoke. Phoebe sat up in horror. Had they just shown the men being killed? To her relief, when the smoke cleared, the men were still on the screen, although two of them were now dragging a third.

"It's awful, isn't it?" Phoebe heard her mother mutter as the newscaster carried on. Phoebe was only half listening as he spoke words such as international condemnation, refugee crisis, and street to street fighting. She closed her eyes as an image of the woman who had died earlier that day floated into her mind's eye. To have managed to escape the horrific scenes on the television and travelled all the way to England, only to die when she arrived. That was awful as well, but it wasn't something she was going to talk about with Teresa.

"I'm going to bed, Mum," Phoebe said as she got to her feet.

"Are you back at the station tomorrow?" Teresa asked as Phoebe yawned. She nodded in response.

"Yes," Phoebe said, glancing back at the television where someone's house was burning down on the screen. There was a swing in the yard in front of the house, and her heart went out to the family who had lived there. A family who had just lost everything, including perhaps their lives. "Yes, I am."

CHAPTER 18

Natasha pushed the pizza box in front of her away, no longer hungry. Sitting next to her, perched on the second bed in the hotel room, was Caleb. He had a mouthful of pizza and his eyes were glued to the television where the news was mid-way through.

They were in a Travelodge hotel not far from Waterloo station. Caleb had managed to get them the last two available rooms before sweet talking the young woman in reception to persuade the chef to get them some food even though he was about to finish his shift. The pizzas had cost almost double what they should have, but Caleb hadn't seemed to mind. The room was functional rather than luxurious. As well as the beds, it had a small table that doubled as a desk, a small kettle with sachets containing tea, coffee, and sugar, and a small en suite bathroom with enough towels for one person. The only real nod to decoration was a stylized picture on the wall that had taken both some minutes to work out was a representation of London's tube system.

"Aren't you hungry?" Caleb asked her, speaking through

his food.

"Not anymore," Natasha replied, nodding at the screen on the wall. Like the rest of the room, it was tired but fit for its purpose.

"We can change the channel to something else?"

"No, it's fine." On the screen, the newscaster had moved on from the piece on Belarus and was now reporting on the latest transfer news from one of the country's premier league clubs. The player had been bought for over a hundred million pounds.

"I don't get soccer," Caleb said. "How can a player be worth that much money?"

"It's football over here," Natasha replied, forcing herself to smile to try to put the images from her home country that had been on the television a few moments previously out of her mind. "They'll get upset if you call it soccer."

"Ah, I see," Caleb said, finishing his mouthful and smiling. He had a crumb at the corner of his mouth, and Natasha was tempted to reach up and brush it away but it dropped into the open pizza box on his lap. "How come you know so much about British culture?"

"My father insisted on teaching us," she replied. "He didn't just want us to understand the language, but also the people. I've tried to carry it on with my son, but he's not that interested."

"You have a son?"

"Yes." Natasha picked up her phone and started scrolling through the photographs for a good one of Mikhail. She needed to find one without her husband in it to avoid the inevitable questions about why he and Mikhail didn't look anything like each other. Anton was a father to Mikhail in every way but biologically, but she didn't want to have to explain this to Caleb. "He's fourteen."

"You don't look old enough to have a teenager," Caleb said. She glanced up at him, hurt by the comment, but saw only kindness in his eyes. "Have I said something wrong?"

"No, Caleb, I'm sorry," Natasha replied. "I was very young, that's all." She looked away, wanting to change the subject. She barely knew Caleb and wasn't going to tell him about what had happened to her that night so long ago. About how Mikhail's father could be one of three young men who had between them both destroyed what had remained of her own childhood and given her the most precious thing in the world. About how Mikhail was older now than she had been when it happened. "This is him. Mikhail."

She angled the phone toward him and watched as Caleb squinted at the small screen.

"He's only fourteen?" he asked. "He looks much older."

Natasha paused, waiting for the inevitable question about Mikhail's father, but Caleb said nothing. She gestured toward Caleb's robe.

"I'm guessing from your clothes that you don't have children?" she asked him. To her surprise, he laughed loudly in response.

"I'm a preacher, not a monk," Caleb said when he had finished laughing. Natasha wasn't sure why he found that funny, and for a moment wondered if she had said the wrong thing.

"Have you always been a preacher?" she asked, keen to change the subject.

"Not always, no," Caleb replied, his smile fading, "but it's been so long now I've forgotten what life was like before." He finished the sentence with a small nod of his head. Picking up on the hint, Natasha changed tack.

"Why do you preach?"

"That's an interesting question, Natasha," Caleb said. "Most people ask what, not why."

"That was going to be my next question," Natasha said with a brief smile which he returned.

"To correct, rebuke and encourage. With great patience and careful instruction."

Natasha thought about what he had just said for a moment before nodding. It wasn't a bad philosophy, and it almost described being a parent.

"But you've not preached to me yet," she said, getting to her feet and gathering the pizza boxes.

"I just did," Caleb replied. "'To correct, rebuke and encourage' is from the second book of Timothy. Chapter four, verse two."

"So you preach to people without them realizing it?" She turned to him with a smile so he would know she was teasing him.

"Sometimes." Caleb had a wry smile on his face. "When the occasion arises, it can be a useful technique." He stood and held his hands out in front of him. "Give them to me. I'll put them in the trash on the way to my room." As she handed him the boxes, their fingers touched and she felt a peculiar sensation in her fingertips. It was warm, but at the same time, numbing. Natasha thought she saw a flicker of concern on his face, but as soon as it appeared, it was gone. "You're tired, Natasha," he said, his smile broadening. "You need to sleep, to rest. You have a long road in front of you." As he said this, she felt the exhaustion descending on her. He was right.

"Yes," she said, looking into his gray eyes. "Thank you for what you did today, Caleb." If it wasn't for the pizza boxes between them, she would have leaned forward and kissed him on the cheek. Not in a sensual way, although if a peck on the cheek turned into something more, she didn't think she would mind. There was something about the way he looked at her that made her feel safe and needed at the same time. She shook her head, blaming her exhaustion for the way it was making her feel.

"You have nothing to thank me for, Natasha," Caleb said, taking the boxes from her. Her fingertips suddenly felt cold, as if she had dipped them into water. "When you lie down, you will not be afraid. When you lie down, your sleep will be sweet."

"Is that from the Bible?" Natasha replied, stifling a yawn but smiling at the same time.

"Yes, it's from Proverbs," Caleb said with a grin, "but then a few chapters later it warns against loving sleep in case you grow poor." He paused for a moment. "Goodnight, Natasha. Sweet dreams, if such a thing is possible."

When Caleb had left, Natasha brushed her teeth and thought about showering. It had been a long day, and she wanted to wash it away. But when she sat on the bed, she realized that sleep was the better option. Natasha remembered she had forgotten to send Mikhail a message. She checked her phone and tapped out a quick text message to Mikhail. It was two hours ahead in Belarus so he would be in bed, but he would get the message in the morning.

Sleep well, Mikhail. Everything's fine here. I'll see you soon xxx

Natasha lay back and gazed at the television where an enthusiastic weather presenter was just starting to tell his audience about the day's weather. She blinked a couple of times, resolving to watch the rest of the forecast.

But she didn't even manage to stay awake for that.

CHAPTER 19

Stepan sat on a fallen tree and smoked as he watched the activity in front of him. There were four personnel, all wearing the same black fatigues that he was, preparing the vehicle that he had escorted almost the entire width of Belarus over the previous day. He had driven, or rather been driven, to meet a small convoy comprised of a single truck and a low-loader on the outskirts of Minsk.

There, in a disused industrial unit, he had taken on the responsibility for escorting the low-loader, it's cargo hidden by a large military tarpaulin, to its destination in the east of Belarus. The truck that had brought it this far had returned to the west, its commander not even bothering to greet Stepan at the handover.

He watched as the crew fussed around their vehicle, a Nona-S mortar system. It was now free from the low-loader which was parked up some distance away. The Nona-S was the size of a small tank, and if Stepan hadn't known better, he would have thought it was a tank except for the large black wheels where tracks should be. It was painted a dark olive green with white numbers stenciled on the side. At the rear of the vehicle was a long, thin, whip aerial and at the front, a cannon some eight feet long. Stepan didn't need to be where he was. His role had been to accompany the low-loader and its cargo to this location. There was another People's Army squad in the surrounding area, providing all round defense just in case any of the locals got any ideas.

They were parked in a clearing behind a small copse just under five miles from their target, a small town which nestled in a valley. Stepan could see the orange of the street-lights reflecting off the clouds and he imagined its residents going about their evenings in blissful ignorance. Some of them would be eating, some would be drinking. Some of them would even be having sex. He started laughing at the thought of a one hundred and twenty millimeter high explosive round punching through the ceiling just as they finished.

"What a way to go," Stepan muttered to himself as he got to his feet. He wandered over to two of the men who were preparing some shells. "What time are your orders for the attack?"

"No idea," one of the soldiers replied, not even looking at Stepan. "Sometime in the night is all we know."

"Shame," Stepan said, more to himself than the soldiers. He would have liked to hang around and watch the action, but it was getting late. His orders for the next day had come through and he was going to be visiting another village where the locals were apparently sympathetic to the resis-tance. With any luck, they might actually be sheltering some of them. This was the main reason for always visiting at dawn, to catch them unawares. With a final look at the Nona-S mortar, he returned to his truck, instructing his driver to take them back to base.

Stepan wanted to get a good night's sleep. If tomorrow

morning turned out the way he hoped it would, he was going to be busy.

CHAPTER 20

Caleb stood outside the elevator in the hotel, watching the numbers counting up. He'd not been able to find a trash can for the pizza boxes, and while he had considered just leaving them on the floor of the corridor for the cleaning team, Caleb thought they probably had to work hard enough already for their money.

As he rode the elevator down, he thought back to the conversation he'd had with Natasha. She was unusual, but in a good way. Most people were full of questions when they met him. Where he was from? Why he wore a robe? What he did for a living? But all that she had really asked him was why he preached.

Caleb exited the elevator when it arrived on the ground floor and searched around for a trash can. He found one in the hotel foyer, deserted apart from a young man sitting behind the reception desk, engrossed in his phone. If he noticed Caleb in the foyer, he made no obvious sign and Caleb wondered what it was on his phone that was so absorbing.

He returned to the elevator, arriving just as the doors

were closing. He could see through the gap in the doors that there were two other guests in the car, and he put his hand between the doors to stop them closing. As he did so, he saw the two people jump apart.

The two guests were very different. The man was older than Caleb, perhaps in his fifties. He was wearing an ill-fitting suit that was too small for his expansive midriff, and had a sheen of perspiration on his forehead. His top button was undone and his tie slightly looser than it could have been. But the most notable thing about the man was that he refused to meet Caleb's eyes, fixing his gaze on the top corner of the elevator.

The woman with him was perhaps too young to be called a woman. Caleb looked at her, estimating her age to be late teens or early twenties at best. His first thought was that perhaps she was the man's daughter, but as he looked at her clothing he realized this was not the case. She wore a tight red dress that showed off the few curves she had under a loose jacket with a handbag over one shoulder. As Caleb entered the elevator, she looked at him, not warily but with a note of caution. He gave her a slight smile before pressing the button for his floor, thinking the girl would be much more attractive without all the makeup she was wearing. For a member of the oldest profession, she had to be one of the younger ones Caleb had seen.

The three of them rode up in an uncomfortable silence. Caleb wanted to say something, but he knew there was nothing he could say. He regarded the girl out of the corner of his eye, wondering how and why her life choices had led to her current lifestyle. As the elevator rose, so did Caleb's anger.

When it arrived at the floor, Caleb let the couple get off. As they walked down the corridor, Caleb used his hand to stop the door closing. He listened until he heard the sound of a door being opened, and then stepped out to follow them. He arrived at the door just before it closed and he put his foot in front of it to stop it from locking.

Caleb stayed there for a few seconds, but neither the man nor the girl had realized the door hadn't closed. He counted to twenty under his breath before pushing the door open and walking in. Both of the room's occupants turned to look at him, her with surprise, him with horror. The man had a bundle of notes in his hand and had been about to hand them to the girl.

"What the hell?" the man said as Caleb strode across the room, snatching the money from him. He handed the cash to the girl and turned his attention to the man, whose face had turned white. "You're robbing me?"

"No," Caleb said, taking a step forward, causing the man to stumble back against the bed. "You've paid her for her time and companionship." He jabbed out his hand, using his extended fingers to poke the man in the solar plexus. Not hard, but hard enough. "They are now both up." Caleb glanced at the girl who had a broad grin on her face. "You can go. But remember, there is another way."

"Yeah, whatever," the girl replied as she stowed the money in her handbag. She wasn't British, but Caleb couldn't place her accent.

Caleb looked at the man in front of him as the girl left the room without another word. Perhaps, Caleb thought as he waited for the door to close behind her, she would see the light. If not today, a different day in the future. He sighed, knowing that was unlikely as long as there were men like the one in front of him.

"Please don't hurt me," the man said. Caleb looked at him to see his lips were trembling. He was afraid. Terrified.

Caleb closed his eyes for a few seconds, imagining beating this man. Raining blows down on his face until the bones beneath his skin crumbled. He opened them, allowing the contempt to flow. That was not the way.

"Give me your wallet," Caleb said.

"I've got no money left," the man replied, his voice wavering. "Not now."

"I don't want your money," Caleb replied. "I'm not a thief. Give me your wallet."

Caleb waited as the man pulled his wallet from his trouser pocket and handed it to Caleb with shaking hands. Caleb opened it and pulled out the man's driver's license.

"Is there a Mrs Rowley, Craig," he asked, "living with you at this address?" The man nodded in reply, his jowls wobbling.

"Look, I'm sorry," the man said, holding his hands up. "This is all some sort of—"

"Shut up, heathen!" Caleb cut him off. He handed the wallet back. "Perhaps I'll pay Mrs Rowley a visit and tell her about her fat, pathetic husband and his penchant for young whores."

"No, you can't—"

"I said shut up." Caleb leaned forward until his face was only inches from the man's. "Your card is now marked, Craig. I will see you again. You may not see me, but I will see you. Therefore keep watch, because you do not know the day your Lord will come." Caleb lowered his voice. "And if you are with another whore when that day comes, then there will be a reckoning. Do you understand?"

The man nodded in reply. Caleb took a few steps toward the door, tempted to punch the man just once, but he restrained himself. Without violence, his words would have more power. As Caleb put his hand on the door handle, he heard the man's voice.

"But what am I supposed to do now?" His voice was plaintive. Pathetic.

Caleb turned to face him, tempering his voice to control his anger. "There'll be a Bible in the nightstand," he said. "Maybe you should read it."

CHAPTER 21

"**M**ikhail! Get up!"

Mikhail jumped in his bed at the sound of a female voice screaming. He'd been dreaming, he thought. Or was he still dreaming? He didn't recognize the voice but as he looked across his bedroom, he saw his aunt. She was clutching a thin robe around her, and she shouted at him again to get up. In the background, Mikhail could hear the rise and fall of the sirens he thought he'd been dreaming about.

"The sirens are going off!" Iĺja shouted, her voice several octaves higher than normal. "Come on!"

Mikhail disentangled himself from his bedclothes as quickly as he could, grateful that he was at least wearing boxer shorts. Iĺja turned and disappeared from his view. A few seconds later, he heard her footsteps thumping down the stairs. He reached out to grab some clothes, bundling them under his arm, and picked up his cell phone from the bedside table. Without even looking at the screen, he ran across the room to the stairs.

Iĺja and Mikhail were lucky in that their house had a basement. It was an older house, built by the Soviets not long after the Second World War. During the war itself, where the house now stood had been part of one of the Jewish ghettos where the Germans herded more than fifty thousand people together. Few of them survived the subsequent deportation to locations such as Auschwitz and Treblinka. By the time the Red Army liberated Hrodna in July 1944, the ghettos were empty and the local residents, perhaps wishing to cleanse the awful memories of what had happened in their town, razed most of the original buildings to the ground. Apart from the newer apartment buildings in the area like the one that Alevtina lived in, the replacement houses all had individual cellars, perhaps built by the Soviets with war in mind.

Mikhail opened the door to Iĺja's cellar to see her sitting on one of the single beds, chewing her fingernails. He closed the door, blanking out the sound of the still-wailing siren, and crossed the small room to sit next to her. The cellar was perhaps five yards by five yards, large enough for a couple of beds. Stacked against one wall from the floor to the ceiling was firewood and on the opposite wall, a series of shelves held essentials such as tinned food, bottled water, and other emergency supplies. A single incandescent bulb illuminated the dingy room and in one corner there was a bucket that Mikhail hoped to never see used for its intended purpose.

"It'll be okay, Aunt Iĺja," Mikhail said as he sat down. "It's probably just another drill like the one earlier."

"At this time of the morning?" Iĺja replied, her voice shrill. "It's only just past dawn."

Mikhail looked down at the screen of his phone to see it

was a few minutes before five in the morning. Iľja was right. There wouldn't be a drill at this time of day. He opened the message from his mother, smiling as he read it. He wanted to reply but the thick cellar walls blocked the cell phone's signal, so he put the phone away, making a mental note to do it later. He and Iľja sat in silence for a few moments, both lost in their own thoughts.

"How long was it between the sirens earlier today, Mikhail?" Iľja asked. She had missed the earlier sirens as her friend's town was too small for such luxuries. Mikhail thought for a moment before replying.

"Ten, perhaps fifteen minutes," he said. "Not long at all." It had felt like much longer at the time, but he wasn't going to tell Iľja that.

"We could move, you know. To Podlipki?" Iľja was looking at him with an earnest expression. "My friend there has plenty of room, and it would be safer."

"The fighting's miles away, Aunt Iľja," Mikhail replied. "We're safe enough here." Just as he said that, there was a high pitched screeching noise over their heads. It was followed a couple of seconds later by a muffled thudding sound. The light bulb jittered ever so slightly although Mikhail could feel no movement under his feet,

Iľja swore under her breath and pulled Mikhail closer to her. He put his arm over her shoulder, just like he had with Alevtina earlier.

"Mikhail?" Iľja said, but he never got a chance to reply. There was another screech, this one much louder and briefer. Almost immediately after it stopped, there was a deafening sound. It was a thunderous noise, as if someone had hit a sheet of corrugated steel with a sledgehammer, but ten times louder. The cellar floor shook under their feet as the light bulb danced for a second, perhaps two, before exploding and plunging them into darkness.

Then the only thing Mikhail could hear was Ilja screaming.

CHAPTER 22

Phoebe gasped as her eyes flashed open. The last vestiges of the dream slipped away, and she closed her eyes briefly to try to hold on to them for a few seconds longer. But it was too late. She was awake.

She sighed in frustration, leaning her head back into the pillow. Phoebe was wrapped up in the sheet which barely covered her, and her pajamas were soaked with perspiration. She laughed, her thoughts turning to what lay in the top drawer of her nightstand buried under her clothes. Something very personal she had bought for herself some months previously. But it wasn't something she was going to use with her mother in the next bedroom. The toy was very good at what it was designed for, but it was hardly discreet.

Phoebe unwrapped herself from the sheet and sat on the edge of the bed, taking a deep breath as she did so.

"Oh, my days," she whispered to herself. It had been a long time since she'd had a dream like that one, and even longer since she'd experienced what she'd dreamed about in reality. She sighed again. Phoebe was more than happy with her own company but on occasion, all she craved was some intimacy and a climax that wasn't homemade.

A few moments later, freshly showered and wrapped in a thin cotton robe, Phoebe made her way into the kitchen. Teresa was sitting at the table, already dressed for the day. On the sideboard, two mugs were sitting next to the kettle which was about to come to the boil.

"Morning," Teresa said. "I was going to bring you a cup of tea in bed."

Phoebe felt her cheeks coloring as she imagined her mother walking in on her *in flagrante.* Then she started laughing as she remembered a previous boyfriend telling her about him waking up as a teenager with a morning call to glory. He'd closed his eyes and rectified the situation only to find, when he opened them again, a cup of tea on his bedside table that his mother had brought in while he'd been busy.

"What's so funny?" Teresa asked, and Phoebe's cheeks colored even more.

"Nothing," Phoebe replied, waving her hand and turning away from Teresa before she said anything about her blushing. "I'll make them. Have you had breakfast?"

"Not yet. I was waiting for you to get up. What time are you at the clinic today?"

"Not until lunchtime," Phoebe replied. The kettle started bubbling and Phoebe busied herself with the teabags. "Why?"

"I was hoping we might nip back to my house for a bit."

"Is there stuff there you need?"

"No," Teresa said. "I want to get someone in to make some adjustments, that's all."

"What sort of adjustments?" Phoebe asked. Her mother lived in a fairly new house in Ealing that backed onto a leafy park. When she was younger, Phoebe used to sneak over the fence and into the park to meet her friends, but she couldn't think of any work that needed doing to the place.

"I want to get some handles put into the bathroom. Just to make it easier for me to get about. Maybe move one of the bedrooms downstairs as well."

Phoebe put a mug down in front of Teresa and sat opposite her.

"You're moving back home?" she asked her mother.

"I can't stay here forever, can I?" Teresa replied. "You need your own space."

Phoebe tried to hide the relief she felt at hearing her mother finally making plans to move back home. She loved Teresa as any child loves their mother, but her apartment was too small for the two of them.

"Okay," Phoebe said with a smile. "I can speak to my friend, Liz, at the hospital. She's an Occupational Therapist so might be able to come round and have a look if you wanted her to? She'll know the best place to put things, and probably knows someone who'll put them in for you."

"That would be lovely, Phoebe, thank you," Teresa replied, placing her hand over Phoebe's and smiling at her. Phoebe instantly felt bad about feeling relieved.

"But you know you can stay here as long as you want to, don't you?" she said.

"That's kind of you, Phoebe." Teresa squeezed Phoebe's hand. "But what if you met some young man and wanted to bring him back here?"

"Mother," Phoebe said, injecting a note of mock warning into her voice but smiling at the same time.

"You can't have a night of wanton debauchery with me in the next room, can you?"

Phoebe felt her cheeks coloring again as she remembered her dream, or at least the few fragments of it that she could. That was the closest she was going to get to any sort of wanton debauchery.

"I'm not that kind of woman, Mother, you know that," she said, still smiling. "Besides, chance would be a fine thing."

Both women laughed at the same time, but Phoebe's laughter was tinged with sadness. She just hoped her mother hadn't picked up on it.

"Why don't we head over there when you've got dressed?" Teresa said a moment later. "We could grab some croissants from the bakery and have breakfast in the back garden?"

"That sounds like a great plan," Phoebe replied as she got to her feet. She started laughing. "But if you think I'm mowing your lawn for you so we can sit out there, you can think again."

CHAPTER 23

Vincuk smoked the last of his cigarette, grinding the butt out into the soft ground of the forest. It had rained at some point during the night, and the earth was still wet. A light mist was rising from the ground as the sun's rays gradually started filtering through the trees. Somewhere in the forest, an animal of some sort called out. A deer, perhaps, or some type of wild boar? A few seconds later, there was an identical reply from another animal which was further away.

He thought of his father, who would have been able to identify the animal, its gender, and probably know exactly where in the forest it was. As would Yuri.

He and his father shared some things in common, at least now they did, even if they didn't when Vincuk's father was alive. They had both spent time hiding in the forest, pursued by enemies of the motherland. Except his father and Yuri were able to live off the land like a true hunter. Whatever beasts had just called out, they would have tracked, killed, gutted and cooked at least one of them.

Vincuk's father had tried to teach his son, but by the time Vincuk was old enough to learn, he was more interested in chasing girls, not animals. Vincuk wondered what his father would think of him now and shook his head in sadness.

The previous day had ended up as an unmitigated disaster. It had started off so well with the success of the training mission. But Vincuk hadn't anticipated being ambushed by the mercenaries on the way back to their base, an abandoned logging hut deep in the forest. He and Yuri had discussed it in depth the previous evening over a bottle of Stoli, but the vodka had only made them more morose. The only thing they could think of was that it had been a random checkpoint that the mercenaries had put up, knowing that there were resistance fighters operating in the area. It was irrelevant.

Vincuk had taken the corner so fast that he'd almost lost control of the van, bullets still thudding into the rear of the vehicle. At least the tires were all intact. If a round had taken one of them out, they would have been captured for sure. Vincuk didn't know what the People's Army would do with captured resistance fighters, but he doubted they would adhere to the Geneva Convention.

"Turn right in fifty yards," Yuri had shouted. Vincuk had looked at the straight road in front of them but trusted Yuri's instructions. As he slowed, sure enough there was a smaller road leading into the forest. It was so narrow that when Vincuk drove the van down it, he could hear branches scraping down the side of the vehicle. It was loud, but not loud enough to drown out the screaming coming from the rear.

It had been a further thirty minutes before Vincuk and Yuri had felt it was safe enough to stop the van. Yuri had guided Vincuk turn by turn, seeming to know the forest like the back of his hand. Vincuk had stopped the van's engine after winding the windows down. Both men had listened intently for the sound of any engines over the whimpering from the back before concluding they were safe, or as safe as they could be.

When Vincuk got out of the vehicle and approached the rear, he could see fifteen to twenty holes punched in the doors and bumper. Each one was perhaps an inch across with jagged shards that reached into the interior. Vincuk had exchanged a relieved look with Yuri, amazed that none of the bullets had come through to the front of the van. When he opened the door, Vincuk saw why.

Three of the four boys in the back of the van were dead. Very dead. One was missing most of the back of his head, the others each had several large wounds in their torsos. The sole survivor—the source of the whimpering—was sitting in the corner of the van. He was covered in blood but, as Vincuk and Yuri coaxed him out of the van, they found that none of it was his.

With the surviving boy sitting in the front of the van, rocking back and forth, Vincuk and Yuri had dug a hurried grave for their comrades. It had only been a couple of feet deep when they had finished, but it was deep enough to cover the bodies with a layer of soil. No doubt their bodies would be uncovered by animals in no time, but they couldn't bury them any deeper in the time they had.

Vincuk turned to see Yuri making his way toward him. He looked like shit, and Vincuk wondered if he had finished off the vodka the previous evening. No one would blame him for that, least of all Vincuk.

"We need a new van," Vincuk said by way of a greeting.

"I'll sort it today," Yuri replied, shaking a cigarette loose from a pack. He offered one to Vincuk who accepted it with a grunt of thanks.

"I'm going to go back to Hrodna," Vincuk said when Yuri had lit both their cigarettes. "We need more soldiers."

CHAPTER 24

Natasha looked around the dining room of the hotel as the other guests swarmed around the breakfast buffet. She was sitting at a table for two, a mug of coffee and glass of orange juice in front of her. While she waited, she examined the other guests to try to imagine why they were in London.

There were several families with small children, one with twin girls aged about six or seven who were dressed as Elsa from the Disney musical, Frozen. The previous evening, she and Caleb had walked past the West End theatre where a live-action version of the musical was being advertised. Natasha smiled at the thought of them and hundreds of other Elsas singing along to the songs.

In the opposite corner of the room were a group of young men, all in their late teens to early twenties, wearing the same colored sports top. A football team, perhaps, or soccer as Caleb would call it. Next to them was a small group of laborers, all wearing high-visibility jackets. Both groups of men had plates that were piled high with food.

Amongst the other guests were a couple of older men wearing suits.

Natasha saw Caleb appear at the entrance to the dining room. He spoke briefly to the member of hotel staff who checked Caleb's room number against his list before he looked up and caught Natasha's eye. Caleb smiled and raised his hand in greeting. She watched him make his way across the dining room, pausing to say something to one of the men in suits. To Natasha's surprise, after Caleb had spoken to him, the man in the suit got to his feet and left, his plate still half full.

"Morning, Natasha," Caleb said as he pulled his chair out to sit down opposite her. "You sleep okay?"

"Yes," Natasha replied. "Did you?"

"Like a log," Caleb said with an easy smile. "You eaten yet?"

"No, I was waiting for you."

"Well then." Caleb stood back up. "Shall we?"

As they made their way to the buffet, Natasha and Caleb walked past the table where the man in the suit had been sitting.

"What did you say to him?" Natasha asked, nodding at the partially finished breakfast. "He disappeared in a hurry."

"I was just asking him if he'd finished the book he was reading," Caleb replied, his smile returning. Natasha looked at him, noticing that his head was freshly shaven. She found it difficult enough to imagine men shaving their faces every day. Shaving your entire head was something else altogether.

A few moments later, they were sitting back at the table with their breakfast. Caleb had opted for what he said was a full English. Bacon, sausages, baked beans, and a fried egg. There was even a small slice of black pudding on his plate which he claimed was an acquired taste. By contrast, Natasha had decided for something lighter and was eating a bowl of cereal.

"So," she said between mouthfuls. "What are your plans for today?" She waited until he had finished an enormous mouthful of sausages that were liberally smothered in beans. She smiled as she watched him. How could he eat so much and remain so slim?

"Well," he said, finally. "I was thinking that we could be tourists for the morning before we go to the station later. Have you ever been to the Tower of London?

"I've never been to London before, so no," Natasha replied with a laugh. "That sounds like fun, though."

"I also want to go to the military surplus store we walked past last night on the way here." Caleb took another huge mouthful of food and chewed it with a thoughtful expression on his face. "Maybe we could go there first, if you don't mind? I want to get some things for the medical clinic to thank them for patching me up."

"Not at all," Natasha replied, looking away so she didn't have to watch Caleb eating. She checked her phone to see if Mikhail had replied to her text message from the previous evening but there was nothing. She did the math in her head and realized that it was only just after five in the morning back in Belarus. She smiled, thinking about how he normally got up about two minutes before he needed to be somewhere, even on the weekends.

A few moments later, once Caleb had used a slice of what looked like fried bread to mop up the last remnants of his breakfast, they both got to their feet.

"Shall we meet in the lobby in a few minutes?" Caleb said. "I just need to grab a couple of things from my room."

Natasha, whose bag was already packed and left in the

luggage room at the hotel, looked down at the cloth bag slung across his chest and smiled. Caleb travelled light, that was for sure, and she wondered what it was he needed to collect.

"Okay," she replied. "I'll wait for you in the lobby." She watched and her smile broadened as she saw some of the curious looks Caleb attracted from the other guests as he walked across the hotel foyer. He was either ignoring them or was immune to them, she wasn't sure.

But she was sure that he didn't care either way.

CHAPTER 25

Mikhail got to his feet, his arms stretched out in front of him. It was pitch black in the cellar, and Iľja's screams were getting louder. He took a couple of steps forward, trying to remember where on the shelves the flashlights were. His hands knocked into one of the shelves a few seconds later, dislodging a couple of tins of food. One of them hit him on the foot and he lurched forward in pain, striking his forehead on a sharp edge.

"Práklon!" Mikhail said with a gasp as he felt a trickle of warmth start to run down his forehead. *Damn!*

"Mikhail, what is it?" Iľja said between screams. "What's going on?"

"I'm finding a light, Aunt Iľja," Mikhail replied just as his hand encircled one of the small flashlights on the shelf. He clicked the button to turn it on, swinging it round to shine it on his aunt. She was sitting on the bed, her arms wrapped around her chest and he could see tears streaming down her face before she brought an arm up to cover her eyes. "Sorry," he mumbled when he realized he'd shone it straight into her eyes. He turned his attention back to the shelf and picked up another flashlight. Mikhail turned it on and handed it to Ilja.

"Thank you," she said, her voice already beginning to calm down. But when she shone the flashlight at him, it went back up an octave. "My God, Mikhail, what happened? Are you hurt?"

"No," he replied, forcing a grin onto his face. "I hit my head on the shelf."

"Come here," Ilja said. "Let me see."

The act of having something to focus on seemed to calm his aunt back down. Mikhail let her turn his head from side to side, tutting as she did so. Then she got to her feet and crossed the room, returning with a small first aid kit.

"What happened?" Ilja asked him as she sorted through the contents of the small green box. "Did we get hit?"

"I don't think so," Mikhail replied. The explosion had sounded loud, but he thought if the shell or whatever it was had hit their house, they wouldn't still be around to discuss it. That wasn't a conversation he was about to have with Ilja though.

"Keep still," she said as she dabbed at his forehead with an antiseptic wipe. Mikhail winced at the stinging sensation and he saw a smile appear on Ilja's face. "You big baby. It's only a scratch."

A few moments later, a fresh band aid on his forehead, Mikhail sat back on the bed and played his flashlight around the interior of the room.

"Perhaps we should use the candles instead of flash-lights?" he said as he noticed a packet of them on one of the shelves. "Save the batteries?"

"Good idea," Ilja replied. She stood and crossed to the shelf before swearing quietly under her breath.

"What is it?" Mikhail asked.

"I left the matches upstairs," she said with a grimace. "In the kitchen."

"I could go up and get them?"

"No!" The vehemence of her reaction surprised him. "No," she said again, more quietly this time. "We should wait for the all-clear to sound, like they told us to on the television.

Mikhail nodded, knowing that she was right. Hopefully, it wouldn't be long. When the air raid had sounded earlier, it had only been a short while before the all-clear. But the earlier siren hadn't been accompanied by artillery. It made no sense to him, them being targeted this way. They lived in a residential district, far away from any military installations, but the bomb had been close enough to shake the entire house. There was no reason at all for either side to target them.

"We should open the door a little," Mikhail said a moment later. "So that we can hear the all-clear when it does sound." Iĺja didn't look convinced at first but she nodded after a few seconds.

"Okay," she said, "but only a couple of inches. And we both keep away from the door just in case."

Mikhail got to his feet and opened the cellar door slightly, just as Iĺja had instructed. He paused, listening for a moment. He wasn't sure, but he fancied he could hear sirens in the distance. Not air raid sirens, but the ones belonging to the emergency services.

He sat back on the bed and turned his flashlight off to conserve the batteries. Then he took a deep breath, wondering how long they would have to wait.

CHAPTER 26

Caleb blinked a couple of times as his eyes adjusted from the bright sunshine outside to the dim interior of the store. The air inside was musty and had a peculiar odor that he remembered from a long time ago. It was a musty smell, not offensive, but slightly cloying in his nostrils. He held the door for Natasha to walk through and then let it go, turning his attention to the contents of the store.

On the walls, stacked in green shelving units, were box after box of equipment and there were racks of clothing containing a variety of uniforms. Some of them he recognized, some of them he didn't. The majority of them had some form of camouflage pattern on them, but there were also items that were navy blue or black.

With Natasha a couple of steps behind him, Caleb started looking through the contents of the boxes.

"Can I help you?" a male voice said from the rear of the store. Caleb turned to see a short, rotund man standing behind a glass-topped counter. He looked to be in his mid-fifties, was wearing an olive green t-shirt, combat trousers, and had the same hairstyle as Caleb did. Both the man's arms were heavily tattooed, but Caleb was too far away to discern what he was inked with.

"Do you have any field dressings?" Caleb asked.

"Sure we do," the man behind the counter said, pointing to the corner of the store. "Just there, in those boxes. Second shelf up."

Caleb walked to where he was pointing and open one of the brown boxes. He pulled out a vacuum packed bandage and turned it over in his hand, smiling at the memory of the item. The box he had pulled the bandage from was one of four, all stacked on top of each other. They all had labels on the outside, lined up with each other.

"Tourniquets?" Caleb asked.

"Next box over on the left."

Caleb looked in the box to the left to see it was full of black military tourniquets, each wrapped in plastic. "How much are they?"

"Fiver each, for the bandages and tourniquets."

"How much for all of them?" Caleb saw a grin spreading on the man's face as he reached for a calculator. He glanced at Natasha, whose nose was wrinkled, as the man stabbed at the calculator with podgy fingers.

"There're about two hundred bandages there. I've not sold many of them. The tourniquet box is full, so there're fifty of them. That should be twelve hundred quid. How does a grand sound?" His grin got even wider. "For cash, obviously."

Caleb whistled through his teeth. A thousand pounds was a lot of money. Far more than he had. He turned to Natasha and whispered. "Can I use the camera on your phone?" He waited as she unlocked her phone.

"Just press the red button there," she replied, also in a whisper.

Caleb started taking photographs of the labels on the outside of the boxes.

"Hey!" the man behind the counter shouted. "What are you doing?" He stepped out from behind the counter and started making his way to where Caleb and Natasha were standing, but by the time he reached them, Caleb had captured all the labels. He handed the phone back to Natasha, thanking her as he did so. "What's your game, pal?"

Caleb didn't reply at first. He was distracted momentarily by the way the atmosphere had changed. As well as the smell of stored clothing, he could now also sense body odor and a faint whiff of stale alcohol. Frowning, Caleb pointed at the labels on the outside of the boxes, each of which had the same text.

NATO Stock Number (NSN): 6510-99-279-9788
Short Item Name: First Field Dressing STANDARD

Underneath the text was a long number which was different on each box. Caleb pointed at the number.

"Do you read scripture, my friend?" Caleb asked. His voice was quiet but firm, and he didn't wait for the man to reply. Caleb was sure he didn't read the good book. "If anyone gives a neighbor silver or goods for safekeeping and they are stolen from the neighbor's house, the thief, if caught, must pay back double." He looked at the man, who was looking confused. "It's from Exodus if you're interested?"

"What the hell are you talking about?" The man had puffed his chest out and Caleb could see him clenching his fists.

"One thing every military is very good at is keeping track

of things," Caleb said quietly, tapping his finger on the number on the box. "That number will be stored somewhere on a spreadsheet in a Quartermaster's department. As will the name of the officer or non-commissioned officer who has signed it off as a loss."

"I've stolen nothing, pal."

"But these items have been stolen," Caleb replied. "And another thing every military is very good at is tracking down thieves. I would imagine if your contact who has supplied you with these items was to come under the scrutiny of the Military Police, it would cause you a problem?" He waved his arms to encompass the rest of the store's interior. "What else, I wonder, might the MPs also be interested in?"

The man sighed as if in resignation and took a couple of steps before turning his back on Caleb and Natasha and walking back toward his counter. Caleb held his hand out to Natasha to make sure she stayed where she was before following the store owner, taking a couple of large steps to make ground on him. By the time the man was behind his counter, reaching underneath it, Caleb was only a yard behind him.

When the man spun round with a knife in his hand, Caleb was already within his arc of movement. Ignoring the look of surprise on the man's face, Caleb's hand flashed out and caught his wrist just underneath the knife. He raised his hand, twisting it clockwise and the man arced his body to try to release Caleb's grip. The knife clattered to the floor as Caleb's other hand shot out and around the back of the man's neck.

Caleb released the knife hand and drove his fist into the man's abdomen, using his other hand to accelerate his movement toward the glass counter as the man doubled over. When his head impacted the glass, which Caleb saw was covering a variety of small and presumably valuable militaria, the counter splintered with a sharp crack but didn't shatter. Caleb raised his eyebrows.

Either the glass was tougher than he'd anticipated, or he was losing his touch.

CHAPTER 27

"What a horrible little man," Natasha said, adjusting the box of tourniquets under her arm. Next to her on the sidewalk, Caleb had the four boxes of bandages in his arms. Natasha could just see his face over the top of them and he was nodding in agreement. "Can I ask you something, Caleb?"

"Of course you can," he replied. The military surplus store was a couple of hundred yards behind them, and they were walking toward Kings Cross station.

"Where did you learn to fight like that?"

"I'm surprised you haven't asked me before," Caleb said. "After what happened in the alleyway."

"I was trying not to be nosy," Natasha replied with a wry smile. "Are you a martial arts expert or something?" She started giggling. "A bald Texan ninja?"

"I have a very particular set of skills," Caleb said. She noticed he had changed his accent. It was now less pronounced. "Skills I have acquired over a very long career." He was also laughing. "Skills that make me a nightmare for people like him."

"Very Liam Neeson," Natasha replied, still smiling. "Seriously, though. Where did you learn that stuff?"

"I learned it a long time ago, in a previous life." She looked at him. He was also smiling but his voice was different, harder in a sense. "A life I rarely think about, and never talk about."

Natasha stopped walking and waited until Caleb did the same. He turned to look at her over the top of the boxes.

"I've offended you," she said, keeping her voice level. "That was not my intent. I apologize."

"You have nothing to apologize for, Natasha," Caleb replied, his voice back to normal. "My philosophy is to not look backward or forward, but to live for the now."

"Is that from the Bible?" Natasha asked, tilting her head to one side.

"Kind of." Caleb smiled. "Come on, let's get these to where they need to be."

They walked on for a while. Natasha was still wondering whether she had offended him with her question. But she was curious. One second, she had seen the man in the store pulling a knife on Caleb. The next, the man was face first into his counter. She'd barely had time to register the movement, and Caleb's robes swirling had hidden much of it.

"Do you really think most of his stock is stolen?" she asked him a moment later.

"Perhaps not all of it," Caleb replied. "Every military has a surplus and disposes of things. But some it will be, for sure. These bandages and tourniquets are, definitely."

"How do you know?"

"They're brand new," he said. "Still in their original boxes, complete with the tracking number on the side. The date of manufacture of the bandage I looked at was only a couple of months ago." He hefted the boxes in his arms.

"They will have disappeared on their way to a unit some-where, marked as *Lost In Transit* and signed off by someone who doesn't get paid enough to care." Caleb sighed. "I was prepared to buy some of them with the money left from the men in the alley, but I changed my mind when I realized he was giving them away. Can't beat that with a stick."

"I don't think he had much choice, Caleb," Natasha replied with a wry smile. "But I wouldn't have thought soldiers would steal things."

"Some will," Caleb said. "It's as old as armies themselves. The Romans had a punishment called fustuarium for thieves."

"Was it a nasty punishment?"

"If you call being stripped naked and beaten to death by your fellow soldiers nasty, then yes, you could say that."

Natasha glanced across at him to see if he was joking, but Caleb's face was serious. A shiver ran down her spine at the thought of men doing that to each other, no matter when it happened.

"Do you think the clinic will be open this early?" Natasha asked him, keen to change the subject from capital punishment.

"I hope so," Caleb replied. She looked at him again to see a smile had appeared on his face. "But if it isn't, we can leave them there."

"It's a kind gesture, what you're doing."

"Well, this lot should help that convoy they're running over there." Natasha saw he was still smiling.

"It will," she replied slowly. Caleb turned his head to look at her. "It's also a chance for you to see that doctor again." Natasha started laughing. "Or am I getting that wrong?" Caleb mumbled something under his breath that she didn't catch. "I'm sorry, Caleb," she said. "I missed that?"

"There's a phrase back home in Texas," Caleb replied, his smile turning into a grin. "Cuter than pig nipples. I won't lie, I think that sums the doctor up pretty well."

"Ah, okay," Natasha said, giggling. "Just one thing, though."

"What?"

"You might not want to tell her that."

CHAPTER 28

Mikhail paced in the cellar, or as much as he could do given its size. Every time he passed the candle in the center of the room, it flickered from the breeze he caused. Earlier, after thirty minutes or so of silence, Ilja had relented and allowed him to run upstairs and grab the matches, on the understanding that he returned immediately. Mikhail had done as instructed, pausing only to listen for a few seconds and check his cell phone for messages.

He could hear the emergency services sirens still in the distance but to his disappointment, his phone was silent and he had no signal. At least he'd been able to reassure Ilja that there was no obvious damage to the house when he had returned. Perhaps, Mikhail had thought, that the explosion had taken out the mobile phone masts or something like that. It was about the only thing he could think of that was of military significance in the area.

"Mikhail, would you just sit down," Ilja said, her voice full of the frustration he felt. "You're making me nervous, all that pacing."

"Sorry," Mikhail said as he sat on the bed opposite her. On the floor between them were a few empty bottles of water, but neither of them were hungry for a breakfast from a tin. "How much longer do you think we'll have to wait?"

"I don't know, Mikhail," Iĺja replied. "But this is exactly why the cellar's stocked up like it is. So that if we have to spend time down here, we can."

"But I don't understand," he said plaintively, jiggling his leg up and down. "Why would anyone drop bombs anywhere near here?"

"I don't understand either, Mikhail, but the sooner we get you out of here and to safety, the better."

Mikhail was just about to reply when they heard a new noise in the distance. It was the wail of the air raid sirens. The all clear.

"Finally," Mikhail said as he jumped to his feet.

He left the cellar as quickly as he could and made his way through Iĺja's house and to the front door. Mikhail flung it open and stepped out into the small front yard. A couple of hundred yards away, he could see a thin plume of black smoke rising into the air so he set off in the direction of the fire to see what was happening. Iĺja called something out to him, but Mikhail didn't catch what she said.

As he walked down the street, he saw a fire truck speeding past at the end of the road, its distinctive red, white, and blue livery a blur. A few seconds later, it was followed by an ambulance. Both vehicles had their sirens and blue lights on, and they were watched by Mikhail and several other local residents who had emerged from their houses.

"What's going on?" an elderly woman asked Mikhail as he walked past her. She was leaning on her front gate, looking up and down the street, with a fearful expression on her face. Her white hair was being blown about by the wind, but she made no effort to move it away from her eyes.

"I don't know," Mikhail mumbled in reply, not stopping his stride.

Mikhail reached the end of the street and turned into a larger street. He looked in the direction he had seen the emergency vehicles rushing down and saw the remains of a residential building around a hundred yards away. His heartbeat quickened as he thought he recognized the building, and he broke into a run to get closer.

When he approached, he could see that the building had been partially destroyed. The top floor, one of three, had a large hole in the center through which black smoke was billowing. All the building's windows had been blown out, and rescuers were clambering over a pile of rubble in front of the ruin. Spread across the area were people's belongings. Mikhail saw letters and cards fluttering in the breeze, and a group of people were gathered together to one side of the building. There was a stench of sewage along with the smell of burning which the faint wind was doing nothing to disperse.

"You can't go any closer," a fireman said as Mikhail tried to join the rescuers. He was wearing a filthy yellowed uniform with a blue hard hat, and his face was streaked with grime. "It's not safe. The building's unstable." Another fireman was trying to string up some tape to form a cordon, but the tape kept catching on debris and shredding. Mikhail took a few steps back and focused on the group of people he had seen. They were all women and children, and he could hear their wailing carrying across the breeze. His eyes flicked between them, but there was no one he recognized. A few yards away from the group were several ambulances and Mikhail could see three stretchers laid out between them, blankets covering whoever was on them.

Mikhail took a few steps toward the group of women and children, determined to talk with them. As he approached, a hush fell over the gathered crowd. He turned to look at the rescuers to see they were preparing to bring another stretcher out from the rubble. One of the rescuers, clad in the same uniform as the fireman but with a bullet proof vest covering his chest, raised his hand in the air. The hush became a silence.

He took a few more steps to get closer to the group, ignoring the glare this elicited from the fireman with the tape. Four men, each of them with a hand on a stretcher handle, started to pick their way carefully over the rubble and make their way toward the ambulances. Mikhail got closer and saw the body on the stretcher was covered with a blanket, heavily bloodstained. The body was smaller than Mikhail, but he didn't think it was a child. One of the stretcher bearers slipped, almost losing his footing on the loose bricks they were walking over. As he did so, the body on the stretcher shifted slightly and Mikhail thought he saw something falling off the canvas material.

But it wasn't something falling off the stretcher. It was something falling from the stretcher. A long braid of fine brown hair that fluttered slightly in the breeze.

It was tied at the end with a small yellow and green ribbon.

CHAPTER 29

Caleb looked around the interior of the station. The concourse was fairly busy with a few harried-looking commuters making their way to work and families with excited children milling about.

He and Natasha walked through the concourse, Caleb smiling as they walked past a Greggs bakery with a line that stretched out of the door of the shop. Few, if any, of the people in the line looked as if they needed anything from the bakery. To one side of the door, a homeless man was sitting with a cup in front of him, munching on a sausage roll that a generous customer had bought for him. Caleb smiled at the man's ingenuity. Even if his cup was empty of any spare change, at least his stomach was full.

It was just after ten in the morning and as Caleb and Natasha made their way to the part of the station where she had arrived the previous day, the crowds started to thin out. They approached a barrier that separated the refugee arrival area where a young man in a bright orange bib stood with a clipboard.

"Morning," the man said with a bright smile. "Can I help you?"

"Good morning," Caleb replied. "We've got some supplies here for the medical center." He waited as the man in the bib looked him up and down with a curious expression.

"You don't look like a delivery driver," he said, nodding at Caleb's robe.

"I'm not." Caleb hefted the boxes in his arms. "These are donations for the convoy they're taking over to Belarus."

"Gotcha," the young man replied. "If you just drop them here, I'll make sure they get to the medical center."

"D'you mind if we take them through ourselves?" Caleb asked. He could see Natasha smirking out of the corner of his eye, but he ignored her. The man in the bib looked uncertain for a few seconds before nodding in agreement.

"Um, sure," he said. "You know where you're going?"

"Sure do," Caleb replied with a smile. "What time is the train due in?"

"The refugee train? It'll be here at two, like always."

Caleb nodded in response and looked over at Natasha. If the train came in at two they probably weren't going to have enough time to be tourists for very long. He thought back to the guy from the Foreign and Commonwealth Office they had spoken to the previous day. He had said the Home Office normally set their desk up half an hour before the train's arrival, so they only had a little over three hours.

"We might need to save being tourists for another day, Natasha," he said as they walked past the man in the orange bib. "I don't think we're going to have enough time."

"Okay, no worries," Natasha replied. He caught a faint look of disappointment on her face, but she hid it well. Even so, Caleb felt bad.

"I'm sorry, that's my fault for going to the military surplus store."

"We can go to the Tower of London another day, Caleb." She smiled at him, and he felt even worse. "It's been there for over a thousand years already. I'm sure it'll still be there for the next few days."

"Even so, I'm sorry."

"Well, don't be."

They walked past the boarded-up store fronts in the sectioned off area of the station concourse and toward the door leading to the medical center. Caleb let Natasha enter first, thanking her as she held the door open for him with a foot. He looked around the waiting area but could only see the nurse from the previous day. There was no sign of the doctor.

"We're not open just yet," Caleb heard the nurse say. She was wearing the same green scrubs as before and was busy restocking one of the shelves.

"We're not customers," he replied. "We've got some medical supplies for your convoy." Caleb nodded at the poster on the wall in response to the nurse's confused expression.

"Ah, I see," she said, smiling brightly. Beside him, Natasha placed her box of tourniquets on the floor and started massaging her forearms. "Could you take them through to the storeroom for me?" The nurse pointed at a door in the rear of the medical center. "It's just through there."

"Sure thing," Caleb turned to Natasha. "Leave that box there, Natasha," he said. "I'll come back for it in a moment."

When Caleb entered the storeroom, to his surprise there was very little in it. A few boxes here and there on the floor, and some packs of diapers in assorted sizes. He placed his own boxes of bandages down and looked around.

It wasn't going to be a very large convoy looking at the meager supplies they had gathered so far.

Caleb pressed his lips together, wondering if he might be able to do something about that.

CHAPTER 30

"It's Jade, isn't it?" Natasha asked as she approached the nurse.

"Yes, that's me," Jade replied with a smile at Natasha. "I'm surprised you remembered." Natasha looked at her. Even though it was the start of her working day, the nurse looked tired. More than tired, she realized. Exhausted.

"Can I help you with those?" Natasha asked, glancing down at the box Jade was using to refill the cupboard.

"No, don't worry, I'm almost done."

Natasha dropped her voice to just above a whisper. She didn't want Caleb to overhear, even though he was in the next room.

"Jade, would you mind if I asked you something?"

"Of course." Jade stopped what she was doing and turned to look at Natasha with a look of concern on her face. "Is everything okay?"

"Everything's fine. I just wanted to ask you something about Phoebe." Natasha gave a furtive glance in the direction of the storeroom door. "On behalf of my friend, Caleb, although he doesn't know I'm asking." She watched as a conspiratorial smile appeared on the nurse's face.

"I'm intrigued. Ask away."

"Is she, er, is she single? Only I think he's taken a shine to her."

Jade's smile broadened and she looked as if she was about to reply when the storeroom door opened and Caleb returned for the box of tourniquets. Both women watched as he hitched his robe up a couple of inches before bending his knees to pick it up. Natasha had to suppress a laugh at the sight. He grinned at them before returning to the storeroom.

"She is," Jade said, grinning as the door swung shut behind Caleb, "but I'm not sure he's her type."

"You won't say anything to her, will you?"

"Of course not," Jade replied. "Mum's the word." Natasha frowned at the unfamiliar expression. It wasn't one her father had taught her, or something she'd ever heard spoken before. As if she realized Natasha might not understand, Jade continued. "I won't say a word to her, don't worry."

"Thank you," Natasha said, taking a couple of steps backward to give Jade room to complete her task. As she did so, her cell phone vibrated. Natasha looked down at the screen to see a text message from her sister back in Belarus.

Can you call me? It's urgent.

"Would you excuse me?" Natasha said to Jade but the nurse didn't appear to have heard her. After a quick glance at the storeroom door to see if Caleb had finished, Natasha took a few steps toward the main door of the medical center, stabbing at the screen as she did so. Caleb reappeared just as she reached it, so she raised the phone in his direction for a couple of seconds before pressing it to her ear. Natasha saw Caleb nodding to show he understood she needed to make a call.

"Iľja?" Natasha said, switching to Belarusian as her sister answered almost immediately. Her first thoughts were of her husband, Anton. Had something happened to him on the front line somewhere? "What's wrong?"

"Oh, my God, Natasha," Iľja said. Her voice sounded desperate and Natasha's heart sank. "We were bombed this morning."

"Is everyone okay? Mikhail?"

"He's fine, we're fine," Iľja replied. "But an apartment block just down the road was hit. People were killed."

Natasha felt her knees starting to tremble and she looked around for somewhere to sit down. Her heart was racing in her chest at the news.

"Do you know who?" Natasha asked, thinking about her neighbors back home as she took a few steps toward the waiting area before sitting down heavily in one of the white plastic chairs.

"No, but I think Mikhail knew some of them. He went out after the all clear and came back in a hell of a state."

"Where is he now? Can I talk to him?"

"He's in his room. I can hear him throwing stuff around. He wouldn't talk to me. What do I do?" Iľja's voice was plaintive and Natasha's heart went out to her. She took a deep breath to try to calm herself down. She knew only too well what Mikhail could be like at times when he was upset or angry. There was no reasoning with him when he was like that. Even if she was there in person, Natasha would have to wait to speak to him.

"Just give him space, Iľja," Natasha replied. "He'll come round."

"I'm going to move, Natasha," Iľja said. "To Podlipki."

"Which one?" Natasha asked. There were several towns by that name in the area.

"The one in Belarus, close to the border. I was there yesterday. At Tatiana and Max's farm?"

Natasha thought for a moment before nodding her head in agreement. She knew Iĺja's friend Tatiana well but didn't really care for her husband after he had made a vodka-fueled pass at Natasha a couple of years ago. Apart from that, they were decent people. Hard working, honest, and in Max's case, apologetic once sober.

"They've got plenty of room," Iĺja continued, "and it's in the middle of nowhere."

"That's a good idea, Iĺja," Natasha said, still reeling from the news about the bombing. She looked up to see Caleb approaching her, a plastic cup of water in his hand. He had a look of concern on his face, but Natasha knew he wouldn't be able to understand what she was talking about. "Thank you," she whispered in English as she took the cup, her hand trembling so much that some of it spilled.

"Is everything okay?" Natasha heard Caleb ask.

No, she thought. *Everything is far from okay.*

CHAPTER 31

Stepan raised his boot and, with a glance at the soldier next to him, kicked at the farmhouse door as hard as he could. The flimsy door splintered and flew in with a loud crash. A few seconds later, he heard similar crashes from the houses on either side of this one. He stepped back, allowing the soldier to enter the house first, before he pulled his pistol from its holster and followed the other man inside.

"Who is here?" Stepan shouted. "Make yourselves known!"

While the soldier searched the downstairs rooms, Stepan started making his way up the stairs to the upper story, deliberately crashing his feet on the wooden floorboards. Like the other peasant's houses he had been in, the interior of this one was minimalist to say the least. The walls were bare with no decoration, and hadn't been painted for some years. Just as Stepan reached the top of the stairs, one of the bedroom doors opened and a large man peered out, his face shocked.

Stepan raised the pistol and pointed it in his face,

tempted to just shoot the man there and then. But from the size of him, getting his body out of the house would be an effort. Then a woman's face appeared behind the man's shoulder. She opened her mouth and screamed, and Stepan was tempted to shoot her instead, but he gestured down the stairs with the pistol after walking onto the landing.

THIRTY MINUTES LATER, just as the sun was coming up over the horizon, Stepan was sitting with one of his patrol in some garden chairs they had found outside one of the houses. The soldier had his gun trained on a group of women in front of them. There were five of them altogether, all sitting on the damp earth in a rough circle still wearing their nightclothes. There was the woman from the house Stepan had been in, a couple of elderly women from one of the others, and a pair of sisters who looked to be in their teens. One of the girls, the younger of the sisters, was staring at Stepan with a look of utter contempt. He put his hand to his holster and gripped the pistol, knowing what was coming next. The women were all looking at the ground or each other but when the automatic gunfire started a few hundred yards away, they all jumped as one.

The echoes of the gunfire burst were just beginning to fade when Stepan heard more shots ringing out. They were single shots, and he knew there would be four of them as there had been four men in the village. One of the women started crying and, when the others realized their menfolk were dead, they all started as well. A couple of times in the past, some of the women they had captured had made an effort to attack the soldiers at this point, but none of these women did so he relaxed his grip on the pistol.

A few moments later, the other three men in Stepan's

squad appeared through the trees from the direction of the gunfire. Stepan saw them laughing as they walked, two of them sharing a cigarette. He waited until they had joined them. It was time for his favorite part of these missions. The education of those left behind.

"You will all be free soon," Stepan said, looking at the younger sister whose expression had turned from contempt to hatred and anger. "You must tell people what happens to collaborators."

"We're not collaborators," one of the woman said with a whimper. Stepan, whose eyes were fixed on the younger girl, didn't see which of them it was. It didn't matter anyway. Nothing they could say would change anything. The only way this situation would be any different would be if they had found members of the resistance in the small village. Then the resistance fighters would be hanging from branches, but the women's fate would be the same. He pulled his pistol from the holster and pointed it at the young girl who was still staring at him.

"You!" he shouted, making sure she was staring right down the barrel of the weapon. Stepan saw her expression change from anger to fear. He heard one of his soldiers sniggering next to him. The girl got to her feet slowly and Stepan gestured with the pistol to the closest house. "Let's go."

CHAPTER 32

Vincuk gunned the engine of his small Lada, cursing as the engine complained with an angry sounding rattle. He cast his eyes over the dashboard but other than the temperature gauge reading high, there was nothing wrong. Perhaps while he was back in Hrodna, he would drop it off with one of his friends to have a look? But that would almost certainly cost money, and that wasn't something that he had much of. If he'd been thinking, he could have saved some of the vodka from the village to use in exchange.

As he drove, the lush green of the Belarusian countryside flying past his window, Vincuk thought back over the events of the previous day. What could they have done differently? What could they do differently next time? Maybe if they had two vehicles they could send one ahead with legitimate papers and no weapons. That way, if there was a mobile checkpoint, the first vehicle could go through it and report back to the following vehicle. They could then set up an ambush and lure the mercenaries into it. Vincuk hadn't been able to see how many men were in the group who had attacked them yesterday, but it couldn't have been more than four or five. If they set up the ambush right, and cut down the majority of them with the first burst of fire, they would be successful. Vincuk made a mental note to run the plan past Yuri to see what he thought about it.

A COUPLE OF HOURS LATER, his Lada engine still rattling but functional, Vincuk entered the outskirts of Hrodna, his home town. Although there wasn't a front line in the truest sense, Hrodna was a long way from any fighting. But Vincuk had heard on the local radio station while he was driving about some artillery shelling during the night, which surprised him. Were the Belarusian army or the mercenaries upping the ante?

The radio news had said nothing concrete about who had fired the shells, or from where. There was some speculation that it was the resistance movement, which had caused Vincuk to laugh bitterly. Where were they going to get artillery weapons from?

As he usually did, Vincuk drove down the road outside his cafe a couple of times, his eyes alert for anything out of place. Although he thought he was well below the radar of the authorities, you could never be too careful. He had a small but trusted circle of colleagues and friends, but anyone could be turned given the right amount of pressure. The Belarus secret police were not an enemy to be taken lightly. Following the protests against the establishment a few years ago, an estimated forty thousand people were arrested. Many of them were still missing or serving hard time in penal colonies for daring to criticize the regime. The authorities response to an armed insurrection would be far worse.

Seeing nothing untoward, Vincuk parked his Lada in a space a hundred meters or so away from his cafe. Then he repeated the same procedure, this time on foot. As he walked past the cafe door, he regarded it out of the corner of his eye. There was a flyer that he'd left wedged under the door before leaving that was still in place. If the door had been opened, it would have been moved. He passed the door, walked on a few more yards, and then turned to return to the cafe.

Once he had let himself into the cafe, Vincuk paused to listen for a moment. The air inside was musty and fetid, but it was still and there was nothing to suggest that he had company. Vincuk thought he was probably being overly cautious, but at the same time he wondered how many of those thousands of people who had been arrested would be in custody if they had been as careful as he was being. He walked through the cafe and into the small office in the rear, glancing at the answering machine on the dusty desk. According to the screen, there were no messages. This disappointed Vincuk. After being away for some days, he had hoped there would be some.

Vincuk booted up his ancient computer and checked the printer for paper. When the computer was eventually ready, Vincuk opened an image file he kept in a hidden folder.

He stared at the woman in the red dress on his screen and smiled. It was only an image and some text, but possession of it could land him ten years in prison. The text below the woman could cost him his life.

But only if he was caught with it in his possession.

CHAPTER 33

Phoebe blipped the locks of her mini, smiling as she saw the brake lights flare to reveal a Union flag set into the glass covering. It was a clever marketing ploy to make people think the vehicle was made in the United Kingdom, as opposed to the parts being made overseas and only put together here, but she liked the local touch it gave her car. With a quick look at the darkening sky, she hurried across the parking lot and into the main doors of the hospital, dodging a small crowd of smokers puffing away next to the sign that declared the site smoke free.

The inside of the hospital was as it always seemed to be. Busy, yet serene at the same time. She made her way through the out patients department and toward her destination, the Emergency Department. Earlier that morning, Phoebe had e-mailed a list of medications that she needed to collect for the clinic. When she reached the doors that led to the department, she paused and looked through the circular windows where she saw a familiar face talking to a young woman.

Thomas Lincoln was a registrar in the Emergency

Department and had worked there for almost as long as Phoebe had. He was a very handsome man, blonde hair arranged in what could only be described as a fop, a triangular torso honed in the gym, and one of the cutest smiles in the entire hospital. Phoebe watched as he used it to full effect on the woman he was talking to, prompting a flirtatious laugh and tilt of the head from her. She knew that smile only too well. Almost three years previously, she had known Thomas in a very different sense for a few short weeks. A biblical one.

Phoebe watched as the two of them chatted, their faces slightly distorted by the glass. The woman Thomas was talking to looked to be a junior doctor, perhaps one of the new rotation of foundation year medics. Senior enough to be called a doctor, but so junior it was really in name only. She saw the junior doctor, a pretty woman with flame red hair, laugh again. This time she accentuated the head tilt by running her fingers through her hair. She was wearing green scrubs, matching Crocs on her feet, and had a bright red stethoscope draped around her neck. Phoebe wondered if the two of them were sleeping together yet. She thought not as the junior doctors' rotation had only just started, but knowing Thomas, it was only a matter of time.

"Like a lamb to the slaughter," Phoebe muttered to herself as she pushed open the door. Thomas looked up as she did so and an easy smile appeared on his face.

"Hey, Phoebes," he said, his educated English accent obvious even from two words. Phoebe sighed. He was the only person who ever called her Phoebes.

"Good morning, Doctor Lincoln," Phoebe replied, glancing at the female doctor who had a look of suspicion on her face. Phoebe almost laughed at the woman. If she thought Phoebe was a rival, she was very mistaken. "How's your wife?"

Thomas's face fell, but only for a split second. From the frown that appeared on the junior doctor's face, Thomas hadn't gotten round to telling her about his wife yet. Just like he hadn't told Phoebe until he'd taken her to bed. Several times.

"Oh, you know," Thomas replied in a nonchalant tone. "Same old, same old."

Phoebe gave them both a smile that she hoped was both aloof and dismissive and made her way to the small pharmacy. There was a hatch in the wall where a perpetually cheerful woman called Peggy was waiting for her. Peggy, always Peggy never Margaret, had been working at the hospital since it opened if the rumors were to be believed. She seemed to spend her days just peering out of the hatch, watching the world go by. But this meant that little got past her.

"Doctor Sokolova," Peggy said as Phoebe approached, a smile deepening the creases in the pharmacy technician's face. She was in her mid-sixties, wore her gray hair in a tight bun, and was constantly on one diet or another.

"Hey Peggy," Phoebe replied, returning the smile. "You're looking well."

"Three pounds this week," Peggy replied, patting her ample stomach. "I'm trying a non-processed food diet." She lowered her voice to a conspiratorial whisper. "But oh my word, the wind."

Phoebe laughed at the earnest expression on Peggy's face. Ever since she'd met her, the pharmacy technician had been trying to lose weight but she seemed to be the same size as that day. Peggy nodded in Thomas' direction.

"I see he's trying to work his way through the new crop

of foundation year doctors," she said as Phoebe's laughter faded away. She glanced in Thomas' direction, aiming for a disinterested look, but she wasn't convinced she'd pulled it off. "Are you still planning on going on that convoy with him?"

"I am," Phoebe replied. When she'd placed an advertisement on the noticeboard of the Doctors' Mess looking for volunteers for the convoy, to her dismay he'd been the only one who'd replied. But she couldn't turn him down with no good reason, or at least one that could be a public one.

"Well, you be careful my dear," Peggy said, putting her hand on top of Phoebe's and glancing at Thomas. "Men like Doctor Lincoln are only after one thing."

Don't I know it, Phoebe thought, hoping that her face didn't give her away. But Peggy's next words and the expression of her face told her it was too late.

"And believe me, Doctor Sokolova, there's no such thing as once bitten, twice shy."

CHAPTER 34

Mikhail, his eyes clouded, sat on the edge of his bed and let the tears flow down his face unhindered. He made no effort to wipe them away. There was no point. There would only be more. As he thought about the blanket he had seen on the stretcher, covering Alevtina's slim form, he balled his fists up and pressed them against his temples. The pain he felt in his chest wasn't imagined. It was as real as her body.

"Why?" he said, the word a mixture of a muffled scream and a sob. "Why her?"

It made no sense. They lived in a residential area, full of houses, schools, shops and civilians. Why would anyone drop shells on them? It had to be Belarus, bombing its own citizens. Or perhaps the mercenaries from Russia he'd heard so much about? Whoever it was, Mikhail hated them. He sat on the bed, trying to focus his grief into something else. Something less painful.

Alevtina was only fourteen years old, the same age he was. She had her whole life ahead of her, but that had now been stolen, as had any future she and Mikhail may have had. He knew he was being dramatic. They had, after all, shared a single kiss. That didn't mean they were going to spend the rest of their lives together, and grow old in a farmstead in the mountains surrounded by children and grandchildren. But Mikhail knew that there was now no chance of that scenario ever happening, no matter how unlikely. He pushed his fists harder against his temple as a fresh wave of tears streamed down his face.

A few moments later, there was a gentle knock at the door.

"Mikhail?" It was Iĺja, but he didn't want to talk to her. "Is everything okay?"

Mikhail took a deep breath to compose himself before replying. "It's fine," he said, keeping his voice as steady as he could.

"Are you sure?"

"Yep."

"I heard about the apartment block," Iĺja said through the door. "Did you know some of the people there?"

Mikhail took another deep breath as the pain in his chest increased and yet more tears threatened. He thought back to when he and Alevtina were in the shelter together. As they had been kissing, she had moved at one point and her breasts had rubbed against his arm. Very slightly, but it was enough for him to sense their shape and what they might feel like. Although there had been plenty of material between their skin, the sensation had sent a jolt of electricity through his body. Now Alevtina would never be touched again. Not by Mikhail, not by anyone except perhaps a coroner.

"I need to get ready for school, Aunt Iĺja," Mikhail replied, even though there was no way he was going to school that day. The only thing anyone would be talking about would be the attack on Alevtina's apartment, and he knew he wouldn't be able to bear that.

"Okay, well just let me know if you need anything."

"I will," Mikhail said, keeping his voice even and nodding even though his aunt couldn't see him.

He waited for a moment until he was sure she had gone and wasn't listening at the door. Then he pulled his hands away from his temples and unclenched his fists before re-clenching his right one. Mikhail hit himself with it hard in the sternum, the way he had seen his father do many times when he was angry. According to his father, it was a way of keeping the anger locked up inside, and not letting it out where it could hurt anyone. There would be a time and a place for it to come out, but Mikhail knew that this was neither the time nor the place.

He glanced across at his tote bag which was lying in the corner of his room, still crammed with last week's training kit which he'd forgotten to put into the washing basket. He needed to get out of the house, to go somewhere he could be alone to think properly. Mikhail looked around his room and at his door which he had imagined Alevtina walking through many times. When they were both alone in the house. Her clothing varied according to his mood. Sometimes she was wearing normal clothes as if they were just friends. Sometimes, she was wearing the types of garments he had seen on the mannequins in the local department store's lingerie department as if they were lovers. Very occasionally, she was wearing exactly what the women he watched on the internet were wearing, before he and Alevtina did what he had watched them do on the internet. But Mikhail didn't really like thinking of Alevtina in that way, not when she was alive and certainly not now that she was dead.

Mikhail got to his feet and crossed to the corner of the room. He picked up the tote bag, undid the fastener, and upended it, wrinkling his nose at the sour smell from the clothes that tumbled out. Then he crossed back to his chest of drawers where he stuffed some fresh clothes into the bag. Mikhail worked quickly, only selecting what he would need for a few days. He had some cash at the bottom of his top drawer which he picked up, but he left his passport where it was.

A few moments later, after a glance in the mirror where he cursed his red-rimmed eyes, Mikhail made his way to the front door of Iĺja's house. He paused as he opened it, turning back to look down the corridor. He could see Iĺja in the kitchen. She looked up at him with a concerned expression and stopped what she was doing.

"I'm going to school, Aunt Iĺja," Mikhail called out, trying to hide the tote bag behind him so Iĺja wouldn't notice how full it was. He saw her taking a couple of steps toward him but he stepped through the door before she could say anything, closing it firmly behind him and half running through Iĺja's front garden.

Mikhail needed to get away. Not just that, but he needed to do something. Something for Alevtina.

CHAPTER 35

Natasha placed the cup of water on the floor before she spilled any more of it. She stared at the screen on her phone which was telling her she had been on the phone to Ilja for less than a minute. They always tried to keep their voice calls brief because of the cost, but it had been long enough to fill her heart with terror.

"What's wrong?" Natasha heard Caleb say. He had dropped to his haunches next to her chair, and was looking at her with a furrowed brow. "Has something happened?"

"There was an air raid at home," Natasha replied, her voice not much more than a whisper. "Some houses got destroyed close to ours. That was my sister, Ilja." She watched as Caleb processed the information for a few seconds.

"Is your son okay?" he asked her. "Mikhail, isn't it?"

"Mikhail's fine. He's just upset. Some people were killed, though." She felt tears starting to prick at her eyes. "Mikhail knew some of them, Ilja said."

Natasha saw Caleb close his eyes for a moment, his lips moving almost imperceptibly. When he opened them, they were full of pain.

"I'm sorry," he said, glancing at her phone. "Can you call him?"

Natasha laughed, a short, sharp bark of a laugh with no humor at all. "He's a teenager," she replied. "They don't speak on the phone. I'll have to message him." She swiped at the screen to bring up her messenger app, selecting Mikhail's name from the very short list of contacts.

Message me when you can, let me know you're okay.

With a swoosh, the message disappeared and Natasha was left staring at a small grayed out tick on the screen. A second tick appeared indicating the message had been delivered, and she waited to see if they would turn green to indicate Mikhail had read the message.

"You must feel completely helpless," Caleb said quietly.

Natasha looked at him for a second. With his words, he had swept her feet out from under her by describing exactly how she felt. Totally and utterly helpless. She was supposed to take care of Mikhail, even more so since Anton had gone off to fight. Mikhail was her son, but her response to the events in Belarus had been to run, leaving him behind. The tears which had threatened now burst from her eyes.

"I should have stayed," she sobbed, "not run like a баязлiўка."

"A what?" Caleb asked, and Natasha realized she'd lapsed into her mother tongue.

"A coward," she whispered.

"You're not a coward, Natasha," Caleb replied, his voice reassuring. His hand was hovering over hers, and she wondered if he was going to touch her. "You're here to prepare for Mikhail getting here." A smile crinkled his face. "In military terms, it's called shaping the battlefield. We need to get you to the Home Office desk to figure out your housing. Then you'll have a place to live, and so will Mikhail once he gets here."

Natasha shook her head in disagreement, even though she knew Caleb was right. She already had a place to live, but it was back in Belarus. A family home where she and Anton had raised Mikhail. A happy place where her husband treated Mikhail like a son before their happiness was torn apart by the conflict. But she was the one who had left her home the moment she could, leaving the most precious thing in her world behind. She should have stayed until they could travel together.

"The exit visas are on a ballot, is that right?" Caleb asked. Natasha nodded her head in reply, not trusting herself to speak. "Then none of this is your fault. You did what you could, which was exactly the right thing to do. Your sister, she's a good woman?"

"Yes," Natasha replied, nodding her head again.

"So, Mikhail is in good hands. They might not be your hands, but they're good hands." Finally, Caleb's hand found Natasha's, and she felt a tingle of warmth in her fingertips.

She looked down at her phone again, but the two small ticks next to her message to Mikhail on the screen remained resolutely gray. Unread.

"What am I going to do?" she asked him, sniffing loudly before apologizing. He took his hand from hers to reach a box of tissues that was on one of the other chairs in the waiting area. Natasha saw him glancing at the clock on the wall as he handed them to her.

"If the train gets here at two, and the Home Office desk

opens half an hour before, we've got some time to kill. I could walk you back to the hotel?" Caleb's voice was sincere, but she'd not meant what she was going to do that morning. She'd meant what was she going to do about the things that were happening back in Belarus.

"But we've checked out," she replied eventually.

"They won't care if you sit in their cafe, though. As long as you buy the occasional cup of coffee." Caleb glanced down at her phone. "They've got the internet there, right?"

Despite the circumstances, Natasha smiled at Caleb's comment. "Yes, Caleb, they've got the internet there. Most places do." She saw Caleb returning her smile.

"Well, that's that, then," he said. "I'll meet you back here at thirteen-thirty." Natasha frowned, not understanding what he was talking about. "Half past one, Natasha," Caleb added helpfully, still smiling.

"What are you going to do in the meantime, Caleb?" Natasha looked at the clock, realizing they had just over three hours until the desk opened.

She watched as Caleb got to his feet, one of his knee joints cracking as he did so. He winced, rubbing at the joint.

"I've got some errands to run, Natasha," he said, "but it won't take long." He held out a hand for her to take. When she did, the tingling sensation returned, slightly stronger than before. It wasn't uncomfortable, but it was a strange feeling.

Natasha stood, remembering what Caleb had just said about Ilja being a safe pair of hands as the tingling started moving into her forearm. When Caleb let go of her hand, to her surprise, she was disappointed.

"I'm sure everything will work out fine, Natasha," Caleb said. There was a note of positivity in his voice, but when she looked at his expression, she realized it wasn't mirrored in his eyes. If anything, he looked as concerned as she was.

Natasha knew at that moment that for all his idiosyncrasies, Caleb was just like any other man. He could lie with his words, but not with his eyes.

CHAPTER 36

"Where to, me ol' china?"

Caleb frowned at the unfamiliar phrase, which made no sense at all to him. He was standing by the taxi stand outside St. Pancras station, talking to the driver of an oversized cab that was more van than it was taxi. Or, at least, he was trying to talk to the driver.

"I'm sorry," Caleb replied, looking at the man behind the wheel. The driver was perhaps in his early sixties, had a shock of white hair Einstein would have been proud of, and a physique that only years of a sedentary lifestyle could achieve. But despite his paunch, the driver was still broad across the shoulders and looked like the type that didn't suffer fools gladly. "What did you say?"

"Ah, you're a septic," the driver said with a laugh, displaying a set of teeth that didn't look as if they'd seen a dentist in years. "Get quite a few of your lot, we do." His accent sounded like Bob Hoskins acting his heart out, with a touch of Michael Caine thrown in for good measure.

Caleb, who only understood the last sentence the man had said, started looking around for another driver. Preferably one who spoke clearer English. As if he sensed he was about to lose a potential fare, the taxi driver continued, this time speaking with a much less pronounced accent.

"It's only an act, fella," the driver said. "For the tourists, you know? They think London cabbie, they want someone who sounds like they're from Eastenders." Caleb nodded. That was one cultural reference he understood. Eastenders was a long running soap opera set in the East End of London where a wedding wasn't a wedding without a fight and every Christmas, one of the key characters got killed off or something equally dramatic happened. "Where are you looking to get to?"

"Ah, okay," Caleb replied with a smile. "I get it. So, what's a septic?"

"Septic tank. Yank," the driver replied, also smiling.

"China?"

"China plate." The smile broadened. "Mate. It's rhyming slang." The driver glanced at Caleb's head. "And if you had any, I'd probably say something about your barnet. Barnet Fair, Hair. Only you've not got any."

"Do people round here really speak like that?" Caleb asked, his curiosity piqued.

"Nah, not really. Like I said, it's only for the tourists."

"Can I hire you for an hour or so? There's some stuff I need to collect."

"It's going to cost you."

Caleb rummaged in his cloth bag to find the money left over from the men in the alleyway. When he withdrew his hand, he had fifty pounds in notes.

"Will this be enough?" The expression on the driver's face said it wasn't. Caleb waited as the man looked him up and down, taking in his robe.

"Are you a monk?" he asked a moment later.

"I'm a preacher."

"Can you put a word in with the man upstairs for me?"

"I can certainly put a word in," Caleb replied with a broad smile. "Whether He'll listen to it or not is completely up to Him."

"Hop in, fella," the driver said. "Let's see how far that fifty pounds gets you, and if him up there knows anything about the three-thirty at Ainsworth, I'm all ears." A few moments later, having established that the three-thirty at Ainsworth was a horse race, Caleb was in the back of the cab. The driver, who had introduced himself as Dave, turned and gave him a yellowed smile through the glass that separated the passenger compartment.

"So, me old china, where to?"

Almost two hours later, the rear of the cab was so full of boxes that Caleb had been upgraded to sitting in the front of the taxi. Dave had turned out to be an ideal companion for Caleb's visits. Not only did he have a near encyclopedic knowledge of London, but at Caleb's first stop, he had accompanied him into the store and stood by the door while Caleb did his business. Once he understood what Caleb was doing, he started taking his role much more seriously.

They had visited seven military surplus stores in total, with Dave becoming ever more menacing as they progressed. Unlike the owner of the store that Caleb and Natasha had visited, none of the subsequent owners had put up much of a fight at all, and it had all been verbal posturing anyway. How much of this was down to Caleb's powers of persuasion and how much was down to Dave lurking over his shoulder, Caleb wasn't sure but they made a good team and had relieved each store of several boxes of supplies, mostly medical in nature. But by the time they reached the eighth store, it was closed even though the lights were on and Caleb was sure he could see someone inside trying to hide behind the counter. Perhaps there was some form of network between them, like a group chat on their cell phones that warned of trouble? He had hammered on the door several times to no effect.

"We'll have lunch here, mate," Dave said as he pulled the taxi to the side of the road and parked it behind a long queue of black cabs. "Best fish and chips this side of the Thames."

Caleb looked through the window to see a grubby looking shop front with a green facade marked with spray painted graffiti. There were shutters above the windows that were no doubt similarly tagged, and the sign on top of the facade read *Masters Superfish*. Despite its shabby exterior, Caleb could see through the windows that it was packed with customers.

Dave locked his cab and made his way into the chip shop, Caleb a couple of steps behind him. With a nod to the man behind the serving area, Dave sat down and picked up a menu, handing it to Caleb once he was seated.

"Have what you want, fella," Dave said. "Ignore the prices. Everything's a fiver if you're a cabbie."

Caleb glanced at the other customers. Almost all of them were wearing lanyards with small oval badges like the one Dave was wearing, embossed with a number between the words *London Cab Driver*. As if he realized what Caleb was looking at, Dave held up his own badge.

"The green background means you've got *The Knowledge*," Dave said. "It's the test that proves you know your way around, and it's a bastard of an exam. But it does get you cheap food in here."

"Why is that?" Caleb asked.

"The bloke that owns it," Dave replied, nodding at the man behind the counter. "His son got stabbed a few years ago. It was a couple of cabbies what took the lad to the hospital. Saved his life, so they did. You see the bloke in the corner?" Caleb looked in the direction Dave was pointing to see a man wearing a green uniform, busily shoveling food into his mouth. "That's the traffic warden. He eats for nothing in return for ignoring the cabs parked outside."

Caleb looked down at the menu with a smile on his face. There were some good people in the world after all.

CHAPTER 37

Phoebe turned her back to open the door to the medical center, nudging it with her butt. She was carrying a couple of large boxes that were heavier than they looked and she was grateful when Jade walked over to take the uppermost one from her.

"Thanks, Jade," Phoebe said with a smile. "They're bloody heavy." They placed the boxes on one of the counters.

"Are these the pharmaceuticals?" the nurse asked.

"Yep," Phoebe replied, tapping the top of one of the boxes.

"You had some more donations for the convoy this morning," Jade said as she opened one of the boxes to look inside.

"Excellent," Phoebe replied, walking in the direction of the storeroom. She opened the door, followed by Jade, and they both peered inside to look at the contents of the small room. "Not got much, have we?"

"Not really." Jade gave Phoebe a wan smile. "But there's

time. You're not due to leave until next week. There's tomorrow, and then there's the weekend."

"I'm off this weekend," Phoebe replied. "I'm not sure who the hospital's sending to cover for me though."

"Okay, no worries," Jade said.

"What's in the new ones?" Phoebe asked, pointing at a couple of boxes in a neat stack that hadn't been there the last time she'd looked.

"Tourniquets and bandages. They were dropped off earlier."

"Fantastic!" Phoebe opened the box on the top of the stack and saw it was crammed with vacuum packed bandages, all wrapped in olive green plastic packaging. "Are these military?"

"I don't know," Jade replied, crossing to stand next to Phoebe. "They look like they might be. It was that weird bloke who dropped them off."

"That doesn't really narrow it down, Jade," Phoebe said with a smile. "Unfortunately, I know quite a few weird men. Can you be anymore specific?"

"The one in the dress who stitched his own stomach up."

Phoebe's smile faltered for a split second, but she managed to hold it in place. "Ah, yes," she said. "I remember him."

"Hard not to," Jade replied, smirking for an instant. "Have you got the paperwork for the pharmaceuticals?"

"Oh, bugger," Phoebe said with a grimace. "I left it all back at the hospital. I'll grab it on the way home if that's okay?" She remembered Peggy waving a folder at her, but Phoebe had forgotten to go back to collect it. Now she was going to have to pay another visit to the place, but hopefully she wouldn't run into Thomas again. Since seeing him again earlier, she had been having some serious misgivings about spending so much time in a van with the man. Three years was a long time ago, but there was something about him she couldn't shake off.

"Don't worry, I'll get them to e-mail it over," Jade said, resulting in a sigh of relief from Phoebe.

"You're a star," Phoebe said. "Thank you. Do you want a cuppa?"

"Go on then," Jade replied.

Phoebe made them both a cup of tea and sat in one of the waiting room chairs while she watched Jade unpacking the boxes of medicines. She knew better than to try to help. The last time Phoebe had offered to help, Jade had stayed behind after the clinic had closed to rearrange the cupboard how she wanted them, which wasn't how Phoebe had laid them out.

"You got any plans for the weekend, then?" Jade asked her a few moments later. "You said you're off?"

"Not really," Phoebe replied. "My mother's moving back home, hopefully." She watched as a smile spread over Jade's face and she realized how that sounded. "I mean, not hopefully. It's been lovely having her to stay while she recovered, but I'm looking forward to having the place to myself again."

"I know what you mean," Jade said, still smiling. "I don't think my husband realizes that when I pack him off to the pub, it's not because I'm being nice to him. It's because I want some bloody peace and quiet." Phoebe saw Jade lining up boxes of medicines in the cupboard, almost with military precision. When the box they had come in was empty, the nurse closed the cupboard door with a satisfied sigh and turned to Phoebe. "Now, don't you dare mess the cupboard up."

"I won't, boss," Phoebe said just as a draft blew across the back of her neck. "Hey, Jade, can I ask you something?"

"Sure," Jade replied, momentarily distracted by something over Phoebe's shoulder. "Um, Doctor Sokolova?"

"The man in the robe," Phoebe said, ignoring her. "What did you think of him? There's something about him that's, well, I'm not sure how to..." Her voice trailed away as she heard someone clearing their throat softly behind her. Then a familiar voice spoke, causing her cheeks to instantly redden.

"Speak of the devil," the voice said, the Texan accent accentuated, "and he's sure to appear."

CHAPTER 38

Natasha sat down on one of the station benches as, around her, people hurried back and forth through the concourse. Everyone except her seemed to be in a hurry and she watched as a harried mother attempted to corral a small child who was very reluctant to sit in his stroller. A smile spread across her face as she remembered Mikhail at that age, and she nudged her suitcase with her foot to push it under the bench and out of the way. She had retrieved it from the hotel while Caleb had been busy as she'd not known what would happen when the Home Office desk was open.

In her hand was a plastic folder that the young man, William but please call me Will, at the Home Office desk had given her. Natasha had realized the desk was open much earlier than she and Caleb had thought, so she had spoken to Will alone instead of waiting for Caleb. She'd got there just as he had finished setting up and getting ready to receive the people from the next train, and the overpriced coffee she'd bought for him from one of the concession stands in the main station had gone down very well. After checking her name and passport details on his laptop, Will had stabbed at a few buttons and the printer next to the computer had whirred into life.

"These are the details of your host family," Will had said as he had handed her the sheets. "They live in a place called Salisbury. Do you know it?" Natasha had shaken her head as she scanned the text on the paper. "It's a lovely part of the country. I think you'll love it there. The family has a teenaged son already, so he'll be good company for your boy when he gets here. Michael, is it?"

"Mikhail," Natasha had replied. "His name is Mikhail."

Natasha leafed through the papers that Will had given her. As well as the details of the host family, there was also a piece of paper she could exchange for a rail ticket from London to Salisbury as well as the contact details for the local liaison officer who would meet her at Salisbury station when she arrived. She swiped at her phone to put the numbers into her contacts, checking WhatsApp first. To her dismay, her earlier message to Mikhail remained unread, the two ticks resolutely gray. Natasha tapped the screen to send a new message to Ilja.

Any news? A few seconds after sending the message, she watched as both ticks turned green. It didn't take Ilja more than thirty seconds to reply.

No, nothing. Mikhail's at school.

Natasha sighed and pressed her lips together. All she wanted was something back from Mikhail. A one word message would be enough. She knew he wouldn't be able to use his phone during lessons, or he would risk a detention, but there was plenty of time between lessons and during breaks for him to respond. Or at least read her message. Natasha shook her head in frustration, knowing that outside of lessons most children Mikhail's age were glued to their phones. Over the last few weeks, she had got used to hearing nothing from Anton, but now she only had Ilja to rely on.

Her thoughts turned to Caleb, and Natasha wondered whether he had finished the errands he'd said he needed to run. Caleb hadn't given her any more information on what it was he was doing, and from the way he spoke, she thought he would rather not speak about it. She glanced back at her phone to check the time, realizing that they were supposed to be meeting at the medical center in a few moments. Natasha got to her feet and started walking slowly through the concourse, lost in thought. Once she had gone to Salisbury, she would probably never see Caleb again. He had no cell phone and appeared to just wander where his life took him. Natasha was envious to a degree. He had no ties to anywhere or anyone. No responsibilities other than to himself. It was, she thought, an interesting way to live. But at the same time, he must be incredibly lonely.

Natasha's stomach rumbled, and she realized she hadn't eaten anything since breakfast. If Caleb hadn't eaten either, then perhaps she could take them for lunch somewhere to thank him for his help over the last few days. It was only prolonging the inevitable, though.

At some point in the next few hours, she was going to have to say goodbye to the man, and Natasha wasn't looking forward to that one bit.

CHAPTER 39

His tote bag between his legs, Mikhail sat on a wooden bench and stared out over the small lake that marked the center of Kronen Park, a small park close to the center of Hrodna. A couple of swans were paddling across the placid water, shepherding a brood of fluffy cygnets between them. As he watched, a large goose got too close to the cygnets and one of the adult swans reared up with its wings and hissed so loudly, Mikhail could hear it across the water.

Kronen Park was one of Mikhail's favorite places to just sit and watch the world go by. The park was almost empty apart from a couple of joggers and people walking their dogs as if the world was entirely normal. As if they weren't living somewhere a shell could come out of the sky with little or no warning and demolish entire families. When he had left his aunt's house earlier, Mikhail had walked past what was left of Alevtina's apartment block. It had been taped off with police tape, and a couple of people in uniform were rummaging through the ruins as a thin spiral of black smoke rose into the air from the rubble. Alevtina, and the other people who had been killed, were long gone. Mikhail swallowed back tears as he wondered who else had died. He knew Alevtina had a smaller sister and that her father, like Mikhail's, was fighting for his country somewhere.

In his pocket, Mikhail's phone vibrated again with a message, but he left it where it was. There was no one he wanted to talk to, even if it was via a text message. Mikhail got to his feet and wandered toward the pond. As he approached it, he noticed a crude flyer had been tacked to a lamp post. It depicted a woman in some sort of red dress with a shawl wrapped around her head. She had one hand raised in the air and the other was holding a piece of paper. Behind her there were guns, fixed with bayonets, and the words *FIGHT FOR FREEDOM!* were emblazoned across the top of the flyer in the same shade of red as the woman's dress. Mikhail walked up to the flyer and started reading the text on the paper the woman was holding.

FIGHT FOR FREEDOM!

Our beloved country is under attack from within. The state has turned Belarusian against Belarusian, using the army not to defeat our enemies but to crush our will. This cannot go on. We must rise up as one and protect the Fatherland.

The text continued with an impassioned plea for citizens to join the Belarusian freedom fighters, and listed a telephone number to call for more information. Mikhail looked around, concerned that even reading the flyer would put him in danger, but no one was paying him any heed. He reached into his pocket for his phone and snapped a quick photograph of the flyer before returning to the bench. Then he checked the image to make sure he had a clear picture of the telephone number before scrolling back through his photographs. When he and

Alevtina had been in the bunker, just before they left he had snapped a photo of her, wanting to capture the look on her face. He zoomed in on the image now, looking at the way her eyes were slightly widened in surprise at him taking her photo so soon after they had been kissing. Her cheeks were red and she had a half smile on her face. Mikhail felt the tears starting to form in his eyes and he blinked them away. Now wasn't the time for tears. Now was the time for action.

"Алло?" a male voice said in Russian after a couple of rings. *Hello?*

"Um, hello," Mikhail replied, his voice uncertain. "I saw a flyer in the park with this number." There was a pause on the other end of the line, and Mikhail was reminded of how distrustful people were of phones in Belarus. "I'm interested."

"Age?" the man asked.

"Eighteen," Mikhail replied, trying to inject a note of confidence into his voice. "My father's already fighting for you."

"Where are you?"

"Hrodna."

"You know Trdlo House?" The man was referring to a small coffee shop in the center of the city. Mikhail had never been there, but had passed by it on his way to the artificial football pitch called *Futbol'nyy Manezh* several times.

"Yes, I do."

"Go there. Ask for Vincuk."

Mikhail started to ask if he needed to take anything with him when he realized he was talking to a dead line. The man had hung up. He looked at the photograph of Alevtina before slipping his phone back into his pocket. Then, with a determined nod of his head, Mikhail got to his feet and slung his tote bag over his shoulder. The cafe was perhaps a twenty minute walk away, less if he hurried.

With Alevtina's picture firmly in his mind's eye, Mikhail set off with a determined spring in his step. He knew he couldn't bring her back, but there was something he could do to make her death mean something.

He could fight.

CHAPTER 40

Caleb looked at Phoebe with a half smile on his face. She looked mortified, but he couldn't work out why. As he watched, she got to her feet and walked quickly over to one of the cupboards on the wall and opened it to look inside. Caleb glanced over at the nurse who just smirked and shrugged her shoulders at him.

"Jade, Doctor Sokolova," Caleb said, nodding first at the nurse and then at Phoebe's back. "Are you all having a good day?"

"All good here," Jade replied, her smirk broadening. "Phoebe?"

"Uh huh," Caleb heard Phoebe reply, but she was still engrossed in the contents of the cupboard.

"I've arranged to meet my friend, Natasha, here. I hope that's okay?" Caleb said. Jade nodded her head in agreement but Phoebe turned round to face him. Her cheeks were red and she was frowning.

"This is a medical center," she said, an obvious tone of reproach in her voice as she put her hands on her hips. "Not a social meeting up point."

The half-smile on Caleb's face faded away. He'd not been expecting her to say that.

"Ah, I'm sorry, ma'am. I can just wait outside in that case."

"Don't ma'am me, Mr. Caleb," Phoebe replied, pointing at the door Caleb had just walked through. "Now if you wouldn't mind, we're busy."

Caleb glanced at Jade who was looking at Phoebe, open-mouthed. Without a word, he turned and left the medical center, closing the door quietly behind him. He didn't know what he'd said to upset the doctor. Perhaps she was still annoyed with him for suturing up his own abdomen, but he didn't think it was that. Through the door, he could hear the two women talking but their voices were too indistinct for him to make out what they were saying. A moment later, the door opened. He turned, expecting to see Jade, but it was Phoebe.

"Um, Caleb," she said as she walked to where he was standing. Her cheeks had now faded to twin points of red where her dimples would be if she smiled.

"Doctor Sokolova," Caleb replied, keeping his face neutral.

"I, er, I wanted to apologize."

"What for?"

"For just now. I was really short with you for no reason."

"No apology is necessary, Phoebe," Caleb said, letting his smile return.

"No, no, it is," Phoebe replied, glancing at the door to the medical center. "Jade just tore me a new one for being rude."

"Are you apologizing because she told you to, or because you want to?" Caleb watched as Phoebe's face started to color again. She bit her bottom lip before a bashful smile appeared on her face. Whether she intended it or not, the expression made her already attractive face even more beautiful, in Caleb's opinion at least. But he knew from the way his body reacted that it wasn't just her face that he liked. It was something far more base than that. An old friend of his, one of the seven deadly sins with four letters. And that wasn't good when you were wearing a robe.

"Can I say both?" Phoebe said, seemingly oblivious to Caleb's predicament. Caleb looked away from her and tried to remember as many of the Texas Rangers Hall of Fame players as he could.

"Are you okay?" Phoebe asked a moment later. "You've got a rather, um, peculiar expression on your face."

"I was just thinking, that's all."

"Penny for them?" Phoebe said, her smile turning broader.

"Ah, okay," Caleb replied with a laugh. "Ian Kinsler, John Blake, Adrián Beltré, and someone called Chuck who does the announcing."

Phoebe laughed and frowned at the same time. "I have got no idea what you're talking about. Anyway, will you let me make up for my rudeness?"

"What're you thinking, Phoebe?" Caleb said, deciding to have some fun with the woman. "A few drinks in an Olde English pub followed by dinner somewhere? Fish, chips, and mushy peas maybe?"

"Um, no." Caleb watched as Phoebe's frown disappeared and she started laughing.

"How about a football game, and I don't mean soccer. Then a stockyard rodeo, and we go somewhere to two-step the night away after?"

"Going to be hard to find those in London, Caleb." Phoebe raised her hand to her head, sliding an errant few strands of hair behind her ear. It was another alluring gesture, for Caleb at least. "I was thinking about offering you a cup of tea."

"You know that's just hot water with some leaves in it, don't you?"

Phoebe put her hands on her slim hips and adopted a look of mock outrage. "You know that's our national drink, don't you? You're not in Kansas anymore, Caleb."

"Texas," Caleb replied with a smile. "Big difference there. Is that a no to dinner or dancing then?"

"You're a funny man, Caleb," Phoebe said, her own smile returning.

"Sure am," Caleb replied. "I'm from Texas. No one normal comes from there."

"Dinner or dancing, though. I thought you were a preacher? A man of God?" Phoebe was giggling as she said this.

"I am a preacher," Caleb said. Then he lowered his voice to a conspiratorial whisper. "But I'm not a monk." He thought briefly about winking at Phoebe, but thought that would be overdoing it. Her giggle turned into a full-throated laugh that Caleb enjoyed the sound of very much. She looked at him with a lop-sided grin, tilting her head to one side as she did so. Then Caleb saw her glancing over his shoulder at something behind him.

Caleb turned to see Dave walking through the station concourse straight toward them. He had managed to find a hand truck from somewhere and had piled the boxes he and Caleb had collected onto it. As he raised his hand to wave at Caleb, the pile teetered and he had to slow down.

"Friend of yours?" Phoebe said as she watched him approaching.

"Yeah, kind of," Caleb replied. "I'm sure he'd like a cup of tea as well, if you're making one?"

CHAPTER 41

Natasha looked at the man working behind the scratched Perspex screen, wondering if he was as miserable as he looked. He was examining the piece of paper she had slipped through the slot in the bottom of the screen as if it was written in a foreign language. Finally, he looked up at her with rheumy eyes.

"You speak English?" he asked. His voice was raspy and she could smell the stale odor of cigarettes coming through the grille in the glass.

"Yes, I do," she replied, looking at him with a frosty smile. All she wanted was the rail ticket the piece of paper said she was entitled to.

"Only not many of your lot do."

"What do you mean, my lot?" Natasha asked, her smile hardening.

"Immigrants," the man replied. "That's what this says you are." He waved the piece of paper, seemingly for effect, but it had none on Natasha.

"I'm a refugee, not an immigrant," she replied. The man just shrugged his shoulders in reply, as if to say *same differ-*

ence. Natasha looked around the dingy ticket office. Did this man really think she would be here if she had a choice? But she didn't want to get into a semantic argument with the man behind the glass. "Please could I have my ticket?"

The man didn't reply, but just tapped at his computer keyboard. "Any seat preference?"

"Forward facing, with a table if that's possible," Natasha said. He nodded and tapped again at the keyboard. She noticed he only used his index fingers to type with, almost as if he was pecking at the keys. A moment later, a printer whirred into life next to his computer screen and a couple of cardboard tickets emerged. He slid them through the slot beneath the Perspex.

"There you go. Platform ten. It's an advance single, so you have to get that train."

"What time does it leave?" she asked.

"In about ten minutes," he replied with a glance at his watch. "The platform closes about a minute before departure, so you've got plenty of time." Natasha saw he was looking over her shoulder, and she turned to see a middle aged man wearing a suit, tapping his foot on the floor. Realizing the conversation was over, she mumbled a thanks and picked up the tickets.

Natasha walked back into the main concourse and looked up at the platform numbers. The ticket office was just by platform one, so platform ten was some distance away. The medical center, where she was supposed to be meeting Caleb, was in the opposite direction. She hesitated, wondering if she would have time to go and see him, even if it was only for a few brief seconds, but realized she wouldn't have time. Cursing under her breath at the pettiness of the man behind the glass, she set off in the direction of the platform, trailing the suitcase behind her.

As she walked, Natasha thought about how she could get a message to Caleb. It didn't seem right for her to just disappear. Maybe she could speak to the local liaison officer when she got to Salisbury and ask them to contact the medical center in the station? Even though Caleb didn't own a phone, she was sure he could use one.

By the time she arrived at the platform, Natasha realized that she would have indeed run out of time if she had gone to the medical center. There was a large queue of people waiting to get through the ticket machines, and it took her several moments to get through the automatic gates. She looked at her ticket to see which coach her seat was on, and made her way to the front of the train. Just as she reached the correct coach, there was an announcement to let the passengers know that the train was about to depart.

Natasha boarded the coach with a heavy heart. Like the train she had been on the previous day, it was almost full. She walked down the aisle to find her seat. When she reached it, she pressed her lips together and mentally cursed the miserable old man in the ticket office.

The seat was not next to a table, and it meant she would be facing backward for the entire journey. Not only that, but the occupants of the seats directly behind her were a toddler with a disinterested-looking mother who was completely ignoring the child as he kicked Natasha's seat over and over again.

It was going to be a long journey to Salisbury.

CHAPTER 42

Stepan spread the map out on the table in front of him. He was sitting in a meeting room in the abandoned industrial complex they had commandeered as the headquarters of the People's Army for the western region of Belarus. The former distribution center had a rag tag collection of buildings in various states of disarray, but they were more than good enough for their needs.

The warehouses where goods had previously been stored made ideal workshops for their vehicles and accommodation for the men, and the small office complex that the meeting room was located in was now an operations room and accommodation for the senior personnel. It had been easy enough to convert the complex into a military compound of sorts, although they lacked the defenses that Stepan would have liked. He was much happier behind a wire with lookout towers, but beggars couldn't be choosers. Besides, who was going to attack them?

He smoothed out a couple of creases on the map and looked at it carefully. It showed the entirety of the area he and the other squads based in their compound covered.

Several of the small villages on the map had gouged crosses through the names, indicating that they had been cleared by Stepan's squad or one of the others. He traced his finger on the map to locate where they had been the previous day and then, more slowly, the location where the white van had appeared. He moved his finger up to the bend where the van had disappeared, and then on to the various roads that led into the forest from the main track.

Stepan sighed. This was pointless. There were too many roads that the van could have taken. They criss-crossed the map like a spider's web, and that was just the roads that were marked on the map. There would be many more, so he needed to take a different perspective. They knew there was a resistance cell operating in the area somewhere. Several of the squads had been attacked, not in a face to face situation, but by stealth. The resistance would hit and then melt away and disappear, just as the van had done the previous day. But as his chain of command said frequently, they were gathering strength, which was why they needed to be rooted out and eliminated before they became a credible threat.

He tried to look at the map through a different lens. If Stepan was a resistance leader, where would he put his base? He doubted they would be located in a village, although it was a possibility. None of the villagers that his squad had interacted with to date had claimed any knowledge of the resistance, even when looking down the barrel of a gun. The more villages they visited, the less likely he thought it was that the resistance would utilize them for anything other than supplies. Stepan looked at the vast areas of green wooded terrain that the map depicted, and tapped his finger in the middle of one of them.

"Somewhere here," Stepan muttered before moving his finger to another wooded area. "Or here."

Stepan thought for a moment, considering the characteristics that he would need to take into account. They would need buildings of some sort, or at least one decent sized building. Stepan doubted they would have the resources to set up and maintain a tented headquarters. The logistics were just too complicated, which was one of the reasons the People's Army had commandeered the industrial complex he was now in. It would need to be a building with power and running water, which ruled out the majority of the simple wooden shacks that were dotted around the map. Like their headquarters, it would need to be relatively central and with access to the road network for mobility.

He spent the next few moments identifying likely sites on the map. Areas deep within the forest, with at least three small buildings or one large one, and not too far away from the road network. Stepan used a pen to circle the locations he thought most likely and then, after tapping the pen on his teeth for a moment, put them into a rough order of likelihood.

It was time to get the rest of his squad together. Although he enjoyed the visits to the villages, as a strategy it wasn't working.

If Stepan could locate their base, then he could cut the head straight off this particular serpent.

CHAPTER 43

"Are you serious?" Phoebe asked when Caleb and Dave had unloaded the hand truck. "This is fantastic."

"There's more in the taxi," Dave said. She watched as he mopped his brow, clearly unused to physical exertion. "I'll be back in a few minutes. Caleb? Can you give me a hand? These boxes are heavier than I realized."

"Sure." Caleb grinned at Phoebe. There was something about his child-like smile that was infectious, and she saw Dave had a similar expression on his own face.

"There'll be a brew waiting for you when you get back," Phoebe replied, smiling at the two men.

"I can't wait," Caleb said with a mock grimace, making Phoebe laugh.

Both men left, Caleb standing back at the door to the storeroom to let Jade enter.

"Well, that looks a bit better," the nurse said as she regarded the boxes which now almost half-filled the room.

"I know, isn't it amazing?" Phoebe ran her fingers down the labels on the side of the cartons. "There're more tourniquets and bandages, as well as a load of military issue first aid kits."

"Did Caleb say where it came from?"

"I did ask him, but all he did was look at his friend and laugh."

"It's not stolen, is it?"

Phoebe's smile faded. She'd not thought of that possibility. But Caleb was a preacher. Surely a preacher wouldn't steal things?

"I'll ask him when he gets back, if I can think of a way of asking him without offending him."

"Oh, so now you're afraid of offending the man? It was only a few minutes ago that you threw him out of the medical center." Jade was smiling as she said this, but she still had a serious look in her eyes. "You've not told me why you bit his head off back then."

Phoebe looked at Jade, feeling her cheeks start to color up again. She thought for a moment about telling her about the dream she'd had the previous night. The one that had caused her to wake up all hot and bothered. The one that featured Caleb, both with and without his robe.

"He just caught me off guard, that's all."

"Really?" Jade replied, crossing her arms and fixing Phoebe with an expression that screamed *liar* at her.

"Yes, really," Phoebe said, forcing a laugh. "There's something about him, though. I'm not sure what."

"Yeah, you were saying." Her expression turned into a smirk. "I would, though."

"You would what?" Phoebe looked at Jade, realizing what she was inferring as her cheeks got even hotter.

"I mean, if I wasn't already in a relationship. If he lost the robe and was in a nice suit." Jade started giggling, and Phoebe knew she'd been rumbled. "Wouldn't you?"

"Jade, stop it," Phoebe replied, trying and failing to sound irritated. "That's unprofessional."

"Phoebe, how can it be unprofessional when we're in a storeroom, chatting as friends," Jade said. "Well?"

"Well, what?"

"Well, you're either going through an early menopause and having a hot flush," Jade replied, touching her fingers to her cheeks. "Or you're blushing like a virgin on her wedding night."

"Would you stop!" Phoebe said, starting to laugh. "I doubt there are many of them anymore, and besides, he'll be back in a minute." She flapped her hands at her own cheeks. "Is it that obvious?"

"It is to me." Jade smirked again.

Phoebe walked to the door, intending to go to the rest room and splash some cold water on her face. She held out her hand, palm outward, to Jade who looked as if she was about to say something else. As Phoebe walked through the medical center to the door to the rest room, she thought back over her conversation with Caleb when she had apologized to him for being short. His comments about dinner and dancing, and in particular the comment about him not being a monk got her thinking. She knew she could be a bit obtuse at times, and heaven knew she was out of practice, but had he been flirting with her? Or was it that she just had an overactive imagination, as her memories of waking up that morning suggested.

She giggled as she pushed open the door to the bathroom. A girl could dream, couldn't she?

CHAPTER 44

Mikhail paused on the sidewalk opposite the cafe. He was perspiring from the walk through the streets and wanted to give himself a moment to cool down in the light breeze. Trying not to look too obvious, he looked at the cafe out of the corner of his eye, but the streets were almost deserted and no one seemed to be paying him any attention at all.

The cafe had seen better days, that much was for certain. The windows didn't look as if they had been cleaned in years, if at all, and were covered in a layer of grime that made it impossible to see inside the building. Perhaps, Mikhail thought, that was the point. It was sandwiched between a boarded up building that looked to have been a bakery at some point in the past, and a taxi firm with a flickering fluorescent sign above the door advertising its presence. The only sign of life in the cafe itself was a cardboard sign in Cyrillic script that read *OPEN*.

A few moments later, Mikhail made his way across the road and tentatively approached the cafe door. Even this close, he still couldn't see inside the windows and as he pushed the door open, a small bell above it tinkled into life. He blinked as he entered the cafe, waiting for his eyes to adjust from the bright sunshine outside to the gloomy interior. When they did, he could see the interior of the cafe was just as decrepit as the exterior. There were four or five tables, each covered with a red and green tablecloth but not a single customer.

"What?" a male voice rang out. Mikhail turned to see a small serving counter in the cafe's corner in front of a door in the wall. Behind the counter was a man who appeared to match the general sense of the cafe in that he looked unkempt and tired. He was perhaps in his mid to late sixties, had a dome of a head without a single hair, and was wearing a grubby apron that matched the tablecloths.

"I'm, er... looking for Vincuk," Mikhail said, attempting to put some authority into his voice. He had, after all, been invited here.

"Who are you?" The man behind the counter hadn't moved a muscle.

"My name is Mikhail. I spoke to a man on the phone. He told me to come here."

With a speed that defied his age, the man crossed the cafe, navigating his way between the empty tables with ease, and flipped the sign on the door to read CLOSED from the outside.

"Sit," he said, pointing at one of the tables.

Mikhail did as instructed and watched the man as he returned to the counter. He bent down to retrieve something from underneath the counter, shoving it into the pocket of his apron before Mikhail had a chance to see what it was. Then he returned to where Mikhail was sitting and sat down opposite him. Mikhail took a couple of deep breaths to calm his nerves.

"I am Vincuk," the man said after staring at Mikhail for a moment. "The man you spoke to on the phone told me you were coming. You are from Hrodna?"

"Yes, I am," Mikhail replied, nodding his head. He held the man's gaze, almost as if they were in a competition to see who would blink first.

"And you want to fight for Belarus?"

"Yes." Mikhail said, nodding again before repeating himself, this time with more authority in his tone. "Yes, I do."

"Why?"

Mikhail paused. It was such a simple question, but at the same time, so complicated. But what was the best answer to give to Vincuk?

"Because it's my country," he said after an uncomfortable silence had started to develop. "My father is already fighting for the Fatherland. I want to as well."

"His name?"

"Anton. Anton Zaystev."

Mikhail waited for a moment as Vincuk pulled a phone from his pocket and appeared to tap out a text message.

"I don't believe you," Vincuk said a moment later. "Your words and your eyes don't match." He shuffled in his chair, and Mikhail realized he was reaching into his apron pocket. "How do I know you're not an infiltrator?" Vincuk pulled his hand out of the apron pocket and, when Mikhail saw what he was holding, his heart started thumping in his chest and his mouth turned to sandpaper. He had never seen a gun in real life before. Now there was one pointing at him. Vincuk was holding it loosely, the barrel of the small black pistol pointing at Mikhail's abdomen, but he was obviously comfortable with the weapon. "I could shoot you here and no one would bat an eyelid. Not at the execution of a spy."

"Because," Mikhail replied, his voice faltering for a

second. "Because they killed one of my friends." He tried to swallow, but there was no moisture in his mouth. "A close friend."

"твоя возлюбленная?" Vincuk asked. *Your sweetheart?*

Mikhail nodded, determined not to cry in front of this man. As he watched, Vincuk's face changed and he realized that he had an approximation of a smile on his face. But the pistol was still pointing directly at Mikhail. Vincuk's phone buzzed, and he glanced down at the screen for a split second before nodding. Mikhail couldn't take his eyes away from Vincuk's hand and the gun he was holding.

He had no frame of reference for such things, but Vincuk's finger appeared to be tightening on the trigger.

CHAPTER 45

Natasha stared out of the window as the gray buildings of London gradually gave way to rolling green countryside. The train had passed through many places, hardly any of which she had heard of. Clapham Junction. Woking. Basingstoke. She could see the affluence of the houses increasing as the train got further away from the city. The size of the houses and their gardens increased while the urban sprawl near the stations reduced. There were even one or two houses with blue swimming pools in the gardens, which given the variable weather in the United Kingdom, Natasha felt was a little optimistic.

The next station is Whitchurch. If you're alighting the train at this station, please remember to take all your personal belongings with you. The nasal tones of the public address system on the train didn't seem to have given the passengers a moment's peace since they had left London. The station announcement was followed by a message to contact the police if they saw anything suspicious so they could *say, see it, sort it*. Natasha closed her eyes and rested her head against the train window. At least the small child in the seat behind had fallen asleep, but any second now, there would be another announcement extolling the virtues of the snack bar in coach B towards the front of the train.

As her head bounced gently against the train window, Natasha's thoughts turned to home. She remembered the agony of saying goodbye to Anton as he had left to fight, not knowing if she would ever see him again. He was a big man, a powerful one. But bullets and bombs had no respect for such things, and if the media reports were to be believed, the Belarusian army and their Russian mercenaries were formidable fighters.

Knowing she wouldn't be able to sleep, Natasha pulled her phone out of her pocket. It took her a few moments to work out how to connect to the wi-fi on the train, but she managed to work it out. First, she checked WhatsApp but there were no messages. Neither had Mikhail read her earlier message.

She navigated her way to the BBC news website in the hope that any reporting from them would be impartial and at least semi-accurate. There was no point looking at Belarusian outlets when they were all controlled to one extent or another by the state. According to the BBC, there was fierce fighting as the two sides wrestled for control of ground to the south of Minsk, the country's capital. The analyst who had written the article was suggesting that whoever held Minsk would win the conflict, but Natasha didn't think it was as simple as that. If, as the article suggested, there was a military coup then everything would rapidly deteriorate. Her homeland might never be the same again.

On the website was a small photograph titled *Resistance Fighters in Southern Belarus*. She scrolled in on the picture, hoping that one of them might be Anton, but she was disappointed. All she saw was a group of exhausted looking men in various uniforms. The article went on to describe the widespread allegations of war crimes, with both sides blaming each other for the various atrocities that were being reported.

The article finished with a stark warning that the world was watching what happened. But apart from the usual platitudes by state actors for peace, no one seemed to be really interested in what was for them a local conflict.

Natasha jumped and almost dropped her phone as it started ringing. Ilja's name appeared on the screen, and Natasha had to swipe a couple of times before she was able to answer the call.

"Ilja?" Natasha said, immediately concerned about receiving a phone call instead of a message. "What is it?"

"Natasha," Ilja replied. "Calm down." Despite her words, Ilja sounded anything but calm.

"Why are you calling me then?"

"I had a phone call from one of Anton's colleagues. From his unit."

"What did they say?" Natasha asked as a cold feeling of dread started descending on her. "Is he wounded?" Was it worse? Ilja paused before replying, and it was the longest few seconds of Natasha's life.

"They don't know," Ilja replied, the dread obvious in her voice. "He's missing."

CHAPTER 46

Caleb looked up at the clock on the wall of the medical center. It was just after two o'clock, and there was no sign of Natasha. They had arranged to meet at one thirty, so either she had changed her mind or something had happened. Caleb wasn't concerned as such —Natasha was a grown woman, after all—but he thought it was unlike her to just change her mind.

He was hungry, despite the enormous portion of fish and chips that he'd eaten only a couple of hours previously, and he looked around the waiting room, wondering when the people waiting there had last eaten. There were only three people in the room, excluding him, and he was tempted to ask them if they wanted any sandwiches but Caleb didn't think any of them spoke English. There was an elderly lady with a cane, the pain obvious on her face, and a woman around Natasha's age with a small child who was fast asleep in her arms. Caleb watched them for a few moments, wondering what they had experienced in the last few weeks that had brought them all the way to England.

Caleb got to his feet, resolving to at least get something

to drink. He could pick up some cans of soda for the people in the waiting room at the same time. If they didn't want them, then maybe there was a fridge in the staff room for the medical center personnel. He was just about to leave the medical center when one of the doors opened, and Phoebe walked into the waiting area, her white coat trailing behind her like a cape. She said something in Russian to the elderly woman, who began to struggle to get to her feet. Phoebe said something else, and the woman sat back down with a grateful expression. Phoebe turned and noticed Caleb standing by the door.

"Did your friend not turn up?" she said, taking a few steps across the room to stand next to him. A light breeze was coming through the door she had just walked through, and Caleb caught the faintest odor of citronella, perhaps from her shampoo.

"Cymbopogon," he said with a grin. It turned into a smile when he saw her starting to frown.

"Sorry, what?"

"Lemon grass," Caleb replied. "I can smell it. I'm not sure which chemotype it is, though." He gave an exaggerated sniff. "Could be Java, could be Ceylon. My money's on Java, though."

"Right," Phoebe said, her frown turning into a smile. "I see what you did there."

"What did I do?"

"Change the subject so you don't have to talk about the fact you've been stood up." Phoebe had a playful expression on her face which Caleb liked very much.

"I've not been stood up," he replied. "My friend, Natasha, is married. Her husband's fighting for their country."

"Oh, God," Phoebe said, the playful expression disappearing in an instant. "I mean, gosh. Not God. That was crass of me."

"No, it wasn't," Caleb replied, regretting his words. He'd not meant it as a reproach, but as a statement of fact. "I was going to get a drink. Would you like one?" He was keen to see that expression back on her face. "A cheeky gin and tonic, perhaps?" To his relief, Phoebe smiled.

"Probably a bit early for that," she said, gesturing at the people waiting in the medical center. "Besides, they probably wouldn't appreciate the smell of booze on my breath."

"How about a can of soda, then?"

"Let me just get Jade to help this woman," Phoebe replied. "I'll come with you. I could do with a leg stretch."

Caleb watched as Phoebe made her way back across the waiting area. She said something to the woman with the cane before disappearing through the door. When she returned a moment later, the white coat was gone and she was wearing a cream colored blouse that accentuated her figure in a way that Caleb appreciated, although he did his best to keep his face neutral.

They left the medical center and walked across the station concourse toward a small store in the corner. To Caleb's delight, Phoebe slipped her hand through the crook of his elbow. He could feel the cool touch of her fingertips through his robe.

"So," she said as they walked. If you're not going to wine me and dine me, then the least you can do is buy me some chocolate to go with my can of Pepsi."

"I did offer to wine you and dine you," Caleb said with an easy smile on his face. "But if I remember right, the only thing that was available was a cup of hot leaf water."

"The only thing that was available?" Phoebe replied, and Caleb didn't need to look at her to know she was grinning.

"If I remember right, and I usually do, there was the suggestion of a few beers and some fish and chips."

"You forgot the rodeo and the dancing."

"Ah, of course. The rodeo and the dancing." Caleb felt her fingertips squeezing his arm. "How long have you been single, Caleb?"

"I won't lie, Doctor Sokolova," Caleb replied. "It's been a while."

"Yes," Phoebe said, squeezing his arm again. "I can tell."

CHAPTER 47

Vincuk looked at the young man sitting opposite him, whose eyes were fixated on the pistol in his hand. He was exactly what the resistance fighters needed. Mikhail was young, looked to be strong, and had a grudge to avenge.

According to the message Vincuk had received from Yuri, his chief recruiter, the boy's father was indeed on the front line but hadn't been seen for several days. Yuri had told Vincuk in his message that Anton had been a fierce fighter, claiming the lives of many of the mercenaries, before going missing while out on a patrol. That was good, in Vincuk's opinion. It would give the young man sitting in front of him an additional ax to grind.

He moved his thumb on the pistol in his hand, noticing that the motion caused Mikhail to flinch. Then he pressed the magazine release lever and let the magazine clatter onto the table between them. Then he racked the slide of the pistol back to eject the chambered round before placing the weapon on the table. Vincuk picked up the round he had ejected and stood it on the tablecloth.

"I need your phone," Vincuk said, his voice as full of menace as he could manage. This was always the difficult part with the youngsters. They were welded to the things at the best of times. Sure enough, he saw the look of surprise on Mikhail's face at the request.

"My phone?" Mikhail said. "Why?"

"Because they will use it to track you." Vincuk held his hand out with his palm up. "Hand it over."

"But it's an iPhone," Mikhail said in a plaintive tone. "They can't be traced, can they?"

"Yes," Vincuk replied. "Of course they can be traced. Even when it's turned off, the chip continues to run." He didn't tell Mikhail, but the resistance had learned this the hard way. "Hand it over."

Mikhail did as instructed, his hesitance obvious. Vincuk thanked him sarcastically and got to his feet, returning to the counter in the corner of the cafe. There he used a pin to eject the SIM card before cutting it in half with a pair of scissors before turning his back to Mikhail. Vincuk pulled a drawer open in the counter and took out a hammer.

"Hey!" Mikhail called out. "What are you doing?"

Vincuk didn't reply but just brought down the hammer onto the phone's screen, shattering the glass. He heard Mikhail call out again as he raised the hammer and smashed the body of the phone.

"That was a present from my father. ублюдок." *Bastard*. Vincuk smiled. The boy was angry, and anger was good. Vincuk was tempted to strike Mikhail for his insult, but he knew it wouldn't make a difference. The anger would be enough, and there was plenty of violence to come in the boy's life.

"It's a small price to pay for our freedom," Vincuk said as he returned to the table. "Now, watch."

He picked up the pistol, pointed it away from Mikhail and put one hand around the top of the slide. Then he pulled the slide back by a tenth of an inch and used his other hand to pull down on the slide lock before removing the slide from the rest of the pistol. He glanced at Mikhail to make sure he was following along. Vincuk had done this so many times he could do it in his sleep.

The spring was next. He removed it and pushed the barrel out of the body of the gun, lining all the components up on the table.

"There," Vincuk said. "It's ready for cleaning."

He picked up the barrel and reassembled the pistol, reversing the steps he had taken to disassemble it. Then Vincuk placed the pistol on the table and spun it round so that the grip was facing Mikhail.

"Your turn."

Vincuk watched as Mikhail hesitated, his eyes flicking between Vincuk's and the pistol a couple of times. Then he reached forward and picked up the gun. Vincuk could tell from the way he handled it that the boy had never used a weapon before. But, to the lad's credit, he managed to disassemble and reassemble the pistol without needing any prompting. Sure, it took him about five minutes, but he seemed to be a quick learner.

Mikhail placed the weapon on the table and spun it round as Vincuk had.

"When does my training begin?" the boy asked. Vincuk smiled and glanced down at the pistol between them.

"It already has, Mikhail."

CHAPTER 48

Natasha took a deep breath in through her nose, trying to expand her abdomen as much as she could.

"One, two three, four, five," she whispered to herself before breathing out, again counting to five as she did so. But she could still feel the nausea in the pit of her stomach and her heart hammering in her chest like a caged bird. She breathed in again, trying to focus only on her breathing as she did so. If any of the other passengers on the train noticed her extreme discomfort, they said nothing. Not that there was anything anyone could say to make a difference.

Anton was missing, Ilja had said. The man who had brought the news knew very little else. Her husband had gone out on a patrol, and not returned. No one had seen or heard from him since. Natasha didn't know if he was injured, captured, or whether it was worse than that. Anton, her beloved Anton, could be dead. A fresh wave of nausea rolled across her abdomen as she considered this. He was her rock. It had been Anton who had saved her from herself, who had guided her through some of the darkest times in her life. He had always been there. Solid, dependable, and always there.

Still focusing on her breathing, Natasha looked around the carriage for three things. A window, a light in the ceiling, and a poster on the wall. Then she listened. She needed to hear three things. The rattle of the train carriage, a muted conversation somewhere behind her in the carriage, and a baby crying somewhere. Then Natasha moved her hands, her feet, and her head. But the distraction technique had no effect on her rising panic.

Good afternoon, ladies and gentlemen, the nasal voice of the conductor on the public address system said. *We will shortly be arriving at our destination, Salisbury. Please ensure you have all your belongings with you when you depart the train. On behalf of everyone at South Western Railway, thank you for traveling with us today.*

Natasha picked up her phone as, around her, the other passengers started to stir into life. She navigated to her contacts and selected Mikhail's number. She needed to speak to him, and as they had agreed that voice calls would only be made in an absolute emergency, Natasha knew he would pick up the phone no matter what. But when she pressed the call button, it went straight through to the automatic voice answering service. She shook her head, not understanding why the call wasn't going through, before trying again. It was the same result.

Her fingers moving quickly, Natasha tapped out a message to Ilja.

I can't get in touch with Mikhail. Where is he??

The three dots that appeared on the screen told Natasha that Ilja was typing.

I don't know.

Natasha could feel a tight band starting to tighten

around her chest. She looked at the clock on the screen. Mikhail should have been back from school at least an hour ago. Where was he? And, more importantly, why wasn't he picking up his phone?

The train began to slow down and, her knees trembling, Natasha got to her feet. She reached up for her suitcase which was in the overhead rack and almost dropped it because her hands were shaking so much. She couldn't wait to get off the train and get some fresh air. Perhaps that would make her feel less like she was about to vomit.

Natasha looked out of the window at the skyline of Salisbury as the train approached the city. At the center was a distinctive cathedral spire, with several other church towers also visible. The sight of the religious buildings made her think of Caleb. She closed her eyes for a few seconds, remembering the strange sensation she had felt when he had taken her hands. For some reason, it calmed her and she felt the band across her chest start to ease a small amount. Natasha thought of him smiling and the gentle expression in his eyes when he did so, and it eased a fraction more. It was as if he was still with her, reassuring her that everything was going to be okay.

But at the thought of how far from okay everything was, the band returned with a vengeance. Anton was missing and she had no way of contacting Mikhail.

In the space of a few short moments, Natasha had lost the two most important people in her life.

CHAPTER 49

P hoebe took a seat in the small cafe and watched Caleb as he lined up to buy the drinks. One thing that amused her was seeing other people's reactions to the robe he was wearing. The garment, along with his shaved head, small cloth bag, and sandals made him a distinctive figure and more than one person had done a double take when they noticed him.

There was a mother with a small child in a stroller waiting to be served. Phoebe saw the child staring at Caleb with the unbridled curiosity of the very young. As she watched, she saw Caleb stick his tongue out at the child after glancing around to make sure no one was watching him. The peal of the child's laughter made Phoebe smile.

"I saw that," she said to Caleb when he walked over to the table, carrying several cans of soda in a plastic bag.

"Saw what?" Caleb replied, a wry smirk on his face. "There're coffees on the way as well."

"Did you get them to go?" Phoebe asked. "Only I need to get back to the clinic." Caleb's smirk turned into a laugh.

"Very American, Phoebe," he said. "I did, yes."

Caleb sat opposite her and placed his arms on the table. "So, here we are."

"Here we are," Phoebe replied, mirroring the way he had crossed his arms. She looked at him for a few seconds, enjoying the way he was looking at her. His gray eyes appeared warm, but at the same time there was the tiniest hint of danger in them that she couldn't really describe.

"What's your story, Caleb?" she asked him. "How did you end up as a preacher?"

Caleb just pointed a finger at the ceiling. "He called me. Obviously, I said yes. Much like He called you."

"Oh, I don't have a religious bone in my body," Phoebe replied with a laugh. "The last time I went in a church, I got a nose bleed."

"But do you not think He called you to become a doctor?"

"I doubt that very much. I had very pushy parents."

"Ah," Caleb replied, the skin around his eyes crinkling as he smiled. "I see."

"In fact, I make a point of trying to sin at least five times a day." Caleb's smile widened as Phoebe said this.

"And what are you up to so far today?"

Phoebe thought for a moment before replying. She was enjoying having such a nonsensical conversation.

"Two, I think. I had a full English for breakfast, so that's greed ticked off." Phoebe pointed at one of the other customers in the cafe. It was an attractive woman with flame red hair, probably a couple of years older than Phoebe. She was standing alone, but her poise exuded confidence. "And you see that woman over there? The one in the green dress?" She waited as Caleb looked at the woman before nodding his head.

"Yes, I see her."

"Well, I would love to be as beautiful as she is. So that's envy."

"There are other sins than the deadly ones, Phoebe."

"I know," Phoebe replied. "But my philosophy has always been to go big or go home."

"That's an interesting philosophy to live by, Phoebe."

Phoebe was about to reply when a member of the cafe's staff arrived at their table. It was a young man, his sullen face pitted with acne, and Phoebe's heart went out to him. There were so many treatments available, but it wasn't her place to say anything. Instead, she thanked him with a broad smile as he placed three cardboard cups of coffee in a cardboard tray on the table, hoping that it might brighten his day at least for a moment. But she didn't think he even noticed her smiling.

"Three coffees to go," the young man said before he turned and left. Phoebe reached forward and picked up the tray.

"How about you, Caleb?" she said as she scraped her chair back, preparing to stand up. "Are you a sinner?"

"We're all sinners, Phoebe," he replied with an almost faraway expression on his face.

"So, come on, spill the beans. Tell me about your last sin?" Caleb glanced at the woman in the green dress who looked over at him. To Phoebe's surprise, she smiled briefly at Caleb before looking away. Phoebe lowered her voice before continuing. "I think I know what it is."

"And what might it be, Phoebe?" Caleb asked, getting to his feet.

"Well, you already told me that you're not a monk," Phoebe replied, looking again at the woman in the green dress. "And I saw you looking at her just now."

"Only because you told me to."

"Is it lust, perhaps?" Phoebe reached out with her spare hand and playfully prodded Caleb in the arm. "Are you having lewd thoughts about the woman over there?"

She watched as a slow smile spread over Caleb's face.

"Do you have the fifth amendment over here, Phoebe?"

"Do you mean the right to remain silent?"

"Yeah, that's the one. Well, I'm taking it."

CHAPTER 50

"Where do you think we're going?" Mikhail asked the man sitting opposite him. They were in the rear of a van, sitting on makeshift seats made out of ammunition crates, as it rumbled along what felt like a rough road of some sort. The man was older than Mikhail by some years, perhaps even as old as his father was. It was difficult to tell in the poor light in the back of the van, which only had a small light in the ceiling for illumination.

They were both wearing army fatigues, but Mikhail's were several sizes too large for him. By contrast, Grigor's looked to be too small. Mikhail had been tempted to suggest they swapped them over, but the older man hadn't seemed to be very friendly.

"I don't know," the man, who had introduced himself as Grigor earlier, replied. "We're not that far from Hrodna. The forests to the north, perhaps?"

Mikhail nodded in reply. They had been in the van for perhaps forty minutes. When they had left the city, ushered into the rear of the windowless van by Vincuk, the roads had started out smooth and fast. They had gradually got slower and more uneven. All Vincuk had said was that they were heading to a training camp. He was in the front of the van with at least one other person who Mikhail hadn't seen, but he could hear occasional snatches of conversation.

"Where are you from, Grigor?" Mikhail asked. The older man looked at him as if he was wondering how much to say.

"Mazyr," Grigor replied a moment later, naming an industrial city in the south of Belarus, not far from the border with Ukraine. "Originally, anyway. My parents were farmers there until Chernobyl."

Mikhail nodded. They had studied the Chernobyl disaster in school, but according to his teachers, the only area of Belarus that had been affected was the area in the south of the country that was now a state park.

"We learned about that in school," Mikhail said. Grigor sneered before replying.

"And what did you learn, boy?"

"About the radiation coming over the border."

"Did they teach you about the crops failing for miles around? The babies who die in their mother's stomachs, even now?" Despite the poor light, the anger on Grigor's face was obvious. "My father tried to find work on the oil pipe-line when the farm stopped even growing weeds. Then the cancer came for him before it came for my mother."

Mikhail said nothing. There was nothing really he could say. None of that had been mentioned in their lessons. He watched as Grigor tipped his head back and rested it against the wall of the van, the conversation seemingly over.

"How old are you, Mikhail?" Grigor asked a few moments later. "Sixteen? Seventeen?"

"I am eighteen," Mikhail replied, nodding his head as he

did so to give some credibility to the lie. But Grigor didn't look as if he believed him.

"Sure you are," Grigor said, closing his eyes. "You should be at home with your mother."

Mikhail felt a flush of anger at what Grigor had just said. He opened his mouth to reply, but couldn't think of anything to say. Instead, he mirrored Grigor and put his head against the van's wall, closing his eyes as he did so.

His thoughts turned to his parents, prompted by what Grigor had just said. Mikhail wanted to get a message to either his mother or his aunt, even if it was just to let them know he was okay. But without a phone, he had no way of doing so. He also didn't know their telephone numbers as they had been stored in his phone which now lay in pieces in Vincuk's cafe. Perhaps, Mikhail thought, he would meet his father somewhere on the battlefield. He would know what to do, of that Mikhail was sure.

Mikhail smiled as he remembered his father saying goodbye to them a few weeks previously. He had given Mikhail a bear hug that was so tight he could barely breathe before telling him that the war would be over in weeks.

"Days, probably, once they give me a gun," his father had said to Mikhail, smiling through his thick beard. "Once they see me coming, they will turn and run back to the border. Squealing like the little piggies they are." Even his mother, tears streaming down her cheeks, had laughed at this.

Perhaps, Mikhail thought as his smile grew, he and his father would fight side by side? Mikhail would no longer be a child, but a man. A soldier, fighting for his country and its freedom. Maybe when it was all over, they would both be given medals for their part in the conflict?

Mikhail slipped into a day dream about standing next to his father on a parade square, a medal being pinned to his chest as grateful crowds cheered their victory. In his day dream, Alevtina was there, also watching and cheering. Years later, when they had children of their own, Mikhail would tell them war stories in the evening.

Stories of how he and his father became heroes of Belarus.

CHAPTER 51

Caleb examined the complicated map on the wall of the underground station. He reached out with his index finger, placing it on the station he was currently at. King's Cross St Pancras. The Kings Cross element of the station name he kind of understood, but he didn't understand the link between the station and St Pancras. If Caleb remembered correctly, Pancras was a teenager who was beheaded for his faith in the fourth century in Rome.

Keeping his index finger on his current location, his eyes roved over the other stations to find the one he was looking for.

"Totten-ham Court Road," Caleb mumbled under his breath, unsure if he had got the pronunciation right. The map appeared to show multiple ways of getting there, none of them direct. His destination seemed to be served by three lines. A red one, a black one, and a clear one but whichever line he took, he would need to change. Caleb crossed to the ticket barrier where a woman in an orange jacket was standing. As the jacket had the London tube symbol on the back, he was sure she would be able to help him.

"Excuse me," Caleb said as he approached the woman. She didn't reply, but just arched her eyebrows. "Can you tell me the easiest way to get to Totten-ham Court Road?"

"Tottenham," she replied, making the word much shorter. *Tott-nam*. "It's pronounced Tottenham."

"Ah, I see. Thank you. I want to go to the British Museum."

"Easiest way is to walk, mate. It's probably less than thirty minutes." She looked at him with a faintly amused expression, as if she was wondering why a man like Caleb would be interested in the British Museum. "If you get the tube, you've either got to get the northbound northern line to Euston, then the southbound northern line. Or go to Liverpool Street, then the central line westbound. Both will get you to Tottenham Court Road. I'd walk if I was you, as long as it's not raining."

If Caleb hadn't been confused by the map, he was confused by her directions. He thanked the woman and made his way to the bottom of the escalator that led back up to the main station concourse. It was a long escalator, perhaps a couple of hundred yards, and Caleb wondered how far beneath the streets of London he was. There was an air of quiet urgency among his fellow passengers, and he realized it was approaching rush hour. Most people were standing on the right, leaving the left hand side for those in a hurry.

Caleb passed the time by looking at the passengers on the escalator next to his which was descending as the same rate his was ascending. Most of them were lost in their own worlds, many of them staring at their phone screens, perhaps knowing that they would lose their signal as they descended further. A few were listening to something on headphones, more than one passenger nodding their heads. Not many of them were looking around as he was. Caleb guessed that they made the same journey every day, and had long since run out of things to look at.

At one point, Caleb saw a young man staring at him. Caleb smiled briefly and nodded his head by way of a greeting. He was used to people being surprised by his appearance, so didn't think too much of it. A few seconds after Caleb had nodded at him, the young man stepped to the left and started hurrying down the steps, a small rucksack on his back hitting several other passengers. Caleb wondered if he had suddenly remembered he was late for something.

A few moments later, just as Caleb's escalator was approaching the end of its journey, he became aware of a minor commotion behind him. Mindful of the approaching transition to sidewalk, Caleb turned to see what was going on. It was the same young man he had seen on the other escalator, except now he was on Caleb's side and running up the steps. The commotion was other passengers reacting to his passing them, as the rucksack hit several of them.

"Oi, mate," one commuter shouted after the man. "Where's the fire?"

Caleb had just stepped off the escalator and was making his way toward some stairs leading to the concourse proper when he heard his name being called.

"Caleb?" Caleb looked over his shoulder to see it was the man with the rucksack. "Excuse me, are you Caleb?"

Caleb stopped and turned to face the young man. He was perhaps in his mid-twenties, slim, and was panting heavily from the exertion. As Caleb watched, the man leaned forward and put his hands on his knees.

"Yes," Caleb said to the top of the man's head. "I'm Caleb."

"I'm Will," the man said, barely able to get the words out. "I need to speak to you."

"Take your time," Caleb replied. "There's no hurry."

Caleb waited for a moment as Will composed himself. When he straightened back up again, his face was still florid but his breathing had slowed and he was no longer gasping lungfuls of air.

"Jesus wept, that was hard work," Will said, wiping his mouth with the back of his hand.

"I'm sure he did," Caleb replied, not caring for the phrase Will had just used. "What with him being crucified."

"Oh, I'm sorry," Will said as he realized what he had just said. "I forgot you're a priest."

"I'm a preacher, not a priest."

"Okay, well, I'm still sorry." Will looked genuinely apologetic beneath his perspiration, so Caleb said nothing more. "Like I said, I'm Will. I work for the Home Office. Do you know Mrs. Zaystev?"

"No, I don't think so. What's her first name?"

"Natalie, I think."

"Natasha?" Caleb asked, suddenly on edge.

"Yes, Natasha. That's her name. You know her, right?"

"Yes, I do. Is she okay?" Given Will's exertions to catch up with him, Caleb was becoming concerned.

"Yes, and no," Will replied. "She needs to speak to you." He took a deep breath. "She needs your help with something. Her liaison officer called me and asked me to look out for you." Caleb saw him glancing at his robe. "She said you were pretty distinctive, and she was right. I couldn't believe it when I saw you on the escalator." Will laughed and reached into his pocket for his cell phone. "What are the chances of that happening, right?"

"It could be chance," Caleb replied, closing his eyes and offering a quick prayer of thanks. He thought he had lost touch with Natasha when she hadn't met him at the medical center, but it didn't look as if that was the case. "It's more likely to be divine intervention, in my opinion." From the look on Will's face, he didn't share Caleb's sentiment, but that meant nothing to Caleb.

"No signal," Will said as he looked at his phone. "We'll need to go up to the concourse. I've got her number."

CHAPTER 52

Phoebe whistled as she walked through Kings Cross station, swinging the plastic bag with the soda cans in it as she did so. Although she had originally intended to return straight to the clinic once their coffees had arrived, Phoebe and Caleb had ended up drinking them in the cafe. She smiled as she thought back over their conversation. Caleb was an easy man to talk to. He had only quoted one verse from the Bible to her, and even that had only been in response to a comment she had made about him not preaching much for a preacher.

Caleb had seemed convinced that Phoebe's choice of profession wasn't her choice at all. His opinion was that it was at the whim of the 'man upstairs' which was a phrase Phoebe had used, much to Caleb's amusement. That had then turned into a playful discussion about whether God was masculine, feminine, or genderless.

"He's referred to as male throughout the Bible," Phoebe had said to him, "which would make Him masculine. And the Bible is the word of God, right?"

Caleb had pointed out that God didn't have a physical

body, so therefore couldn't be assigned a gender. Phoebe had nodded, conceding the point, before going on to say that if God didn't have a physical body, then he couldn't actually exist.

"Q.E.D., Caleb. That's all I'm saying," Phoebe had said, smiling at him.

"Nice try, Phoebe," Caleb had replied, laughing. "But there's a lot more to it than that."

Her smile broadened as she remembered how easily the conversation had flowed right up until the point they finished their coffees. Then Caleb had taken hold of Phoebe's hand, transporting her for a split second back to the dream she'd had about him. But before she could even think about it, Phoebe was transfixed by the way he was looking at her. His eyes were like infinite pools of cool water and his expression was the most earnest she had ever seen.

"Never forget, Phoebe, that everything you do is His work," Caleb had said, his voice almost a whisper but at the same time, a resounding voice that echoed inside her head. She felt a warm sensation in her solar plexus, not an uncomfortable sensation but most unusual. Then Caleb let go of her hand, his eyes returned to normal, and the sensation faded away. Phoebe had opened her mouth, about to ask him what had just happened, but Caleb was already getting to his feet, the moment seemingly forgotten.

Phoebe frowned as she pushed the door to the medical center open. The waiting room was almost full with perhaps fifteen or twenty people sitting in it. They turned to look at her, almost as one, as she walked across the waiting area.

"Where have you been?" Jade asked when Phoebe walked into their small staff room. "You've been gone for ages." The nurse looked frustrated rather than angry.

Phoebe looked at the clock on the wall and realized that

she had been sitting with Caleb for almost a whole hour. She was convinced it had been less than ten minutes.

"I'm so sorry, Jade," Phoebe said, placing the bag of soda down and retrieving her white coat from the back of a chair. "These are for the fridge. I think Caleb wanted the patients to have them, but there's not enough to go round."

"We can keep them for the kids," Jade replied. "How was your date with the Buddha?"

"We went for a coffee, Jade," Phoebe said with a smile. "It was hardly a date, and Caleb's nowhere near fat enough to be the Buddha."

"Isn't that blasphemy? Calling the Buddha fat?"

"Er, I'm not sure," Phoebe replied. "I'll have to ask Caleb next time I see him."

"So you are going to see him again?" Jade had a mischievous smile on her face as she spoke.

"He said he might stop by at some point, so probably."

"We've had a load more stuff donated for the convoy as well. A taxi driver dropped off four more boxes."

"The same one from earlier?" Phoebe slipped her arms into her coat and adjusted it before draping her stethoscope around her neck. "What was his name again? Dave?"

"No, it was a different man. It's mostly nappies and baby food, stuff like that. He said some of his colleagues might be by later with some more stuff."

"That's great news. I wonder how he found out about the convoy," Phoebe replied. The smile on Jade's face just broadened.

"He said a man in a robe sent him."

CHAPTER 53

Stepan sat in the passenger seat of his truck, watching as the young soldier who was sitting on the front fender got the drone ready. They had already looked at, and discounted, one of the potential locations for the resistance fighters' base. The second location was several hundred yards away, deep in a copse. According to the map, there were at least three buildings there, and from the look of the road, vehicles passed down it regularly.

The drone's propellors started whining and a moment later, the small gray aircraft lifted into the air. It was a drone that could be bought in any electronic shop, so not large enough to carry any sort of weapon, but the camera was phenomenal and when it was a hundred yards up in the sky, it was invisible and silent. They could always return with a larger drone if necessary, but if they found any resistance fighters, Stepan wasn't planning on a sneak attack. They would go in all guns blazing. With their better training and superior firepower, any resistance would be short lived.

The soldier's attention was fixed on the screen of the phone he was using to control the drone, and he didn't hear

Stepan step out of the vehicle. When Stepan spoke, the young man jumped and almost dropped the phone.

"You see anything?" Stepan asked. In response, the soldier moved slightly so that Stepan could see the screen.

"There're the three buildings on the map," the young man said. "But there's not much else there."

Stepan squinted to look at the screen. The soldier was right. There were no signs of activity at all. No vehicles, no people. There was nothing. Stepan sighed.

"Okay, just get some footage of the area while we're here. Just because they're not here now doesn't mean it's not a base for them," he said. The young man nodded in response and returned his attention to the screen. Stepan knew that the footage might be useful in the future if they ever needed to return. He put his hands on his hips and looked at the trees in front of them where the rest of his squad were sitting, playing cards from the look of it. Somewhere in these woods, the resistance was hiding. Stepan knew it. It was just a case of finding them.

Stepan returned to the passenger seat and picked up his phone to call in the results of their reconnaissance.

"Ops?" a male voice said when the call was answered.

"This is Bravo Zulu," Stepan said, using the code for his squad. Even though they didn't think the resistance was able to monitor their calls, they might have some outside help who could. "I'm at location four. Nothing seen. Confirm?"

"Confirm, location four is cold. Stand by."

Stepan tutted at effectively being put on hold by a junior soldier. Not just a junior one, but one who was sitting fat and happy back in a proper headquarters. Not out in the field like he was. To pass the time, he thought about his experience that morning with the girl at the village. She hadn't taken long to give up and submit. None of them did.

"Bravo Zulu, are you ready to receive some coordinates?" the man on the phone asked a moment later, just as Stepan was mentally getting to the best part of his memory. Stepan scrabbled for a pen and something to write on.

"Go ahead." He listened as the soldier read out a series of numbers before Stepan read them back to him.

"Confirmed," the soldier said. "Proceed with caution to that location. Reports of armed men in the area."

"Do we have any assets in place?" Stepan asked. The last thing he wanted to do was waste time tracking other squads from the same side.

"Negative, Bravo Zulu."

Stepan ended the call and leaned over to press on the horn of the truck. This time, the soldier sitting on the front did drop his phone, but he recovered it quickly.

"On me, squad," Stepan called out of the truck window to summon the rest of his soldiers. "We've got some work to do."

CHAPTER 54

"I'm sorry," Natasha said as her cell phone vibrated in her hand. According to the screen, it was a withheld number. "Do you mind if I take this?"

"Of course not," replied the woman with her, a sprightly woman who had to be twenty years older than Natasha, but wore it well. Natasha was sitting in the woman's office, a satellite of the main Home Office in London. "I'll give you some privacy. You take as long as you need."

The woman, Natasha's liaison officer, stood and left the room with a cheerful wave. Natasha sat back in the armchair she was sitting in and answered the call.

"Hello?" When she heard Caleb's voice reply, she gave a huge sigh of relief. Even the sound of his voice was reassuring.

"What's going on?" he asked her, the concern obvious in his tone.

"It's Anton, my husband."

"Is he okay?"

"That's just it," Natasha said, her voice breaking. "I don't know. They've said he's disappeared."

"Who is they?"

"The unit he's fighting with. The resistance army, or whatever it is they're calling themselves. I can't get in touch with Mikhail, either."

There was a long pause on the end of the line, and Natasha was about to check that the call was still active when Caleb replied.

"Did they say what happened when your husband disappeared?" he asked.

"He went out on a patrol and never came back." Natasha brushed at a tear that was slowly making its way down her cheek. "And Mikhail's not answering his phone. I'm so worried, Caleb. What should I do?"

"Do you think the two things are connected?"

"No, I don't see how they can be. Mikhail was upset about a friend who was hurt. Perhaps even killed."

There was another long pause, but this time Natasha just waited to see what Caleb said. As she did so, she started to feel foolish. What was Caleb supposed to do about something happening so far away, in a country he didn't know? It wasn't only that, though. Caleb himself was also hundreds of miles away, still in London.

"Does your sister speak English?" Caleb asked eventually.

"Of course," Natasha replied, forcing a smile onto her face as she saw the liaison officer peek in through the door to check on her. "Not quite as well as I do, but almost."

"Would you mind if I spoke with her?"

"No, if you think it might help. I just don't know what to do." Natasha lowered her voice so that the liaison officer wouldn't hear her. "I'm thinking perhaps I should go home."

"But what would that achieve, Natasha?"

"At least. I would be there. Closer than I am now."

"What if they don't let you leave?" Caleb replied. "You could be stuck there in Belarus, and how would you be able to help Anton and Mikhail then?"

His voice was reassuring and Natasha knew he had a point. She knew she could get into the country easily. The borders were open in that direction. But with the ballot system for leaving Belarus, she doubted she would be able to get back across the border to safety if she needed to.

"Can you text her number to this phone?" he asked her. "And what's her name?"

"Her name's Iĺja," Natasha said. "I'll send her a message so she knows you're calling. Thank you, Caleb."

"I've not done anything yet." She could tell from the way he spoke that he was smiling. "Let me speak to Iĺja to see if I can get some more information." Natasha could hear his voice speaking, muffled as if he had his hand over the phone. "Will is going to buy me a phone so I can stay in touch with you. Once I have it, I'll send you the number."

Natasha thanked Caleb before ending the call. Just as she said goodbye, the liaison officer appeared. She had obviously been loitering outside the door, waiting, and Natasha wondered how much of the conversation she had overheard.

"Now then, my dear," the woman said. "We need to get you to your host family. They're a lovely couple. Are you ready?"

Natasha nodded but she felt far from ready. Was she about to start a new life?

On her own?

CHAPTER 55

Mikhail paused for a moment, jamming the spade into the soft earth and leaning on the handle. A few feet away from him, Grigor did the same thing, reaching into his pocket for a packet of cigarettes.

A few yards further up the trench were Dmitry and Ruslan, who were, according to Vincuk, the other two members of their squad. Dmitry was the squad leader by virtue of age. He was in perhaps his early thirties, whereas both Grigor and Ruslan were in their twenties. But all three of them shared similar characteristics in Mikhail's opinion. They were all rough-looking men and he was pleased they were on the same side as him.

"You want one?" Grigor said, holding the pack out to Mikhail. Mikhail looked at them for a few seconds. He'd never smoked a cigarette before, but then, he'd never been a soldier before. He took one a few seconds later, angling his head for Grigor to light it as he'd seen so many people do on the television.

Mikhail puffed before inhaling a mouthful of bitter,

acrid, smoke. He coughed once, and then again. It turned into a coughing fit that made Grigor laugh, but it wasn't a nice laugh. It was as if he was enjoying Mikhail's discomfort.

"You've smoked before, right?" Grigor said with a smirk.

"Of course," Mikhail replied between coughs. "These are just stronger than the ones I'm used to."

"Sure they are," Grigor replied.

"Leave the мальчик alone, Grigor," Dmitry, who had walked across to join them, said. He was using the Russian term for a young boy, and Mikhail wasn't sure if it was a nickname or a derogatory title. If it was the former, Mikhail was happy. He'd read somewhere that often, in the military, soldiers used nicknames as a sign of belonging. But from the disparaging look that Dmitry gave him as he said it, Mikhail thought it was more likely to be an insult. "Here," Dmitry said to Mikhail, holding out a water bottle. "Have some of this."

"You shouldn't smoke," Ruslan said to Grigor as he approached them. "It's bad for you." Ruslan was the closest to Mikhail in terms of age, and of the three men, he seemed to Mikhail to be the friendliest. They were all wearing the same army fatigues, no ranks or insignia on them. Dmitry had taken his jacket off to hang on a tree while he worked, and Mikhail glanced at the tattoos that almost covered his chest. Central to them, right over Dmitry's sternum, was a crude depiction of a knight on a charging horse. It was a Pahonia, the historical coat of arms of Belarus that in recent times had become a symbol of opposition to the president. From the way the ink was slightly faded, Dmitry had had the tattoo for a few years, but Mikhail knew he could still be persecuted for wearing it.

"So what?" Grigor replied. "The cancer will be coming for me one day, so why not enjoy life while I can?"

"How are you enjoying life as a soldier so far, Mikhail?" Ruslan said. Mikhail turned to him, grinding the cigarette out beneath his foot.

"So far, so good," Mikhail replied, scratching at his chest. The fatigues were uncomfortable, and the perspiration from the exertion of digging made them ten times worse. "I didn't think we'd be digging trenches, though."

"You'll be glad of them when the shelling starts," Dmitry replied with a cruel laugh. "Somewhere safe to shit yourself."

Earlier on that afternoon, before they had started the task that Vincuk had given them, Dmitry had told the others that they were in a forest to the north of Minsk. The Belarusian army was perhaps two miles away, but the forest was a good position for them to hide in to launch attacks on the neighboring villages that were harboring both the Belarusian army and the Russian Mercenaries.

"We can strike them hard and melt back into the trees before they know we're there," Dmitry had said, punching his fist into his other hand for emphasis. He had then given Mikhail a hard look. "That's when we'll be able to separate the men from the boys."

CHAPTER 56

Caleb sat on the park bench, wondering briefly who Lewis Fountain was and why he had a bench dedicated to him. The bench was in a park close to Kings Cross station that was full of people. There was a small group of women, all with mats laid out on the grass, who were either practicing Tai Chi or yoga, Caleb wasn't sure. He watched them for a few moments as their instructor led them through a sequence of moves. When he saw them start to drop into a kua squat, he smiled. Tai Chi it was.

He had spent almost twenty minutes on the phone with Natasha's sister, Ilja. Will hadn't seemed to mind the effect this might have on his mobile bill, saying that the King was paying it anyway. When the call had finished, Will had taken Caleb to a small mobile phone shop next to the station where Caleb had bought a small cell phone and SIM card. The Asian man who ran the shop had taken the time to both charge the phone and teach Caleb how to use it, even though it was the cheapest phone in the store. Caleb could make and receive calls, which was all he really needed the cell phone for.

Caleb relaxed on the bench, watching as an overweight female jogger wobbled by. A young couple on another bench sniggered as she passed them, which Caleb found faintly amusing. The woman might be carrying a few extra pounds, but at least she was doing something about it. He stretched his arms out on the back of the bench and closed his eyes, enjoying the warmth of the sunshine on his face. Caleb needed to think, and he thought best with the sun on his face.

He needed some courses of action. Three, ideally. During the phone call with Iĺja, Caleb had mostly listened, only asking questions when it was absolutely necessary. By the time the call was finished, he had as much information as possible. It wasn't enough to fully develop mature courses of action, but it was enough. He was used to working with what he had, not necessarily what he needed.

Caleb's potential first course of action, as always, was to do nothing. He thought about this for longer than he normally did as it was a viable option. It wasn't a case of not wanting to help, but a case of not being able to. Both Natasha's husband and son were in a country miles away. A country where Caleb didn't speak the language and was in the middle of some sort of revolution. If Anton was dead, which Caleb thought was probably the case, then there was nothing he could do to resolve that situation. Her son, Mikhail, was probably doing what Caleb was doing. Sitting somewhere quiet, thinking. If Mikhail had lost a friend, which Iĺja seemed to think was the case, again nothing Caleb could do would help with that. He owed Natasha nothing. In fact, he barely knew the woman.

The do nothing option was rarely one that was taken, in

Caleb's experience. It was designed to present a commanding officer with a worst case scenario. It was designed to persuade a senior officer why action must be taken. But in this scenario, it was a viable course of action to take. Caleb contemplated it for a few moments before nodding his head.

Next was the third option, usually known as the nuclear option. This was the most extreme course of action, and often involved extreme violence of one form or another. It was the right of arc to the left of arc that was doing nothing. Caleb frowned as he started to put the option together. It would involve several stages. First would be to get to Belarus somehow. Then he would need to locate and navigate to Anton, assuming he was still alive. If he was, then Caleb would need to extract the man from the country, locating and collecting Mikhail on the way. Caleb's frown deepened as he thought through this course of action. As always with the third one, it was by far the most difficult, and usually served to temper the enthusiasm of the senior officer.

Course of action number two was almost always the one that was selected. It presented a middle ground, a way of not doing nothing, but not reacting to a situation in an extreme way. If formulated correctly, it presented a considered response. Caleb brought up a mental image of Belarus and its neighboring countries to think about where he might be able to generate an effect from. Russia was out, obviously. Lithuania was problematic as well, as far as he knew. That only left Poland and Ukraine, both of which he had visited but for very different reasons.

Caleb's thoughts turned to Poland. When he had been there, he'd been impressed with the country. He'd not met a single person who didn't speak English, and they had much better roads than the country he was currently in. They were also very used to conflict in the countries next door to them, so would have an infrastructure that was used to receiving people. Perhaps he could base himself there and enlist the help of some of the local people with ties to Belarus? Reach into the war-torn country remotely and locate both Anton and Mikhail that way?

His eyes snapped open a few moments later when he had revisited all the options in his mind. Caleb blinked a couple of times, looking at a large seagull that was standing on the grass of the park, looking menacingly at passers by. The bird turned to look at Caleb, who nodded his head three times, once for each course of action. Then he got to his feet.

Caleb had a plan.

CHAPTER 57

"They look soft to me," Vincuk said, pointing at the four men with a stick. He and Yuri were sitting on a log a hundred yards away from the group digging the trench. "Except for him. The oldest one."

"Grigor?" Yuri replied. "He's certainly the most capable. Got a proper thousand yard stare."

"Prison does that to a man," Vincuk said. They exchanged a knowing look, both having served time in at least one of Belarus' jails. "But there's no fire in his eyes. Not like the boy." He pointed his stick at Mikhail. "You really think he's eighteen?"

"It doesn't matter." Yuri shrugged his shoulders. "As long as he fights like a man."

"He'll certainly bleed like one," Vincuk replied with a laugh, although he didn't want to be responsible for a child. "Now come, we have work to do."

The two men turned their attention to a map that was laid out on the ground in front of them, each corner secured with a stone. Vincuk used his stick to point to an area on the map. He slowly traced the outline of a small village.

"This is Halitsa," Vincuk said. "Thirty kilometers to the south." He tapped the stick at another couple of villages on the map. "The mercenaries have already been to these places. It stands to reason Halitsa will be next. They're operating in death squads of between five and seven soldiers. Every place they visit, they leave shallow graves behind."

"What time did they visit these other settlements?" Yuri asked.

"Always at dawn."

"How many people live there?" Yuri asked.

"Thirty-five. Forty, perhaps? But the houses are very spread out, like the other places." Vincuk watched as a scowl appeared on Yuri's face. "They seem to hit groups of houses, always leaving someone behind to tell others what has happened. As a warning to them not to assist us."

"Are you sure it's only a squad of mercenaries that's heading here?" Yuri asked, tapping at the map with his own stick. "One hundred per cent? What if we're heading into a trap?"

"I'm as sure as I can be," Vincuk replied. He didn't mind being challenged by Yuri. If anything, he welcomed it. The man was a solid second in command, and one of the few men who Vincuk trusted with his life. He had saved it on more than one occasion, a debt Vincuk would repay in a heartbeat.

"When do we go in?"

"Tomorrow morning, perhaps the day after," Vincuk replied with a glance at the four men who were still digging. "We'll do weapons training with them this evening, except for Grigor. But the sooner we get them into action, the better. There are three other groups moving into position." He stabbed at the map with his stick as if to indicate where the groups might be.

Vincuk knew that the resistance, such as it was, wasn't yet ready to take on the mercenaries face to face in combat. The mercenaries were too powerful, and the resistance too fragmented. The Belarusian army was not a threat. Although at the start of the conflict, they had been relentless, things had slowly changed when the soldiers realized their government wanted them to kill their fellow countrymen. Vincuk had even heard talk of a potential military coup, which would mean the only thing they needed was time.

In the few skirmishes that the resistance had with the Belarusian army recently, there had been no casualties on either side. When the resistance realized that the army was firing over their heads, they did the same. But the mercenaries were completely different. They were well-armed, skilled in combat, and utterly ruthless. They shot to kill.

"We should be documenting what they're doing," Vincuk muttered under his breath, using his stick to trace around the village of Halitsa again. He glanced at Yuri who nodded in assent. The only way to defeat the mercenaries was to turn opinion against them. "These are war crimes. The outside world should know what they are doing."

"This isn't a war, Vincuk," Yuri replied, his scowl returning. "I don't think the outside world cares."

CHAPTER 58

Phoebe sighed as she closed the doors to the medical center for the final time that day. She was exhausted, and from the look of her, so was Jade. There had been more patients than they had expected on the most recent train, including several who had been in hospitals over in Belarus. Things must be bad if they were starting to evacuate them as well as people who could move under their own steam.

"You got any plans for tonight, Phoebe?" Jade asked as she put her jacket on over the top of her scrubs.

"I was thinking a glass or two of wine, a microwaveable lasagne, and the *Great British Bake Off* final on the television, " Phoebe replied with a grin. "How about you?"

"Oh, God, that sounds heavenly. What wouldn't I give for an evening like that? I'm afraid the other half's cooking, so not only will I still be hungry afterward, but the kitchen will look like a bomb's hit it."

"Ah, I see," Phoebe replied with a giggle. She'd not met Jade's husband, but the more she heard about him, the more she liked the man. "He's not a chef then, I take it?"

"He has many talents," Jade replied with a mischievous look, "but cooking's not one of them."

The two women walked across the waiting area and into the examination room. Phoebe started checking that the cupboards with the drugs in were locked and properly secured. A few weeks earlier, someone had broken into the clinic in the night and stolen a lot of controlled drugs. Since then, they'd had CCTV and a much better cupboard installed. She had just checked the final cupboard when she heard the doors to the waiting area opening.

"We're closed," Phoebe called out loudly before Jade could say anything. A moment later, there were two light taps on the door of the examination room.

"I said we're closed," Phoebe said as she walked across the room to open the door, putting a stern expression on her face as she did so. She flung the door open to see a man wearing a hoodie, running pants, and trainers standing there. It took her a second or two to realize who it was.

"Oh, hi Caleb," Phoebe said, looking him up and down. "You look, er, different." She smirked at him. "Almost normal, in fact. What happened to the robe?"

"I'm having it dry cleaned," Caleb replied with a brief grin. He glanced at Jade, who raised a hand to wave at him. Caleb returned the gesture and turned back to Phoebe. "I need your help, Phoebe," he said under his breath.

"What, again?" Phoebe replied, turning her smirk into a smile. Caleb didn't return it though.

"Can we talk?" he asked her, his expression serious.

"Do you mind if I leave you two to it?" Jade asked, buttoning up her jacket. "Dinner's going to be bad enough already without it being burnt."

"Sure," Phoebe replied, looking at Caleb with concern.

He was worried about something, and she'd not seen that expression on his face before. "I'll see you tomorrow, Jade."

"Sure," Jade replied. As she walked past Phoebe and Caleb, Phoebe saw her also look Caleb up and down before turning her attention to her. "Don't do anything I wouldn't do," Jade said with a glint in her eye.

"Goodbye, Jade," Phoebe replied firmly, stifling the smile that was threatening. She waited until she heard the medical center doors closing before she said anything else. "What's the matter, Caleb?"

She watched him as he paused for a moment. He did look completely different without his robe, and she thought back to what Jade had said about him previously. Something about put him in normal clothes and he'd be a different man. Looking at Caleb now, Phoebe could see that she was right.

"Like I said, I need your help," Caleb said a moment later.

"Are you sick?" Phoebe asked. "Injured?"

"No, not that sort of help," Caleb replied with a look of frustration.

"Well, how can I help you?"

"This convoy of yours. When does it leave?"

"In a couple of days' time. I'm not sure I would call it a convoy, though. There's only one van. Why?"

Caleb looked at her intensely, his gray eyes boring into hers. For an uncomfortable split-second, Phoebe was sure he could see right into her soul and access her innermost thoughts. Then, just as quickly as it had appeared, the sensation vanished.

"I want to come with you."

CHAPTER 59

Natasha sat on the edge of the armchair and regarded her surroundings. She was sitting in an elegant room, which the woman who had answered the door had described as their drawing room. It had yellow painted walls, a white ceiling with an elaborate chandelier, and everything about the decor just oozed quality. The house itself was a grandiose dwelling on the outskirts of Salisbury.

Almost square, it had pale limestone walls and a dark gray slate roof. The windows in the front were enormous, and the garden surrounding the house seemed to be almost as large as the park Natasha had taken Mikhail to when he was a child.

"Georgian," Natasha's liaison officer had said, nodding at the building as their taxi had approached on the gravel driveway. Then she had lowered her voice as if she didn't want the taxi driver to overhear. "Grade two listed as well." Natasha had just nodded, not understanding the phrase.

Natasha looked up as the door to the room opened and the house's owner walked in. She had introduced herself earlier as Heidi, explaining that her husband was away at work in London but would be back at some point in the next few days. The dress Heidi was wearing was a light, summery garment with long sleeves. Natasha looked at it with envy. Not only would she not be able to afford anything like it, but she knew she wouldn't look anywhere near as good as her host. In Heidi's hands was a silver tray which she placed on the coffee table in the center of the room, centering it on a crocheted ornamental mat.

"I've made us both some tea," Heidi said. Her accent was unusual, and not one that Natasha had heard before. She spoke very precisely, almost as if she was pronouncing each word with deliberate care. "And would you like some cake? It's lemon drizzle."

Natasha looked down at the tray to see two small slices of cake on fine china plates. The cake was the same color as the walls.

"Thank you, Heidi," Natasha said as she regarded the plates the slices of cake were on. They were incredibly thin, and matched the teapot and cups which came with saucers. The ensemble was completed by a small bowl of sugar lumps with a small pair of tongs next to it. "This looks lovely."

"We only bring it out for special guests," Heidi replied with a kind smile. She was a few years older than Natasha who knew if she wore the same dress, she would just look frumpy. Natasha watched as Heidi poured the tea in precise steps. Tea first, then milk. Then she looked at Natasha with her eyebrows raised, the tongs in her hand. "Sugar?"

"Please," Natasha replied, eyeing the cup and saucer warily. She was terrified of dropping them, breaking the fragile-looking china and spilling tea onto the deep cream rug under the coffee table. "You have a lovely house."

"Thank you," Heidi replied, picking up her own cup and saucer. She took a dainty sip from it. "I'm pleased you like it. We don't use this room very often, though. Only for guests." Heidi took another sip as Natasha looked again at the tray. "I'll show you round properly once we've had our tea."

"What does your husband do?" Natasha asked, finally plucking up the courage to pick up the cup and saucer. It wobbled slightly in her hand, but she managed to not spill any.

"Lawrence?" Heidi replied. "He works in the City. Intelligent wealth management, whatever that is." She gave Natasha a conspiratorial smile. "I don't understand exactly what it is, but it pays well."

"Do you work?" Natasha asked. She wasn't sure, but she thought she caught a flicker of disappointment on Heidi's face.

"No, not anymore. I used to, before we got married."

"What did you do?"

"I was a teacher."

Natasha smiled broadly at Heidi. "That's what I do. What did you teach?"

"I taught primary school children, so pretty much everything." Heidi returned Natasha's smile.

"Do you miss it?" Natasha asked. This time, it wasn't a flicker of disappointment on Heidi's face, it was an obvious expression.

"Every day, if I'm honest. But Lawrence says I don't need to work." Heidi glanced around the opulent room and opened her mouth to say something else when Natasha's hand slipped and the cup and saucer went flying. As the cup hit the table, it cracked into several shards of china, depositing its contents on the cream rug just as Natasha had feared. Her hands flew to her mouth.

"Oh, no. I am so sorry!" she said, mortified, as she stared at the growing stain on the rug. When she looked up at Heidi, to her surprise, the woman was laughing.

"Oh, don't be," Heidi said as she put her own cup and saucer down. She looked at Natasha with a broad grin on her face. "I've hated this tea set ever since Lawrence's mother bought it. At least now I've got the perfect excuse not to use the bloody thing again."

CHAPTER 60

Caleb stepped out of the pub for a few moments, keen to get some fresh air. The pub, which according to its advertising, had been selling beer there since the fifteenth century, was full of people who had finished work. He also needed to make a phone call.

He walked a few yards down the sidewalk to find a place where he could speak without being overheard, and also hear properly. Caleb studied the handset, thinking back to his impromptu lesson in the shop, and pressed on the button with the number one on it. He kept his finger down as the assistant had shown him and was rewarded with a message on the screen.

Calling Natasha

Caleb's eyebrows went up at how simple it was. But he still didn't want to own a cell phone long term. He could see no use for it with his lifestyle. When he moved on from a place, which he always did, he wanted to leave nothing behind.

"Hello, Caleb?" Natasha's voice sounded from the handset. With a laugh, Caleb pressed it against his ear, hoping no one was watching him.

"Hi, Natasha," he replied. "Are you free to talk?"

"Give me a moment."

Caleb nodded and then, when he remembered Natasha couldn't actually see him, he replied.

"Sure."

Caleb listened for a moment until Natasha's voice came back on the line. "I'm here," she said, and Caleb could tell from the way her voice sounded that she had moved location.

"How are things?" he asked, unsure of the etiquette of phone calls. Was some small talk required before the meat of the conversation, like in real life?

"All good here," Natasha replied. Perhaps small talk was okay, after all. "The house I'm in is really posh, though. I managed to break something within ten minutes of getting here."

"Oh dear," Caleb said with a smile. "Nothing too precious, I hope?"

"A cup. It could have been Ming china for all I know. But Heidi didn't seem too bothered."

"Heidi?"

"She's my host. They've put me into a guest apartment in the grounds of the main house." It could have been his imagination, but Natasha sounded uncomfortable. "It's bigger than my entire house back at home. She's lovely, though. I've not met the husband yet. He works in London doing some sort of banking thing."

Caleb nodded. From what Natasha had told him of the house, that didn't surprise him. Caleb didn't know many bankers, but the ones he had come across never seemed to be short of money. "Did you speak to Iĺja?" The small talk part of the conversation was obviously over.

"I did, yes," Caleb replied.

He went on to tell her about his plan to get to Poland and base himself on the border. What he was actually going to do when he got there, he'd not quite worked out, but he knew he had a few days to think about it while they traveled over. At first, Natasha had been against the idea, saying that it was too much for Caleb to do, but he had been quietly insistent that this was what was going to happen.

"So you're going with the doctor?" Natasha asked.

"Yes," Caleb replied, "and one of her colleagues from the hospital. I've not met him yet."

They chatted for a few moments, agreeing to stay in touch regularly and to call the moment there was any news.

"Are you okay, Natasha?" Caleb asked as the conversation was winding up.

"I'm fine," she replied, but there was no conviction in her voice.

"I mean," Caleb said, "are you really okay?"

She paused for a moment before replying.

"I will be, Caleb," Natasha said with a sigh. "I will be."

Caleb ended the call as the sales assistant in the shop had showed him and slipped the cell phone back into his pocket. He paused for a moment, closing his eyes and saying a prayer for Natasha. When he was finished, he made his way back to the pub.

When he opened the door, the noise of the drinkers inside hit him like a wall of sound. He blinked a couple of times to adjust to the change in atmosphere and made his way through the crowd to the rear of the building. At least here it was slightly quieter. Caleb paused and looked at the table he was sitting at. Phoebe was still there, with her drink and his in front of her. But she had been joined by someone else. A younger man, late twenties in Caleb's estimation, and from what Caleb could see of him, a good looking one. He was talking to Phoebe, leaning forward with his arms on the table. Her posture had changed from when she had been talking with Caleb a few moments before, and she was leaning back with her arms across her chest. Then she looked up and saw Caleb. A smile appeared on her face and she beckoned him over.

"Caleb," she said as he approached, nodding a greeting at the new arrival. "Your ears must be burning. We were just talking about you."

Caleb watched as the man sitting with Phoebe got to his feet. He stretched out a hand for Caleb to shake.

"Caleb, this is Thomas," Phoebe said. "Thomas, meet Caleb."

Caleb grasped the man's hand to shake it. He saw the other man's mouth moving, but he didn't hear what he said. A greeting of some sort, which Caleb would need to reply to. Thomas' grip was firm, slightly too much so as if he was asserting dominance. But Caleb couldn't care less about that. He closed his eyes, focusing on the sensation that the touch had sparked off in his core.

There were few people Caleb instantly disliked, either deliberately or intuitively.

Thomas was most certainly one of them.

CHAPTER 61

Mikhail closed his left eye and shuffled his position so that he was as stable as possible. He was lying on the forest floor on a makeshift firing range, holding the rifle just as Yuri had told him to. In front of him, perhaps fifty meters away, was a picture tacked to a tree. It was a woman, bare chested and crouched down in a pose typical of the magazine it had been torn from.

"That's it," Mikhail heard Yuri say. "Breathe in through your nose, and out through your mouth. But only half way." Mikhail did as instructed and tightened his finger on the trigger. "Don't snatch at it," Yuri said, his hand resting lightly on the small of Mikhail's back. "Just squeeze it lightly, as if it was a woman's nipple."

Mikhail, who had never touched a woman's nipple in his life other than as a baby, lined up the sights and squeezed on the trigger. He was determined not to mess this up. When the gun fired, he couldn't help but flinch, but in front of him, the corner of the picture exploded with a shower of paper.

"Again," Yuri said. Mikhail ignored the ringing in his

ears and the strange sensation in his shoulder, and pulled the trigger again. This time, a hole appeared in the picture, a couple of inches above the woman's head. "Excellent. One more." This time, the bullet creased her shoulder.

Yuri patted him on the back and shuffled over to Ruslan who was lying a couple of meters away from Mikhail. A few seconds later, Mikhail heard a shot ring out, but he couldn't see where the bullet had landed. Wherever it was, it had been nowhere near the picture tacked to the tree. Ruslan's second and third shots also appeared to miss.

"Give me that." Mikhail looked up to see Grigor standing next to him. He handed him the rifle and the two of them swapped places. "You need your elbows further apart," Grigor said. "Watch."

Mikhail watched as Grigor demonstrated a slightly different pose. Then he got to his feet and handed the rifle back to him. Mikhail's next round punched through the woman's left breast, causing Grigor to laugh.

"That's gonna hurt," Grigor said with an appreciative look at Mikhail. "Nice."

When they had finished the training session, Mikhail sat down on a log to the side of the firing range and placed the rifle on the ground in front of him. He was pleased with himself. By the time they had got to the end of the session, he was able to group his rounds in a tight circle, even from fifty meters away. When Vincuk and Grigor approached him, he got to his feet. To his surprise, Grigor clapped him on the back.

"Got ourselves a proper sharp shooter here, Vincuk," Grigor said with a grin that showed off his yellowed teeth. "Reckon he could give the mercenaries a right headache." As he said this, he pointed his index finger to Mikhail's forehead and made a noise like a child would when pretending to fire a gun.

"Yuri says you're one of the best shots he's taught since all this began," Vincuk said. "And believe me, he's not keen on paying compliments so you must have impressed him. Grigor?"

"Yes, boss?" Grigor replied.

"Clean the boy's rifle for him," Vincuk said. Mikhail saw Grigor's face fall slightly at his request, but he bent over to pick up the weapon without another word. "Mikhail, come with me."

Mikhail followed Vincuk as he walked over to a dirty white van that was parked behind the range. When they reached it, Vincuk opened the door and pointed in the back. Mikhail leaned over to see a long, black case. As he watched, Vincuk opened it.

"This," Vincuk said as Mikhail looked at the long, sleek rifle in the case, "is a Dragunov." The weapon had a wooden hand guard and stock, part of which was cut away. "Effective range is anywhere between six hundred and fifty and one thousand four hundred meters." Mikhail whistled softly as he took in the weapon, Vincuk pointing out the main components like the optical sight on the left of the weapon and the clamp-style bipod legs on the front of the barrel. Vincuk unlatched the sights and handed them to Mikhail to look through.

"The rangefinder is on the lower left and the chevrons in the middle are for distances beyond a thousand meters," Vincuk explained.

"What are the markings to the left and right of the reticule?" Mikhail asked. He saw Vincuk smile at the question. Finally, all the hours Mikhail had spent playing *Call of Duty* on his PlayStation had come to fruition.

"They're called stadia marks. They're for windage."

"So they help you adjust the scope for the wind?"

"Very good, Mikhail," Vincuk said, taking the scope from Mikhail and reattaching it to the rifle.

"Can I fire it?" Mikhail asked.

"Well I've not brought you here to look at it," Vincuk replied. He pointed at a plastic bag in the rear of the van. "There're some glass bottles in there. Grab the bag, and let's see if you're as good a shot as Yuri thinks you are."

CHAPTER 62

Phoebe sipped her glass of wine and sighed, relaxing back in her armchair. She had put some light music on her music system, more for background noise than anything else. It was a playlist she'd not listened to for some time, and she tried to relax into the music. She was freshly showered, was wearing a slip that she'd not worn before under a dressing gown that her mother had bought her months ago, also unworn.

She thought back to the moment in the pub when Thomas and Caleb had met for the first time and sighed again. Thomas had been his usual self. An arrogant prick trying to hide behind a cocky exterior. And Caleb, although he had hidden it well, had seen straight through it. It was going to be a difficult trip if they didn't get along, and their dislike for each other was obvious even from the few moments they'd spent together in the pub. Phoebe raised her glass to her lips and paused before taking another sip.

"Bollocks to it," she whispered to herself before she drained the glass in one long swallow. Just as she had refilled the glass, there was a soft tap on the lounge door.

"You don't need to knock," Phoebe called out. The door opened and her guest walked in. Phoebe pointed at the glass of wine she had already set out for him. "I poured you a glass."

"Thank you," Caleb replied. "I do appreciate you letting me stay here." He was wearing a fresh set of running pants and a t-shirt that showed off his lithe arms very well. Phoebe looked away from him, embarrassed at the thought that had just popped into her head.

"Like I said, there's no point wasting money on a hotel room when I've got a spare bedroom," she said, taking another sip and resisting the temptation to drain the glass again.

"Well, I appreciate it." Caleb picked up his glass and raised it. "Cheers, as I think you say over here."

"Yes, that works," Phoebe replied, raising her own glass. "You can also say chin chin or down the hatch."

Caleb took a tiny sip of his wine before putting his glass back down.

"So," Phoebe said a moment later. "What did you think of Thomas?"

"Thomas, yes," Caleb replied. Phoebe smiled, wondering how Caleb was going to approach this one. "Is he your boyfriend?"

"No!" Phoebe replied, shocked by the question. That wasn't at all what she'd been expecting him to say. "Whatever makes you think that?"

"But you have history, yes?"

"Did he say something to you in the pub? While I was in the bathroom?" Phoebe set her glass down and stared at Caleb, trying not to be angry with him for something that Thomas might have said.

"He did, yes," Caleb replied, holding his hand up in the

air. "But what he said is between he and I. And no, I'm not going to tell you what he said."

"He's a bastard," Phoebe muttered, taking a much larger gulp of her wine than she had intended to. "Let's talk about something else."

"Were you married?" Caleb asked as if he'd not heard what she had said.

"Oh, he was," Phoebe replied with a sharp laugh. "Just not to me."

AN HOUR LATER, Phoebe was right in the sweet spot between being tipsy and drunk. She'd had almost an entire bottle of wine, while Caleb had barely touched his. She wriggled to her feet, almost losing her balance, and put a hand on Caleb's shoulder as she walked past him to the kitchen.

"I'm going to get another bottle," she called out over her shoulder at him.

A few moments later, both their glasses refilled, she sat back down. If Caleb noticed that there was already a glass missing from the bottle, he said nothing, but just looked at Phoebe with an amused expression.

"I gotta question for you, preacher man," Phoebe said, a lop-sided grin on her face.

"Shoot."

"This God of yours, he's omnipotent, right?"

"Apparently so," Caleb replied.

"So he knows everything we're thinking, even if they're sinful thoughts?"

"Yes."

Phoebe closed her eyes for a moment before opening them again.

"He knows what I was thinking just now?"

"No."

"No?" Phoebe looked at Caleb and frowned. "But you said he was omnipotent."

"Not on a Thursday evening."

"What do you mean?"

"He has Thursday evenings off." Caleb put on an awful English accent. "He goes down the pub with his mates on a Thursday."

Phoebe started laughing and leaned forward, her gown falling away slightly as she did so. Caleb's eyes never left hers.

"I think you just made that up, preacher man," Phoebe said, looking at him.

"No, I didn't," Caleb replied. "It's in the Bible."

"Which chapter? Which verse?"

"I forget."

"Now I know you made that up, Caleb," Phoebe said, smiling at him. Her mouth was dry, and she took another sip of wine. She leaned forward some more, and her gown fell away even more. Caleb's eyes never left hers.

"What do you want, Phoebe?" Caleb asked, his voice low and soft. Phoebe felt the heat rising to her face. She couldn't tell him what she wanted. What if she was completely misreading everything? What if he was horrified about what she wanted?

"I..." Her voice trailed away. "I don't really know." She suddenly felt foolish about the situation she had put them both in. The right thing to do would be to tie her gown and go to bed. But she didn't want to do that.

"Is it something you want, or something you need?" Caleb asked, his eyes still fixed on her face. Phoebe knew from the draft across her chest that the gown wasn't covering much, and the slip she was wearing left little to the imagination.

But Caleb's eyes never left hers.

CHAPTER 63

Vincuk twisted the cap off the bottle he was holding and tipped some of the clear liquid into two metal mugs. He handed one to Yuri who took it with a nod of his head. The two men were sitting on a log next to the range, the last rays of the day filtering through the trees. Vincuk's father had always said that a man should see the sunrise and sunset at least once a year.

"It will remind him of how insignificant he truly is," he had always said with a sad expression. Vincuk raised the mug to his lips and took a sip of the fiery liquid, wincing as it burned the back of his throat.

"My God, Yuri," Vincuk said as he lifted the bottle to examine it. "There is no way this is genuine Stoli vodka."

"I never said it was genuine, only that it was cheap," Yuri replied with a smile. "What would you rather have? Birch sap?"

Vincuk chuckled. "It's better than birch sap, that's for sure." He took another sip, this one less harsh on his throat as if the first had anesthetized it.

"How did the boy get on with the Dragunov?" Yuri asked.

"He's good for about a thousand yards," Vincuk replied. "Beyond that is a bit shaky, but he'll get there."

"A thousand yards?" Yuri asked, his mug paused half way toward his mouth. "With one lesson?"

"Well, he's got an excellent tutor," Vincuk said with another deep throated chuckle. He saw Yuri nodding in agreement. Vincuk had been joking, but at the same time, he was a good tutor and he knew how to shoot. "A thousand yards is far enough, though."

"When are you thinking? First light?" Yuri asked. Vincuk nodded in response. "Both villages?"

Yuri was referring to the villages they had discussed earlier that day. The one with the mercenaries who, as far as they knew, were still there. And the village they had left. Of the two villages, Vincuk wasn't looking forward to visiting the second one but it had to be done.

"Yes," Vincuk said. "We'll leave before dawn. Strike at the mercenaries first and then we'll loop back round to the other place."

"All of us?"

"I think so. Ruslan can go on point to watch for checkpoints."

The previous evening, a young man who Yuri knew had dropped off a motorcycle a couple of miles away from their base. Yuri and Vincuk had gone to collect it, with Vincuk riding the bike back to the camp. It'd been years since he'd ridden a motorcycle, and the Minsk MMVZ model was a far cry from the one he'd had as a teenager. Vincuk had said nothing, but he had enjoyed the ride more than he thought he would.

Of the younger men, Ruslan and Mikhail were the only

ones without criminal records and Mikhail had never ridden a motorcycle. That left Ruslan as the one in front, with no weapons and legitimate papers. Vincuk and the others would follow them with enough distance between the vehicles to be alerted to any checkpoints. Yuri had not thought much of Vincuk's plan to lure any mercenaries into an ambush.

"It's too early for them," Yuri had replied when Vincuk had floated the plan past his second in command. "We have no idea how they'll react under fire." Having an advance party though, Yuri had conceded, was a good idea.

Vincuk raised his mug and drained it, coughing as he swallowed the last of the vile liquid. "I'm going to bed," he said. "Don't drink too much of that swill." He ignored the disparaging look Yuri gave him and made his way to the woodsman's cabin the two of them were using as their accommodation. As he walked through the forest, he passed some small tents with the rest of the team. Vincuk paused to listen for a moment. All of them had been given a generous helping of Yuri's Stoli vodka. Enough to help them sleep, but not enough to make them shabby. He nodded as he heard the soft sound of snoring coming from one of the canvas tents.

A few moments later, Vincuk was in bed, looking at the ceiling of the cabin. He blinked a couple of times, willing sleep to come. If he didn't get to sleep before Yuri came to the cabin, his snoring would mean Vincuk got little sleep. And the more vodka Yuri drunk, the louder his snores.

Vincuk closed his eyes and took a deep breath. Tomorrow morning was going to be an interesting one. Two planned villages, both very different. Grigor could perform under pressure, Vincuk had no doubt of that. Ruslan should be okay on point. All he had to do was ride the motorcycle. But the boy, Mikhail?

Vincuk's last thought just before he dropped off to sleep was that by this time tomorrow, Mikhail would know what it was like to take a life.

CHAPTER 64

Stepan looked at the two men standing in front of him. They both had their hands in the air, and were terrified, but as they had several guns pointing at them, that wasn't an unreasonable response. They looked to be father and son, the father perhaps in his mid-forties and the son late teens or early twenties. Both men were dressed in typical farmer's clothing. Their clothes were old, worn, and heavily patched. At their feet were two bolt action rifles and a few yards behind them, a string of rabbits lay on the forest floor.

He looked at the rifles, both of which were older than he was. They were bolt action, five shot military rifles known as Mosin–Nagants. The weapons were like the peasants clothes. Old but functional. Stepan knew the Mosin rifle was a very popular weapon, variants of which had been in use for over a hundred years. He'd never used one, preferring something less archaic to kill things with.

"You have a license for these rifles?" Stepan asked, gesturing at them. The older man shook his head.

"No, we don't. We don't need one."

Stepan looked at the rest of his squad, hoping that one of them would know more about the gun licensing laws in Belarus, but all he saw were blank faces. He raised his eyebrows at the peasant to encourage him to continue.

"Explain?" Stepan said when the man didn't take the hint.

"We're hunting on common land," the man said. "It's allowed without a license." Stepan looked at him carefully. Despite his fear, he thought the peasant was telling the truth. They were in the location that Stepan had been given, but if they were resistance fighters, they weren't being subtle about it. They had made no attempt to fight or run when Stepan's squad had approached earlier. Stepan's men had tracked the two men through the forest for a couple of hundred yards before apprehending them. All they had seen them do was hunt rabbits.

"We're going to confiscate those," Stepan said, nodding at the string of rabbits. At least he and his men would eat well that evening. He saw the look of disappointment on the men's faces as they realized that they wouldn't, but they were hardly in a position to do anything.

"May we keep one or two of them?" the younger of the men asked, earning a harsh look from the other. "For our pot?"

Stepan laughed at the youngster's bravado. He was facing a squad of heavily armed men and still had the balls to try to negotiate. Stepan liked that.

"Yes, you may," Stepan replied. Why not cut the lad a break? There were plenty of rabbits for the squad. "You may keep the smallest one."

"Thank you," the young man replied, almost but not quite smiling.

"Have you seen anyone else in the area?" Stepan asked

as he prepared to dismiss the two hunters. "People with weapons who are not hunting?"

"No," the older man replied, but Stepan noticed that as he spoke, the younger one's expression changed. It was only a flicker, but it was noticeable. Stepan pointed his gun at him.

"You?" Stepan said. "Have you seen anyone?"

"I've not seen anyone," the young man replied, nodding to his right, "but I have heard there are some men camping out in the woods."

The older man said something in a language that Stepan didn't understand, Belarusian perhaps, but he fell silent as Stepan glared at him.

"Which woods?" Stepan asked the boy. In response, the young man nodded again to his right.

"Around five miles that way," he said, ignoring the dark look the other man gave him. "There's a small wood on a hill, around a mile due north from the gas depot."

"Very good," Stepan replied. He would need to look at the map to identify the area, but he had a rough idea of the geography. If he was correct, it wasn't one of the locations he had identified. Stepan looked at the rest of his squad and nodded at the truck to signal it was time to go. Then he returned his attention to the two hunters. "Why don't you take two rabbits? For your pot."

CHAPTER 65

Natasha looked down at her phone which was vibrating on her bedside table. She picked it up to see Iĺja's face on the screen. It was an incoming video call, which meant Iĺja was somewhere with a Wi-Fi connection. Too tired to bother what she looked like, Natasha swiped at the screen to answer the call and turn on the camera.

"Iĺja," Natasha said, forcing a half smile onto her face. "Is there any news?" She saw her sister shaking her head and sighed. "Where are you?" She knew Iĺja didn't have the internet in her house. No need for it, she had always said.

"I'm in Podlipki," Iĺja replied. "At Tatiana's house."

"But what about Mikhail?" Natasha said, her face falling. "Has he come back? You said there wasn't any news?"

"No, he's still missing."

"But what happens when he does come back?" Natasha replied, her voice going up by an octave. "How will he know where you are?"

"Relax, Natasha," Iĺja said, using a patronizing tone that grated on Natasha's nerves. "I spoke to him about coming here, and I've left him a note. All he needs to do is call me when he gets home and I'll go and get him."

"No." Natasha shook her head emphatically. "No, Iĺja. That's not what we agreed." She saw her sister's face darken on the small screen.

"That was before we started getting shelled," Iĺja shot back. Natasha shook her head again. The thought of Mikhail returning from where ever he was to an empty house filled her with fear.

"Is there any more news on what happened?" Natasha asked.

"It was an apartment block a few streets away that was hit. Six dead, including a girl at Mikhail's school."

"Oh, God," Natasha gasped. "How awful. Those poor people." She felt sick at the news, and suddenly felt bad about berating her sister. But, Mikhail was out there somewhere. He could be in danger. "Have they said who did it?"

"The authorities are blaming the insurgents, and the insurgents are blaming the authorities," Iĺja replied with a deep sigh.

The two women chatted for a while before Iĺja ended the call, promising to call or send a message the moment there was any news. Natasha stared at the screen for a few seconds after they had finished. She was still angry that Iĺja had moved to Podlipki, but the more Natasha thought about it, the more she understood why she had moved. Just as Natasha replaced the cell phone on the bedside table, there was a soft knock at her bedroom door.

"Is everything okay?" It was Heidi. She was wearing pajamas with sleeves so long they almost came down to her fingers. "I came to check if you needed anything and I heard voices."

"I was just talking to my sister," Natasha said with a note of anger in her voice that she'd not intended.

"Ah, okay," Heidi replied with an apologetic look at Natasha. "I wasn't listening. Sorry."

"No, it's not that," Natasha said. She looked at Heidi, wondering how much of what was going on to share with the woman. There would be nothing Heidi could do other than listen, and Natasha wasn't sure that was fair. "Just a bit of an argument, that's all."

"I know that feeling," Heidi said with a wan smile. "I'm the youngest of three and always seemed to get it the worst." She took a couple of steps toward the bed and Natasha moved over to give her space to sit down. Natasha watched her, realizing that she was a lot thinner than she'd thought. She almost had the build of a long distance runner, but her calves lacked the definition of one.

Heidi didn't say anything but just pulled at her cuffs. When she looked at Natasha a few seconds later, her eyes were full of sympathy. To her dismay, Natasha felt a lump starting to form in her throat. "Do you want to talk?" Heidi asked, her voice mirroring her eyes.

That was all it took to start the tears.

CHAPTER 66

Caleb looked at Phoebe who still hadn't answered his question. He kept his eyes fixed on hers, knowing that her gown was barely covering her chest. Even when she closed her eyes for a few seconds, he focused on her face, not trusting himself to do anything else. Caleb knew she wouldn't be able to answer what he had just asked her. It wasn't that it was an unanswerable question, it was that the answer was she both wanted and needed something and Caleb wasn't sure that something was him.

Phoebe opened her eyes and, to Caleb's surprise, a tear ran down her cheek. He instinctively reached up and wiped it away with a finger.

"Why are you crying?" Caleb asked.

"I don't know," Phoebe replied, moving her arms to replace her gown over her chest. "I just feel so, I don't know, foolish. This is ridiculous." She took a deep breath which dislodged another tear. "I'm ridiculous."

"No, Phoebe, you're not," Caleb said, wiping the fresh tear with his thumb. Her skin was soft, and he wanted to slip his hand around her neck and pull her toward him. "He counts each one, you know?"

"Each what?"

"Each tear. They all get written into a book." He saw Phoebe smile but her eyes still looked sad. "Psalm fifty-six, chapter eight."

"I thought He was off on Thursdays."

"So He is," Caleb replied.

Phoebe's smile broadened and her dimples appeared. Caleb slid from his armchair and knelt in front of hers, picking up the bottle of wine and refilling her glass as he did so. Then he refilled his own, although it wasn't even half empty.

"Chin chin," he said, raising his glass.

"Down the hatch," Phoebe replied. He watched in amazement as she half drained her glass. "Oh my God, I needed that. Um, sorry."

"Don't be," Caleb said with a smile. "But tell me, why did you say you're ridiculous just now?"

Phoebe paused for a moment before replying, as if she was weighing up her options. He watched her thinking, wondering if she was putting together some courses of action in her head. There would be the do nothing option, of course. Then there would be the safe middle ground. Or there was the nuclear option.

"Do you remember your dreams, Caleb?" Phoebe asked eventually.

"I don't believe so, no," he replied. In truth, Caleb didn't think he'd ever dreamed, much less remembered them.

"I had a dream the other night. About you." She bit her lower lip and looked at him.

"I know you did."

Phoebe's mouth opened and her lips formed a circle for a few seconds.

"How do you know I did?" she asked.

"Because I was there. In your dream."

She looked at him with an incredulous expression.

"Seriously?" she said, a frown forming on her forehead. "You were there?"

"Yes," Caleb said, allowing a smile onto his face. "You just told me I was." He laughed. "Q.E.D."

"Ah, very good," Phoebe replied, taking a sip of her wine. "I see what you did there." A smile was playing over her face but, as Caleb watched, it faded and was replaced by a look of determination and something else he didn't recognize.

"So, what was your dream about?"

"Um, well, you were in it. And so was I."

"Obviously."

"The reason I feel ridiculous, Caleb, is because..." He saw her swallow. "Because in my dream, we were, um, you know."

"I know what?"

"Oh, Jesus, Caleb. Sorry, I didn't mean to say that."

"What were we doing, Phoebe?" Caleb grinned, enjoying her discomfort. She looked at him and he knew at that moment exactly what she wanted and needed. And he very much wanted to be able to fulfill that. "The crossword in the paper?"

"No," she replied, her voice almost a whisper. "But I thought maybe after I'd dreamed about it, maybe, well, maybe something might happen."

"Something might happen." Caleb deliberately made sure it didn't sound like a question, but a statement.

"Do you think it might?" Phoebe said, leaning forward again. This time, her gown stayed in place but Caleb looked down anyway. Just in case. When he looked back up at her face, he could see twin spots of red on her cheeks, right where her dimples were when she smiled. "I mean, He is off on a Thursday evening."

"I've thought of little else since the moment I saw you for the first time, Phoebe," Caleb said, adjusting his position on so he was kneeling closer to her armchair. Phoebe's lounge suddenly seemed much smaller than it had done a few moments before.

She raised her hands to his face and he could feel her fingertips trembling on his skin. Phoebe bit her bottom lip again before running her tongue over her lips.

"Here?" she whispered.

"Here," Caleb replied, tugging at the belt of her gown.

And Caleb's eyes never left hers.

CHAPTER 67

Phoebe arched her back, grinding her teeth together as she did so. Another wave of pressure was building in her lower abdomen. It was like an ocean wave. Unstoppable, relentless, and at some point in the next few seconds, it would peak. She groaned, a deep guttural noise that she had no control over and beneath her, she felt Caleb's hands on her hips. He adjusted the angle they were moving at, and she felt the wave start to intensify, approaching its peak more quickly.

She looked down at Caleb's face, illuminated by a shaft of early morning light that was streaming in through a small gap in her bedroom window curtains. He had his eyes closed and a look of serene concentration on his face. Phoebe gasped, knowing that what was about to happen was an inevitable physiological response. All she could do was to go with it. Just as the wave reached the top of its path, and the pressure became almost too much for her to bear, Phoebe's doorbell rang.

Phoebe was too far in the moment to do anything other than jam her hand into her mouth to try to stifle her moans.

But they came anyway, as did she. The doorbell rang again but the world could have ended at that point in time, and she wouldn't have noticed.

Afterward, her body still trembling, Phoebe laughed. Partly with pleasure, partly with relief. A thin stream of perspiration made its way down her chest and she giggled when Caleb raised his head to lick it from her skin.

"Whoever that is at the door," she said, still giggling, "has got the worst timing ever."

"Mmm hmm," Caleb replied, sliding his hands from her hips to her thighs.

"Did you...?" Phoebe asked him but, as she shifted her position slightly, she could feel that he hadn't. That was a situation she was going to have to remedy once she had dealt with her visitor

The doorbell rang again as they disentangled themselves. Then, a few seconds after that, her phone started buzzing on her bedside table.

"Oh, for fuck's sake," Phoebe muttered as she picked up her phone. "It's not even seven in the morning."

"Who is it?" Caleb asked. If he was tired, and by rights they both should have been exhausted, it didn't show in his voice.

"Bloody Thomas," Phoebe replied.

"Let me get the door," Caleb said, sitting up in the bed. "Can I borrow your dressing gown?"

"But then he'll know we've—"

"So what?" Caleb replied. "You're a grown woman, Phoebe. He's going to find out sooner or later, so he might as well hear it direct from the horse's mouth."

Phoebe said nothing as she watched him squeeze himself into her dressing down, adjusting the front to maintain his dignity. If it had been anyone else at the door, the scene would have been comical, but it was Thomas. The previous evening, one thing she'd not really thought through was any potential awkwardness at being in a van with two men she'd slept with. By the time she did realize it could be difficult, it was too late.

She lay back in the bed, blowing her breath out through her cheeks. What a night she had just had. What a morning she had just had to follow it. Phoebe smiled as she remembered elements of it. It made her erotic dream seem like a distant memory. Caleb had seemed to instinctively know what she liked. What she wanted. What she needed. For a man of the cloth, he seemed to have a very good understanding of the female anatomy. Which buttons to press, and exactly when to press them.

Phoebe listened but couldn't hear anything. She was expecting to hear either Caleb or Thomas' voices, perhaps both. Perhaps even raised. But there was silence. All she could hear was her heartbeat in her ears as her body slowly came back from where it had been. Then she heard the kitchen tap being turned on. Once, and then again.

When Caleb returned a moment later, he was carrying two glasses of water in his hands. He had even added some ice from the freezer.

"I thought you might be thirsty," he said as he placed one of them down next to her phone. Then he shrugged off Phoebe's robe and slid back into bed.

"Thank you," Phoebe said, putting her arm over his chest. "What did Thomas say?"

"He's going to call you later."

"Was he surprised to see you?" She watched as a smile played over Caleb's lips.

"You could say that, yes."

Phoebe ran her finger over the puckered scar in Caleb's shoulder. "Was this a bullet?"

"It was, yes."

"What happened?"

"I got shot."

"Ha ha, very funny. Where?"

"In my shoulder. I thought you were a doctor?"

"I am a doctor," Phoebe said with a grin as she ran her finger down his chest and to the scar in his abdomen, still with the stitches holding it together. "I forgot about this. I hope we've not disturbed it."

"I don't think we have." His eyes closed as Phoebe ran her finger further down his abdomen and underneath the covers. She leaned in and kissed his earlobe before whispering in his ear.

"So," she asked. "Where were we?" She smiled and he said nothing as she felt him respond to her touch. Another inevitable physiological reaction, but one which she very much liked. She slid the sheet from him and straddled him. A moment later, they both gasped in unison. "Somewhere around here, wasn't it?"

"Mm hmm."

"We've got three hours until I need to go to work," Phoebe whispered, her hands flat on his chest. "So why don't you lie back and think of England."

"The way you're making me feel right now, Phoebe," Caleb replied, his voice languid, "we're only going to need about thirty seconds."

CHAPTER 68

Mikhail wriggled on the uncomfortable camping mat. It and the thin sleeping bag he was in were not giving much in the way of relief from the hard forest ground. There were roots or something digging into the small of his back but even if there hadn't been, he didn't think he would have slept much anyway. Not with Ruslan's constant snoring.

He could hear someone moving around outside, so Mikhail decided to get up. It was light outside and he needed the bathroom anyway. Not that they had a bathroom. A few hundred yards away from their camp was a hurriedly constructed deep trench latrine. It was nothing more than a plank of wood balanced on some logs either side of a stinking ditch and there was zero privacy. All the more reason to use it before everyone else got up, in Mikhail's opinion.

Mikhail got out of his sleeping bag, moving slowly to avoid waking Ruslan, and unzipped the tent as quietly as he could. With a nodded greeting at Vincuk, who was starting a small fire in the center of their camp, he made his way to the latrine to complete his business. When he returned, Vincuk had got the fire going and was staring at a kettle that was balanced precariously over it.

"Good morning, Vincuk," Mikhail said, eager to sound polite. Vincuk didn't reply, but just stared balefully at him. "Um, did you sleep okay?" He should have as Mikhail had seen the beds in the cabin the previous day. They looked a lot more comfortable than a thin sleeping mat.

"No," Vincuk replied. It was more of a grunt than a word. "Yuri snores like a pig."

"Do you want me to cook breakfast?" Mikhail asked, looking at the shopping bag next to the fire. He could see some plastic packaging inside with what looked like sausages in it, but he hoped that Vincuk would decline his offer. Sandwiches were more Mikhail's forte, not a cooked breakfast. But he wanted to impress Vincuk, as he thought he had done the previous day when he'd used the sniper rifle.

"No," Vincuk replied with another grunt. "You'll only fuck it up."

THIRTY MINUTES LATER, with the exception of Yuri, the group was sitting around the fire. Grigor looked like shit and Dimitri wasn't far behind him. It seemed to Mikhail that only he and Ruslan were not suffering from the effects of Yuri's vodka. Vincuk was holding a frying pan, shaking it over the fire, and the delicious smell of cooking sausages filled the air.

"Here," Vincuk said, holding the pan in Mikhail's direction.

"Thank you," Mikhail replied as he speared a piece of overcooked sausage with a fork, transferring it to his mess tin. "Smells lovely." He watched as Vincuk offered the pan to Grigor and Dimitri, both of whom declined. That was fine by Mikhail. More for him and Ruslan. "What are the plans for today, Vincuk?"

He watched as Vincuk glanced over to the cabin, as if he was thinking about waiting for Yuri to surface. Then Vincuk looked at each of them in turn before pointing at Mikhail with the spoon he'd used to cook the sausages.

"You, young man, are going to put that Dragunov to work." Then he pointed at Grigor, Dimitri, and Ruslan. "And you three are going to have some fun in one of the villages." Mikhail saw a smile spreading on Grigor's face, but the other two young men just looked confused. Vincuk's spoon returned to Ruslan. "You're on point on the Minsk."

"What does that mean?" Ruslan asked, beating Mikhail to the question.

"It means you'll be out in front, on the motorcycle. If the mercenaries have got any roadblocks set up, you'll let us know. We'll be a half mile or so behind you in the van."

Mikhail nodded, realizing why Yuri had asked them the previous day which of them could ride a motorcycle.

"Isn't that dangerous?" Ruslan asked, his nervousness obvious. Vincuk didn't reply, but just gave the young man a glare.

"Finish your breakfasts," Vincuk said a moment later, spooning another sausage into both Mikhail and Ruslan's mess tins. "Wash up, and get ready to go." Mikhail saw him look at his watch. "We leave in thirty minutes."

As Vincuk got to his feet, Mikhail nudged Ruslan before leaning over to whisper in his ear.

"Today's the day, Ruslan," Mikhail said. "We're going to see some action at last."

CHAPTER 69

Caleb sat at Phoebe's kitchen table and watched her as she rummaged through one of the cupboards. She stretched up on to her tip toes and he admired the way it brought her profile into relief. She was wearing a long t-shirt with nothing underneath, and when she raised her arms, he could just see the swell of her buttocks.

"Can I help you with anything?" he asked, hiding a grin at the sight.

"No, I'm good," Phoebe replied, glancing at him. He managed to move his gaze a split second before she caught him leering at her. Caleb didn't think she would mind given what they had been up to last night and that morning. He'd said thirty seconds, but things had taken a lot longer than that. "I'll fix us some breakfast."

"That would be awesome," he replied. "I'm famished. I'll probably skip the blood pudding, though. Black pudding, you call it?"

Phoebe turned to look at him. In her hand was a brown

box. "It's not that sort of breakfast, Caleb. Sorry." She held up the box. "You like All Bran?"

"What's that?"

"The clue's in the name." She shook the box and grinned at him. "It's bran."

Caleb was just about to reply when Phoebe's phone started buzzing on the kitchen table. He nudged it toward her. When she picked it up, she looked at the screen before mouthing the words *It's Thomas* at Caleb. Then she turned and walked out of the kitchen.

As he waited, Caleb thought back to what Thomas had said to him in the pub, when Phoebe had gone to use the bathroom. He had stared at Phoebe's butt as she walked across the pub before turning to Caleb.

"You like what you see, preacher man?" Thomas had asked him with a leer on his face. "Would you ever sympathy fuck something like that?" Caleb had said nothing in return, but smiled as he recalled their conversation that morning at Phoebe's front door. It had been a lot shorter.

While he waited for Phoebe to return, he picked up the box of bran she had left on the table. Caleb examined the contents, realizing Phoebe hadn't been joking. He wasn't sure he wanted to boost his digestive health that much, though. Perhaps once Phoebe had gone to work, he could find a cafe somewhere. He made a mental note to ask her if there was anywhere local where he could buy an American breakfast. Caleb's mouth started watering at the thought of pancakes, drizzled with syrup, or some chicken fried steak with sausage gravy on the side. Surely there was somewhere in London that served southern food.

"That was Thomas," Phoebe said as she walked back into the kitchen. She had a mock frown on her face, but was smiling. "Unfortunately, he won't be able to come to Poland with us."

Caleb sighed with relief. His message that morning had obviously hit the spot.

"Oh, that's a shame," Caleb said. "I was looking forward to getting to know him better. Is he okay?"

"He's got laryngitis, apparently."

"He sounded okay the other night. That's come on quickly."

"Well, he sounds awful now," Phoebe replied as she returned to the cupboard, emerging with two bowls. "His voice is all croaky. Says he's got a really sore throat." She poured bran into both bowls before splashing milk over the cereal.

Caleb looked uncertainly at the brown flakes floating in the milk. "Am I allowed sugar?"

"On bran?" Phoebe replied with a laugh. "No." She gestured at his bowl with her spoon. "Stop complaining and eat up."

He took a spoonful of the cereal which, as he suspected, tasted of nothing. Caleb ate slowly, unlike Phoebe who finished her bowl in no time.

"Have you got a driving license?" she asked a moment later.

"I've got an American one, yes. Will that be okay?"

"I think so," Phoebe replied. "I'll have to phone the rental company."

"Can you get an automatic?" Caleb asked her. "I can't drive a stick shift."

"Seriously? Why ever not?"

"Just never learned," Caleb replied with a shrug of his shoulders. He pushed the half-finished bowl of cereal across the table. "I'm done. No more cardboard for me."

"I'm going to get dressed," Phoebe said, getting to her feet. "Can you drive the coffee machine?"

"That I can do," Caleb replied with an easy grin.

As he put the coffee on, Caleb considered Thomas' sudden withdrawal from the trip. He grinned as he thought about the doctor's sudden onset of laryngitis. Thomas had obviously said nothing to Phoebe, which was no surprise. Caleb knew exactly the moment that Thomas' laryngitis had started.

With the coffee pot bubbling away on the counter and the smell of fresh coffee filling the kitchen, Caleb smiled to himself. Thomas' sore throat and croaky voice had started just after Caleb had answered the door.

A swift punch to the trachea would do that to a man.

CHAPTER 70

Natasha yawned, stretching her arms above her head as she did so. She was tired and almost tempted to go back to bed for a while, but it wasn't an option. She had far too much to do today. The previous evening, she and Heidi had talked long into the night. Natasha had ended up telling her about Anton and Mikhail, both missing in action in their own ways. Heidi was an easy person to talk to, and Natasha had almost shared more than she'd originally intended. But there were some things, such as Mikhail's actual parentage, that Natasha would never share, no matter how much of a good listener the other person was.

She straightened the bedspread on her bed, trying to get it to the same level of perfection as it had been when Heidi had first showed her the room. But try as she might, Natasha couldn't quite achieve the look. She left the bed as it was and made her way downstairs, where she met Heidi in the hallway. Natasha's host was busy with a can of spray polish and a yellow duster, working on a small table. She jumped when Natasha said good morning.

"Oh, my," Heidi said with a smile, her hand held to her chest. "You startled me."

"Sorry, I didn't mean to."

"Don't be daft," Heidi replied, waving the duster dismissively. "I was miles away." She returned her attention to the table which, as far as Natasha could see, was spotless. "Lawrence is coming back this evening. He does like things just so." Heidi smiled at Natasha, but there was a nervousness behind it that she'd not seen before.

"I was wondering if I might be able to use your computer. And perhaps your printer?" Natasha asked. "There's some stuff I need to get for a friend of mine."

"Of course, Natasha," Heidi replied, placing the polish and the duster on the table. "Let me show you where it is."

Natasha followed Heidi through the house to a room she'd not been shown the previous day. It was a small office off the kitchen with an antique desk and matching chair. The desk was in front of a large window which gave an uninterrupted view of the impressive gardens beyond. Natasha saw a man on a rider lawn mower making his way around a large oak tree near the bottom of the garden, and she wondered if Lawrence's impending arrival also necessitated the grass being cut. On top of the desk was a huge aluminum gray iMac computer and keyboard. Heidi moved the keyboard and reached into a drawer to pull out a laptop which she placed where the keyboard had been.

"That's Lawrence's computer," Heidi said, nodding at the iMac, "but I have this one. It's hooked up to the printer over there so you're all good to go."

Natasha glanced in the direction Heidi was pointing to see a small wireless printer in the corner of the room.

"Thank you," Natasha said. "There'll only be a few bits. I can pay you for the ink."

"Absolutely not," Heidi said. "Will you be okay?"

"Is there a password?" Natasha asked with a nod at the laptop. Heidi had opened it and there was an Apple logo on the screen.

"Oh, no," Heidi replied with a laugh. "There's no need for one."

Natasha waited until Heidi had left before she opened up the browser on the laptop. First, she navigated to a couple of Belarusian news sites, most of which were covering a rocket attack on a hospital in the north of the country. Much like Ilja had said previously, both sides appeared to be blaming each other. Not that it helped any of the poor people she could see in the few images there were of the aftermath, nor the families of those who had died.

She brought up a blank Word document and started to make a list of all the places that Mikhail frequented. Or at least, the ones she knew of. It would be a starting point for Caleb who, according to the text message he had sent her earlier, was departing for Poland the next day. Then she opened Apple maps and started taking screenshots of the locations, printing each one out as she did so. The place where he practiced football with his friends, the parks she knew he liked to hang out in. Natasha even included some locations that she knew were popular with teenagers. Even if Mikhail didn't use them regularly, he could be at any of them with friends.

By the time she had finished, Natasha had a bundle of papers almost half an inch thick. She looked around for a pen to start labelling the maps, but apart from the keyboard and computer, there was nothing on Lawrence's desk. Natasha paused for a moment with her hand on one of the drawer handles but when she tried it, it was locked. They all were.

She got to her feet and, gathering the bundle of paper together, Natasha set off to find Heidi. Her host was still in the hallway and had moved on to polishing the tops of the picture frames. As she approached, Natasha coughed slightly, not wanting to startle Heidi again.

"Did you get what you need?" Heidi asked with barely a glance in Natasha's direction.

"I did, but I have a favor to ask."

"Of course, Natasha," Heidi replied. She finally stopped cleaning and turned to face Natasha.

"I need to get to London," Natasha asked, holding up the sheaf of paper. "Before tomorrow morning."

CHAPTER 71

Vincuk watched through the binoculars at the small village at least five hundred yards in front of him and Mikhail. They were on a bluff that overlooked the settlement, one of several that surrounded it. Through the scopes he could see the buildings start to come to life. Lights came on in windows, smoke started spiraling up from a chimney. Eventually, one of the front doors to a house opened and someone stepped out.

"You see him?" Vincuk whispered to Mikhail. He looked down at the young man who was lying prone, his eye pressed up against the scope of the Dragunov rifle.

"Civilian, I think," Mikhail whispered back. Vincuk nodded in agreement. The man who had stepped outside his house was wearing brown trousers and a smock of some sort. A farmer, perhaps? Definitely not a mercenary. The two of them watched in silence as he lit a cigarette and stood on his doorstep to smoke it. "There's someone else coming," Mikhail said a moment later.

Vincuk saw a woman appear at the door, a baby

wrapped in a blanket in her arms. She said something to the man who flicked his cigarette onto the ground before turning and stepping back inside.

"Vincuk," Mikhail whispered, the urgency obvious in his voice. "Third house from the left. In the yard. There they are."

Vincuk switched his binoculars to the house Mikhail had indicated. Yuri's informant, a man who had called in the small hours of the morning to let him know there were mercenaries in the village, had been right. In the small yard behind the house, two men clad in black uniforms were loading something into the back of a truck while a third watched them, leaning against a log pile. He adjusted his focus to see what the men were loading into the vehicle. It was shovels.

He felt bile rising in his throat as he saw movement in another part of the village. On the other side, there was a group of men, all walking in single file toward the forest behind the dwellings. They were dressed in a similar way to the man they had seen smoking, but the main difference was these men all had their hands in the air and were being escorted by two black-clad men with rifles.

"What do I do, Vincuk?" Mikhail asked. "They're going to kill them."

"I know," Vincuk whispered. He looked again at the men in the black uniforms. There were five of them altogether that he could see, so part of a squad. There would be others in the same squad, and there would be other squads in the area making up a full platoon. What they were about to do was very risky, especially when they didn't know the location of the remaining soldiers in the squad they were watching, or the other squads. They could be anywhere in the area. All Vincuk could do was hope they were not in the same part of the forest that they were.

"The one leaning against the log pile," Vincuk whispered. "Take him out." It was the obvious choice. He was the only man not actually doing anything. Therefore, he was probably the one in charge. Vincuk focused on the man leaning against the logs and took a deep breath, almost as if he was taking the shot himself. If he was younger and still had his eyesight, he would have been.

A few seconds later, there was a loud gunshot which reverberated around the trees and off the other bluffs. Vincuk saw a puff of smoke rising from the Dragunov out of the corner of his eye, but his attention was focused on the man in black whose head had just exploded in a fine puff of red mist. The two mercenaries with him both dropped to their knees and scrambled for cover, looking around them as they did so. It was a good sign as it meant they didn't know the direction the shot had come from.

The men with the prisoners also dropped at the sound of the shot. Vincuk could see them wriggling on their stomachs, trying to find cover. Snipers were a soldier's worst fear. The thought that a shot could come from hundreds of yards away, totally unannounced, was a horrible one. The group of men they had been escorting took the opportunity to run and, a few seconds later, Vincuk saw the man with his wife and child doing the same thing, hurrying across their own yard for the relative safety of the forest.

There was another shot from Mikhail, the sound again rebounding and echoing around the area.

"What are you doing?" Vincuk said, more loudly than he had intended. "We need to get out of here." He turned to look at the houses and saw that Mikhail had put a round through the radiator block of the truck the mercenaries had been loading. It was a risk, but it was one worth taking. "Come on," he said, injecting as much urgency into his voice as he could. "We need to go."

CHAPTER 72

Phoebe had to stifle a laugh at Jade's words. They were sitting in the medical center, having a mug of tea. Phoebe and Caleb had arrived thirty minutes earlier, just as the van they'd hired for the trip to Poland had arrived.

"Seriously, Phoebe," Jade had just said when Caleb had left to check the van. "I saw him looking at you just now. He definitely likes you."

It's a bit late for that, Phoebe thought, but she knew she couldn't say anything to Jade. "He's a man of the cloth," she replied, but Jade just smirked.

"Yeah, but he's still a man, if you know what I mean."

Phoebe stood, not wanting the conversation to continue in case she gave herself away. She crossed to the sink and made herself look busy, washing some mugs from the previous day.

"What time is your ferry?" Jade asked.

"Not until this evening," Phoebe replied. "We'll be leaving about lunchtime. This time tomorrow, we'll be approaching Poland, I think."

"Are you driving through the night?" Jade asked, a mischievous smile appearing on her face, "or are you going to find yourselves a little guest house somewhere?"

"Enough, Jade," Phoebe said, throwing a dish towel at Jade, who was laughing at her. "That's enough."

Jade was just about to reply when the door to the medical center opened and Caleb walked in. He glanced at the mugs of tea on the table.

"Do I get a mug of hot leaf water?" he asked, looking at Jade with a hopeful smile. Phoebe also looked at her, expecting her usual response to a request for a cup of tea, which was *make it yourself*. But to her surprise, Jade nodded her head.

"Sure. How do you like it?"

"Um, I'm not sure," Caleb replied. "I didn't know it came in different ways."

Jade just laughed and made her way to the kettle.

"Everything okay with the van?" Phoebe asked Caleb.

"Sure," he replied. "It's not got a stick, which is good. It means we can share the driving. The steering wheel's on the wrong side, though."

"No, Caleb," Phoebe said with a grin. "It's on the right side. Everyone else's is on the wrong side."

"Why do you guys drive on the wrong side of the road over here, anyway?"

"We don't. Like Phoebe said, it's everyone else who's on the wrong side," Jade called out, joining in the conversation from the other side of the room.

"Guess this isn't an argument I'm going to win anytime soon," Caleb replied.

"Not if you know what's good for you," Phoebe said with a smile at Caleb. He smiled back, lowering his voice so Jade wouldn't hear.

"Oh, I know what's good for me, Phoebe."

The look in his eyes as he said this caused an immediate flush to appear on her face. "I'm just nipping to the bathroom," she said, hoping that it wasn't obvious.

"Why do you call it a bathroom?" she heard Caleb ask as she walked to the door. "You don't have a bath in there, do you?"

"Well, you don't go there for a rest, either," Phoebe heard Jade reply.

In the bathroom, which as Caleb had pointed out had no bath, she looked at herself in the mirror as she patted cold water on her cheeks. What had happened the previous night was very out of character for her. She had practically thrown herself at the man. Sure, she could blame the wine, but she'd not been drunk. Slightly, perhaps, but not out of control. She'd known what she'd wanted, and Caleb had delivered it in spades. Now she was going to have to spend the next few days with him, in a van. Jade's comments about finding a guest house came back to her.

Phoebe grinned at herself in the mirror. What she and Caleb had done wasn't a crime. It might be a sin, but as Caleb didn't seem too bothered about that, neither was Phoebe. She heard the bathroom door open and turned to see Jade's head peeking in.

"You nearly done?" Jade asked her. "Natasha's back. She needs to speak to you and Caleb. Says it's urgent."

CHAPTER 73

Natasha was mid-yawn when she looked up to see Phoebe walking into the medical center. She got up from the table where she had been sitting with Caleb and smiled.

"Phoebe," Natasha said. To her surprise, Phoebe pulled her into a hug.

"Natasha," Phoebe replied a few seconds later. "I didn't think we'd be seeing you again. Certainly not so soon."

"I needed to see Caleb before he goes to Poland." She saw Phoebe and Caleb exchange a brief glance before they looked away from each other. "I've got some information that might be useful."

Natasha had to stifle another yawn. It had been an early start. Heidi had given her a lift to the train station in time for Natasha to catch the first train from Salisbury to London. She'd tried to sleep on the train, but every time she closed her eyes, images of either Anton or Mikhail, sometimes both, flashed across her eyes.

"Sit down, Natasha," Caleb said. "You look exhausted. Are you settled in your new home?"

Natasha paused before she replied. She'd not been there long enough to call herself settled, and the atmosphere in the house had changed when Lawrence had arrived home the previous evening. He was exactly how Natasha had imagined him to be, strait-laced and prim, and Heidi had been so deferential to the man that it had made Natasha uncomfortable. But she was a guest in their home, and such behavior was none of her business.

"Everything's fine," Natasha said with a sigh. She looked at Caleb who, from his expression, didn't believe her, but he said nothing. "I've brought some information." She reached into her bag and pulled out the sheaf of papers. Natasha had spent the time on the train marking them with annotations to describe what the various locations were, and as she spread them out on the table, she saw both Caleb and Phoebe look at them with interest.

"Are these places Mikhail might be?" Caleb asked a moment later, having studied one of the printed maps. Natasha nodded, picking up the piece of paper he had been looking at.

"Yes," she replied, pointing at a location on the map that was marked with the letter *I*, surrounded by a small circle. "This is Iĺja's house. I've marked it the same way on all of them." Then she pointed at another location, this one marked with an encircled letter *F*. "This is where a boy called Felix lives. He's Mikhail's friend. I've written some information on the back of the maps to explain what each one is."

Natasha saw Caleb nodding at her explanation. He spent a few moments looking through all the sheets of paper, passing each one to Phoebe when he had looked at it. Something had definitely changed between the two of them.

It was subtle, but the way they were interacting was different. They seemed to Natasha to be closer, and she found herself smiling at the thought.

"These will be really useful, Natasha," Caleb said as he handed the last sheet of paper to Phoebe. "Thank you."

"I want to come with you," Natasha replied, earning a curious look from Phoebe. Natasha turned her head to look directly at the doctor. Despite what Caleb had said, it was her trip, not his. "Please, Phoebe? Is there room for me?"

"No, Natasha," Phoebe replied after a brief glance in Caleb's direction. "We changed the van for an automatic so Caleb could share the driving. There're only two seats in the front."

Natasha looked at Phoebe, wondering if she was telling the truth. Was this something they had discussed already? But they hadn't known Natasha was coming, so they couldn't have. Natasha sighed, feeling bad about thinking Phoebe might be lying. Caleb had been right. She was exhausted.

"Natasha," Caleb said, reaching out his hand and taking hers. "This information is amazing. If Mikhail is at any of these places, I'll be able to find him."

"But how?" Natasha replied. "How can you do that from Poland? You don't speak Polish." She could feel she was on the verge of tears.

"Most Polish people speak English, Natasha," Phoebe replied, taking her other hand in hers. "And my Polish isn't too bad for those who don't. If Caleb needs to speak to anyone in Belarus, I can translate if needed."

"Natasha, listen to me," Caleb said. She looked at him, feeling his eyes boring into hers. "I will find him and bring him home."

"How do I know you'll be able to do that, Caleb?" She watched as a slight smile appeared on his face.

"This isn't my first rodeo, Natasha."

CHAPTER 74

Stepan winced as he took the skin off both his knees as he hit the ground. Keeping himself as low as possible, he crawled as fast as he could toward the trees that the villagers were now running through. He needed cover. A second shot rang out a few seconds after the first, but his focus was on getting somewhere safe.

He could hear shouting from the houses, recognizing the voices as belonging to his men. When Stepan got to the relative safety of the tree line, the soldier who had been accompanying him with the villagers was already there. He was young, no more than twenty years old, and his face was ashen.

"What's happening?" the soldier asked, breathless from the exertion of crawling.

"Sniper," Stepan replied, the disgust obvious in his voice.

"Where?"

"Could be anywhere."

Stepan cursed under his breath. He'd not even wanted to come to this village, but HQ had insisted. He'd spoken to the control room the previous evening, telling them what the hunters had told him. Stepan had identified on the map where he thought the resistance fighters were reported to be camping and, as he was the one who had identified the location, he thought he should be the one to attack it. But the control room had been insistent that the priority was to keep looking in the villages.

"But we can hit them while they're still asleep," Stepan had said, pleading his case. The only concession he'd been able to get was that the request would be passed up the chain of command, but orders were orders, which was why he was currently cowering amongst tree trunks.

"What do we do now?" the soldier asked.

"We wait," Stepan replied. The resistance had tried this tactic before. It was usually a single shot, and then they melted away to wherever they had come from. The fact there had been two shots in rapid succession was new, though. Stepan peered around the tree trunk, half expecting another round to come his way, but there was nothing. Now that the sound of the second shot had dissipated, all he could hear was high-pitched screaming. He wasn't sure whether it was one of the women from the village, or one of his men. "Come with me," Stepan said to the soldier.

Half crouching, the two men scuttled across the ground to the houses where their truck was parked. As Stepan approached, he realized that the screaming was coming from one of his own men. The soldier was sitting on the ground, cradling the body of one of his colleagues who was missing the bulk of his head. Stepan swore under his breath at the sight.

"Come on," Stepan shouted at what remained of his squad. "Let's get him in the wagon and get out of here." They needed to move. Not only did the resistance know where they were, but they also had a bead on them by someone who knew how to shoot.

"The truck's fucked, sir," one of the squad members said. "They shot out the engine block."

Stepan swore again, reaching into his pocket for his phone. "Right, get into an all round defense position. I want a tight ring around the village. And stay in cover!" He kicked the foot of the soldier cradling the body. "You! Pull yourself together while I call this in." The young man stopped screaming but just looked at Stepan, wide-mouthed, so he kicked him again.

Using the engine block of the truck as cover, Stepan crouched down to make the call. While he waited for it to connect, he realized he didn't care what HQ or his chain of command said anymore.

Stepan knew where the resistance was, and he was going after them.

CHAPTER 75

Caleb pulled on the strap in the back of the van to tighten the ratchet and secure the remaining few boxes in place. Thanks to the additional supplies that had been brought in by a small army of taxi drivers throughout the morning, the rear of the van was full. He nodded in satisfaction as he pulled down the shutter and locked it. The van was in a small loading bay that belonged to Kings Cross station, and should be secure enough, but Caleb wasn't going to take any chances with the precious cargo.

"Are you happy?" Caleb heard a female voice say. He turned to see Phoebe leaning against the door that led back into the main station.

"I am," Caleb replied with a grin. "Nearly time to get our knees in the breeze."

"I have no idea what that means," Phoebe said, also grinning. "But are you ready for some lunch?"

"Sure am," Caleb said. "Eat when you can, sleep when you can."

He looked at her for a moment, his mind drifting back to

the previous evening. And first thing in the morning. As if she sensed what he was thinking about, Phoebe started blushing.

"Why are you looking at me like that?" she asked him, a frown appearing on her face. Caleb looked away. He'd not meant to make her uncomfortable.

"Sorry," he replied. "I was just, uh, just thinking about last night. To his relief, her grin reappeared, and she pointed a finger upward.

"Have you told the man upstairs yet? He'll be back at work by now."

"Oh, He already knows," Caleb replied. "I think we're good, though. You can kind of tell when he's pissed. Revelation, chapter sixteen, verse eighteen."

"Humor me?"

"And there were flashes of lightning and sounds and peals of thunder, and there was a great earthquake."

Phoebe took a couple of steps toward Caleb and stood in front of him. He wanted to reach out and hold her, but the yard was too public for that.

"Are you talking about the wrath of the man upstairs?" she said, reaching out and brushing something from his face. Then she lowered her voice to almost a whisper. "Or are you talking about last night?"

TWENTY MINUTES LATER, Caleb was sitting in a Greggs bakery on the main concourse of the station. He had commandeered a table for four and was looking suspiciously at an item on his plate that Jade had just placed in front of him. It was around six inches long and made of puff pastry, but it wasn't something he recognized. Both Natasha and Jade were watching him, while Phoebe was already laughing.

"What is it?" Caleb asked Jade as he poked his finger at the item.

"It's a sausage roll," she replied with a grin. "Sausage meat, wrapped in pastry. Do you not have them over the pond?"

"We have pigs in a blanket, but the pastry's harder."

"Pigs in blankets don't have pastry over here, Caleb," Phoebe said, reaching under the table and squeezing his knee. "That's a sausage wrapped in bacon. There's no pastry involved. Are you going to say grace and eat?"

Caleb closed his eyes briefly and did as instructed before he picked up the sausage roll and took a tentative bite. Then, after a nod of appreciation, he took a larger one. The pastry was buttery and flaked onto the plate, while the meat filling was slightly spicy. Caleb finished it in no time and then had to wait for the others to finish theirs. He smiled as he watched Phoebe eat. She seemed determined not to drop a single flake of pastry on her plate.

A few moments later, a silence descended over the table. It was time for Caleb and Phoebe to leave. The silence was broken by Natasha. She looked at both Caleb and Phoebe in turn, before her gaze settled on Caleb. His heart went out to her when he saw her pained expression.

"Thank you," Natasha said quietly. "Thank you for what you're doing for me."

Caleb said nothing. They had done nothing for Natasha yet. But he did have a plan.

He'd just not been entirely honest with Phoebe about exactly what his plan was.

CHAPTER 76

Mikhail retched again, but there was nothing left in his stomach to bring up. He glanced back at the truck where Vincuk and the others were waiting for him. Yuri was standing next to Vincuk, both smoking cigarettes. As Mikhail put his hand on his brow to wipe the perspiration away, he saw Yuri walking toward him. They were around twenty miles away from the village where the mercenaries had been. Twenty miles from where Mikhail had killed a man. He felt another spasm of nausea at the thought.

"You did well, Mikhail," Yuri said a moment later, resting a fatherly hand on Mikhail's back. "Your first time, yes?" Mikhail could hear the smile in his voice as Yuri spoke, and he nodded his head in reply. "It gets easier, my friend."

Mikhail took a deep breath and watched as Yuri sat on the ground, offering him a bottle of water. He took the bottle gratefully and sat down near Yuri, careful to avoid the puddle of bile he had deposited on the ground. They were in a turnout next to a main road, hidden from view, but Yuri appeared to be in no hurry.

"You'll always remember your first kill," Yuri said, his expression grim. "It's like your first kiss." His face softened for an instant, but it soon returned to a hardened expression. Mikhail tried to push away the image of Alevtina that the man's words had summoned in his mind, but he couldn't.

"Right," Mikhail said noncommittally, wishing that Yuri hadn't just linked the two events in his head.

"It was a righteous kill, Mikhail," Yuri said. "Look at me."

Mikhail did as Yuri told him, sipping his water as he did so.

"There are five, perhaps more, men who are alive because of what you did." Yuri's gaze was unwavering. "Five or more sons, brothers, or husbands who are not lost, as well as one less murdering bastard in the world. That's what I mean by righteous."

"There's one more murderous bastard as well," Mikhail said, still holding Yuri's eyes with his. "Me."

"Nonsense," Yuri spat back. "That was an armed man preparing to murder innocent civilians. His death was his responsibility. You were just the instrument that fulfilled it."

Mikhail thought for a moment, taking another sip of his water. He glanced over at Vincuk, who gave him an appreciative nod. Had he and Yuri discussed this pep talk? Mikhail shook his head sadly, knowing it didn't matter. He'd not thought that it would feel like this, killing someone. He had thought he would feel heroic, like a man. But all he felt was sadness.

"Like I said, Mikhail," Yuri said, getting to his feet. "It gets easier, my friend. We're safe enough here. You take your time, and think about what I've said."

Mikhail scuttled around so that his back was facing the group by the truck. He could feel them looking at him, but he didn't care. He forced himself to think about Yuri's words. Sure, Mikhail had taken a life, but it was the life of a soldier who would have known the risks when he picked up a weapon, just as Mikhail knew the risk he was taking. At the same time, he had saved lives. The lives of innocent people who wanted no part of this conflict. Alevtina had been innocent, and she had died. Would Mikhail have killed for her? He knew the answer to that question a million times over.

He got to his feet a few moments later, brushing dirt from his backside as he did so. Then he took another swig of water, testing his stomach, but it felt fine. Taking his time, he ambled back to where the others were waiting for him.

"How are you doing?" Vincuk asked, his expression almost fatherly.

"I'm thinking," Mikhail replied, looking at each of them in turn, "that's it's time to go and kill some more of these murderous bastards."

CHAPTER 77

Natasha stared out of the train window as the gray monolithic buildings of London gave way to the suburbs. She looked at her phone to see it was just past two o'clock in the afternoon. Caleb and Phoebe should be well on their way to Dover by now. Despite the assurances that Caleb had given her, Natasha was struggling to see how he was going to be able to locate Mikhail. She certainly didn't share the confidence he seemed to have.

She scrolled through her phone, checking her WhatsApp messages for what must have been the twentieth time that day, but her original message to Mikhail, and the ones she had sent subsequently, remained resolutely unread. More worrying, none of the messages she had sent in the last twenty-four hours appeared to even have been delivered to his phone. They all had a single gray tick next to them. It was almost as if at around this time the previous day, his phone had disappeared. Perhaps the battery had run out and, wherever he was, he wasn't able to recharge it?

Natasha put her phone back into her bag and rested her head against the seat. She felt utterly helpless. Closing her eyes, she tried to tune out the low hubbub of conversation in the carriage and doze for a while. Natasha was just on the cusp between being awake and asleep when she realized her phone was ringing.

"Hello?" she said as she answered the call, forgetting to look at the screen to see who it was.

"Natasha, it's me." It was Iĺja.

"Iĺja?" Natasha said, shaking her head to clear it. "What's happening?" If her sister was calling her, she must have some news.

"I've found out where Anton is."

Natasha heaved a sigh of relief. Iĺja knew where her husband was. She'd not said that he was dead. If he was, she would have said she'd found out what happened to him or something similar.

"Is he okay?" There was the briefest of pauses at the end of the line, and Natasha thought her heart had stopped beating until she heard Iĺja's reply.

"He's injured, but I don't know how badly."

Natasha fought the rising sense of panic in her chest.

"He's alive though?" she asked.

"Yes, Natasha, that's what I was told. I called the hospital, but they wouldn't tell me anything." Iĺja's voice was calm and measured, and it reassured Natasha no end. "They won't talk to me because I'm not a direct relative."

Natasha pressed her hand to her sternum at the news. Anton was alive. That was all that mattered.

"Will they talk to me?" she asked Iĺja. "Where is he? What happened to him?"

"They might talk to you, yes. He's in a hospital in Lida, but I don't know what happened to him. He could have broken his leg playing football for all I know."

Natasha laughed, a sharp noise that earned her some

disapproving looks from her fellow passengers. But she couldn't care less what they thought. Her husband was alive, and in a hospital not too far from Hrodna.

"Can you text me the number? I'll call them now," she asked Iĺja.

"Of course," Iĺja replied. "I'll do it now."

A short time later, after listening to on-hold music for what had felt to Natasha like hours but was in reality only minutes, Natasha was talking to one of the nurses on the ward where Anton was being cared for. The woman sounded harried and distracted, but at the same time, there was an edge of sympathy to her voice. Natasha had told her she was asking for information about her husband, Anton Zaystev.

"What's his date of birth?" the nurse asked. Natasha had to think for a moment, but she managed to retrieve the information. There was a pause on the end of the line and she could hear papers being rustled. "Yes, we have an Anton Zaystev," the nurse said eventually. Natasha let out an enormous sigh of relief at the news.

"Is he okay? What happened to him?" she asked. There was another pause on the line, this one much longer.

"I can't discuss how he was injured or the nature of his injuries, I'm afraid."

"But he's okay?"

What the nurse said next struck fear into Natasha's heart.

"He's very sick," the nurse said. "It could go either way."

CHAPTER 78

P hoebe blipped the locks for the van and watched while Caleb checked to make sure that the rear door was secure. They were parked in the bowels of the cross-channel ferry that would be taking them to France. Around them, cars and vans were being shepherded into position by ferry employees. It was a well-practiced operation that ensured every inch of space on the parking decks was used.

"So, what now?" Caleb asked her. He had a wry smile on his face. "Do we get a cabin?"

"No, Caleb," Phoebe replied with a laugh. "It takes about an hour and a half to cross the channel. We're not getting a cabin."

"We could get up to a lot in an hour and a half," Caleb said, his smile broadening.

"Well, there are no cabins, so you're out of luck. We'll just go up to the passenger deck and grab a drink."

Phoebe and Caleb had stopped at a motorway service station not far from the port of Dover for some food. Phoebe still had some bad memories of the restaurants on cross-channel ferries from a school trip she'd been on many years ago, and she didn't think things would have improved.

"I was as sick as a dog all the way from Calais to Paris," she had told Caleb as they tucked into a burger and fries. "It had to have been the food on the ferry."

She made her way to a stairwell that led to the upper decks. It was busy, and she felt slightly claustrophobic as they made their way up the narrow staircase. When they reached the passenger deck, to her relief, there was a lot more space.

"Do you want to grab a table?" Phoebe asked Caleb. "I'll get us a couple of coffees."

"Any preference for seating?"

"A window seat would be good, but you'll need to be quick."

"Yes, ma'am," Caleb replied with a mock salute. "Popping smoke now."

Phoebe shook her head and laughed before making her way to the restaurant. The passenger deck was filling up fast and there was a large group of school children who looked to be aged ten or eleven, all with stickers on their chests with their names on them. As she got in line, she watched them for a while, envying their excitement. She certainly didn't envy the teachers who were attempting to control them. It must be like trying to herd cats, Phoebe thought as she watched a woman becoming more and more exasperated with her charges.

Eventually, Phoebe reached the front of the line and bought two overpriced cups of coffee. She glanced at the hot plate as she paid for them. Getting some food before they got on the ferry had been the right move. It took her a few moments to find Caleb, but he had found a table next to a window at the stern of the ship and was staring through it at the iconic white cliffs of Dover. His cell phone was on the table, on top of the papers that Natasha had given him.

"One coffee," Phoebe said, placing the cup down next to the paperwork. "You've been on a cross-channel ferry before, right?"

"No," Caleb replied, turning to look at her. "The last time I crossed the channel, the boat I was in was a bit smaller than this one." Phoebe was about to ask him a question about it when he changed the subject. "What's your plan when we get to Poland?" She frowned at his choice of words. He had asked her about her plan, not their plan.

"There's a large World Health Organization depot in a town called Kuźnica," Phoebe replied. "It's not far from the border with Belarus. They're acting as a distribution hub for aid being sent to the country." She watched as Caleb nodded.

"Makes sense," he said, sipping his coffee.

"How about you?" she asked him. "What are your plans?"

"This coffee is lovely," Caleb replied. Phoebe folded her arms across her chest and stared at him. "What?" he asked with a grin. "What did I do?"

"Don't try to change the subject," she said, suppressing the grin she could feel forming on her own face. "I asked you what your plans are. How are you intending to find Mikhail?"

Phoebe waited as Caleb appeared to consider the question. He was looking at her intently as he did so, as if he was waiting for her to say something else. But Phoebe said nothing. A moment later, she raised her eyebrows to try to elicit a response. At the same time, the ship started juddering slightly as the propellors began to drive, causing ripples to appear on the surface of their coffees.

"I'm not sure," he said eventually. "I'm thinking that with the information I've got, I can maybe recruit someone to look for him." Phoebe regarded him carefully, wondering what to say next. In the end, she just decided that honesty was the best policy.

"Caleb?" she said, finally smiling. "You know something?"

"What?"

"You're a shit liar."

CHAPTER 79

Vincuk's mood, like that of everyone else in the truck, was somber despite their relative success earlier that day. Following the attack on the mercenaries at the village, he and his squad had traveled to another small group of dwellings that had been visited by the People's Army a few days previously. It had been a contact of Yuri's who had let him know about it.

In Vincuk's pocket was a flash drive full of photographs. They were not the type of photographs that the press would ever publish, but they needed to be made public. When they had arrived at the group of houses, a woman had led Vincuk and Yuri to the shallow graves in the forest close by. Vincuk and Yuri hadn't asked the rest of the squad to get involved on the grounds that, with the exception of Grigor, they were too young. But the boys had joined in anyway, disinterring the bodies for them to be photographed. They were all male, civilian, and they had multiple gunshot wounds in their backs. Although nothing was said, Vincuk also knew that a horror had been visited on the woman who led them to the graves. He could tell from her demeanor that she was broken somehow and Vincuk didn't need much imagination to understand how.

"That was a tough one, Vincuk," Yuri said from his position in the passenger seat as if he could tell what Vincuk was thinking. Vincuk just nodded, keeping his eyes focused on the Minsk motorcycle a few hundred yards in front of them. In Vincuk's opinion, Ruslan had been the most affected by the sights and smells they had all witnessed. Grigor and Dmitry had remained impassive and said nothing as they worked, while Mikhail just seemed to become angrier and angrier.

"We'll need to keep an eye on the boy," Vincuk said. Yuri nodded in response and they drove on in silence for some moments. "What happens next?" Vincuk asked Yuri eventually.

"I'll take the flash drive to Hrodna," Yuri replied. "I have a friend there who can get it over the border to Poland. There's a journalist there who he knows."

"Will it be enough?" Vincuk asked.

"It should be." Yuri shook a cigarette free from his pack, offering one to Vincuk, who took it gratefully. "The camera's got a GPS chip so they can verify the location they were taken. Also, the time and date is built into the photos somehow."

"We can trust this journalist, can we?" Vincuk thought back to the broadcast he'd listened to about the resistance possibly being responsible for the shelling a day or so ago. "He won't try to turn it round and use it against us?"

"It's a she, not a he," Yuri replied. "And as to whether we can trust her, we don't have a choice."

In front of the truck, the brake light of Ruslan's motorcycle flared and Vincuk tapped his own brakes. But Ruslan was just slowing down for an approaching bus. As it passed them a moment later, Vincuk looked at the faces of the occupants. His thoughts turned to Mikhail when he realized the bus was full of people who looked to be around his age, perhaps a year or two younger. They were laughing and joking with each other as they didn't have a care in the world. Why should they? They were children.

Vincuk shook his head in sadness. This needed to end.

CHAPTER 80

Caleb looked at Phoebe who regarded him with a faintly amused expression, but her eyes were hard. Behind her, he could see a group of schoolchildren all with their faces glued to the windows as they watched the port moving away.

"Do you think I'm stupid?" Phoebe asked, a definite note of irritation in her voice.

"No, of course not," he replied. "I just figured I'll work something out when I get there."

"That's total crap, and you know it. You're not the sort of person who works something out when he gets there." She used her fingers to make air quotes as she paraphrased his statement.

Caleb sighed. He'd been hoping to have this conversation with her much later. Phoebe could just refuse to take him any further when they got to France, and then where would he be? He held up his hands as if surrendering.

"I'm planning on going to find Mikhail in person."

"In Belarus?" Phoebe's face was incredulous, and any trace of amusement had vanished.

"In Belarus," Caleb replied.

Phoebe said something in Russian that he didn't understand, but it didn't sound polite. She switched back to English.

"I was asking you how well you speak Russian or Belarusian, Caleb?"

Caleb opened his mouth and closed it again, knowing there was nothing he could say to that question. "There's a mission in Hrodna. A Catholic mission that I'm going to approach for help. I'm hoping they'll be able to provide me with someone who can speak English to help me search."

"A mission?" Phoebe replied with a laugh. "What, like on *Call The Midwife*?"

He looked at her with a bemused expression.

"Call The Midwife?" he asked.

"It's a television program about a bunch of nuns having babies," Phoebe replied, waving a hand as if it was irrelevant.

Despite the situation, and Phoebe's obvious anger, Caleb started to laugh.

"Nuns having babies?" he said. "That sounds like a novel plot."

"Not having babies, you idiot," Phoebe replied. To his relief, he could see the traces of a smile around her mouth. "Delivering babies. So, let me see if I have this right. Your plan is to go to Belarus, find a nun—preferably one who speaks English—and wander round until you find Mikhail?"

"Well," Caleb said. "I don't think it's that kind of mission, and I do have a plan for the search."

"Oh, well, that's alright then." He watched as Phoebe leaned back in her chair and took a sip of her coffee. Above their heads, the ship's horn sounded with a deep, resonant blast that was followed by an excited cheer from the school-children. "How are you planning on getting him back across the border?" Caleb pulled the corners of his mouth downward. That was something that he didn't have a plan for just yet. He watched as she started giggling.

"What's so funny?" he asked her.

"I was thinking," Phoebe replied, "you could always dress him as a nun."

Caleb laughed politely and got to his feet. "I'm going to find the bathroom."

Leaving Phoebe still giggling, he made his way across the crowded deck, side stepping people as he did so. As he walked, he thought about what Phoebe had just said. There was much that he'd not told her. He'd not told her that he had a very good idea what Mikhail was doing. If the young man had lost someone close to him, as Natasha had said, then he would be angry as well as grieving. And in Caleb's experience, angry young men wanted to do one thing, which was to fight. He'd been one himself, although it was years ago. Natasha's husband had joined the fight, so it stood to reason that Mikhail would want to either join him or at least follow in his footsteps.

Caleb knew from his experiences in war-torn countries that networks were quick to emerge among the local population. They were a vital way for information to be passed around, and there would be a network of some sort for the fight against the authorities. If he could tap into that network, and this was where he would need some local help, then he could locate Mikhail. Caleb knew he couldn't make Mikhail return with him, and there was still the problem of getting over the border, but he would do his best to persuade him. Caleb had many skills, and the art of persuasion was one of them.

All he needed Phoebe to do was to get him to the border.

CHAPTER 81

"Right, listen in, squad," Stepan said, looking at each member of them in turn to make sure he had their undivided attention. They were sitting on plastic garden chairs in their makeshift ops room gathered around an easel that Stepan had pinned a map of the area to. A black *X* on the map marked the location where the hunters had reported the resistance was camping. Stepan tapped the cross with a sharpie. "This is our primary objective."

The site Stepan had just tapped the pen on was a small forest some thirty kilometers north of Hrodna. It was isolated with the nearest obvious buildings at least a couple of kilometers away, but the entire area was criss-crossed with logging roads. Stepan hadn't looked at it before as he'd thought it was too far away from civilization, but as he regarded the map now, he realized it was a good choice for the resistance. It was remote enough for them not to be discovered accidentally, but central enough to give them the mobility they needed.

"Looking at the map, there's an area just here which

would be a suitable location for reconnaissance." He tapped the sharpie on another, much smaller forested area to the northwest of the primary objective. It had roads close by, but none running through it. "This would be suitable and is well within range of the drone. Any thoughts?"

The squad remained silent, and all Stepan got in return were sullen stares. There was a replacement for the soldier who had been killed due in at some point that day, and Stepan pitied anyone who was joining this group. He placed the pen on the easel and pulled up a chair before sitting down and facing his men.

"Right," he said, trying to sound sympathetic. He was going to have to speak to them less like a soldier, and more like a father. Stepan paused, suddenly realizing he didn't know the first name of the soldier who had died. "We lost a man today, and that's tough. But we're soldiers." He thumped his chest with his hand. "We fight, and some of us die. That's what we're paid to do."

"Tomas wasn't paid enough for what happened to him," one of the men said. Stepan looked at him, mentally thanking him for the reminder of the dead man's name.

"I know, Daniel," Stepan replied, looking at him directly. "Tomas was a good man. A good soldier. But what, we're just going to let his death go unpunished?" He glanced at the map on the easel behind him. "Or are we going to go and find the man who did this to Tomas and punish him?"

There were a few sullen nods from the men. It was hardly an enthusiastic response, but Stepan wasn't sure what else he could say. He looked at their drawn faces and tried to hide his frustration. They were supposed to be soldiers, but they looked far from that now. They just looked like miserable young men who had only just realized how dangerous what they did for a living could be. He got to his feet and walked away as his irritation with them grew. They weren't complaining when things were going their way, and now they were downcast because they had lost a single man. Where was their fight?

Perhaps, Stepan thought as he paced, perhaps when they were face to face with the resistance, that would put a fire in their bellies? He thought back to the first firefight he had been in. Not the first time he had fired a gun in anger, not the first time he had killed a man. But the first time he had gone toe to toe with an enemy. It had been many years ago, back in the early 2000s, when the Chechens had tried to wriggle away from the direct control of Moscow. That had been a proper fight, and he remembered the enthusiasm he had felt following it.

Stepan made his way outside to smoke, waving away one of the soldiers who looked to be following him. He wanted a few moments alone to think. His original plan for the resistance had been to simply round them up and hang them. But would that ignite his squad in the way he wanted? Would that make them men? He puffed on his cigarette, shaking his head. They needed to fight, not just to round people up. To know what it was like to be under fire, and to be victorious.

When he returned to the ops room, Stepan had a change of tactics to tell them about. They were still going to visit the resistance campsite, but they were going to approach it very differently.

CHAPTER 82

Natasha was surprised when a female voice answered the phone. She'd been expecting Caleb to pick up. Had she got the wrong number?

"Hello?" the voice said.

"Ah, I was expecting Caleb," Natasha said, unsure of herself.

"Natasha? It's Phoebe," the voice said. Natasha breathed a small sigh of relief. She had the right number. "He's just in the bathroom. Is everything okay?"

"Kind of, yes," Natasha replied. "I spoke to Iĺja, my sister. My husband's been found."

"Is he alright?"

"He's wounded, but he's alive."

"Oh, that's fantastic news," Phoebe said and Natasha could hear the genuine relief in her voice. "You must be so relieved."

"I am, yes," Natasha said, pausing for a few seconds before continuing. "I spoke to the hospital he's in, and he's quite sick."

"Did they say what happened to him?"

"No, they wouldn't tell me. Just that he had been wounded and was suffering from a serious infection."

"Okay, well, depending on his wounds and what the infection is, that should be treatable," Phoebe said. "I did my residency in Russia and people who were, er, wounded but made it to hospital almost always survived."

Natasha was grateful for her attempt to reassure her. She was a doctor, but she didn't know the full story.

"They hardly have any supplies, Phoebe," Natasha said. "The nurse said they don't have the right antibiotics to treat him properly." There was a pause at the end of the line before Phoebe spoke.

"Can they move him? To a hospital that does?"

"No," Natasha replied. "No one's allowed over the border unless they've got a ballot ticket."

"Not even casualties?"

"Especially not casualties who are men." Natasha heard Phoebe sigh as she said this. "Do you have antibiotics in your van? Maybe there would be a way of getting them to him?"

"It would depend on the type of infection, Natasha, but no, I don't. If your husband has been wounded in combat, then the infection is most likely resistant to the ones I have," Phoebe replied. Her voice was starting to crackle and distort, and Natasha had to concentrate to hear her. "Listen," Phoebe said. "I've got some friends at the Red Cross. Maybe I can make some calls, see what I can do? And perhaps I can speak to the doctors at the hospital as well? They might give me some more information. Can you message the details through to this phone?"

"That's really kind of you, Phoebe, but I don't know what they can do," Natasha said, trying not to sound too downbeat. Phoebe was only trying to help if she could. "I think the line might be going. I'm on a train at the moment."

"I don't know how much longer I'll have a signal for either, Natasha," Phoebe replied. "We're on the ferry, so at some point, the signal will disappear. But we'll be able to pick up the message when we get to France."

"You'll tell Caleb?"

"Of course I will."

Natasha thanked Phoebe and ended the call. She switched to her messaging app, checked to see if her messages to Mikhail had been delivered or read, and fired off a message to Caleb's phone with the details of the hospital where Anton was. It was good for Phoebe to offer to try to speak to her contacts, but Natasha knew there would be nothing that she could do.

Then she opened her browser and started searching for flights to Poland. There was no way she could stay in England now.

CHAPTER 83

Caleb washed his hands and exited the bathroom, holding the door open for a couple of school-children who were chattering animatedly. He smiled, envying their excitement. The only school trip he'd even been on was to the Big Bend National Park, and he couldn't remember much about it other than it was hot and dusty and a boy called Jimmy had crapped himself in the bus on the way there and again on the way back.

When he got back to the table where Phoebe was sitting, she had his phone in her hands and was examining the small screen with a frown on her face.

"Everything okay?" he asked her as he sat down.

"I just spoke to Natasha," Phoebe replied, putting his phone down. "Sorry. That's your phone. I wasn't, er, I was just reading a text she sent. You can put a passcode on the handset if you want to."

"There's nothing on that phone, Phoebe," Caleb said with a grin. "No secrets there for you to find." He saw her blushing slightly. "So no need for a passcode. Is Natasha okay?"

"She's found her husband."

"Is he okay?"

"He's alive, but he doesn't sound okay. Natasha spoke to the hospital and apparently he's got a bad infection of some sort, but they don't have the right antibiotics and there's no way of getting him over the border. Perhaps if he got to Poland, they could treat him there. He's not that far from the border." Phoebe slammed her hand on the table. "This is so bloody frustrating."

It was the first time Caleb had seen proper anger on her face. "We've got antibiotics, right?" he asked, keeping his voice neutral. He sensed his plans might be about to change.

"That's what Natasha asked," Phoebe replied, "but we've only got basic ones. If he's got combat injuries, he's almost certainly got multi-drug resistant organisms in his system." She sighed and Caleb could see the frustration in her expression. "Nothing we've got will touch them. I've now lost the phone signal. Sorry, I mean you've now lost the phone signal. But I did manage to forward the message on to my phone before the signal disappeared."

"What difference will that make if there's no reception?" Caleb asked.

"Because, Caleb," Phoebe said, pulling her own handset out of her bag, "my phone can connect to this magical thing the ferry has that's called the internet. Which I can use to make calls with."

"Ah, yes," Caleb replied. "I've heard of that sorcery called the internet. Isn't it just full of pornography and African princes wanting to give you money?"

"Very good, Caleb," Phoebe said with a lopsided grin that he liked a lot. She picked up his phone again and held it side by side with hers, her eyes moving from one to the other. "Would you excuse me for a moment? I'm going to try to speak to the hospital her husband is in." She peered at Caleb's screen. "Anton. Anton Zaystev."

"Sure," Caleb replied, moving to stand up.

"You don't need to leave, Caleb. You don't speak Russian anyway, unless you learned it in the bathroom just now." Phoebe smiled at him as she said this, and he sat back down.

Caleb watched Phoebe as she made the call. At one point, she put her hand over the handset and mouthed the words *I'm on hold* at him. He smiled. Why had she not just said that? A few moments later, she was speaking to someone in rapid-fire Russian. Caleb couldn't even make out the individual words she was speaking, other than the occasional *ara* which he thought meant yes. Then there was another pause in the conversation, longer than the previous one. He raised his eyebrows and this time, she spoke to him.

"I'm waiting to speak to the doctor who's looking after Natasha's husband."

Caleb nodded in reply. It must have been five minutes later when Phoebe started speaking again. The conversation appeared to be going well, but gradually Phoebe's voice became less animated and her phrases became shorter. At the same time, the frown lines on her forehead became deeper. By the time she ended the call, her expression was as dark as he had ever seen it.

"It's not good, Caleb," Phoebe said, looking at him with pain in her eyes. "Anton's got multiple gunshot wounds, and all of them are deeply infected. The doctor treating him thinks he's got three or four days left."

Caleb considered what Phoebe had just said for a moment. He closed his eyes, offering up a silent prayer to St. Michael the Archangel. St. Michael was the patron saint of soldiers, but from what Phoebe had just said, even the Archangel was going to struggle.

"How long can you stay in Poland, Phoebe?" Caleb asked her. "Before you have to return to England?"

"A couple of days, I guess. Maybe more. Why?"

"You said if Anton could get to Poland, he might be okay," Caleb said. "If I can get him across the border, could you get him into a hospital?"

"I'm sure I could, yes. But even if you can get him to the border, how are you going to get across it?"

"Yeah," Caleb said, relaxing back into his chair. "Not quite worked that part out yet."

CHAPTER 84

Mikhail tossed and turned in his makeshift bed. He had adjusted it to try to avoid the root he'd slept on the previous evening, but all he'd managed to do was to find another one. In the distance, he could hear the muted conversation of the others above the rustling noise his tent made in the gentle breeze. As he rolled over, he heard Grigor's distinctive laugh and wondered what they were talking about. It was still light outside, although the sun was beginning to set. Mikhail had gone to bed early, claiming to be tired, but in reality, he wanted some time alone.

He had killed a man today. Ended a life using his own hand. Despite what Yuri had said earlier, and despite what he had said to the others, Mikhail was hurting inside. Somewhere, there might be a mother grieving for her son. A wife for her husband. The man's status as a soldier wouldn't matter to them. Their grief would still hurt, as Mikhail's grief for Alevtina did. Wasn't he supposed to feel a sense of vengeance, not a sense of loss?

Mikhail belched, which caused a burning sensation in

the back of his throat as he tasted the vodka Vincuk had
given him earlier.

"It'll help you sleep, Mikhail," Vincuk had said. But so
far, all it had done was give Mikhail indigestion. If he was at
home, or at his Aunt Iĺja's house, he could get up and fetch a
glass of cold milk. But here in the forest, they didn't even
have a fridge. He turned again, closing his eyes, but images
and sounds started appearing in his mind's eye. The graves
they had dug up earlier. The sound of the camera shutter
whirring as Vincuk had photographed the bodies. As
Mikhail lay there, he imagined he could still smell them.

Only a few days previously, he had been in school,
listening to Felix telling dirty stories about Mrs. Ananič.
Mikhail forced himself to smile, remembering the expression on her face as she had been about to sentence Felix to
a detention when the sirens had sounded. His smile faded as
he remembered what happened in the bunker, when it was
just him and Alevtina. How soft her lips had felt as he had
kissed her. The warmth of her body against his. Mikhail
rolled onto his back and unzipped his sleeping bag. He
knew there was no way he would be sleeping anytime soon,
and he didn't want to be alone anymore. Besides, he needed
a pee.

After he had used the deep trench latrine, finishing his
business as quickly as he could to get away from the stench,
he joined the rest of the group who were sitting around the
remnants of a fire. Yuri had left earlier, taking the motorcycle to Hrodna to deliver the photographs to one of his
friends. If he had taken the truck, it had been Mikhail's
intention to ask if he could go as well. While Yuri was
speaking to his friend, Mikhail had thought he might be
able to go and see his aunt. Sure, she would scream and
shout at him, but at least she would know he was okay. Or

something close to it. Aunt Iĺja would also be able to let his
mother know that he was safe. Doing his bit for his country
like his father was.

"Thought you were sleeping, Mikhail," Grigor said as
Mikhail took a seat on a log near the fire. Mikhail just
shrugged his shoulders in response. On the other side of the
fire, Dmitry and Ruslan were sitting side by side, their
weapons leaning against the log they were sitting on.

"Where's Vincuk?" Mikhail asked. Grigor nodded at the
cabin.

"He's in there," he replied, "planning our next attack, I
think." Mikhail watched as Grigor extracted a cigarette from
a pack and tried to light it with a burning stick from the fire.
But every time he brought the flame close to his face, it went
out. "Has anyone got a light?"

"What does it feel like, Mikhail?" Ruslan asked, shifting
his position to put his hand in his pocket. When he pulled it
out, he had a small plastic lighter, which he tossed at Grigor.

"What does what feel like?" Mikhail replied.

"What does it feel like to kill someone?"

Mikhail shrugged his shoulders again.

"Doesn't really feel like anything, to be honest."

Grigor started laughing. He lit his cigarette, keeping it in
his mouth as he returned Ruslan's lighter. Then he put his
hands on either side of his head and made an exploding
noise as he pulled them away.

"That's not what that soldier thought," Grigor said with
a laugh. "The last thing that went through his head was a
bullet." With the exception of Mikhail, they all laughed.

As the laughter died away, the four of them sat in an
almost companionable silence. Mikhail could hear the
noise of the forest around him, but he thought there was
something else. Something much fainter than the rustling

of the tree branches, but there was definitely something. Grigor opened his mouth so say something, but Mikhail hushed him.

"Can anyone else hear that?" Mikhail asked, his voice a low whisper. He saw a look of concentration on their faces, but they all shook their heads.

"Hear what?" Grigor asked, his voice also low. Mikhail met his eyes, not wanting to look up in case he was right.

"I think I can hear a drone."

CHAPTER 85

Phoebe tapped her finger on the screen of the GPS, double checking she had the spelling of the town they were heading for correct. Then she sat back in the driver's seat and waited for the route to be calculated. When she saw the summary appear on the screen, she whistled.

"Ouch," she said to Caleb, who was watching her with interest. "Fifteen hours. That's going to hurt."

"Which countries are we going through?" he asked her.

"France, obviously, but not much of it. Then Belgium, Holland, pretty much all of Germany, and then pretty much all of Poland," Phoebe replied, scrolling through the route on the screen.

"So, about lunchtime tomorrow?"

"Probably later, with rest stops," Phoebe replied. Jade's earlier comment about finding a guest house came back to her, and she smiled. "I don't think I've even been to five countries in one day before." She turned to look at Caleb as, in front of them, the large doors to the ferry started to open. He was looking at her with a curious expression. "What?"

"Nothing," Phoebe said. "Just something Jade said, that's all."

A few moments later, the cars in front of them started to ease their way off the ferry. Phoebe put the van into drive and followed, nervous about driving over a ramp even though she knew it was quite safe. But when the wheels of the van reached firm ground, she breathed a sigh of relief. Next to her, Caleb was looking out of the window at the high chain-link fences on either side of the road that were topped with razor wire. They were illuminated by both the orange street lights and also floodlights in the ground.

"It looks like a prison," he muttered. There were even fences on the bridges that crossed above their heads.

"It's to keep the migrants away from the port," Phoebe replied, "but it doesn't seem to stop them. They just come over in small boats instead. I can't imagine being that desperate." She glanced at Caleb to see he had a thoughtful look on his face, but he said nothing.

They drove past signs in both English and French, reminding them to drive on the right. Then there was a larger sign at the side of the road.

Bienvenue en France. Welcome to France. Beneath it was some graffiti sprayed on the sign in black paint. *Bienvenue en Europe*. Welcome to Europe.

A few miles on, the fences disappeared, and the traffic from the port started to thin out. Phoebe followed the instructions on the screen, which took them around the town of Calais. What little she could see of the place looked pretty industrial. She followed the signs toward Dunkerque and Lille until a couple of miles further on they joined the E40. The dual lane highway made the driving easier, as she didn't have to concentrate quite so much about which side of the road to drive on.

As she drove, Phoebe's thoughts turned to Anton, Natasha's husband. The doctor she had spoken to in the hospital had told her that his patient had been confirmed as having a gram-positive infection of some sort, but they weren't able to identify exactly what type of organism was causing it. She tried to remember back to the infection module she had done at medical school, but the only thing she could remember from the warfare section was an infection called clostridial myonecrosis, also known as gas gangrene. If that was what Anton was suffering from, his prognosis was very poor. Three or four days was optimistic, but if she remembered correctly, it was actually quite rare.

"Clostridium perfringens," Phoebe muttered under her breath, surprised she could remember the actual name of the bacteria species that caused the horrible infection.

"Sorry, I missed that?" Caleb asked her. His voice sounded sleepy, and she felt bad that she'd woken him up.

"I didn't mean to wake you," Phoebe replied. "I was just thinking about Anton and trying to remember the names of the bacteria that cause wound infections. Clostridium perfringens is one of them."

"That's easy for you to say," Caleb said, laughing.

"You had any more thoughts about how you're going to get Anton across the border?"

"A few," he replied, sounding more awake. "There's no such thing as an impenetrable border. You can build all the razor topped fences in the world, and people will always find a way through." He yawned and stretched his arms out. "Even a twenty mile stretch of water can't keep people out."

"True," Phoebe replied, conceding Caleb's point. "But if he's as sick as he sounds, it's not going to be easy."

CHAPTER 86

Stepan leaned over Daniel's shoulder to see the small screen in the young man's hands. They were lying down at the edge of the forest, their truck hidden a few hundred yards behind them in the trees. Stepan thought the chances of anyone driving down the roads they had taken to get to their location were slim, but he wasn't going to take the risk. The rest of the squad were also lying down, spread out in a semi-circle on either side of Stepan and Daniel.

"No smoking, no talking," Stepan had told them all. "We're in enemy territory here, and don't forget it." There had been one or two disbelieving looks, but as he looked at the screen now, Stepan and the hunters had been right.

"There're four of them here," Daniel whispered, pointing at the center of the screen with his fingertip. "Sitting in a circle. You see the weapons?"

Stepan couldn't, but his eyes were at least a decade older than Daniel's.

"Can you get in any closer?" Stepan asked.

"Not really, no. We can't risk them hearing the drone."

On the screen, the two men watched as one of the figures on the screen got to his feet and made his way to the cabin. As he did so, Stepan saw him picking something up. Daniel had been right about the weapons.

"What else is there?"

The figures on the screen got smaller as Daniel increased the altitude of the drone. "There's a vehicle here," Daniel said. The view shifted as he manipulated the controls. "Four tents. One per man."

"Plus the building. There could be accommodation in there," Stepan said.

"It's not much more than a hut, so there can't be many. They could be two man tents, of course."

"Okay, so we're looking at up to ten people."

Daniel nodded, but Stepan had been thinking out loud, not addressing him. He gestured to Daniel to bring the drone back. If there were up to ten resistance fighters in the makeshift camp, then they were outnumbered. He didn't think there were that many. Four sitting down, perhaps two inside the small cabin. But even with six, an assault wouldn't be straightforward. His original plan to assault the campsite was not going to work and besides, they were losing the light. A dawn attack would be better but if he needed more men, then he was going to have to call it in to headquarters and more soldiers wouldn't be available for a day or two at the minimum.

Above his head, Stepan heard the familiar whine of the drone getting louder as Daniel piloted the craft back to their location. He looked up into the sky but couldn't see the craft. Stepan knew it should have red and green navigation lights on it, but they were covered up with tape for obvious reasons.

Daniel expertly piloted the drone to the ground and cut

the engines. Stepan whistled softly, two short tones to signify they were all about to withdraw to the truck. He looked to his right to see two of his soldiers crouching and almost waddling backward, their weapons still trained in front of them. He nodded as they dropped back into the prone position around twenty yards away. Then, to his left, the other fire team maneuvered the same way, this time going further back than the first. They were doing exactly as they had been trained, and Stepan made a mental note to congratulate them later.

Stepan wriggled back until he was within the tree line and got to his feet slowly. Even though the resistance fighters were several hundred yards in front of their position, he wasn't taking any chances. Followed by Daniel, he made his way back to the vehicle. When they arrived, he could smell a faint odor of cigarette smoke in the air, but he didn't press the issue. His men had done well. They had located and positively identified one of the resistance hideouts.

Now they knew where they were hiding, they could wipe them all out.

CHAPTER 87

Caleb raised his hand from the steering wheel and rubbed his eyes. They were gritty from driving, but he wasn't tired. Next to him, in the passenger seat, Phoebe was curled up and snoring softly, while in front of him the sky was just beginning to lighten. There were streaks of red and orange starting to form and an airplane high above him was leaving dual contrails behind. Caleb wondered for a moment about the plane. Where it was going, and who was on it. He imagined excited families going on vacation, bored businessmen and women traveling to and from work, and people just going from point A to point B.

"But the path of the righteous is like the light of dawn, which shines brighter and brighter until full day," Caleb muttered under his breath, not wanting to wake Phoebe. "Proverbs, chapter four, verse eighteen," he added, unable to help himself.

Caleb glanced at Phoebe, wondering if she was dreaming and, if she was, what about? When he returned his eyes to the road, the sun had just appeared on the horizon, sending its rays upward. Caleb smiled at the dawn of a new day, but his smile faded as he considered what it might bring.

A few moments later, Phoebe started stirring next to him. He looked over at her and saw that she was trying to stretch, but didn't have enough room. As he watched, she opened her eyes and smiled at him. Perhaps she had been dreaming of him, Caleb knew it was self-indulgent, but he appreciated that her first waking act had been to smile at him. She looked beautiful in the early light of the sun, but he couldn't look at her for as long as he wanted to. He was supposed to be driving.

"Morning," Caleb said as he turned his eyes back to the road.

"Morning," Phoebe replied. "What time is it?"

"Well, looking at the angle of the sun, I'd say it's just before five."

"You can tell that from the angle of the sun?" Phoebe asked as she yawned.

"That, and the clock on the dashboard."

"It's too early for jokes, Caleb," Phoebe replied with another smile.

"Are you hungry?" Caleb asked her. They had passed a sign for a service station a mile or so back, so could stop if she wanted to.

"I'm bursting for a pee, and a coffee would be good. You should have woken me earlier. It must be my turn to drive by now." Phoebe yawned again. "Where are we?"

"Somewhere in Germany," Caleb replied, looking at the GPS. "We passed Berlin about half an hour ago, so it's not too much further to the Polish border."

"You should have woken me," Phoebe said again. "You've been driving for ages."

"But you look so peaceful when you're asleep."

"Hmm," Phoebe replied with a smirk. "That's not creepy at all."

They drove on in silence for a few moments, passing another sign for a service station, which was five miles ahead.

"Can I ask you something, Caleb?" Phoebe said. He turned to look at her, surprised by how serious she sounded.

"Sure. Ask away."

"What happens to us when this is all over?"

"How d'you mean?" he replied, unsure what she meant.

"I mean, let's say we get to where we're going. You find Anton and Mikhail and get them to safety somehow so they can live happily ever after," Phoebe said. He looked at her again, but she was staring out of the passenger window. "What happens after that?"

"I don't know," Caleb replied, deciding honesty was the best approach. "I don't know what happens after that."

"I suppose it depends what the man upstairs has in mind for you." The way Phoebe said this made Caleb feel sad, and he wasn't sure why. "Whether He has a plan?" Caleb didn't reply, knowing it wasn't a question for him to answer. There was a silence that lasted just long enough to feel uncomfortable before Phoebe continued. "I'm sorry, Caleb," she said. "I'm not usually maudlin."

"Perhaps you're tired."

"Perhaps." Phoebe sighed, adjusting her position in the passenger seat. "I just don't want what happened to be a one off, that's all. What happened between us, I mean."

"It doesn't have to be," Caleb replied. "When I asked you how long you could stay in Poland, perhaps I had an ulterior motive?" He looked at her and let a smile play over his face, but it wasn't returned by Phoebe.

"I've never had a one-night stand in my life, Caleb," she said. "I've never slept with someone that I've only just met." Her tone was clipped and he could sense the anger she was trying to suppress. "Until I met you."

Caleb drove on in silence for a few moments as they approached the turnoff to the service station.

He wasn't often lost for words, but he had absolutely no idea what Phoebe wanted him to say.

CHAPTER 88

Natasha stared, open-mouthed, at the large television screen. It was showing the BBC news channel which had a moving *BREAKING NEWS* banner across the bottom of the picture. Heidi was sitting next to her on the sofa, also intently watching the anchor.

"The BBC has received information, which it has been able to independently verify, about the deaths of civilians in Belarus that appear to be war crimes," the stone-faced woman on the screen said. "In the village of Metlichino to the northeast of Minsk, the bodies of several civilians have been recovered by members of the local resistance. The footage is too graphic for us to show in detail, but the BBC has shown it to a forensic examiner who has suggested that the male victims were all shot in the back at close range."

The footage on the screen changed from the studio to a shot of a forest floor. Three areas of the shot were blurred out, but the shallow grave the bodies had been exhumed from was obvious.

"Oh, my God," Natasha said, her voice trembling. She

felt sick and briefly considered running to the bathroom. "I know that village."

"International pressure is mounting on the Belarusian authorities to stand down the so-called People's Army, the private mercenaries who they are using to try to regain control of the country," the anchor went on to say. "In London, the Belarusian ambassador has been summoned to Number Ten Downing Street to account for the alleged crimes. The situation in the country is being described as a tinderbox by the Prime Minister, who has said that the international community must not stand by and watch. His sentiments have been echoed by the President of the United States, who has called for the country's borders to be opened to allow refugees from the conflict to flee." The screen changed to a shot of a destroyed building, smoke still spiraling into the air from the ruins. "Elsewhere in Belarus, there has been renewed shelling of civilian residential areas, with numerous fatalities reported. The BBC has not been able to verify this, but the shelling is also thought to be the work of the People's Army."

"Natasha, you cannot go back there," Heidi said. Her voice was shrill as she spoke. "Look at what's happening!"

"I have to go back there," Natasha replied, her voice harsher than she intended. "My son and husband are both there, and Anton is sick. I have to see him before..." Her voice tailed away. She wasn't able to say the words *before he dies*. Although she knew it was irrational and unfair, Natasha wanted to shout or scream at her. To highlight how privileged she was, sitting in her nice, big, safe house in England. But none of that was Heidi's fault, just like none of what was happening to her family was Natasha's fault.

"But you can't get them out," Heidi barked back. She

looked to be on the verge of crying. "All you will be doing is putting yourself in danger."

"What if it was your family, Heidi?" Natasha said. "What if it was Lawrence in a hospital bed? What if it was your son who was missing?" The moment the words left Natasha's mouth, she wished she could take them back. Heidi's face crumpled and tears began to run down her face. Natasha reached out and took Heidi's hand. "I'm sorry. I didn't mean that."

"No, you're right," Heidi replied with a sob. She gripped Natasha's hand so hard it hurt. "But it's just so awful, what's happening."

LATER THAT MORNING, Natasha and Heidi were walking in Heidi's garden, their arms linked. Natasha had apologized again to Heidi for her outburst, but Heidi had dismissed it as not being important.

"What's important, Natasha," she had said, "is that you do whatever you need to do."

"I can get the train to the airport tomorrow," Natasha said as they paused by a flower bed that was crawling with bees.

"Nonsense," Heidi replied. "I wouldn't dream of it. I would have driven you to London to visit your friend, but getting into the city is a nightmare. It's not the same with the airport."

They watched the bees for a few moments. Natasha was envious of the simplicity of their lives. Their only concerns were to find nectar and make honey. As they walked away from the flowerbed, Natasha's thoughts turned to Caleb, and she wondered where he and Phoebe had got to in their journey. She'd heard nothing since her conversation with

Phoebe the previous evening, so assumed they were still on the road. Natasha thought again about the change in the way they interacted when she'd visited them. It was ever so subtle, but definitely there.

"Do you think he'll be able to find your son, this friend of yours?" Heidi asked a moment later.

"I don't know, Heidi," Natasha replied. "I hope so, but all I can do is have faith in the man."

CHAPTER 89

"You're sure it was a drone?" Vincuk heard Yuri ask Mikhail. The three of them were in a disused cabin a couple of miles away from their normal base where Vincuk had been watching the news on Yuri's laptop. It was showing a stream from NBC where the footage Yuri had given to his contact was top of the news.

"I think so," Mikhail replied. Vincuk turned his attention from the laptop to the two of them. Mikhail had come to the cabin the previous evening to tell Vincuk he thought he'd heard something but by the time they went outside, there was nothing. "My friend Felix had one before he crashed it into a lake. They make a pretty distinctive noise."

"But you didn't see anything?" Yuri asked.

"It was almost dark, Yuri," Vincuk said.

"But if it was dark, then a drone wouldn't be able to see anything," Yuri replied. "So, why would they bother?"

"I said it was almost dark, Yuri." Vincuk could see where Yuri was coming from, but he was still concerned about what Mikhail had told him. Concerned enough to quietly round up his men and relocate to the cabin they were currently in. If the People's Army had known where they were, they could have attacked them at any moment. "Besides, according to young Mikhail here, some drones have thermal cameras." Vincuk saw Mikhail nodding in agreement.

"Mikhail, you said you think you heard a drone," Yuri asked. "How sure are you?"

Vincuk watched Mikhail as he considered his reply. He'd asked the same question the previous evening and had seen the uncertainty in the boy's eyes. It was this uncertainty that had stopped him from moving the entire camp. The position their original camp was in was a good one. The cabin and woods were on a rise that would be difficult for the People's Army to encircle and it would be reasonably easy to defend. But any defense was reliant on a small force assaulting. If the People's Army came in numbers, it would be a short battle and not one they could win. By contrast, their current location wasn't anywhere near as suitable and Vincuk was nervous just being there.

"I can't be a hundred percent sure," Mikhail replied, repeating what he had told Vincuk. "It was very faint."

"Okay, thank you, Mikhail," Vincuk said. "That'll be all. You can re-join the others."

Vincuk waited as Mikhail got to his feet. When the cabin door had closed behind him, he turned to Yuri.

"What do you think, Yuri?" he asked his second in command. Yuri paused for a moment before replying, a thoughtful expression on his face.

"If it was a drone, and the People's Army know where we were, wouldn't they have attacked by now?"

"Probably," Vincuk replied. "I would have attacked at dawn." That was exactly the reason why he and Yuri had spent a very damp and chilly couple of hours in the woods overlooking their original camp as the sun had risen. Apart from a family of deer passing through the area, there had been nothing at all.

Yuri spread his arms out, gesturing at the cabin. "This place isn't good enough. It's too close to the roads. Our original site is much better."

"You think we should return there?"

"It would be different if the boy was sure he'd heard a drone," Yuri replied. "Or you'd seen something." Vincuk opened his mouth, but Yuri held his hands up. "It was dark, I know. You told me."

"It's a risk," Vincuk said.

"Everything's a risk. We'd have to find somewhere new and start from scratch."

"Digging trenches and filling sandbags is good for morale," Vincuk replied with a chuckle. "That's what my Praparščyk used to say, anyway." He was referring to his old Senior Non-Commissioned Officer, a brute of a man in every sense which made him an ideal SNCO.

"That sounds like exactly the type of thing a Praparščyk would say," Yuri said, also laughing. "But let's not do it unless we have to. How about we mount some static patrols further out from the base at the same time this evening? If it was a drone, it'll probably be back. They won't attack at night, and if we do hear a drone, we just relocate."

"That sounds like a plan, Yuri. The youngsters can do the patrol while we're drinking Stoli."

CHAPTER 90

"It says it's closed for deliveries," Phoebe said, translating the sign tacked to the gate of the humanitarian aid warehouse. "It reopens at four o'clock." She sighed in exasperation. They'd had such a long journey to get here, and it was closed. Beyond the fence, she could see several trucks, all with magnetic signs attached to the doors with the familiar emblem of the World Health Organization on them. There were several people milling about, some of them with hand trucks full of supplies stacked on them.

"It's the same as a quartermaster's department," Caleb said. "They need time to load up the trucks before they can accept more deliveries." She turned to look at him and saw he had his fingers looped through the chain links of the fence and was watching what was going on around the warehouse with interest.

"But what do we do now?" Phoebe asked him. "Four o'clock is hours away."

"We could do a recce of the border crossing," Caleb replied.

"A reconnaissance, you mean?"

"Sorry, yes. Maybe have a look at the rest of the border for a couple of miles in either direction."

Phoebe thought back to his earlier comment about porous borders and nodded. "We need to find some food and accommodation as well." It had been hours since they'd had breakfast in the service station. She had apologized again for her mood, blaming it on fatigue. Caleb had seemed to accept her explanation, but their conversation as they had eaten had been stilted. When they had returned to the van, it had been Phoebe's turn to drive and Caleb had appeared to fall asleep within minutes. When he awoke, it was as if the conversation had never happened.

She walked back to the van and approached the driver's door.

"Isn't it my turn to drive?" Caleb said, resting his hand on her forearm before she could open the door.

"You do the reconnaissance thing, Caleb," Phoebe replied, enjoying the touch of his fingers on her skin. She made no attempt to move away, and they stood in the same position for a couple of seconds. Caleb said nothing, but just looked at her and she wondered what he was thinking.

"Okay, that makes sense," he said, removing his hand.

A short while later, they were sitting in a parking lot near the border crossing between Poland and Belarus. It was a utilitarian military affair, all fences and gates, and she was reminded of the security they had seen around Calais. Bored looking men in uniforms with weapons slung around their necks were milling about as a long line of cars waited their turn to be processed. As they watched, one of the vans from the warehouse they had just left approached the border crossing and was waved through, bypassing the line.

They watched for several moments, but there was nothing more really to see.

"I could do with some binoculars," Caleb said. "It's not really possible to see what's happening on the other side."

"Isn't looking at military installations with binoculars dangerous?" Phoebe asked him.

"Only if you get caught," Caleb replied with a grin. He pointed out of the passenger window at a small hill that overlooked the crossing point. It was bisected by two tall fences, around fifteen yards apart. "Can we get up there?"

AN HOUR LATER, having driven up and down the border in both directions for several miles, she sensed that Caleb was becoming frustrated. The tall fences that marked the border itself appeared to be continuous. They observed several patrols on either side and earned some curious looks from one on the Polish side, but Phoebe had just continued driving. Caleb had been able to see some of what was happening on the Belarusian side of the border crossing, as had Phoebe. The line of cars was much longer and didn't appear to be moving at all, but apart from that, it looked like a mirror image of the Polish side.

"Have you seen enough?" Phoebe asked Caleb. He nodded, looking resigned. "Let's find somewhere to stay. There were a couple of hotels back there. Shall we try them?" Caleb just nodded again.

The first hotel they visited was full, probably because it was a cheap looking affair that reminded Phoebe of some of the Russian hotels she had stayed in. From the various insignias on the vehicles in the lot outside, it was full of people from non-governmental organizations.

The second hotel was much grander and had its own

restaurant. Phoebe paid for a room, handing Caleb one of the key cards.

"Do you want to get some food?" she asked him.

"As long as it's not All Bran," Caleb replied, grinning at her.

They sat in the restaurant and while they waited for some sandwiches to be prepared, Phoebe asked Caleb what he thought about what they had seen earlier. She saw a look of disappointment on his face as she asked the question.

"I don't think it's going to be as straightforward as I thought," he said. "Perhaps if we find somewhere more remote, the border fences might not be quite as robust?"

Phoebe nodded in encouragement, but the fences she had seen looked pretty solid to her.

"We'll drop the medical supplies off at the warehouse," she said. "Then we can go for another drive if you want. A bit further this time?"

"Okay, that sounds like a plan. How are you feeling? You look pretty tired."

"I am," Phoebe replied. "Ready for bed, that's for sure."

"Me too," Caleb said. "I could do with some sleep." She looked at him, thinking back to their earlier conversation and what she had said to him in the van. Then she decided to throw caution to the wind.

"Who said anything about sleep?"

CHAPTER 91

"I don't understand," Mikhail said, leaning on his spade. "Why are we digging yet more trenches?" Grigor just laughed as he shoveled another mound of earth out of the ground.

"Because Vincuk told us to," the older man said, "and he's the boss."

"But why here?"

They were a couple of hundred yards away from the camp, and Mikhail could just see the cabin in the distance through the trees.

"It's a listening post," Grigor replied. "A small trench to hide in and listen out for the drone you heard last night. If you'd been paying attention in the briefing, you'd know that."

"I think Mikhail should be digging all the trenches," Ruslan said, also stopping to lean on his spade. Mikhail turned to look at him, but he had a smile on his face, as did Dmitry. "Seeing as it was him that heard the drone." With the exception of Mikhail, they all laughed.

"Come on you two," Grigor said, heaving another

mound of earth out of the shallow trench. "Keep digging. We've got more to do after this one."

THEY WERE JUST FINISHING the trench when Yuri walked over to join them some moments later. He nodded in appreciation at their efforts.

"Very good," Yuri said, pointing at the mound of earth they had produced. "That needs to be flattened out and then the trench needs to be covered with branches." Mikhail saw him looking around. They were close to the edge of the forest and there would be a good view of the surrounding terrain from the trench. "It's quite exposed here and we need to make sure we can't be seen."

"What do we do if we do see a drone, Yuri?" Ruslan asked. "Shoot it down?"

"If you want to give our exact position away to whoever's operating it, why not?" Yuri replied with a sneer. "No, Ruslan. You don't shoot it down. I've seen you shoot, anyway. The chances of you actually hitting it would be pretty slim." Mikhail saw Ruslan's face coloring as the others laughed at him.

"Mikhail could probably hit it," Grigor said. To Mikhail's surprise, Yuri nodded.

"He probably could," Yuri said, "but no one's taking pot-shots at a drone. If we see or hear anything, we leave."

"Why do we always have to run, Yuri?" Grigor asked. "Why don't we fight? That's what we signed up to do." Mikhail saw Grigor looking at him, Dmitry, and Ruslan in turn. "At least, that's what I signed up to do. I don't know about these children." He had a look of contempt on his face as he looked at them.

"Grigor," Yuri said, a note of frustration in his voice.

"There are six of us. We've got hardly any weapons, and the ones we have got are small arms. We've got nothing larger than a sniper rifle to fight with. The People's Army is much better armed, better trained, and there're more of them."

"I'm just saying," Grigor replied, "that just doing sneak attacks here and there isn't going to beat them."

"Sneak attacks here and there are debilitating," Yuri replied, and Mikhail was reminded of the way Mrs. Ananič used to speak to him and Felix when they didn't understand something. He would give anything to be back in her classroom now, not standing in a forest listening to Grigor and Yuri arguing. "It's not just about sneak attacks, though. Those photographs we took yesterday in the village?"

"What of them?" Grigor asked, his disdain still obvious.

"Those photographs and reports from other groups are on the news headlines around the world." Yuri lit up a cigarette, but didn't offer one to any of them. "The media is calling them war crimes, which is exactly what they are. World leaders are talking about them." He pointed his index finger at Grigor, prodding him hard in the chest. "We did that, Grigor. If we can't beat them with force, we can beat them with information."

"A few pictures of dead peasants isn't going to make a blind bit of difference, Yuri." Grigor took a pack of cigarettes from his own pocket and made a point of offering them around, but Mikhail declined. "The only thing the People's Army will understand is violence. The more we fight, the more people will join us. That's how we'll beat the People's Army."

"You're wrong, Grigor," Yuri said with a sigh. "Now, enough talking and more digging. Come back to the cabin when you've finished this trench. Vincuk is making us food."

Mikhail watched as Yuri walked away, watched by Grigor, whose expression hadn't changed.

"You heard the man," Grigor said as he ground his cigarette into the earth. "Let's just get this done so we can have some lunch."

CHAPTER 92

Caleb lay back on the bed, his eyes closed. He was exhausted but exhilarated at the same time.

"Well, that was a new one on me," he heard Phoebe say with a laugh. Caleb opened his eyes to look at her. She was wrapped in a sheet from the bed, wearing it like a makeshift toga. Her face and neck were flushed, and she was smiling broadly, showing off her dimples. Her hair was still damp from the shower, which was where they had begun. "My legs are already starting to ache. That was, erm..." Caleb waited as she searched for the right word to use. "Enthusiastic?"

"Especially when the hot water ran out," Caleb replied, remembering how Phoebe had squealed from the cold water. He had managed to turn the shower off, but they were both too caught up in the moment to leave the cubicle. The steam in the small bathroom had suited their mood perfectly.

"So, not a one night stand anymore, right?" he said. Her smile flickered, but only for a second.

"I already apologized for saying that, Caleb," Phoebe replied, leaning over to kiss him. "We fit together quite well, don't we?"

"I think we're designed to, Phoebe."

"Please, at least let my heart get back to normal before you quote anything at me, Caleb." Phoebe was smiling as she said this, fanning at her face with her hand. "I'm so warm. I think I need another shower." Caleb leaned forward and cupped her breast. He could feel her heart thudding in her chest and it pleased him as it matched his own. Phoebe was right. They did fit together very well.

"Me too," he murmured in her ear. "But I'm not sure the water will have heated back up yet."

"I meant, on my own," Phoebe replied. "We should get dressed. It's not long before the warehouse opens. Come on, lover boy. Get some clothes on."

Caleb laughed. "I've never been called lover boy before," he said, watching as Phoebe tried to get off the bed without the sheet sliding from her body. "Is that a British thing?"

"Is what a British thing?" she asked him.

"We've just shared the most intimate act that two people can share. I've touched every inch of your body, and you mine, and yet you seem embarrassed by your nakedness."

In response, Phoebe got to her feet and let the sheet slide to the floor. She stood, naked, and looked at him with her head tilted to one side.

"Happy now?" she asked, but his eyes never left hers.

"You're beautiful, Phoebe," Caleb said. "Every inch of you."

She looked at him, color returning to her cheeks, for a few seconds. She looked thoughtful, almost wistful. Caleb hadn't said that to reassure her, or to make her think of anything. He'd said it because it was true.

"Thank you, Caleb," Phoebe replied, her voice soft. "That's a lovely thing to say. Then a wry smile appeared on her face as she stooped to pick up the sheet. "I could make a joke about every inch of you," she said, her smile widening. "But that would be crude, and I'm not that kind of woman."

CHAPTER 93

Stepan examined the bullet ridden car which was half on and half off the road about fifty yards beyond their checkpoint. The air was full of the smell of cordite from the machine gun they had used to stop it and there were wisps of smoke rising from the wreckage.

"What do you think?" he heard one of his soldiers asking. He turned to see it was Daniel who was fast proving himself to be a competent young warrior. It was he who had initiated the firing on the vehicle when it had careered through their makeshift roadblock. "You think they're resistance?"

"They could be," Stepan said as he pulled his pistol from its holster. "Why else would they charge through the checkpoint?" He vaguely remembered seeing a woman's terrified face in the passenger seat of the car, but that meant nothing. Stepan was only too aware that the resistance could have women as well as men. What he would give to capture one of them. But from the amount of rounds that had thumped into the car, he doubted anyone inside it would have survived. "Come on, on me."

Stepan walked slowly toward the vehicle, Daniel a few yards to his right. Both of them had their weapons trained on it just in case. As he approached, he could hear the engine block ticking as it cooled down. The car was blue apart from where the bullets had chipped away the paint to expose the metal beneath. He could see the license plate hanging down, its Belarusian flag on the left hand side visible. There were at least ten holes in the rear window, and he was surprised it hadn't imploded. Several of the rounds had also impacted the windshield.

He slowed as he approached the driver's side of the car. There was a man slumped over the steering wheel, obviously dead. In the passenger seat was the woman he had seen, also motionless. Splashes of blood had painted the interior of the vehicle.

"Stepan?" Daniel asked, his voice quiet. He was on the other side of the car, peering into the passenger window. "Have you seen what's in the back?"

Stepan took a couple of steps forward and looked in through the rear window. There were two children's seats strapped into the seat, both of which were occupied. But apart from the ticking of the engine block, there was silence.

"Guess they weren't resistance, then," Stepan said to Daniel. He looked at the young soldier, whose face was ashen. "They shouldn't have tried to run, Daniel," Stepan said. "They brought this on themselves. Have you got a phone?"

Daniel nodded, although his eyes were fixed on the two car seats.

"Yes, of course," he replied.

"Take some photographs," Stepan said. "We can claim the resistance did this."

Stepan watched as Daniel slung his rifle across his back

and pulled out his phone. His hands were trembling as he took some photographs.

"We can claim we came across the resistance and went after them when we saw what they had done." Stepan saw Daniel nodding again, but he didn't look convinced. "Once you're done, go back to the roadblock and get the others. We need to push the car off the road. Maybe if we flip it onto its roof, it would look better?"

Daniel put his phone back into his pocket and started walking back to the rest of the squad. His head was lowered and he was staring at the ground as he trudged along the road. Stepan was shaking his head, wondering how best to toughen him up, when he heard a soft whimper coming from the car. He flipped his head around to look inside, his pistol aimed straight out in front of him. It was the female passenger who had made the noise. Stepan watched as she moved her arm a couple of inches and he adjusted the pistol so the barrel was pointing directly at her. Her eyelids fluttered as she struggled to open them. When they finally opened, Stepan saw they were as blue as the water of Lake Bailkal where he had holidayed as a child. She blinked once and opened her mouth as if to say something.

Stepan swore under his breath as he pulled the trigger.

CHAPTER 94

Caleb watched as two men, both wearing blue coveralls, approached the van. He had already opened the rear door after Phoebe had parked it in the loading bay of the warehouse. A couple of the boxes had shifted at some point during the journey, but nothing appeared to be damaged.

"Good afternoon," he said to the first of the men who just looked at him curiously. "Do you want me to help you?" The man shrugged his shoulders before saying something to his colleague in a language Caleb didn't recognize. They walked up to the rear of the van and started unloading the boxes, waving Caleb away when he went to help them.

With nothing to do, Caleb looked around the loading bay. Their van was one of several being unloaded, and Caleb was impressed at the quiet efficiency of the people doing the unloading. They worked almost in silence, depositing the boxes in a cluster in the center of the bay where a man with a clipboard inspected their contents before directing most of the boxes somewhere within the warehouse itself. Some sort of triage area, Caleb assumed.

Some of the boxes were loaded straight into World Health Organization vans, their logos clearly visible on the doors. The man with the clipboard nodded in appreciation as he pulled out a packet of bandages that were impregnated with a quick clotting agent from one of Caleb's boxes. When he saw Caleb watching him, the man raised a thumb in acknowledgement.

A little way from the van, Phoebe was on her cell phone, deep in conversation with someone. Caleb wandered over to her, realizing she wasn't speaking English, but her enthusiasm told him the conversation was going in the right direction. He felt slightly left out, not understanding what anyone around him was saying.

While he waited for Phoebe to finish her call, Caleb thought back over their reconnaissance mission earlier that day. He'd not said anything to Phoebe, but it hadn't gone anywhere near as well as he'd hoped it would. They had driven perhaps three or four miles along the border but the fences had remained in place. He could see from the tracks on either side of them that they were regularly patrolled, even in areas a long way from any sort of civilization. Caleb had hoped that as the area got more remote, the fences would have become less secure, but this wasn't the case.

He'd seen a pair of cameras every few hundred yards. One would be a normal camera, the other would be an infra-red camera, and both had motion sensors mounted below them. Caleb knew there wouldn't be anyone continually watching them, but he imagined there would be a control room somewhere. The moment any motion was detected, an alarm would sound and trigger a response. Caleb doubted the entire border was so secure. They were going to have to look further afield for the opportunity to cross, but time wasn't on their side.

Caleb crouched down to look underneath the van, wriggling himself underneath it. On the news in England a few days previously, a prisoner had managed to escape from a high security prison by strapping himself under a food delivery truck, but this van had no room for a similar attempt. Even if it had, if Anton was as sick as Phoebe seemed to think he was, he would be in no position to be strapped underneath a vehicle. In addition to that, there was the issue of getting over the border itself.

"What on earth are you doing down there, Caleb?"

Caleb turned to see Phoebe's feet next to him. He shuffled out from under the van and got to his feet, brushing some dust from his knees as he did so.

"I was just looking under the van," he replied. Phoebe looked at him as somewhere in the distance, a bell tolled. Around them, the men who had been unloading the vans stopped and started walking toward a door. Caleb glanced in the back of their own van to see there were only a few boxes left to unload.

"Looks like it's coffee time," Phoebe said, watching them leave. Then she turned to face Caleb. "I spoke to the hospital here. If we can get Anton to them, they can treat him." He looked at her, wondering how best to tell her that getting him there might be an issue. "Do you want to grab those boxes?" Phoebe said, nodding at the van. She had a peculiar expression on her face which piqued Caleb's curiosity, but he said nothing about it.

"Sure," Caleb replied. He walked to the rear of the van and climbed into it. There were only four boxes left, so it wouldn't take more than a couple of journeys to deposit them in the sorting area. He stooped over to pick up the first box when he heard the van's roller door starting to rattle. By the time he turned around, the door had been closed.

"Phoebe?" Caleb called out. "What are you doing?" There was no reply. All Caleb heard was the sound of the van door being locked.

CHAPTER 95

Phoebe put the van into park and breathed a sigh of relief. That had been a lot more nerve wracking than she had imagined but at least Caleb had got the message to remain silent pretty quickly. She opened the driver's door and climbed out, taking a few deep breaths as she did so. Then she walked around the van to the rear and unlocked the door, sliding the rolling door up.

In the rear of the van, sitting on a box with a furious expression on his face, was Caleb. She looked at him and, not being able to help herself, she laughed. It was partly in relief at what she had just done, and partly because of his face. He uncrossed his arms and got to his feet, still looking more irritated than she'd ever seen him.

"I hope you're going to tell me what that was about," Caleb said as he clambered down from the van. Phoebe was still laughing as she watched him taking in their surroundings, blinking in the bright sunshine. The van was parked just off a main road in open countryside. "Phoebe, would you stop laughing and tell me what the hell is going on?"

"I'm sorry, Caleb," Phoebe replied, still giggling. "It was a spur-of-the-moment decision."

"What was? To lock me in the van like a prisoner?"

"No, to do what I did. It was when I saw the workers disappearing that I decided." Phoebe spread her arms out at the countryside. "What do you think?"

"What do I think about what?" he replied, his anger starting to fade.

"What do you think about Belarus?" Phoebe said with a broad smile. "Quite nice, isn't it?"

"What?" Caleb asked, his expression morphing instantly to surprise. "We're over the border?" She just nodded in response, still smiling at him. "How?"

Phoebe took a couple of steps to the side of the van, pulling Caleb with her. Then she pointed at the driver's door. She saw his eyebrows go up as he took in the magnetic World Health Organization sign that now covered the hire company logo.

"We just drove through," Phoebe replied. "All I got from the guards was a friendly wave." She saw him glance at the lanyard hanging around her neck. It had the words *World Health Organization* on the material, and the photograph on the ID card was of a man, not a woman, but no-one had looked at it. She felt bad about taking the lanyard, but it had been on the driver's seat of the van she'd peeled the magnetic signs from. All she had done was wave it in the direction of the guard.

"You're joking," Caleb said, a smile finally appearing on his face. "You just drove across the border. How are we going to get back?"

"The same way," Phoebe replied. "As I was coming across the border, I passed another van with the WHO logo coming in the other direction." She didn't tell Caleb that the van had been stopped, and that she had seen the driver handing something to the Belarusian guard. The van had been too far away for her to see exactly what it was that had changed hands, but her guess was that it was cash.

"That's genius. The KISS principle in action." Caleb's smile gave way to a laugh as he hugged Phoebe, briefly lifting her off her feet.

"Put me down, you big oaf," Phoebe said, slapping him on the shoulder. "What's the KISS principle?"

"Keep It Simple, Stupid," Caleb said as he let go of her. "So, what, we go and get Anton and drive him back over in the van?"

Phoebe nodded her head. "Yep, why not?"

"What if the hospital won't release him?"

"Trust me, they will," Phoebe replied. "The doctor I spoke to said they were full to overflowing and had hardly any supplies. If we turn up and offer to take a seriously injured patient off their hands, they'll be happy to let him go." She watched as Caleb processed the information for a few seconds. Then he nodded.

"It could work," he said quietly. "But what if they stop us at the border? I don't know about you, but I don't fancy spending time in a Belarusian jail."

"Me neither, but we've got to give it a go." She playfully punched his arm, but her face was serious. "Have some faith, Caleb."

Caleb closed his eyes and Phoebe saw his lips moving briefly. When he reopened them, his eyes were dark and full of foreboding.

"Okay, Phoebe," he said as he walked around the front of the van. "Let's do this."

CHAPTER 96

Caleb thought about Phoebe's plan as they drove toward Lida where the hospital Anton was being kept in was located. He had been surprised when he realized the maps on the GPS included Belarus, but there was no reason for them not to. Using Phoebe's phone, he had tapped in the address of the hospital, which was just over an hour away.

As they passed through several small villages, Caleb looked out of the passenger window to see people going about their business. The fact that life had to go on, despite conflict, was lost on many. But people had to eat, to work, and to live as normally as they could. Compared to Poland, the houses looked older, more run down, and there were fewer businesses at the side of the road. The ones that were there looked to be pretty informal. They drove past a farm truck laden with vegetables, a small crowd of women gathered round it. There was a cafe which looked to be being run from someone's house with a pair of elderly men sitting outside in plastic chairs. They both stared at the van as it passed them, neither returning Caleb's wave.

"It's a bit different, isn't it?" Phoebe said as they jolted over a large pothole in the road.

"It is, and it isn't," Caleb replied. He'd been to many similar areas in the past, both officially and unofficially. "Different to Poland, yes, but the same as a lot of other places."

They approached a large sign on the side of the road. Caleb saw Phoebe nodding at it.

"Isn't that where Natasha lives?" she asked him. Caleb looked at the sign which was telling them Hrodna was only five miles away. He thought it was, but he consulted Natasha's printed information to double check.

"Yes, it is," he replied.

"I could drop you here to start looking for Mikhail if you want?" Phoebe said. "I could carry on to Lida to get Anton and meet you in Hrodna somewhere?"

"No, I think it's better if we stick together. We'll need someone in the back with Anton." He saw Phoebe nodding in agreement.

"Okay, I just wanted to check."

An hour later, Phoebe maneuvered the van into an ambulance bay outside the hospital in Lida. The hospital itself was housed in a squat, utilitarian building consisting of four floors. Caleb knew precious little about architecture, but the building looked to him to be a large concrete block surrounded by several smaller concrete blocks. An awning covered the main entrance and, as they made their way toward it, Caleb saw Phoebe hiding the identification badge she had borrowed in her blouse, leaving only the lanyard and its text visible.

The change in Phoebe as she approached the reception desk was remarkable. Although Caleb couldn't understand anything she was saying to the dour-faced receptionist,

Phoebe's tone was commanding. She sounded like a woman who was going to take no nonsense and, in no time at all, they were making their way to the ward where Anton was. The interior of the hospital matched the exterior and they passed several medical personnel, including one with streaks of blood down the front of his scrubs. Tattered posters lined the walls with Cyrillic script on them that Caleb didn't understand. There was an underlying sense of resignation on the faces of the medics they passed, and Caleb wrinkled his nose at the smell in the corridor. It was mostly disinfectant, but there was something just underneath the acrid smell of antiseptic. Something much more fetid.

When Caleb and Phoebe arrived on the ward, they had not exchanged a single word. A nurse pointed them toward one of the single rooms.

"I'll find the doctor," Phoebe said, her voice low as if she didn't want the nurse to hear them speaking English. "You go and introduce yourself to Anton."

Caleb nodded and walked over to the door the nurse had indicated. He paused, not wanting to walk straight in, and rapped his knuckles softly on it. When he heard a male voice calling out, Caleb opened the door and walked in.

The only thing inside the room was a single bed with a bedside table a couple of yards away from it. On the ceiling, a pair of florescent tubes hummed, but apart from that, the room was silent. Lying listlessly on the bed, beyond the reach of the jug of water and glass on the table, was a swarthy man in mismatched pajamas. His face was florid and mottled, and a thin sheen of perspiration could be seen on his forehead.

"Anton?" Caleb said as the man regarded him with dark eyes. "Natasha has sent us to get you out of here."

The man said nothing, and Caleb suddenly realized he might not speak English. But then noticed his eyes had widened slightly at Caleb's words.

"Thank you," Anton replied a few seconds later, his accent heavy.

Caleb took a few steps into the room. He picked up the jug of water and filled the glass before pushing the table to within Anton's reach. Then he stood and watched as Anton picked up the glass, his fingers trembling, in case the man needed any help.

As he stood there, Caleb tried to keep his expression neutral, but he was finding it difficult. The smell from earlier, the odor underneath the antiseptic in the corridors, was much stronger in this room. Caleb had smelled it before.

It was the smell of death.

CHAPTER 97

"I need to speak to Doctor Suskevich," Phoebe said to the nurse sitting behind the desk who was regarding her with a look of suspicion. Phoebe knew her accent was very good, but it wasn't a Belarusian one which was probably the reason for the distrust. "Could you tell him that Doctor Sokolova is here to see him?" She smiled at the nurse, but tried to keep her eyes determined. Phoebe was hoping that the use of the formal title would do the job.

The nurse slowly got to her feet. Like the other medical personnel Phoebe had seen, the woman looked exhausted but Phoebe didn't have time for any sympathy.

"He may be in surgery," the nurse replied, "but I will check for you."

"Thank you."

A few moments later, the nurse returned to her desk. She was followed by a slim man in his early forties who was wearing a white coat several sizes too large for him over green scrubs. He had a stethoscope around his neck and a pair of bright orange Croc shoes on his feet. He had one hand extended before he even reached Phoebe and was clutching a manila folder in the other.

"Doctor Sokolova," the new arrival said. "I'm Doctor Suskevich. Yefrem, please."

"Pleased to meet you, Yefrem," Phoebe said as she shook his hand. She liked the nervous energy he was exuding. It was a sharp contrast to every other member of staff she had seen in the building. "I'm Phoebe. We spoke on the phone?"

"We did, we did. You are Russian?" Yefrem asked.

Phoebe laughed. Whether he'd intended it or not, she would take the compliment. "No, I'm English, but I lived in Russia for a while. I trained in Moscow."

"Me also," he said, his eyes lighting up. "Which school?"

"Moscow Medical Academy."

"Ah, I went to Moscow State University. We are rivals, yes?"

"Only at Bandy," Phoebe replied with a laugh. She remembered the exuberance of the annual Russian Hockey competition between the two medical schools well. If there wasn't at least one fractured bone per side, it was declared a non-event even though they were all doctors. "Can we talk about Anton Zaystev?"

"Of course," Yefrem replied, pointing at the same door that Caleb had entered. "He's in there."

"I know, my colleague is with him."

"He's a doctor, your colleague?" Yefrem asked. Phoebe paused for a second before nodding her head.

"Yes," she replied. "We want to take him with us. To Poland."

"To Poland? Do you have transport?"

"Yes, we have a..." Phoebe stopped herself just in time. She'd almost referred to their van. "We have an ambulance outside."

Yefrem gestured to a couple of tatty seats near the nurses' station. They both sat down and he opened the manila folder in his head.

"So, Mr. Zaystev suffered a mine blast just over a week ago," Yefrem said. Phoebe raised her eyebrows, surprised he'd survived this long from her earlier conversation with the doctor. "He's got a tangential shrapnel injury of the outer surface of the left knee joint with soft tissue defect. There's also a fracture of the upper third of the tibia with fragment displacement." She watched as Yefrem ran his finger down the medical notes in the folder. "Compartment syndrome of the left shin of moderate severity. Two rounds of surgery so far, but the wound is deeply infected."

Phoebe shook her head in sadness. The chances were that even if Anton survived the next few days, he would lose his leg. "I'm surprised you've not amputated."

"That was going to be our next step, but he's become septic, so it's probably too late for that without the right antibiotics." Phoebe shook her head again. Sepsis was a life threatening condition where the body's immune system overreacted to an infection. It was treatable in many cases, but the mortality rate was high. Without the right antibiotics, it was almost a hundred percent. "When do you want to transfer him?" Yefrem asked.

"Now?" Phoebe replied. If Yefrem was surprised by her reply, he didn't show it.

"Okay, I'll need to do a discharge summary."

"There's no need, Yefrem," Phoebe said, resting her hand on his arm for a few seconds. Then she tapped the manila folder. "It's all in there, right?"

"Yes, but you'll want the x-rays." Yefrem called out to the nurse, who got to her feet reluctantly. While they waited for her return, Yefrem asked Phoebe why she was doing this. "Why this man?" he asked. "What is he to you?"

"His wife is a friend of my colleague," Phoebe replied.

"You've got the paperwork to get him over the border?" Phoebe didn't reply, but her eyes obviously gave her away. "Have you got any paperwork to get over the border?"

"No, but I have got a plan of sorts."

Yefrem beckoned to Phoebe to get her to lean in closer to him. Then he whispered in her ear.

"It wasn't a mine strike that caused the wounds," Yefrem said. "It was a bullet. I know because I took it out myself. But I didn't write that in the notes. This so-called People's Army?" She saw him glance at the desk where the nurse had been sitting. "They have eyes and ears everywhere."

She nodded as he continued talking and as the nurse came back with a folder full of x-rays, he looked at her and smiled. The nurse hadn't noticed him pressing something into Phoebe's hand.

"Good luck, Doctor Sokolova," he said. "You're going to need it."

CHAPTER 98

Natasha was sitting in Heidi's armchair, more asleep than awake, when she realized her phone was ringing. The television was on in the corner of the room, showing a game show with an over enthusiastic host who was trying his hardest to get the audience going, but the sound was turned down. She picked up the phone to see it was an incoming WhatsApp call from a British number she didn't recognize.

"Hello?" Natasha said after swiping at the screen.

"Natasha?" a female voice said. "It's Phoebe."

"Phoebe?" Natasha replied, blinking and sitting up straight in the chair. "Is everything okay?"

"Everything's fine, Natasha," Phoebe replied in Russian. "I'm going to turn the video on. There's someone who wants to talk to you."

Natasha pulled the phone away from her ear and stared at the screen. It flickered a couple of times, and she gasped loudly when she saw whose face was on it.

"Anton! Oh, Anton!"

Natasha reached out with her index finger and

traced his face as she saw him smiling weakly. Her finger shaking, she managed to turn her own camera on. A few seconds later, when her face appeared in a small window on the screen, his smile broadened. He looked awful. His skin was blotchy and the red patches looked like sunburn, but he was alive and he was smiling at her.

"Hey, you," Anton said, just as he had done hundreds of times over the years. It was how he always greeted her. Even when he woke up next to her, the first words he said were *hey, you*.

"Hey, you," Natasha whispered, tracing his face again. "How are you doing?" She watched as his smile faded for a few seconds before he made a concerted effort to hike it back up.

"I've been better, to be honest. How's Mikhail? Ilja? Are they well?" Anton's voice was almost indistinct, and she could tell he was struggling just to talk.

"They're fine, everything's fine," Natasha said. Now wasn't the time to let Anton know Mikhail was missing.

"Good," Anton replied, closing his eyes. "That's good to hear." His face relaxed and his smile faded away.

The screen shifted slightly and the next face she saw was Caleb's.

"I think he's asleep," Caleb said, his face flickering. "We're leaving for Poland in a few moments, but he wanted to speak to you before the journey."

"Oh, Caleb, I can't thank you enough," Natasha replied, switching to English. The tears that had been threatening started running down her face. To her surprise, Caleb laughed.

"No, I can't take the credit for this." The phone moved again and Natasha could see Phoebe, her face next to

Caleb's. "This is all on Phoebe. All I've done is come along for the ride."

"I've arranged a bed in Poland for Anton," Natasha heard Phoebe say. "I just spoke to the nursing staff there and they're waiting for him. They'll start treating him the moment he arrives."

"I'm flying to Poland tomorrow afternoon," Natasha said. "Into Warsaw, but I'll hire a car. Can you message me the hospital's details?"

"Of course," Phoebe replied. Natasha saw her and Caleb exchange a smile. "And I'll send you a text the minute we get to the hospital."

When she ended the call, Natasha put the phone on the chair and held her face in her hands. She sobbed loudly, her relief almost overwhelming.

"Is everything okay?" Heidi asked from the door to the lounge. Natasha put her hands down and looked at her.

"Anton's okay," she said. "I just spoke to him."

"Oh, Natasha, that's fantastic news," Heidi said, crossing the room and throwing her arms out. Natasha got to her feet and let the other woman hug her, which only prompted more tears. Then Natasha pulled back from the hug and looked at Heidi with an expression of horror on her face.

"What is it?" Heidi asked her. "What's wrong?"

Natasha felt sick as she realized she'd completely forgotten to ask about Mikhail.

CHAPTER 99

C aleb sat on the box in the rear of the van as it drove along, swaying from side to side. The only illumination was from a small overhead bulkhead light in the ceiling, and in the dim light, Anton looked even worse than he had back at the hospital. His florid face appeared ashen, and several times, Caleb caught himself studying the man carefully to make sure he was still breathing. They had been in the van for a couple of hours, so they couldn't be that far from the border.

He closed his eyes and started mentally reciting a version of the ritual prayers of the *Commendation of the Dying and Prayers for the Dead*. Caleb was careful not to speak out loud in case Anton heard and recognized the words, although he doubted he would. From what Phoebe had told Caleb after they had carefully loaded Anton into the back of the van, helped by Doctor Suskevich and a hospital orderly whose only distinguishing feature was the gold cross he wore around his neck, Anton might not survive the journey. Caleb had chosen the Catholic version of the prayers purely because he was familiar with them.

Given their location, the Eastern Orthodox prayer of *The Office at the Parting of the Soul From the Body* may have been more appropriate, but prayer was prayer and Caleb knew God was always watching and listening. Even on a Thursday evening, but Caleb would make up that particular earlier transgression in due course.

"Are you praying?" Caleb heard Anton whisper above the low thrum of the van. He looked at him, but Anton's eyes were still closed.

"I am, Anton, yes," Caleb replied.

"Why?" Anton asked, opening his eyes by only half an inch.

"It's what I do."

"Am I dying?" Anton asked.

We're all dying, Anton, Caleb thought. *Death is like comedy. It's all a matter of timing.* He smiled, but didn't think Anton saw him doing so.

"We're talking now, so you're still alive." Caleb replied in a soft voice.

"Are you a religious man?" Anton's voice was so low, Caleb struggled to hear him. He leaned toward the man and tried to ignore the sour smell of his breath and the underlying scent of decay.

"Not really," Caleb said, "but I am a man of faith."

"My father used to tell me," Anton replied, "that when death is approaching, God sends a messenger to those who he courts." Caleb said nothing, reflecting on the language Anton had just used. God courting people close to death wasn't a concept he was familiar with. In Caleb's experience, it was usually the other way round. "But so does the Devil." Anton took a deep breath and then opened his eyes fully. "Who sent you, Caleb?"

"No one sent me," Caleb replied after taking a few

seconds to consider the question. Natasha hadn't asked him to come, and she certainly hadn't sent him. Given Anton's statement about either God or the Devil sending a messenger to collect souls, it wasn't a question he was going to answer. "I am just here."

"But why?"

"Because I have to be somewhere," Caleb said. "You should rest, Anton. Preserve your strength. Natasha is flying from England to see you."

"So she got a ballot ticket." Caleb saw a faint smile on his face. "And my son?" Anton asked. "Mikhail? Where is he?"

"I don't know," Caleb replied. This wasn't the time to lie to the man. "But as soon as you're in hospital in Poland, I'm coming back to look for him."

Anton closed his eyes again after nodding his head once. As he watched him, Caleb heard three soft knocks on the divider separating the front and rear of the van. It was Phoebe warning him the van was approaching the border. A few moments later, the vehicle began to slow down, and he heard a muffled male voice shouting something in Russian.

The van slowed to a halt, and Caleb closed his eyes, muttering another prayer under his breath. But this one wasn't for Anton, not directly anyway. It was for Phoebe.

It was time to see if her plan worked in both directions.

CHAPTER 100

Phoebe's heart was in her mouth as she watched the Belarusian soldier approaching the van. She clenched and unclenched her hands on the steering wheel before winding down the driver's side window. She'd hoped that they would just wave her through as she had seen previously, but there was no mistaking the soldier's raised hand or the barrier that was blocking the road in front of her.

"Good evening," Phoebe said, hoping her nervousness wasn't obvious in her voice. She looked at the soldier as he peered inside the front of the van. He was younger than her by a couple of years and had a single stripe on his sleeve. While Phoebe had no idea about the rank structure of the Belarusian army, his age and the single stripe would make him relatively junior.

"Good evening," the soldier replied, his expression blank. "Identification, please?"

Phoebe fumbled for her lanyard as her heart rate increased. Her plan was to wave the identification card at him quickly and hope the poor light would help her, but to her dismay, he held his hand out for the card. Then he pulled a small flashlight from his pocket and used it to examine the photograph. When his eyes met hers, he had a look of surprise on his face.

"This isn't you," he said, glancing at a small hut where a small group of soldiers was standing.

"Yes, it is," Phoebe said quickly, trying to get his attention away from the hut. "May I?" She gave him the sweetest smile she could as she took the card back from him. Then, hoping she wasn't overdoing it, she let a look of horror appear on her face. "Oh, no. I don't believe it." The soldier said nothing, but at least his attention was on her and not on the other soldiers. "It's my boss's lanyard. I must have picked it up by mistake." She allowed a quiver into her voice, again hoping she wasn't overdoing it. "He's going to kill me."

"Do you have your identification card?" the soldier asked.

"He's a monster," Phoebe replied, trying to sound as if she was on the verge of tears. "I am going to be in so much trouble if he finds out." As she spoke, she made a show of pretending to look for her own identification card.

The soldier glanced again at the hut, but when he turned to look again at Phoebe, there was the faintest hint of sympathy on his face.

"Is there anything you can do?" Phoebe asked, also looking at the hut. She aimed for a conspiratorial look at the young man. He would have a boss, perhaps at the hut, and would no doubt know what it was like to be on the wrong end of a tongue lashing. "My identification card must be back at the World Health Organization depot. Is there anything you can do to help me?"

"Do you have any other identification?" the soldier asked.

"Of course," Phoebe replied, brightening her voice. "I have my passport." She fumbled in her bag, looking down to make sure she pulled out her Russian passport, not her British one. Phoebe handed the document to the soldier. "Please don't laugh at my photo."

His expression didn't change at her joke and the sympathetic expression she thought she'd seen had disappeared. The soldier glanced at the passport and handed it back to her.

"This is highly irregular," he said, his face hardening. "You have no paperwork to go with the passport." The soldier looked again at the hut with his colleagues and, as Phoebe followed his gaze, she saw one of the other soldiers staring back at them.

Phoebe reached back into her bag and slipped something into the passport. Then she handed it back to the soldier.

"I'm sorry, I forgot," Phoebe said, Yefrem's words in the hospital coming back to her. "The paperwork's in there now."

When the soldier handed the passport back to Phoebe, the two hundred roubles she had slid into the back were gone.

He took a step back and waved his hand at the soldiers by the hut.

Phoebe wasn't able to see exactly how he was waving, but a few seconds later, the barrier started rising. She started the van, pressing her lips together to stop the smile she could feel forming.

They were through.

CHAPTER 101

Caleb and Phoebe were watching the activity in the resuscitation room through a porthole style window in the door. She was gripping his hand tightly, and Caleb knew that she wanted to be in the room with the other medical personnel, but this wasn't her hospital so that wasn't an option. Beyond the window there was a team of men and women, all wearing green scrubs, bustling about a gurney on which Anton was lying.

When they had arrived at the hospital a few moments earlier, it had been a couple of members of this team who had unloaded Anton from the mattress he was lying on, placing him on the gurney. Caleb and Phoebe had tried to help, but had been politely pushed away. The only thing they could do was follow the gurney as it was pushed into the Ostry Dyżur, or emergency department. At the door to the resuscitation room, one of the medical staff had stopped them.

"You can look in through the window," the nurse or doctor had said, "but you must remain outside."

"What are they doing?" Caleb asked Phoebe. He was

bemused by the activity. It was like some sort of ballet, with the medical personnel moving around each other as if they knew not only their own roles, but everyone else's as well. There was a man at the head of the gurney holding an anesthetic mask attached to a bag over Anton's face. To his left, another man was preparing some sort of medication in syringes and at the foot of the gurney, a woman was standing by a chart mounted to an easel. Every minute or so, she was looking at a screen attached to the wall which had a multitude of colored lines. Next to the screen was a medic wearing a light blue surgical mask who was just watching what was going on.

"I think they're going to intubate him," Phoebe replied. "Put him into a medical coma."

"What, a life support machine?" Caleb asked. His thoughts turned to Natasha, who would be on her way to Poland in less than twenty four hours. Should he call her and tell her to get an earlier flight?

"Of sorts, yes."

Caleb watched as Anton was given a cocktail of drugs through a cannula in his forearm. The man holding the mask squeezed the bag several times before placing it down and tilting Anton's head back. He used a stainless steel contraption to open Anton's mouth before sliding a blue plastic tube into his throat. Caleb looked away. It wasn't that he was squeamish. He just felt uncomfortable seeing how vulnerable Anton was.

As if she sensed his discomfort, Phoebe squeezed his hand.

"He's in excellent hands, Caleb," she said. "Why don't we go and get a drink while they're working on him?"

Caleb allowed Phoebe to lead him away from the door to the resuscitation room. A few moments later, they were sitting in a waiting area with a vending machine, sipping strong coffee from plastic cups.

"I've watched a lot of resuscitations, Caleb," Phoebe said as she looked at him over the top of her cup. "That team is excellent. They were working almost in silence. Did you see the woman in charge?"

Caleb thought for a moment before replying. "Was she the one by the chart, writing everything down?"

"No," Phoebe replied with a smile. "That's probably the most junior medic in the room. It was the one in the surgical mask."

"But she wasn't doing anything."

"That's my point. She didn't need to. Like I said, that's a very competent team." She sipped her drink. "One of the unintended consequences of the war in Ukraine," Phoebe said, "is that there's a whole new generation of medical personnel who are experts in combat trauma."

Caleb nodded in reply. He'd not thought about it like that.

"Are you hungry?" he asked her. "We should get some food."

"You have to try some pierogi while you're in Poland," Phoebe replied.

"What's that? Please don't tell me it's some sort of blood pudding."

"No, it's boiled dumplings with a filling. I'm not a massive fan, but it's pretty much the national dish."

"Okay," Caleb said, nodding his head. "And after that?" He looked at Phoebe and she gave him a wry smile.

"You want to head back over the border, don't you?"

"Ideally, yes."

"We can't look for Mikhail at night, Caleb."

"We could make a start. There were a couple of hotels in

Hrodna," Caleb said. "I can't see them being full, can you? We could check a few places this evening and then be in place for first thing tomorrow."

"Why don't we wait until Anton's settled on the ward," Phoebe replied, taking another sip of her coffee. "They'll be transferring him to the intensive care unit." Then she sighed and looked thoughtful for a few seconds. "We'll leave after that."

Caleb smiled at her, knowing she would rather have stayed in Poland for the night.

"You're the boss," he said, hoping she would return his smile.

"But I get to choose the filling in your dumplings," Phoebe replied a moment later, finally doing as he had hoped. "And you have to eat them."

CHAPTER 102

V incuk wrinkled his nose at the fetid odor coming out of the deep trench latrine. He made a note to himself to get the youngsters to dig a new one the next day, and fill this one in. Vincuk knew they would complain, but this trench had run its course. He finished his business and zipped his fly, wiping his hands on the back of his trousers as he did so. It wasn't as if they had anywhere to wash them, and they had some hand sanitizer back in the cabin, anyway.

He turned and walked back in the direction of the cabin. The last rays of sunlight were just about to disappear from the sky, and he thought about the four young men lying in the ditches they had constructed earlier. All they had been told to do was to watch and listen for any signs of a drone. It was about this time the previous evening that Mikhail had reported hearing one. If the boy had been right, Vincuk knew it wouldn't be an isolated incident. The People's Army wouldn't only do a single reconnaissance mission. They would do several to try to establish their targets daily routine. That was why he had left Yuri sitting by the fire, pretending to cook.

As he approached the fire, he realized he couldn't see Yuri. Vincuk swore under his breath.

"One job, Yuri," he muttered. "I gave you one job." Of all the men in his small squad, Vincuk expected Yuri to follow orders. Then he heard his second in command calling out in a stage whisper from the direction of the cabin.

"Vincuk," Yuri said. "You need to get in here and listen to this."

Vincuk made his way to the cabin where Yuri was standing in the doorway, waiting for him.

"What is it, Yuri?" Vincuk said when he reached the door. "You're supposed to be by the fire. What if the drone comes back?"

"Never mind the drone, Vincuk," Yuri replied, and Vincuk caught the note of excitement in his voice. In his hand, he was clutching his phone and Vincuk saw the screen was lit up. "Come on."

Vincuk walked into the cabin, which was full of cigarette smoke. Yuri followed him, placing the phone on the table on top of the map. Then he poked at the screen.

"Uladzimir?" Yuri said into the handset. "You're on speaker." Vincuk knew whoever Yuri was talking to, they weren't called Uladzimir.

"Is your number one there?" a male voice replied.

"Yes, he's here," Yuri said. "Can you repeat what you just told me? I have the map here."

"Number one? Listen in. There's a compound we've identified." As the man on the phone spoke, Yuri indicated an area on the map with a fine pencil line already drawn around it. "It's the main base for the People's Army in the area. We estimate twenty to thirty men, several vehicles. Mostly small arms weapons, some machine guns and what we think are RPGs."

Vincuk whistled through his teeth. "You're sure?"

"Affirmative," the man replied. "We've had eyes on for a few days now and are tracking their movements. You'll tell him the rest, number two? We've been on this line for long enough already."

Vincuk looked at Yuri, who was grinning broadly. "Yes," Yuri said. "I'll take it from here."

There was an electronic click as Uladzimir, or whatever his name was, ended the call.

"Okay," Yuri said, shaking a cigarette loose from his pack and offering one to Vincuk. "There'll be five groups of us in total." He pointed his unlit cigarette at an area on the map to the north of the compound. "We've got this sector. The attack signal is a white flare."

"When do we attack?" Vincuk asked him, feeling nervous but excited at the same time.

"1600 hours tomorrow."

"Why the afternoon?" Vincuk asked. "Wouldn't it make more sense to go in at dawn? While they're all sleeping?" Although dawn was the most obvious time to launch an attack, it was also the most effective.

"Because many of the groups will have left before sunrise," Yuri explained. "They pre-position themselves near the villages they're hitting. 1600 is when they're all in the compound."

"We could attack during the daytime," Vincuk said. "Destroy their compound and capture a lot of their equipment."

"Uladzimir said 1600, Vincuk." Yuri's voice was even but

Vincuk understood the mild rebuke. He'd not been questioning Uladzimir's judgement, but thinking out loud.

Orders were orders, so 1600 it was.

CHAPTER 103

P hoebe handed the youths standing in front of her and Caleb a photograph of Mikhail.

"Do you know this boy?" she asked them in Russian, watching as they examined the photograph. "Or where he might be?" Both of them shook their heads.

"No, sorry," the one she had handed the photo to replied with a nervous look at Caleb. They were standing in a park close to the center of Hrodna, one of the locations Natasha had said Mikhail went to quite often.

"Ask him if he knows anyone who's fighting for Belarus?" Caleb asked Phoebe in English.

"No, Caleb," Phoebe replied. "They're jittery enough already, and apparently I have a Russian accent. If I ask them that, they'll just run." She looked again at the two boys. They were perhaps the same age as Mikhail, and Caleb's presence was obviously making them uncomfortable, probably because he was speaking English. But there was no way she was going to wander around a park at night in any city on her own.

The previous few hours had been fruitless. They had

crossed the border without incident, the same guard as before waving the van through. He had even smiled at Phoebe as he had done so, no doubt anticipating a further contribution to his wallet if he was still on duty when she returned. Phoebe knew two hundred rubles wasn't a lot of money—around eighty US dollars—but she intended to take some cash out of an ATM, both to pay Yefrem back and to have some for the return journey. A journey which hopefully would be with Mikhail accompanying Caleb in the rear of the van, but that wasn't looking likely just yet.

Their first stop in Belarus had been at one of the hotels Caleb had seen earlier that day. In comparison, the Polish hotel they had stayed in was almost opulent, but this one was also much cheaper. They'd not even seen the room yet, but had checked in and had keys, so at least they knew they had somewhere to sleep. Their second stop had been to the house where Mikhail's best friend, Felix, lived but the house was empty when they visited.

Caleb reached into his pocket and pulled out two miniature bottles of vodka. Phoebe glanced down at them, realizing they were from the minibar back in the Polish hotel. He jiggled them in his hand to ensure that the two boys saw them.

"Ask them to take another look at the photograph," Caleb said. He nodded at one of the youths. "Especially that one. He barely looked at the photo."

Phoebe did as Caleb asked, wondering if he had emptied the entire minibar into his pockets. She handed the photograph of Mikhail back to the boys, this time handing it to the one Caleb had indicated. He was the younger of the two, and Phoebe couldn't help but wonder what they were doing in the park at night, and whether their parents knew where they were. As she watched, the boy with the photo in his hand muttered something to his friend.

"Do you know him?" Phoebe asked the boy, trying to keep her voice as friendly as she could.

"I think I might have seen him in Kronen Park a couple of times," the youth said. "With a girl. I can't be absolutely sure, and I don't know him. I remember her more than I remember him"

"Thank you," Phoebe said before switching to English.

"Caleb, is Kronen Park one of Natasha's locations? Do you remember?" She nodded at the boy. "He thinks he might have seen Mikhail there."

"I'm not sure, but we should go there anyway. Is it far away?"

Phoebe asked the boy and he gave her detailed directions to the other park, but they included footpaths and she realized he would not have driven there

"We can find it," she replied to Caleb. Then she nodded at the bottles in his hand. "Are you going to thank them?"

Caleb reached out his hand and gave each of the boys a miniature.

"Spa-see-ba," he said slowly. She grinned at his attempt to speak Russian, as did the two boys. *Thank you*.

They turned and started walking back to the parking lot where they had left the van.

"You want to go there tonight, Caleb?" Phoebe asked him. "It's getting late." She saw him smiling at her in the orange glow of the street lamps. His face was animated, and she knew what his reply would be before he spoke.

"No time like the present, Phoebe."

CHAPTER 104

S tepan walked to the rear of the room, watching as Daniel got to his feet to give the briefing to the rest of the troops. The young soldier waited until Stepan was seated before clearing his throat. Stepan looked at the backs of the heads of the twenty or so soldiers in front of him. They were sitting on chairs laid out in neat lines, all facing forward, with their weapons leaning against their legs. All the men were motionless and staring at Daniel, no doubt cognizant of their superior sitting at the back of the room.

"Okay," Daniel said, looking at Stepan. Stepan lifted his hand and moved it up in the air a couple of times to indicate the soldier needed to speak up. "Okay," Daniel said again, this time receiving a thumbs up from Stepan. "Let's confirm callsigns. Fire team alpha?" Stepan saw five hands being raised in the air. "Fire team bravo?"

When Daniel had confirmed all four fire teams, he turned his attention to a large piece of paper pinned to an easel. On the paper was a crude map with a rectangle and several drawings of what looked like clouds to Stepan.

Between the clouds were a couple of zig-zag lines and some oval shapes. Daniel picked up an extendable baton and pulled it out to its full extent.

"This cabin here is their main headquarters," the soldier said, resting the end of the baton on the rectangle on the paper. "There are woods here, here, and here." Each of these was highlighted with a tap on one of the clouds. "Trenches here and here." The baton rested on the zig-zag lines briefly before coming to rest on the ovals. "Tented accommodation is here. Any questions so far?"

Stepan smiled at Daniel's technique, although calling the ramshackle cabin he had seen on the drone footage a main headquarters was a bit of a stretch. He watched as Daniel leaned the baton against the easel and picked up a sharpie. He used it to draw an arrow from the top of the paper to one of the clouds, writing the letter A next to the arrowhead. Then he drew another arrow, this time to another cloud and with the letter B.

"Fire teams alpha and bravo will advance to these positions." The letters C and D were drawn at the top of the paper. "Charlie and delta fire teams will remain in position here to provide support." Daniel leaned in to the easel and drew a cross over the rectangle denoting the cabin. "The signal to commence the assault will be an RPG into the main headquarters. Fire team alpha will then provide immediate covering fire from a static position while fire team bravo assaults the tented accommodation." Daniel used the baton to tap on the oval shapes again before using the sharpie to draw some more arrows with the arrowheads covering the tents. "Yes, you?"

Stepan looked to see one of the soldiers in the audience had his hand raised.

"Which fire team is commencing the assault with the

RPG?" the soldier asked. There were a few heads nodding in agreement. Daniel looked directly at Stepan as he responded.

"That will be our commanding officer. He will be collocated with fire team alpha." Daniel then returned his attention to the drawing. "Fire teams charlie and delta will monitor for any fighters attempting to flee. If seen, they are to be followed and neutralized, but clear firing lines must be observed at all times."

Stepan watched as Daniel then launched into a question and answer session. He posed a question, paused, and then pointed at a soldier in the audience to answer.

"What is the signal to commence the assault?" Daniel said, letting his eyes rove around the room before they landed on a soldier in the front row. "You."

"The RPG into the cabin," the soldier responded.

"What comes after that?" Daniel pointed the baton at a soldier in the middle of the room. "You."

"Fire team bravo assaults the tented accommodation."

Stepan let the briefing continue, pleased with what he was seeing. Daniel had performed well, and the soldiers in the room appeared to be responding well to him. Stepan looked at his watch. It was almost ten in the evening, and dawn was a few moments before seven the next day. With travel time, the men could get a full night's sleep before the attack. It was a simple assault on a group of untrained men who would be asleep, but it would send an important message to any Belarusian who was thinking about taking up arms against them.

They would be found, and they would be killed, no matter who they were.

CHAPTER 105

In contrast to the previous park they had been in which had a few groups of people hanging around, Caleb could see no one in this one. It was much smaller, and it had only taken he and Phoebe a few moments to circle the small lake in the center.

"We should have brought some bread," Phoebe said. She had her arm linked through his as they walked.

"What for?" Caleb asked.

"For the ducks."

"I can't see any ducks."

"That's because we didn't bring any bread." Phoebe sighed and pointed at a small bench that overlooked the lake. "Can we sit down? I'm exhausted. It's been a long day."

"Sure," Caleb said, changing direction and walking toward the bench. Phoebe was right, it had been a long day. But a productive one, with Anton now being treated in a well-equipped and well-staffed hospital. When they had spoken to the doctor in charge of his care at the intensive care unit, she had been quietly optimistic.

"He's got a long way to go," she had said, "but I think

he'll pull through. He'll need more surgery on that leg though." Caleb had seen the doctor and Phoebe exchange a look at that point in the conversation, and Caleb had wondered if they had already spoken about Anton's wounds, perhaps while he had been in the restroom.

"We'll sit for a few moments," Caleb said as they approached the bench. "Then we'll head to the hotel."

"Sounds good to me," Phoebe replied. She sat down with an exaggerated sigh. "My feet are killing me."

"We could start here tomorrow morning, maybe?" Caleb said as he sat next to her. "I can see why Mikhail might come here. It's very peaceful."

"Where do you think he's gone, Caleb?" Phoebe asked.

"I think he's gone to fight," Caleb replied after a short pause. "Or at least, to try to."

"Why do you think that? He's only a child."

"He's a young man who's lost someone close to him to an enemy his father was fighting." Caleb paused again. "It's what I would have done."

Phoebe said nothing in reply, and the two of them sat in a comfortable silence for a few moments.

"Is the man upstairs telling you anything?" Phoebe asked. He turned to see she was smiling.

"That's not quite how it works, Phoebe," Caleb replied, also smiling. "It's not like I can call him or anything like that."

"Isn't that what prayer is, though?"

"In a sense, I guess," Caleb said. "Although it can feel like a one way conversation at times."

"Maybe he could send you a sign?" Phoebe asked, still smiling.

"What sort of sign?" Caleb put his hands out in front of him and waved his fingers at the lake. "Nope. Nothing."

"What were you doing that for?"

"To see if I could get the lake to part like the Red Sea."

"Oh, I remember that from Sunday School. Wasn't there a burning bush as well?" Phoebe yawned as she said this.

"Different bit of the Old Testament, but it still had Moses in it." Caleb waggled his fingers again, this time at a small bush. "Sorry, nothing there either."

"Maybe He's annoyed with you," Phoebe said.

"What for?" Caleb asked.

"Lying with a woman," she replied, a faint smile on her face.

"He could well be," Caleb replied, "but I have committed many worse sins than that."

"But have you repented for them?" Phoebe asked. "Have you been forgiven your trespasses?"

"Hey," Caleb said. "I'm the preacher here, not you."

Phoebe laughed and adjusted her position on the bench so she was sitting closer to him. In response, he put his arm around her shoulder. They sat there for a few moments, Caleb appreciating the fact Phoebe was seemingly content to just sit with him.

"Can I confess something?" Phoebe said eventually, her voice quiet but playful.

"I'm not a priest, Phoebe," Caleb replied with a smile. "I don't really do confession, but try me anyway."

"I quite like it when you trespass against me."

Caleb chuckled at her comment, wondering if she understood the true meaning of trespass in a Biblical sense. It wasn't the time or the place for that discussion, though.

He extracted his arm from around her shoulders and got to his feet.

"Come on," he said, "let's go back to the hotel and get some sleep. We can come back here tomorrow." He reached down and took Phoebe's hands, pulling her to her feet. She sighed as she linked her arm back through his.

As they approached the parking lot where the van was parked, a gentle breeze blew across the park's grass. It picked up a piece of paper trash which fluttered toward them. As it approached, Caleb put a foot out to stop it. There was a trash can in the parking lot where he could put it. He stooped to pick up the paper, realizing as he did so that there was some Cyrillic writing on it underneath a picture of a woman in a red dress with what looked like a phone number beneath that.

Caleb showed Phoebe the piece of paper.

"What does this say, Phoebe?"

CHAPTER 106

Vincuk was just on the verge of sleep when he heard Yuri's phone ringing on the other side of the cabin. It wasn't Yuri's standard ringtone, though.

"For God's sake, Yuri," Vincuk muttered. "Can't you shut that thing up? I'm trying to sleep here." He heard Yuri rustling in his bed and a few seconds later, the phone stopped ringing.

"Hello?" Yuri said, causing Vincuk to swear under his breath. He'd meant for Yuri to turn the phone off, not to answer it. There was a pause for a couple of seconds before Yuri spoke again.

"No, no women," he said. Vincuk looked across the cabin and saw he had ended the call and put the phone back down.

"Who was that?" Vincuk asked.

"Some Russian woman," Yuri replied, turning over in his bed. "I don't know. Just go to sleep, old man."

Vincuk thought about responding to the insult but, at the same time, Yuri had a point. Vincuk smiled to himself as he too turned back onto his side, only to be disturbed a moment later by Yuri's phone ringing again. As Yuri picked up the handset, Vincuk reached over the bed and picked up one of his shoes, flinging it across the room but missing Yuri by some distance.

"I said no women," Yuri said as he answered the call. Vincuk could see he had his finger over the screen, ready to disconnect the call when whoever was on the other end of the line said something that got Yuri's attention.

"What?" he said. "Say that again?"

Vincuk sat up in his bed, suddenly curious. He asked Yuri what had been said, but his second in command just held up a hand to silence him. Vincuk watched as Yuri listened intently, a deep frown appearing on his face as he did so.

"How do you know him?" Yuri said with a look in Vincuk's direction. Then he went back to listening.

Vincuk swung his legs off the bed and sat on the edge, reaching out for his cigarettes. He lit one and then flicked the pack over to Yuri, who didn't even seem to notice.

"I will call you back. This number?" Yuri said. After a brief pause, Yuri ended the call. He reached for the cigarettes and tapped the carton.

"Vincuk," Yuri said as he placed the cigarette between his lips and lit it. "We have a problem."

"What is it?" Vincuk asked, now fully awake. Yuri rarely said they had a problem. Issues, difficulties, or complications, sure. But rarely problems.

"Mikhail," Yuri said. "He's only fourteen."

"Shit, you're kidding," Vincuk replied. "He said he was eighteen. He looks eighteen, for God's sake. Who was that on the phone?"

"A woman called Phoebe," Yuri replied, struggling to

pronounce the unfamiliar name. "She says she's a friend of his parents."

"She was Russian?"

"She spoke with a Russian accent, but another accent as well." Yuri inhaled and puffed out a cloud of smoke a few seconds later. "Not Belarusian, that's for sure. There was a man with her. I could hear him in the background, speaking in English."

"Shit," Vincuk replied. "He's going to have to go. I won't be responsible for a child." He saw Yuri looking at him with a frown.

"He's the size of a grown man, Vincuk. You're not his father."

"I said, I won't be responsible for a child," Vincuk replied, fixing Yuri with a stare to make it clear this wasn't a topic for negotiation. "It doesn't matter how big he is. He's a child. He'll have to go."

"But what of the attack tomorrow afternoon?"

"What of it?"

"He's the only one who can shoot the Dragunov."

"That doesn't matter," Vincuk replied. "There'll be a man in one of the other squads who can, or I can shoot it myself."

"Which would be fine if it was a barn door we were attacking."

"He'll have to go, Yuri, and that's the end of it."

"Okay, okay," Yuri replied in resignation.

"We can take him to a village tomorrow. Halitsa has a small church. Call the woman back and tell her Mikhail will be there tomorrow at noon. Ruslan can take him on the motorcycle and be back with plenty of time to spare."

Vincuk finished his cigarette as Yuri made the call.

Then, now wide awake, he retrieved his shoe from where he had thrown it at Yuri and put it on with the other one.

"Need a pee," Vincuk said, prompting Yuri to laugh. "What's so funny?"

"I said you were an old man," Yuri replied. "Your bladder's shrunk along with your brain."

CHAPTER 107

Phoebe laced her fingers behind her head and tried to make herself comfortable in the bed without waking Caleb. He was snoring softly beside her like a small child. Every few moments, he would make a noise of some sort and she wondered if he was dreaming. Phoebe had looked at her phone around an hour ago to see it was two in the morning, but despite their long day, she was far from tired, at least mentally.

The exhaustion she had felt in the park had disappeared when she had called the number on the poster and located Mikhail, and Caleb trespassing against her when they got back to the hotel hadn't had the same soporific effect that it seemed to have had on him. Their love making had been quite different from before. The frantic nature of their previous times together had been replaced by something more languid and measured, perhaps even comfortable. But that was exactly what Phoebe had wanted at the time, so perhaps that was what Caleb had picked up on. It had been no less enjoyable given the change in nature, but different nonetheless.

With Caleb snoring beside her, Phoebe thought about Anton and wondered how he was getting on. He would be asleep in the medically induced coma for the next day or so, of course, but how was he doing physically? Were the antibiotics working yet? Phoebe knew as a doctor how his body should be reacting to the treatment, but she was finding it difficult to see him as just a patient. It was if he was more to her than that. She considered for a moment getting up and calling the hospital to speak to one of the nurses to see if he was okay, but she decided against it.

Phoebe was looking forward to meeting Mikhail later that day. The man she had spoken to on the phone had sounded surprised when she had told him about Natasha's son's real age. When he had called back to arrange the meeting they had planned, he had told her that Mikhail had told them he was eighteen and they had no reason to disbelieve the boy. He was almost apologetic. Caleb had been right. It had been Mikhail who had called the same number on the poster she had called, wanting to do his bit. Wanting to fight like his father. She smiled as she imagined Anton, awake and sitting up in his hospital bed, being reunited with Natasha and Mikhail. They still had to try to get them back to England, which wasn't going to be easy, but they could cross that bridge when they got to it.

She tried to fix the image of the happy family in her head, hoping that perhaps it would help her drift off to sleep. A moment later, though, there was a noise outside the hotel room. It started almost like a low wail, which gradually increased in both pitch and volume until it was so loud she couldn't even hear herself think. Caleb jerked in the bed, sitting bolt upright with a look of surprise on his face. He listened to the wailing for a few seconds as the pitch started to lower and the look of surprise faded.

"What is it, Caleb?" Phoebe asked, instinctively scared, but she wasn't sure why.

"It's the air raid sirens," Caleb replied, lying back down on the bed. Phoebe could feel her heart rate increase instantly at the confirmation of what she had been thinking.

"What do we do?" she said, almost shouting over the top of the noise. She looked frantically around the room. Her clothes were in several different locations and it would take her a moment to gather them all.

"Nothing," Caleb replied as he closed his eyes. "We'll just wait."

"Caleb, for fuck's sake," Phoebe said, shaking his shoulder. His eyes flicked back open and he looked at her, his calm expression not doing anything to allay her fear. "What do we do?"

"Phoebe, there's nothing we can do," he replied. "There's no shelter in the hotel. If the room had a bath, we could get into that, but there's only a shower. So we just wait. At some point, the all clear will sound and then we can go back to sleep."

"But there could be bombs, or shells, or whatever they're called?"

"There could be, yes." He reached out and took her hand. "But there probably won't be and, even if there are, the chances of them landing on us are tiny."

"But they have to land somewhere." Phoebe was on the verge of tears. At any second, a shell could come through the ceiling of their hotel room and vaporize them both. "Just like you have to be somewhere, so do they."

"Phoebe, He chooses where we are. Just as He chooses where the shells or bombs are. All I can do is hope that He makes sure both locations aren't the same place."

"Seriously, that's your plan? Believe in your invisible friend?"

If Caleb was offended by Phoebe's comment, he didn't show it. He just nodded his head in response as the noise of the sirens started to fade. They had done their job, which was to inject terror into the hearts of everyone who heard them. She knew she was being irrational, that the sirens were just inanimate objects, but this wasn't something she'd ever experienced before. The sirens ended on a low wail and cut out, leaving behind a silence that was, in Phoebe's mind, even more deafening.

Phoebe put her hands to her face, not knowing what to do. Then Caleb sat back up and put his arms around her, pulling her back down so she was lying beside him.

"We just wait, Caleb?" Phoebe said in a whisper, her cheek against Caleb's. "We just lie here and wait, knowing that we could die at any moment?" She felt his arms tighten around her.

"We just wait, Phoebe," Caleb replied, also whispering. "We just wait."

CHAPTER 108

Caleb lay on the bed, holding Phoebe tightly to him. He didn't have to be touching her to know she was terrified. He could almost smell the fear coming from her in waves, but her being so scared was understandable. She was, after all, a civilian.

The air raid sirens, when they had sounded a few moments before, had surprised Caleb. They sounded different to the ones he was used to, but at the same time, they sounded the same. Back in the old days, his reaction would have been to hit the floor, put his helmet and body armor on, and make his way to the nearest bunker or building with a hardened roof. But they were in a hotel room in Belarus. He had no helmet or body armor, and there was no bunker or hardened roofs.

"Mors Ab Alto," Caleb muttered under his breath. It wasn't a quote from the Bible, though. It was Latin for *Death from Above*, the motto of the 7th Bomb Wing from Dyess Air Force Base back home in Texas, and was exactly what Phoebe was so scared of. Caleb remembered watching the B-1B Lancer sweep wing heavy bombers known as Bones taking off from the base, their cruciform tails distinctive against the blue sky. He had heard they had a range of over seven thousand miles, putting most of America's enemies well within their range. But people had been scared of death from above for far longer than the B-1B Lancers had been flying.

Caleb listened, waiting to hear the incoming crump of shell fire, but other than the occasional engine noise from the road close to the hotel, there was nothing. He wondered briefly if the air raid sirens sounding was an attempt by the Belarusian authorities to scare the population into submission, but he doubted it. Once the novelty of the sirens sounding had worn off, people generally just ignored them and went about their business. It was as if they knew there was little point in doing anything else. If death was to come from above, it would come.

He remembered a friend in Afghanistan who had left his bunker for a smoke and to read a letter from his girlfriend. A Chinese 107mm rocket, fired into the base by insurgents in the low foothills surrounding the area, had landed only a few yards from where the soldier had been sitting. Apparently, they had been finding bits of him for days following the attack.

"Are you okay, Phoebe?" Caleb asked in a low voice.

"No," she replied, her voice muffled. "No, I am not okay. This is horrendous." There was little he could say to that, so he remained silent for a few moments.

"This time tomorrow, Phoebe, we'll be back in that hotel in Poland," he said eventually. "We'll pick up Mikhail from the village, scoot back across the border with you working your magic on the guards like before, and reunite him with his parents."

"Uh huh," Phoebe replied. "All we need to do is live that long."

Caleb took a deep breath but said nothing else. He could have told Phoebe that from what he had seen on the news, shelling was not very common in this conflict. He could have told her that depending on their air defense systems, the sirens could have been triggered by a flock of birds. He could have told her that the chances were the air raid sirens had sounded across the entire country. But he knew she would not really hear what he was saying, so he remained silent.

They lay in the darkness for what seemed like hours, but was in reality only around thirty minutes. At one point, there was a sudden bang from close by which made Phoebe jump, but it was only a car backfiring on the road. Then the mournful wail started back up. This time, instead of undulating, it rose to a single pitch and stayed there.

"That's the all clear," Caleb said over the noise of the siren. "We can relax now, Phoebe." She disentangled herself from him and sat up, for once not covering herself as she did so. Caleb saw her cheeks were streaked with tears.

"Relax?" she said, her incredulity obvious. "How can we relax?"

CHAPTER 109

Working as quietly as he could, Stepan used his combat knife to slice open the seal of the cardboard box in front of him. He lifted out a blue tube, the booster which would propel the warhead that Daniel was holding for him. Stepan screwed the booster onto the end of the olive green warhead, tightening it as hard as he could. The last thing he wanted was the booster going in one direction and the warhead going in another.

When he was satisfied it was as tight as it could be, he slid the assembled artillery into the front end of the RPG launcher, lining it up with the trigger mechanism. The grenade on the end had a point initiating, base-detonating piezoelectric fuze which would explode on impact with something. Which in this case was the cabin around three hundred meters in front of them, barely visible in the early dawn light.

"Are the fire teams in position?" Stepan whispered to Daniel, who was packing the cardboard box away. There were other grenades and boosters in the box, but they would only be using one. If everything went to plan, and Stepan had no reason to think it wouldn't, they would only need one. Besides, in the time it would take Stepan to change position and reload the RPG, the firefight would be over.

"Yes, they are all in position," Daniel whispered back. Stepan peered through the trees they were hidden in. He could barely make out the other members of fire team alpha in the gloom. It wasn't helped by the camouflage paint they had smeared on their faces. The five men were all crouched down in the undergrowth, their weapons pointed in the direction of the campsite. Stepan put his thumb up and received four thumbs in return. Then he pointed at his watch and raised both hands in the air, fingers and thumbs splayed. Ten minutes.

"Okay, get into position, Daniel," Stepan whispered. "We just need a bit more light and we'll attack. You ready?"

"Born ready, boss," Daniel replied with a grin. Despite Daniel's cliche, Stepan returned the grin and turned his attention to the cabin. This was going to be fun.

IT WAS SLIGHTLY LONGER than ten minutes until they had the light Stepan wanted. Fifteen, perhaps twenty minutes later, the sky had lightened to the point the cabin could be clearly made out. Stepan could see the window, which was where he wanted to put the rocket. His intent was for it to go through the window, which he knew wouldn't trigger the impact fuse, and strike the opposite wall of the cabin before exploding. That way, the explosion would be inside the building, not against the wall of it.

Stepan looked over at Daniel to make sure he was watching. When Daniel raised his thumb, Stepan got himself into a kneeling position and raised the launcher to his shoulder. The sight was a basic one with a soft cushioning ring around the eyepiece, but it lacked the forehead guard that later ones had. Stepan looked through the sight at the numbered grid. He estimated the height of the cabin to be just over two meters, meaning the window was around a meter and a half above the ground. Using the vertical numbers on the grid, he lined up the crosshairs to account for the height and distance. Then he took a deep breath to steady the weapon and gently pulled the trigger.

The whoosh, when it came, was much louder than Stepan remembered. The launcher kicked back against his shoulder painfully, and the top of the sight rammed into his forehead just above his aiming eye. Stepan ignored the pain as he watched the smoke trail in front of him. Less than two seconds later, the rocket slammed through the window and exploded. To Stepan's delight, it took the roof off the building and blew the door out, which cartwheeled across the ground. The roof hadn't even come back down onto what was left of the cabin when Stepan heard the bark of rapid small arms fire. He could hear screaming above the noise of the weapons, but he knew it was his men charging forward into battle, just as soldiers had always done.

Stepan threw the empty launcher to the ground and ran through the trees in a parallel direction to the campsite. Although he doubted anyone would have seen, the flash and smoke trail from the firing of the RPG would instantly identify his position, and he wasn't taking any chances. As he ran, he pulled his own AK-12 assault rifle slung on his back into position and selected the two-round burst mode. He could hear that both fire teams alpha and bravo were using full auto as instructed.

With smoke and now flames billowing from what remained of the cabin, Stepan burst out of the trees and started running toward fire team bravo. As he approached, he saw they were strafing the small tents which were now tattered with bullet holes and barely standing. Daniel's fire team were shooting into the cabin, just as instructed, but there was not much left for them to shoot at.

"Cease fire!" Stepan shouted. "Cease fire!"

The silence as the men stopped shooting was a welcome relief. The only sound was the crackling of the wood from the cabin as flames consumed it. Stepan looked at his men. They had done well.

Stepan grinned. He had been right.

That was fun.

CHAPTER 110

Natasha wrapped her hands around the mug, grateful for the warmth from the tea inside, and stared out through the kitchen window. The garden beyond was calm and a light mist was rising from the grass. She knew it would soon be burned away by the sun, but she enjoyed the view while it lasted.

"Good morning." Natasha turned to see Heidi at the kitchen door. She was wearing long-sleeved pajamas and, despite the hour of day, looked fresh.

"Morning, Heidi," Natasha replied. "Sorry about the early start. Can I make you some tea?"

"That would be lovely," Heidi said with a smile. "Thank you."

"Can I make one for Lawrence as well?"

"He's left already," Heidi replied. "Had to be in London for an early meeting."

Natasha busied herself with the kettle as Heidi sat at the kitchen table. She'd not heard Heidi's husband leave even though she didn't think she'd slept much the previous night, but at the same time, she was relieved he wasn't there. She wanted to speak to Heidi before leaving, and had planned to have the conversation in the car, but this would be much better.

"There you go," Natasha said a moment later, placing a mug of tea down in front of Heidi. She sat opposite her at the table. "Heidi," she said. "I wanted to thank you for all that you've done for me."

"I've hardly done anything for you," Heidi replied with a smile.

"You have," Natasha said. "More than you know. Perhaps there's something I can do for you?" She saw a look of confusion on Heidi's face.

"There's nothing you need to do for me."

"I could help you, perhaps?"

"Help me with what?" Heidi's look of confusion deepened.

"How long has it been going on?"

"I'm sorry, Natasha, you've lost me." Heidi attempted a laugh, but Natasha knew it wasn't genuine.

"Lawrence," Natasha said, looking directly at her. "How long has he been beating you?"

Heidi didn't reply at first, which was all the confirmation Natasha needed. It had been exactly the same with Ilja and her husband. Her now ex-husband.

"Lawrence doesn't beat me," Heidi replied, her voice almost a whisper.

"Then why do you always wear long sleeves, even in your pajamas? It's almost summer. And the compulsive cleaning before he comes back?"

Natasha remained silent as she watched Heidi thinking. Her brow was furrowed and Natasha sympathized with her, even if she couldn't really empathize with her. Although Natasha knew only too well what it was like to be a victim of male violence, her experience had been a different one. Heidi would be thinking about whether she should talk to Natasha about it. Ilja had been through the same struggle, and Natasha hoped that Heidi's response would be the same as her sister's was.

"He just gets so angry sometimes," Heidi said eventually as she fiddled with the sleeves of her pajama top. "He doesn't mean to."

"That's what my sister said." Natasha reached out and took Heidi's hands in hers. "It doesn't have to be this way, Heidi. Does anyone else know?"

"No," Heidi replied, shaking her head. "I don't really have anyone to talk to. Not anymore."

"Heidi, I am coming back. I don't know when, but I will be coming back." Natasha knew there was little she could do for Heidi other than let her know that someone else knew what she was going through. Someone who would be able to help her. "You're not alone."

"Can we not talk about this please, Natasha?" Heidi looked at her, all her confidence gone.

"I didn't want to leave for Poland without telling you that I know, Heidi," Natasha replied. "All I want you to know is that you're not alone. Perhaps we can talk properly when I come back?"

Heidi remained silent for a moment before nodding her head.

"Yes," she whispered. "Yes, I think I'd like that."

CHAPTER 111

The sound of the cabin exploding made Mikhail jump so much he almost dropped the Dragunov. Next to him, Vincuk rested a hand on his forearm as the firing started. A few seconds later, Mikhail heard small bits of debris, presumably from the cabin, landing around them on the forest floor.

"Wait," Vincuk said, his voice low. "Not yet." Next to Vincuk, Mikhail could see Ruslan with his rifle in his hands, crouched in what looked to be a very uncomfortable position. They were lying in the trenches they had dug to observe for the drone, having been woken in the middle of the night by Yuri.

"We're relocating to the outer trenches," Yuri had said as Mikhail had shaken the sleep from his head. "If the People's Army attack the camp, it'll be at dawn."

Mikhail and the others had crept to the outer trenches, passing the ones closer to the camp as they did so. They moved in silence, crawling into the shallower trenches and pulling branches over the top of their heads. Mikhail, Ruslan, and Vincuk were in this trench, while Yuri, Dmitry and Grigor were in the other. Then they had lain there for at least two hours, awake but exhausted, as they waited for the dawn. Sure enough, about thirty minutes before the sky started to lighten, a group of armed men had moved past them. It had been a few nerve wracking moments as they passed by, with all of them knowing that if their location was discovered, all hell would break loose. It would only have taken one of the enemy soldiers to step on the branches covering the trenches, or to hear something, and they would have lost the element of surprise.

He watched as Vincuk, moving slowly, moved one of the branches covering them and raised his head above the parapet. Then he looked back at Mikhail and Ruslan and gestured for them to do the same thing. Mikhail shifted his position and got to his knees, still trying to be quiet although the noise of gunfire was all pervasive in the trees. When he raised his head and looked over the top of the trench, he could see two groups of men silhouetted in the light from the flames that were consuming what was left of their cabin.

"Two teams," Vincuk said to both of them. He pointed at the group closest to them who were currently destroying their tents with automatic fire. Mikhail's mouth dried up at the sight. Only a short time before, they had all been fast asleep under the canvas that was now hanging in ribbons from the tent frames. "Ruslan, you and I will take the team closest to us on the left. There are five of them. You see them all?" Mikhail saw Ruslan nodding in response. "Yuri and the others will take the other team."

"What do I do?" Mikhail asked, realizing that Vincuk had excluded him from his instructions.

"You, young man, will stay here," Vincuk replied.

"But I don't want to stay here," Mikhail said, trying not to sound petulant. "I want to fight." He watched as Vincuk turned around and pointed at the ground behind him. There was a grassy area of three hundred meters which sloped up toward a tree line.

"Mikhail, I need you facing this way," Vincuk said. "If they have reinforcements, they'll come from that direction. You have the scope and the sniper rifle. If you see anyone coming, just holler."

Mikhail nodded, pleased to have something to do. But at the same time, it seemed to him that Vincuk was excluding him from the fight for some reason.

"Cease fire!" a male voice rang out from the campsite. "Cease fire!"

Mikhail saw Vincuk turn and rest his rifle on the parapet of the trench. Beside him, Ruslan did the same thing.

"On three," Vincuk said. "One, two, three!"

Even though Mikhail was expecting the noise, the bark of the automatic fire still made him jump.

CHAPTER 112

Acting more on a soldier's instinct than anything else, Stepan threw himself to the ground when he heard the first bursts of fire from behind him. Next to him, one of his soldiers stiffened before dropping in a heap, his rifle clattering to the ground beside him. Stepan glanced at the man. He was dead, probably before he'd even hit the ground.

"What the fuck?" Stepan shouted, momentarily confused. His head darted from side to side as he looked for cover while, all around him, he could hear the zinging noise of rounds flashing past. They were being attacked, but from the direction they had just come.

He leopard crawled a few feet toward one of the defensive trenches the resistance had constructed. Just as he was about to roll into it, another one of his soldiers also started crawling toward his position.

"Return fire, damn you!" Stepan screamed. The soldier paused and looked at him for a second. Then Stepan saw the young man's tunic puffing several times as rounds slammed into him. He fell to the ground, his eyes still fixed on Stepan's.

Stepan rolled into the trench as bullets showered small clods of earth into the air. He crawled to the end of the trench before raising his head above the edge to try to see what was going on. In the few brief seconds he was able to look, all he could see was flashes of light from muzzles fifty meters away from them. Stepan didn't understand. They had traversed that ground, and there had been nothing there. Stepan opened his mouth to shout some more instructions when he felt a white hot pain in the side of his head. He fell to the floor of the trench with a gasp. Had he been hit?

He raised his hand to the side of his head where the pain was increasing. When he pulled it away, he could see it was covered in blood. But he was still alive, so the wound couldn't be that bad, could it?

"Shit, shit, shit," Stepan said as his hands scrabbled for his trouser pocket where there was a field dressing. His fingers shook badly as he tore open the packaging, but he was able to wrap the bandage around his head. Stepan didn't know if the dressing in the bandage was against the wound, but he didn't care. Around him, the gunfire had lessened but continued, sporadic bursts echoing around the forest. Somewhere, a man was screaming in pain.

"Mama!" the soldier shouted. "Mama!"

Stepan had an unwanted flashback to his basic training where one of the instructors had told him that, when wounded, men wanted three things, all beginning with the letter *M*. Their mothers, a medic, and some morphine. Usually in that order. Suddenly, the screaming stopped as another burst of automatic fire rang out.

He needed to move. Stepan didn't know how many men

he had left, if any. There had been no return fire from his squad, and the fire they were under was relentless. Although he was in a trench, he was still exposed. The resistance had dug this trench, so they would know where it was. Also, at least one of the attackers knew he was in it. The one who had creased his head with a bullet. He knew that the other two fire teams would react to the gunfire, but as they did so, he would be in their line of fire. He had no option but to move.

Stepan moved to the end of the trench that was the furthest away from the gunfire. Then, bracing himself for incoming fire, he put his hands on the edge and pulled himself out of it. Staying as low to the ground as he could, he ran across the forest floor, fully expecting to be shot at any moment. But although the gunfire was continuing behind him, it didn't appear to be aimed in his direction.

He had covered around fifty meters when he saw the dark outline of another trench in the floor of the forest. Stepan changed his direction to aim for it, grateful to find a safe location where he could wait for the arrival of the other fire teams. He could let them deal with their assailants and then emerge, victorious.

As he approached the trench, Stepan crouched down lower still, sliding over the edge and into the darkness. He realized two things as he landed in the trench. The first was that it was deeper than the other one he had hidden in. The second was that the bottom was full of knee deep sludge. As the stench rose up around him, Stepan swore. He might be able to emerge from his location victorious, but he wouldn't be smelling of roses.

CHAPTER 113

Mikhail squinted down the scope of the Dragunov rifle. Had he seen something moving in the tree line? He moved the sniper rifle slowly from left to right, and then back again. As he swept the trees, he stopped and focused on one particular area. There had been movement. A few seconds later, he saw some men in black fatigues emerge from in between the tree trunks. They were moving slowly, almost uncertainly. He waited until they were ten yards in front of the tree line.

"If you see anyone, just holler," Mikhail said between clenched teeth as he pulled the trigger.

The soldier in the front of the line of men dropped to his knees as a puff of red mist emerged from his mid-thigh. Around him, almost moving as one, the rest of the group all threw themselves onto their stomachs. Mikhail moved the scope again to see another group of men close to a different line of trees. They were all kneeling, rifles pointing in his direction, but Mikhail thought he was far enough away to be safe. He loosed off another round, this time catching one of the second group in the shoulder, spinning him round before landing him hard on his backside.

Mikhail returned his attention to the first group of soldiers. He could see two of them trying to drag their wounded comrade back to the relative safety of the forest, and Mikhail hovered the reticule of his scope over one of them. His finger tightened on the trigger, but he eased the pressure a couple of seconds later. They were trying to help a wounded soldier, and he wasn't about to shoot them while they were doing that. Instead, he focused on one of the other men who was half hiding behind a trunk. Mikhail put a round into the trunk a couple of feet above his head and laughed as he saw the soldier scrabbling to get into better cover.

Behind him, the shooting had died away and he could hear footsteps approaching. He maintained his watch on the soldiers, all of whom had now reached the tree lines they had emerged from, as Vincuk slid into the trench next to him.

"I told you to shout, not shoot," Vincuk said, his anger obvious.

"Why?" Mikhail replied. "Look. Their so called reinforcements are running away like the cowards they are."

"It was an order, Mikhail," Vincuk spat back. "You should have followed it."

"I'm not a child, Vincuk," Mikhail replied.

"Yes, Mikhail," Vincuk said, his voice softening. "You are a child. I know how old you are."

"I'm eighteen, I told you that."

"You're fourteen."

Mikhail looked at Vincuk feeling like a child with his hand caught in the cookie jar. The older man's expression was kind but hardened at the same time, and Mikhail instinctively knew the game was up. He suddenly felt stupid holding the sniper rifle, so he placed it on the lip of the trench.

"How do you know?" he asked Vincuk. "Who told you?"

"A friend of your mother," Vincuk replied. "She has sent some people to come and get you. You'll be taken to Halitsa later this morning. Your war is over." Mikhail saw Vincuk looking at the ground between them and the trees that the People's Army had melted back into. "But it has ended well."

CHAPTER 114

Caleb looked down at Phoebe who was finally fast asleep with a sheet wrapped around her. She had one hand close to her face, almost as if she were sucking her thumb. He moved quietly, not wanting to disturb her, and got dressed. Caleb was hungry, and needed coffee. Unlike the hotel back in Poland, there was no kettle in the room.

He left the hotel room and made his way to the reception desk where a middle aged man was sitting, staring at a television. He was wearing a uniform of sorts, a plain turquoise shirt with the hotel logo embroidered over one side of his chest. As Caleb approached, he realized he was younger than he'd first thought, and was probably about the same age as he was. Caleb glanced at the television screen to see it was showing a ruined building with several people picking through the wreckage. The man behind the desk noticed Caleb and said something to him in Russian.

"Do you speak English?" Caleb asked hopefully. The man looked at him balefully for a few seconds.

"Of course," he replied in a thick accent. "You are with the World Health Organization?"

"Um, yes," Caleb said. "Yes, we are."

"There were some kids messing about near your van this morning," the receptionist replied, "but I chased them away."

"Thank you. I appreciate that."

"You're welcome." The man returned his attention to the television screen.

"Hey, do you know where we can get some coffee? Maybe some breakfast?"

The receptionist sighed as he looked at his watch.

"The kitchen's not open until nine," he said. "That's if the chef bothers to turn up." Then he said something in Russian which Caleb assumed to be a swear word from the way he said it. "There's a diner half a mile down the road that opens at eight. I'd go there if I were you. At least the food will be hot."

"Okay, thank you. How about some coffee?"

"Sure," the receptionist replied, pointing at the television. "After the news."

"What's happening?" Caleb asked. The man looked at him with a frown, and Caleb wondered if he'd understood the question. "On the news?"

"More shelling," the receptionist replied with a sigh. "More people dead."

"Was that during the air raid last night?"

"Yes. Another apartment block. Near Lida this time."

Caleb thought about the hospital they had visited the previous day and remembered the medical team who had worked on Anton. He closed his eyes and offered a quick prayer for their safety, although it was a little late for that.

Fifteen minutes later, having watched the rest of the

news with the receptionist even though all Caleb could do was watch the pictures, Caleb was walking back to the room with two cups of what smelled like very strong coffee in his hands. When he reached the door, he tapped it with his foot.

"Room service," he called out. A moment later, Phoebe opened the door, the sheet wrapped around her. She looked disheveled and tired, but still beautiful in Caleb's opinion.

"Is that coffee?" she said, looking at the cups in his hands and smiling. "My prayers have been answered."

Caleb walked into the room, nodding at the sheet as he did so. "You look pretty good in a robe," he said as he placed Phoebe's cup down on a small table. "Do you fancy some breakfast? There's a diner down the road, apparently."

"I might get dressed first, Caleb," Phoebe replied. "I'm not sure the world is ready to see me wrapped in a sheet. Or wearing a robe, for that matter."

"Don't see why not," Caleb said with a grin. "It works for me."

He walked to the window and looked out, sipping his coffee. Caleb could hear rustling behind him as Phoebe got dressed, and he wanted to turn and watch her, but he didn't. Instead, he ran through their itinerary for the day. It was around 0830 now. They could take a leisurely breakfast and leave around 0930. That was plenty of time to get to Halitsa and find the church.

The receptionist had used the word diner when he'd told him where to get some food. Perhaps it was a proper diner? One with a black and white checkered floor, red tables and chairs, and a row of bar stools next to the counter? Caleb smiled as he imagined being served biscuits and gravy by a waitress who called everyone *honey*.

"What are you grinning at?" Phoebe asked as she walked to join him at the window.

"Just thinking of home," Caleb replied, his smile fading. "Or at least a version of it."

"When were you last in Texas?"

"A long time ago."

"I'd love to go there. It looks amazing in the films." Phoebe had a faraway expression on her face as she said this.

"Like I said, Phoebe, there's different versions of it."

"We could get married in Las Vegas," Phoebe said.

"That's not in Texas."

"I know," she said, slapping his arm playfully. "But we could get the Greyhound there and get married in a drive through by a man dressed as Elvis." Phoebe started laughing.

"I did go to Vegas once," Caleb replied, joining in with her laughter.

"What happened?"

"I played some roulette and put everything I owned on red," he said. "Came up black. Lost everything including the shirt on my back." Caleb started laughing. "That's when I started wearing a robe."

CHAPTER 115

Phoebe had to suppress a laugh as she watched Caleb pushing his potato pancake around the plate. It was draniki, a simple fried dish with only a few ingredients. Flour, potatoes, milk, onions and some seasoning. On the side of his plate was a large dollop of sour cream which Caleb was doing his best to avoid, and a small side dish with some fruit.

"I thought Americans like pancakes?" she said as she forked a large piece of draniki on her own plate, putting it in her mouth after dipping it in the cream.

"Ours are a bit different," Caleb replied, slicing a tiny sliver of pancake and holding it up in the air. "I can't see these going together with maple syrup."

"It could have been worse," Phoebe said with a grin. "They've got khaladnik on the menu as well."

"What's that?" Caleb put the slice of pancake in his mouth and chewed it thoughtfully.

"Cold beet soup," she replied, and his grimace made her laugh. She pointed her fork at the sour cream on Caleb's plate. "Served with some of that and a sprinkle of chopped dill. It's bright pink and often served with a hard-boiled egg on the top."

"Sounds delightful," Caleb said, slicing a larger piece of pancake and loading it onto his fork. "This isn't too bad, though."

The diner they were in was a lot nicer on the inside than it looked from the parking lot. It was spotlessly clean with mis-matched tables and chairs, a small but functional serving area, and a flat screen television on the wall that was muted, but Phoebe could see it was playing the news. They had sat near a window that looked out onto the parking lot where their van was the only vehicle. When Caleb had told her about the boys the receptionist had seen, she'd been concerned but when they examined the van, they had seen nothing untoward. The diner's menu ran to six pages, with the waitress telling Phoebe that they could rustle up whatever they wanted from it. But as they were the only customers, it wasn't as if they were rushed off their feet.

"Anything interesting on the news?" he asked her. Phoebe watched the screen for a few moments. Although it was on mute, subtitles were running across the bottom of the picture.

"Growing international condemnation over alleged war crimes in Belarus," she translated for Caleb. "World leaders are meeting in Geneva for some sort of summit, as if it will make a difference."

"Ah, I see."

"I added the last bit about it making a difference. That's not what they're saying on the television."

"Yeah, I figured that."

They finished their breakfasts, Caleb eating almost all of the pancakes but leaving the sour cream and fruit untouched, and Phoebe waved at the waitress to indicate she wanted to pay. The waitress, a silver-haired woman who looked to be in her late sixties, waved back before disappearing into the kitchen. When she came out a moment later, she had two packages wrapped in greaseproof paper in her hands. She approached the table, giving Phoebe a gummy smile, and placed them on the table.

"We've made you some sandwiches," the waitress said to Phoebe in Russian. "For your lunch."

"Oh, thank you very much," Phoebe replied. "How much do we owe you?"

"No, these are on the house. So is the breakfast." The woman nodded at the van in the lot outside. "You people are doing God's work. The least we can do is feed you while you're doing it."

Phoebe instantly felt bad. They didn't work for the World Health Organization, so didn't deserve to receive this hospitality. "Please, let me pay you," she said, looking at the woman.

"Does he speak Russian?" the waitress asked, prompting a laugh from Phoebe.

"He can say thank you in a really poor American accent," Phoebe replied.

"He is your husband?" Phoebe laughed again.

"No, he's not."

"But you're together. I have the sight. I can tell." Phoebe watched as the waitress folded her arms over her ample bosom and looked at Caleb who was smiling and frowning at the same time. The waitress nodded her head and turned back to look at Phoebe. What she said next made Phoebe's cheeks color. "You should keep him. He is a good man."

The waitress turned and walked back to the kitchen. Phoebe reached into her purse and took out more than enough rubles to cover their breakfast and the sandwiches.

She wasn't paying for them, she reasoned. She was leaving a tip.

"What did she just say to you then?" Caleb asked as they got to their feet.

"Nothing important, Caleb," Phoebe replied with a sigh. "Nothing important."

CHAPTER 116

Stepan slammed his fist on the steering wheel in frustration. He couldn't believe what had happened back at the resistance campsite. Both fire teams involved in the attack were lost, and of the two teams who were supposed to be providing support, two of the men were injured. One of them was screaming in the back of the truck. And to add insult to injury, Stepan's legs were caked in shit.

"Shut him up, for God's sake!" Stepan shouted.

"But he's been shot," one of the soldiers replied. "He's bleeding badly."

"I don't care. Just shut him up."

Stepan knew that when he got back to their base, there would be hell to pay. Not only was he going to have to explain what had happened to his commanders, but the rest of the men there would forever know him as the man who had led his men into battle and seen them annihilated in the process.

He didn't understand what had just happened. How had the resistance known they were coming? Stepan wanted to blame it on a collaborator, a spy in their ranks, but apart from he and the command chain, none of the men had known the location of the camp. He thought for a few seconds, trying to drown out the screaming that was still ear-piercing. Had Daniel known about the attack? Stepan couldn't remember whether he had or not, but as he had been the first to die, he doubted it. If there had been a collaborator, he would have made sure that he survived.

"For fuck's sake, give him some morphine or something," Stepan shouted, punching the steering wheel again. His was the first in a convoy of two trucks, and he should have put the wounded man in the second, so he didn't have to listen to him squealing like a pig.

"He's already had some."

"Well, give him some more."

"But he's had both his auto-injectors." The soldier who had replied sounded frantic, and Stepan realized that the screaming wasn't only getting to him, but to all of them. That was why a wounded man was more challenging than a dead one. Dead men couldn't scream and bleed.

"Then give him yours!" Stepan shouted. All the soldiers carried two morphine auto-injectors for their own personal use. The rule was that the men never used them on another soldier. If they did, and then they too were wounded, they would have no pain relief. "That's an order, soldier!"

Twenty minutes later, Stepan and what was left of his soldiers pulled into the compound that served as their base. Of the twenty men who had left with him before dawn, only ten remained. He pulled in next to the disused meat packing plant that served as their makeshift hospital and parked the van. Then, leaving the soldiers to unload the trucks and take the wounded inside, he made his way to the ablutions to shower the shit and piss from his legs and get a fresh uniform and some clean boots.

When he got to the operations room, finally rid of the awful smell from the trench he had hidden in, one of the other squad leaders was there with a small group of his men. As he walked in, they all looked at him, the disdain obvious on their faces. Bad news obviously travelled fast.

"What are you looking at?" Stepan barked at them. The other squad leader, a dour faced man called Konstantin, waved his men to the door and waited for them to leave. He was older than Stepan, wearing the same black fatigues, and had a lot more experience that was evident in his deeply lined face. He was looking at Stepan with an inscrutable expression.

"What happened?" Konstantin said finally. His voice was deep and graveled.

"We were ambushed," Stepan replied, his voice still shaking with anger. "Somehow, they knew we were coming. It should have been a textbook attack, but it all went to shit."

"You lost ten men."

"Yes," Stepan said, "and two wounded." Too late, he realized it hadn't been a question.

"No such thing as a textbook attack," Konstantin replied, reaching into his pocket, and retrieving a hip flask. He handed it to Stepan who took it gratefully. "I was in Sudan a few years ago. We were providing security for a gold convoy going to the Central African Republic when we got hit. Lost a lot more than ten men that day."

Stepan sipped from the flask, relishing the burning sensation in his throat. It was vodka of some sort, but not a cheap one.

"Thank you," he said as he handed the flask back. "I needed that."

"You've called it in?" Konstantin asked as he slid the hip flask away. Stepan nodded. It had been the first thing he had done once he had found the remaining fire teams and got to a safe location. "What did HQ say?"

"Nothing. They want me to take a new squad out on patrol later."

"That's good. They can't be too pissed with you if that's the case."

Stepan saw that Konstantin was looking at his boots. He glanced down at them himself, realizing that for a man who had just come from the battlefield, they were remarkably clean.

"So, it's true, then?" Konstantin asked, a smile spreading on his face.

"What's true?"

"That you hid in a deep trench latrine to escape the resistance?"

Stepan said nothing. He could feel the color rising to his cheeks, so he turned away from the older soldier.

"I'd crush that rumor pretty quick if I were you," Konstantin said as Stepan walked toward the door. "You know the men have already got a new nickname for you?"

"Thanks for the advice," Stepan mumbled, walking away before he could find out what it was.

CHAPTER 117

Phoebe looked at the GPS to see they only had a couple of miles to go until they reached Halitsa, the village where they were to meet Mikhail. The area they were driving through was remote and mostly uninhabited, and the only traffic they had seen in the last twenty minutes had been an old farmer with an equally ancient horse that was pulling a cart laden with produce.

"They have hard lives, some of these people," she had remarked to Caleb as they had passed the rickety cart.

"They do, and that's without people killing them," Caleb had replied. "I can sense the evil in the air. It's like ozone before a thunderstorm."

Phoebe had looked at him, wondering if he was pulling her leg, but his face was deadly serious.

"Not far now," Phoebe said, and she saw Caleb glancing at the GPS. "I wonder what Mikhail will be like."

"I think it will depend on what he's seen. What he's done," Caleb replied. "He'll probably play the tough guy and try to hide the fact he's still a kid."

"What were you like when you were a teenager?" Phoebe asked him.

"At that age it was all about how far I could get my hand up a girl's skirt before she slapped me in the face," Caleb replied with a grin.

"At fourteen?"

"It was Texas. Not much else to do in the town where I come from. How about you?"

Phoebe thought for a moment before replying. All she could really remember about that age was acne, braces, and unrequited love.

"I'm not really sure," she said, "but I know if you'd tried to put your hand up my skirt at that age, I wouldn't have slapped you in the face." Phoebe saw Caleb's smile broaden, but it faded as she continued. "I'd have punched you in the testicles."

"Classy," Caleb mumbled, but there was still the hint of a smile on his face.

They turned a bend in the road and saw a couple of houses a few hundred yards away. Phoebe was just thinking that this must be the outskirts of Halitsa when she realized there was something not quite right about them. They were houses, but at the same time, they weren't. It wasn't until they got closer that she realized they were burned out shells.

"Look at that," Phoebe whispered, slowing the van as they approached. "Isn't that awful?" Caleb just nodded his head but said nothing. Phoebe brought the van to a stop and stared through the windshield at the blackened remains. In front of one of the houses was a child's swing attached to a tree branch. As they watched, it moved slightly in the wind and Phoebe wondered what had happened to the child or children who had played on it. "This was someone's home."

"Perhaps one day, it will be again," Caleb replied. "When this is all over, maybe they can return."

If they're still alive, Phoebe thought, but she said nothing.

She pulled away and they drove on in silence for a few moments.

"Why would anyone do that, Caleb?" she asked a moment later. "I don't understand. I mean, soldiers fighting other soldiers I kind of get. But why burn someone's house down?"

"Like I said earlier, Phoebe, evil is in the air. I can smell it. His messengers are close by. I can smell their foul odor."

"Whose messengers?"

Phoebe looked across at Caleb to see his eyes were hard and fixed on the road ahead.

"Satan's messengers," he replied, his voice low. "They truly walk among us."

CHAPTER 118

Vincuk hid a smile as he watched Grigor and Dmitry saying goodbye to Mikhail. He and Yuri were too far away to hear what the men were saying to the boy, but he could see Mikhail nodding in response. The youngster held out his hand to Grigor for him to shake, but Grigor ignored the offered hand and pulled Mikhail into a bear hug.

"He'll be missed, the boy," Yuri said. "He should be a soldier when he's older. I think he would make a good one."

"I think he already has," Vincuk replied. "He's certainly seen and done a lot for a boy of his age." Earlier that morning, in an attempt to protect Mikhail, Vincuk had asked him to wait in the truck while they cleared up the campsite, but the next time he looked, he saw Mikhail and Ruslan carrying one of the dead People's Army soldiers. They had placed the body in a trench, almost deferentially, before Grigor started covering the corpse with earth. They were taking a risk by remaining in the area, but Vincuk wasn't going to leave a dead soldier on the battlefield without so much as a thin covering of earth. The dead soldiers might have been on the opposing side, but no soldier deserved that indignity.

"You think he'll be okay?" Yuri said, watching as it was Dmitry's turn to hug Mikhail. A few yards behind Vincuk and Yuri, Ruslan was waiting on the motorcycle.

"He told me he'd lost someone close to him," Vincuk replied, lighting a cigarette. "If he considers the man who he killed to be his avenging act, then perhaps." Beside him, Yuri nodded his head.

"An eye for an eye, a tooth for a tooth," Yuri said. "It's from the Bible."

"Really?" Vincuk replied in a disinterested tone. "Something like that, yes."

His goodbyes complete, Mikhail started to walk toward where Vincuk and Yuri were standing. Vincuk saw Mikhail's hand come up to his face briefly, and he wondered if the boy was crying. After everything they had been through, Vincuk wouldn't have blamed him. He had seen men with much less combat experience than Mikhail in tears when they had to say goodbye to their brothers in arms. It wasn't something most civilians would ever understand, which was one of the reasons soldiers did what soldiers did. So they wouldn't have to.

"I guess this is goodbye," Yuri said as Mikhail approached. He held out his hand, which then turned into another bear hug. Vincuk saw Yuri slap Mikhail on the back as he whispered something in his ear. Vincuk didn't hear what it was, nor did he try to. It was between Yuri and Mikhail. The boy nodded his head but didn't reply. Then he turned to face Vincuk.

"Mikhail," Vincuk said, looking at him with a smile. "Mikhail. If I were to ever have a son—"

"You'd have to find a woman first, Vincuk, and hope

there's still lead in the pencil," Yuri said, interrupting him but forcing a laugh from Mikhail. Vincuk turned to Yuri, grinning.

"You and me both, Yuri. You and me both. Now, hush." He returned his attention to Mikhail. "As I was saying, if I were to ever have a son, I hope he would become half the man you are. Then I would be proud." Mikhail didn't reply, but just nodded his head. "When all this is over, you come and find me. We will drink vodka together, and not the cheap stuff Yuri here tries to pass off as the real thing."

"Maybe go out and find some women?" Mikhail replied, smiling. Vincuk turned to Yuri and both men laughed.

"Maybe, maybe," Vincuk replied, putting his hands on Mikhail's shoulders. "Although I think the odds are stacked in your favor."

As he pulled Mikhail into a bear hug, Vincuk whispered in his ear.

"You are a hero of Belarus, my boy." He squeezed him like the son he didn't have. "Never forget that. A true hero of Belarus." Vincuk released Mikhail and made a flapping motion with his hands. "Now go, back to school. Tell your teachers Yuri and I say hello."

"Especially the female ones," Yuri added, slapping Vincuk on the back and laughing loudly.

Mikhail took a couple of steps toward Ruslan, who stirred into life, kicking the motorcycle from its stand and putting his hand on the ignition key. Before Ruslan started the engine, Mikhail turned to look at Vincuk and Yuri.

"Thank you," he said with a single nod of his head. "Thank you, and good luck."

CHAPTER 119

Caleb had felt his mood darkening over the last couple of miles. He had tried to hide it from Phoebe, but he could tell from the way she was looking over at him more frequently that she had picked up on it. When he had told her earlier that he could smell evil in the air, he'd not been joking. There was a darkness descending on him that he had no control over, nor did he wish to. He knew what it meant, and it confirmed that at that moment in time, he was exactly where he was supposed to be. Where He wanted him to be.

Through the van windshield, Caleb could see more houses coming into view. Unlike the ones they had passed previously, these were intact houses with people still living in them. Laundry was being hung out in gardens, children were playing on undamaged playthings, and dogs were being walked. Caleb saw a bearded man, holding his side in obvious discomfort, walking a small Dachshund but from the excited look on the dog's face, it wasn't clear who was walking who. A few hundred yards ahead of them, a small cross was visible on top of a plain looking building with white-washed walls. Other than the cross, there was nothing to advertise it as a church, but it was right where the GPS said it was supposed to be.

"There," Phoebe said, pointing at the church. "That's it." Unlike many of the churches Caleb had seen in the area, some with ornate domed roofs and elaborate turrets, this one was very underwhelming. But Caleb had no time for churches anyway, even when his mood was brighter. The church was located on one side of a small square, which he assumed was the center of the village.

He said nothing as Phoebe pulled up to the building, parking the van in the small lot in front of it.

"Caleb?" she said as she turned off the engine. "What's the matter? Have I said something wrong?"

"No, Phoebe, not at all," he replied, forcing a smile onto his face. "I just get like this sometimes. I'm sorry."

"Okay, as long as I've not upset you."

"Back at the diner, the waitress said something to you as we were leaving," Caleb said. "What did she say?" He looked at her and saw a brief flash of what looked like disappointment on her face before it was replaced by a smile.

"She said you were a good man," Phoebe replied. Caleb knew she wasn't telling him everything the woman had said, but he let it go.

"Well, she would be an excellent judge of character," Caleb said. "Even though I wasn't able to say a single word to her."

"She said she had the sight."

"Perhaps she does," Caleb replied, wondering if the waitress could also feel the same darkness he could feel.

The clock on the dashboard told them it was just before

twelve, so they had timed their journey well. Caleb got out
of the van to stretch his legs, followed by Phoebe. He turned
in a slow circle to look around the square. In addition to the
church, there was a single story shop with pale orange walls
and elaborate white grilles, badly in need of painting,
covering the windows. Opposite was what Caleb thought
was a garage of some sort and the last side of the square was
occupied by houses. All of them were in a state of disrepair
and echoed the general ambience of the village, which was
of a place that was exhausted.

Caleb heard an engine approaching and turned to see
two young men, both helmet-less, riding into the square on
an old motorcycle.

"That's him," Phoebe said, her excitement obvious.
"That's Mikhail on the back."

They both watched as the motorcycle came to a halt
right outside the church. The young man on the back of the
motorcycle climbed off and looked around, his eyes resting
on Caleb and Phoebe. He stood there, uncertain what to do,
as the rider of the motorcycle said something to him. Then
they shook hands and Mikhail's friend rode off in the direction he had come from.

Caleb let Phoebe approach the young man left behind,
reasoning that he would prefer to hear someone speaking
his own language. But when Phoebe greeted him, it was in
English.

"I'm guessing you're Mikhail," she said, smiling at the
young man. As he got closer, Caleb recognized him from the
photographs that Natasha had shown him. He looked a lot
older than fourteen. Not just physically, but he had the eyes
of a much older man.

"I am Mikhail, yes. Who are you?" Mikhail replied in
almost perfect English. His mother had taught him well.

"I am Phoebe, and this is Caleb," Phoebe said, still smiling. "We've been looking for you."

"Well," Mikhail replied with a look that indicated to Caleb that he didn't entirely trust them. "Now you've found me."

CHAPTER 120

Natasha picked up the last of her belongings from the plastic tray that had carried them through the security check and, double checking to make sure she had her boarding card, walked to where large television screens were hanging from the airport roof. It took her a couple of seconds to locate her flight, but when she did all it told her to do was to wait. The gate for her flight wasn't yet allocated.

With a sigh, Natasha made her way to a spare seat in one of the waiting areas. She could do with some sleep, but wouldn't get the opportunity. Perhaps she could grab some on the airplane if it wasn't too busy? She had hoped she might be able to sleep a little in the car, but despite saying she hadn't wanted to talk, Heidi hadn't stopped. It was as if the floodgates had been opened and in no time at all, Natasha had almost her entire life story. It had been a happy one, right up to the point she said the fateful words *I do*. Then it had spiraled downhill from there, in a story that was depressingly similar to Natasha's sister's story.

Natasha sat down, tempted to ease her shoes off, but

she decided against it. The airport wasn't as busy as the train station had been, and she walked past a couple of armed policemen, one of whom smiled at her. At first, she had thought it was an appreciative smile, but she soon realized he was smiling at everyone, presumably to reassure them they were safe in his hands. She rummaged in her handbag for the charger to her phone when she noticed there was a small charging point built into the seat. Although she had only made one call to the hospital since it was charged up, she didn't want the battery draining. Natasha smiled as she remembered the conversation with the nurse earlier that morning. Anton was doing well, she had said. He still had a breathing tube but they might be taking it out later, and he seemed to be responding well to the treatment already.

She plugged the phone in and it vibrated in her hand. At first, she thought it was because it was charging, but as the phone started ringing, she realized it was an incoming call. Natasha looked at the screen before swiping it and a few seconds later, Phoebe's face appeared. She looked to be outside from the blue sky and off-white building with a cross on top of it behind her.

"Natasha?" Phoebe said. She had a broad grin on her face as she spoke. "I've got someone here who wants to talk to you." The image on the screen wobbled slightly and a familiar face came into view.

"Mikhail!" Natasha screamed, causing several people around her to jump in alarm. The armed policemen both whirled around, their eyes alert, but when they soon relaxed when they saw it was just someone on the phone. "Mikhail," Natasha said again, this time in a voice that was as close to normal as she could manage. "My God, you're okay."

"Of course I'm okay, Mother," Mikhail replied, using the

voice he used when he thought she was over reacting about something. Natasha knew she was, but she didn't care.

"Oh, my God," Natasha said, pressing her hand to her sternum where her heart was beating like a bird's. "Oh, my God. Where have you been?"

"I've been staying with some friends, Mother," he replied, smiling the way he did when he was lying.

"I've been so worried," Natasha said. "What happened to your phone?"

"I dropped it in the toilet." Mikhail was still lying, but it didn't matter to her. All that mattered was that he was okay. "I had it in a bowl of rice, but it's as dead as a Dodo."

Natasha laughed, remembering taking Mikhail to the National History Museum in Minsk when he was about six or seven. There had been the skeleton of a Dodo there that he'd become obsessed with, more so when he'd discovered they were extinct.

"Have you heard from Dad?" Mikhail asked. Natasha paused before replying. Did Mikhail know Anton had been injured? She didn't really want to tell Mikhail that over the phone.

"Yes," she replied. "I spoke to him last night."

"Oh, cool," Mikhail replied. "He's back, then?"

"He will be," Natasha said, thinking about when they would all be together again and grinning. "I need to let Ilja know you're okay."

"Phoebe's boyfriend is doing that now," Mikhail replied. "The weird man with no hair?"

"That's Caleb," Natasha said, smiling at the way Mikhail had described him. So, she'd been right about Phoebe and Caleb, after all. "Can I speak to Phoebe quickly?"

"Sure," Mikhail replied, waving at the camera. "I'll see you soon."

"I'll see you soon." Natasha blinked back a tear. "I love you, Mikhail."

"Yeah, love you too."

The screen adjusted again, and Phoebe's face reappeared. She was still smiling.

"Everything okay?" Phoebe asked.

"It is now, Phoebe," Natasha replied. "I can't thank you both enough."

"We're leaving for the border now," Phoebe said. "What time's your flight?"

"In about forty minutes. I'll get a cab from Warsaw to the hospital." Natasha knew she could barely afford the luxury, but nothing was going to stop her seeing her family reunited. "Can you tell Mikhail about Anton for me? I spoke to the nurses there. He's doing really well."

"Of course I will, and that's great news. I think we'll be there before you."

"Will you thank Caleb for me as well?"

"You can thank him yourself, Natasha," Phoebe replied. Natasha saw her glance at someone off camera and grin. "Although, to be honest, he's not done much."

CHAPTER 121

Mikhail sat in the center seat of the van, promising Phoebe that he wouldn't mention to his mother that it had three seats. The strange American Caleb was in the driver's seat, and Phoebe was on the other side of Mikhail. There wasn't much room in the front of the van, and Phoebe's thigh was pressed against his. He could feel the warmth of it through his trousers and although he didn't mind it at all, he had a feeling that Caleb might. The village of Halitsa was some miles behind them, and they were driving through a wooded area that reminded him of the road to their campsite.

When Caleb had introduced himself back in the village, he had shaken Mikhail's hand. But it wasn't like any other handshake Mikhail had ever had. He'd noticed a strange sensation in his fingertips and when he looked at Caleb, the man had his eyes closed and his lips were moving ever so slightly. Then he had opened them and let go of Mikhail's hand, a strange smile on his face that was somehow reassuring and frightening at the same time.

Before they had left Halitsa, Mikhail had watched Phoebe enter an address in Poland into the GPS. When he realized it was a hospital that she had entered, he had asked her why.

"Your father's been injured, Mikhail," Phoebe had replied, "but he's okay. We managed to get him over the border into a Polish hospital. We're going to meet your mother there."

"Injured how?"

"He's hurt his leg, but he's doing really well."

Mikhail had nodded at the news. Knowing his father, he'd probably fallen over after slightly too much vodka. It wouldn't have been the first time.

"Have they re-opened the borders then?" Mikhail had asked Phoebe.

"Not yet," she had told him, "but we've found a way across."

In front of them, the road was becoming narrower and the trees on either side were almost touching in the middle.

"We didn't come this way, did we?" Caleb said. Mikhail looked at him to see a frown on his forehead.

"I don't think so," Phoebe replied. She leaned across Mikhail to check the screen of the GPS, and the pressure on Mikhail's leg increased. "I definitely put the right address in. But we came here from Hrodna, not from Poland." To Mikhail's relief, she sat back in her original position. "That'll be why it's a different route."

"Do you follow soccer, Mikhail?" Caleb asked. Phoebe groaned but was smiling at the same time.

"Of course I do," he replied. "Dinamo Minsk all the way."

"Who's your favorite player?"

"Got to be Dusan Bakic." To Mikhail's surprise, Caleb

nodded in response. Surely he couldn't know anything about Belarusian soccer?

"Shame you lost Vladislav Lozhkin to FK Turan." Mikhail laughed out loud, partly because Caleb was right, but more because he obviously did know about Belarusian soccer.

"Seriously, Caleb?" Phoebe said, leaning forward and looking at Caleb with an incredulous expression. "You know this how?"

"Dinamo Minsk is my second team," Caleb replied. "When in Rome and all that?" Mikhail saw Caleb grinning broadly as Phoebe started swiping at her phone. He looked down at her lap to see she was checking her browser history. On the screen was the home page for Dinamo Minsk.

"Very good, Caleb," Phoebe said. "Pick the closest big team to Hrodna and do some research."

"Hush, Phoebe," Caleb replied. He was still grinning. "We're bonding."

Mikhail sat back in the seat and smiled. He was beginning to like Caleb a lot.

They drove on in silence for a few moments, the road in front of them remaining narrow. The trees had now started to meet in the middle, giving the impression they were driving through a tunnel. Mikhail had noticed that the van's lights had come on automatically and was about to say something about it when they turned a corner and Caleb started to slow the van.

"Damn," Caleb said.

"What is it?" Phoebe asked, her attention still focused on her phone. Mikhail looked through the windshield and his heart sunk. He knew exactly why Caleb had sworn.

A hundred yards in front of them, parked at an angle across the road, was a white truck. Mikhail looked at Caleb to see him staring at the wing mirror before his eyes returned to the road in front of them.

"Behind us as well," he said. Caleb's voice was low.

"What is?" Phoebe said, finally looking up from her phone. Mikhail saw her jaw drop as she saw what was in front of them.

Caleb brought the van to a halt.

Mikhail knew there wasn't much else he could do when there was a heavy machine gun pointing straight at it.

CHAPTER 122

Stepan looked at the van that had pulled up about fifty meters in front of his checkpoint. As it had started to slow, he had seen the second part of his squad emerge from the trees behind the van, effectively blocking the van from going in either direction. With large trees on either side of the narrow road, it was the ideal point for an impromptu checkpoint, which was exactly why he had chosen it.

He leveled his AK-12, using his thumb to ensure that the double shot mode was selected, and pointed it at the driver of the van. Then he jerked it to the side a couple of times to indicate that he should get out. The man did as instructed, even going so far as to raise his hands in the air without prompting. With a glance over his shoulder to make sure the rest of the squad was covering him, he took a few steps toward the man. As he was doing so, the passenger door opened and two people got out. One of them, to Stepan's delight, was a woman.

Walking slowly, Stepan approached the group, stopping a couple of yards in front of them. The driver was staring at him intently, his gray eyes inscrutable and the sun reflecting off his shaved scalp. He wasn't a local, nor was the woman. That much was obvious from their clothes. The young man with them was aged in his late teens or perhaps early twenties, and he had a slightly Slavic look about him. He had high cheekbones and a long, straight nose and looked angry, rather than scared. By contrast, the woman looked terrified.

Stepan said nothing for a moment, taking his time to examine the strange group. Then he took a couple of steps to one side so he could see the logo on the side of the van which belonged to the World Health Organization. With the nearest village some distance away, he couldn't think why the WHO would be driving down this particular road.

"What's in the van?" Stepan asked the driver. There was no reply. He was just looking at him. To make the point he expected a reply to his question, Stepan raised the weapon a couple of inches.

"Medical supplies," the woman replied. "Not many, as we've dropped most of them off."

"You're Russian?" Stepan asked, still keeping his eyes fixed on the bald man.

"I speak Russian," she said. "My name is Doctor Sokolova." Finally, Stepan turned his attention to the woman. A doctor could be useful. Particularly with two wounded men back at their base.

"And these two?" Stepan asked, pointing his gun at the two men.

"The young one is Mikhail. He is an intern working in our hospital. The man is Doctor Caleb." Then she said something in English which Stepan didn't catch. His English was not too bad, but she had spoken too quickly for him to understand what she had just said. The bald man nodded his head.

Stepan gestured behind him, waving for one of the soldiers to come forward. "Turn around, all of you." The young man did as instructed, but the bald man waited until the woman said something else in English before doing the same. "Zip tie them all," Stepan said to the soldier. "They're coming to the base with us. Search the van, put them in it, and then follow us."

Stepan waited as the soldier secured the wrists of their three captives behind them. Then he walked around until he was standing behind them, the bald man's gray eyes following his every move. Stepan pressed himself up against the female doctor, his pelvis against hers. The action of securing her wrists behind her had caused her chest to be pushed forward, and he slid his hand around her before resting it on her breast.

"Doctor Sokolova," Stepan said as he squeezed lightly. He saw her close her eyes as he did so. "I am very pleased to meet you. We have some medical work for you to do, and then I will thank you in the way that only a man can thank a woman." He pressed his pelvis against her harder, hoping that she could feel his intention through their clothes.

When he moved away, he saw that the driver was still staring at him. A jealous lover, perhaps? His eyes, previously gray, had changed to the point of becoming almost black. His expression remained inscrutable, and Stepan knew he couldn't have understood what he had just said. But with his hands secured behind him, what could he do?

Stepan laughed, staring at the driver as he did so. He took a couple of steps toward the man and grabbed his jaw in his hand, squeezing it tightly. The driver's eyes closed in response. Stepan knew exactly what the man could do when Stepan thanked the doctor.

He could watch.

CHAPTER 123

The moment Caleb heard Phoebe say *I told him you're a doctor*, he understood what her plan was. He nodded in response to show her he understood, and then started to consider his courses of action. The problem was that he was zip tied, had several guns including a heavy machine gun trained on him, and had no idea what the soldier in front of him was saying. Option one —do nothing—was his only viable course of action. But Caleb wasn't fazed by that. He'd been in similar situations before and managed to find a way out. He decided to spend the time observing instead. The best of the courses of action would come later.

The man talking to Phoebe was obviously in charge. It was partly the way he was talking, and partly the way the other soldiers responded to him. The young soldier who had tied their wrists together had been nervous, and the sense Caleb got was that his nerves were not because of the situation, but because of the man doing the talking. None of the soldiers looked to be far out of their teens and, as their boss touched Phoebe's breast, he saw several of them exchanging worried looks. He filed the observation away on the basis it could come in useful.

Caleb watched as the soldier who had tied them up picked his weapon up from the ground where he had put it. He wasn't handling the weapon like an experienced soldier would. Instead of picking it up by the stock and checking the safety was still on, he picked it up like a baseball bat, grabbing it barrel first. Another useful observation.

But it was when the soldier grabbed Caleb's jaw that the real intelligence started to flow. Caleb closed his eyes, concentrating on the touch of the man's skin. A series of images flashed across Caleb's eyelids. A shallow grave, soon to be filled. A woman, screaming in pain and humiliation as someone grunted rhythmically. A pair of the bluest eyes Caleb had ever seen and the life being snuffed from them in a heartbeat. Caleb could smell cordite, fear, and shit. By the time the soldier released Caleb's jaw, his death sentence was signed, sealed, but not yet delivered. But Caleb would deliver it. This man, if you could call him that, was going to die, and it was going to be at Caleb's hand. Or Caleb was going to die trying. Only the man upstairs would know how that was going to play out, and He had looked after Caleb up to that point.

The soldier barked something in Russian, and another couple of the group standing by the machine gun approached. Caleb allowed himself to be led toward the rear of their van, and he stood watching as it was searched. There were only a couple of boxes left in the rear from when Phoebe had locked him inside it to cross the Polish border. That had only been a couple of days before, but it felt like a lifetime ago. The search complete, he, Phoebe, and Mikhail were bundled into the back of the van and the door closed, the click of its lock audible. A few seconds later, they heard the engine starting.

"Caleb, what are we going to do?" Phoebe said as Caleb started wrestling with his zip ties. They were tight, but not as tight as they would have been if he had applied them. When he had placed his hands behind his back, he had clenched his fists and faced his palms down, hoping this would make his wrists bigger and create some room. There was some wiggle room but from the feel of the plastic, the ties were pretty industrial.

"What did he say? The soldier?" Caleb asked her as he turned his wrists so they were facing inward. He tried as hard as he could to slip one of his thumbs out, but there wasn't quite enough room.

"He said he had some medical work for us to do. That was why I told him you were a doctor as well. They'll be less likely to harm us if they think we're both doctors."

Caleb glanced at Phoebe in the dim illumination of the vanity light. There was a logic behind what she had said that he couldn't fault, but at the same time, he wasn't sure their status would make any difference at all.

"That's excellent, Phoebe," Caleb said, trying to reassure her.

"I mean, you've had some medical training, right?" she replied. Caleb could tell she was now trying to reassure herself. "You can pretend to be a doctor."

"Sure," Caleb said, trying to maneuver his thumbs into a different position. "How hard can it be?"

"Those men," Mikhail said in a quiet voice as the van bounced along the road. "They're from the People's Army."

"How do you know, Mikhail?" Phoebe asked him, but it was Caleb who replied.

"Because he was fighting them not long ago," Caleb said,

fixing Mikhail with his eyes. "And unless I'm mistaken, you've killed at least one." He ignored the look of surprise on Mikhail's face. "You might find yourself doing it again. We're not going to get out of this easily."

CHAPTER 124

Phoebe sat back in the van, trying and failing to make herself comfortable. She watched as Caleb continued to wriggle, determined to get himself out of the zip ties, but his struggles appeared to be in vain. Eventually, he gave up, and sat in silence, seemingly deep in thought.

"A spot of divine intervention would be good, Caleb," Phoebe said.

"Don't I know it," Caleb replied before, to her surprise given the circumstances they were in, he smiled. "But at least it's not a Thursday night. I'm sure He's keeping an eye on what's going on."

Beneath them, the road the van was traveling on had appeared to become rougher, and Phoebe wondered if they had turned off the main road. She listened as the automatic transmission shifted itself down a notch. A few moments later, she felt the van slowing down before it stopped. It shifted to one side as someone got out of the front and then the rear door was unlocked and flung open. Bright sunshine streamed into the back of the van, causing her to blink several times. It wasn't as if she could put her hands over her eyes.

"This way," the young soldier standing outside the van said in Russian. Phoebe shuffled to the rear of the van and swung her legs out, looking at the soldier as she did so. He was young. Not as young as Mikhail, but only a few years older. "I'm sorry," he muttered under his breath as she stood.

Phoebe looked around to see a random group of buildings, all badly in need of maintenance. They were in some sort of industrial complex, long abandoned from the look of it. There were a few soldiers milling about, and a small collection of vehicles parked in a straight line close to the largest building.

"This way," the soldier said to her in heavily accented English, gesturing to one of the smaller buildings with his weapon. "Please?" he added when she didn't move.

Phoebe set off in the direction the soldier had pointed with his gun, followed by Caleb and Mikhail. She could hear the soldier who had been in charge back at the checkpoint shouting orders at someone.

"He's your boss?" Phoebe asked quietly as she walked.

"He is now," the soldier replied, a note of reluctance in his voice. "His name's Stepan, but we call him the shit magnet. Is that how you say it in English?"

"Yes, it is. What's your name?" she asked him. She saw Caleb smiling at the nickname.

"Timofei," the young man replied. "Timofei Stasevich."

"I'm Phoebe, Timofei," she said with as much of a smile as she could muster, given the weapon that was pointed in her direction. Then she nodded at Caleb and Mikhail who were walking behind them with another soldier behind them. "That's Caleb and Mikhail. Caleb's the one with no hair." There was the flicker of a smile on the young man's face, but it was gone as soon as it appeared.

Timofei led them into the building. As soon as the door opened, Phoebe smelled the familiar metallic odor of blood. She looked around the room to see a collection of disused fridges, all with their doors open, and some sort of assembly on the ceiling with long rails. When she saw the hooks hanging from the rails, she realized she was not in a hospital, but some sort of slaughter house. Close to the fridges were two tables pushed against each other to form a larger table, and on this table was a soldier lying motionless.

"You, cut her free," a male voice shouted. Phoebe turned to see it was Stepan. He took a couple of strides across the room and stood in front of her as Timofei cut her zip ties. She massaged her wrists once they were free, grateful for the release in pressure on her shoulders from the unnatural position she had been in. "Get their medical supplies from the van and send someone to get the idiot with the hole in his shoulder," Stepan barked at Timofei who disappeared without a word. "Doctor? See to him. He's been shot in the leg." He was pointing at the soldier on the table. "If you can't save him, put him out of his misery."

"Wait," Phoebe called out as Stepan turned away from her. "I can't do this alone. I need someone to help me." She nodded at Caleb. "Can you cut him free as well?"

"No, I don't think so," Stepan replied, wheeling around to face her. He walked over to Caleb and dragged him to the side of the room. Then Phoebe saw he was securing Caleb's arms to a thick pipe on the wall.

"What are you doing?" Phoebe said. "He's a world renowned trauma surgeon."

"I don't trust him," Stepan replied as he checked Caleb's restraints. "I don't like his eyes."

"Cut the intern loose then," Phoebe said, injecting a note of authority into her voice. This might be his base, but if this room was their hospital, then she was in charge. "Do you want me to save your soldier or not?"

Stepan stared at her with hatred in his eyes. "Do as she says," he said to the other soldier who had remained in the room. "But if they try anything, just shoot them."

As the other soldier made his way to where Mikhail was standing, Stepan walked over to Phoebe. When he spoke, he was close enough for her to smell his fetid breath.

"We will have some fun later, you and I, doctor," he said before nodding in the direction of the man on the table. "But if he dies, then so do you."

CHAPTER 125

Mikhail watched as the soldier called Timofei returned to the makeshift hospital, the two boxes from the rear of the van in his arms. He had his rifle slung loosely over his shoulder and Mikhail looked at it, wondering if he could wrestle it from the man. But when he glanced at Caleb, standing by the wall, he shook his head slightly as if he knew what he was thinking.

Timofei upended the boxes onto a table and the contents fell out, some of them spilling to the floor. Mikhail saw Phoebe look at what had just been tipped out. There wasn't much in the boxes. He could see some metal medical instruments, wrapped in some sort of plastic, a few white packages of what looked like bandages, and some boxes of medication.

He saw Phoebe approach the soldier who was lying on the tables. She put her hand on his shoulder and shook him gently, but there was no response. Then her hand slid to his neck, and he saw she was checking his pulse. When Phoebe looked at Mikhail, her expression was serious.

"His pulse is weak and thready," she said. "I think he's going into shock. Get me one of those scalpels." Phoebe was nodding at the medical instruments on the table. Mikhail rifled through them to find a scalpel and he tore open the wrapper as Phoebe was working her way methodically from the wounded soldier's neck to his chest. "Timofei?" she called out. "Is there any oxygen here? Intravenous fluids?" Timofei just shook his head in response.

Mikhail watched as Phoebe exposed the wounded man's chest, observing it carefully for a few seconds. Then her hands moved down to his leg where a large, blood soaked bandage was wrapped around his upper thigh. Mikhail thought back to that morning, when a round from his sniper rifle had torn into a soldier's upper thigh. He felt sick to his core. He had done this.

"How long has this tourniquet been on?" Phoebe asked Timofei as she used the scalpel Mikhail had handed her to slice through the bandage.

"A couple of hours, I guess," the soldier replied with a shrug of his shoulders.

Mikhail felt even more nauseated as Phoebe peeled back the bandage to expose a fist sized ragged hole in the man's thigh, causing the wounded man to moan softly. It was a sticky maw of a hole with yellow tissue and bright red flesh showing, but the skin surrounding the wound was mottled and discolored.

"We need to release the tourniquet," Phoebe said. "Are there any artery forceps in there?" She was nodding at the equipment on the table. "I can see the end of the femoral artery. It needs to be clamped."

"What do they look like?" Mikhail asked her, swallowing a lump of bile back as he looked again at the wound he had caused.

"They're like scissors, but with a clamp between the arms," Phoebe replied. Her hands were covered in the soldier's blood. "Timofei? When I release this tourniquet, it could cause toxins to rush into this man's body. I need to speak to Doctor Caleb. I need his advice, or this man might die."

Mikhail watched as Timofei considered her request. He tightened his grip on his rifle before nodding his head. As Phoebe walked over to Caleb, followed by the muzzle of Timofei's weapon, Mikhail sorted through the equipment on the table. He found what he thought were the forceps Phoebe was referring to. They looked like scissors, but they didn't have blades on the end. Instead, there were flattened edges that looked like pliers. Mikhail unwrapped them and held them up in the air. He waited for a moment for Phoebe to finish speaking with Caleb.

"They're the ones," Phoebe said when she returned to the table the wounded soldier was lying on. She took the forceps from Mikhail, almost dropping them as she did so. He could see her fingers were shaking, but the look on her face was one of pure determination. "Now, I want you to slowly release the tourniquet. Can you do that for me? Just slowly unwind that spindle." Mikhail looked down at the tourniquet to see what Phoebe was referring to. He could see a black piece of plastic, secured in place with a small tab.

"Yes, I think so," Mikhail replied. He grimaced as Phoebe inserted the forceps into the soldier's wound, causing another soft moan. Mikhail heard her apologizing to him.

"Now, Mikhail," Phoebe said, tightening her grip on the forceps.

Mikhail slowly released the spindle, hearing a metallic click from the forceps as he did so.

The next thing Mikhail heard was a thunderous roar

from outside the building as the windows imploded, showering them all with fragments of broken glass.

CHAPTER 126

"Left by fifty meters," Vincuk shouted, his eyes glued to his binoculars. The mortar round had landed far too close to the building he had been watching. Beside him, he saw the mortar team from the Belarusian army adjusting their aim and reloading the mortar. The next round, when it left the mortar tube with a characteristic popping noise, slammed through the roof of the building adjacent to the one he had seen Mikhail and the other prisoners being led into. "Direct hit. Repeat!"

The scene that Vincuk was watching through the binoculars was chaotic. He could see soldiers running between the buildings in total disarray. He heard the distinctive boom of the Dragunov rifle from somewhere behind him, and a soldier fell to his knees before pitching forward onto the ground. There was one soldier, an officer perhaps, who appeared to be trying to coordinate the others. Another boom sounded, and the officer whirled around before falling in a crumpled heap.

Vincuk had been on the ridge overlooking the compound for several hours as the rest of the resistance had slowly moved into position. To his surprise, they had been joined by several groups of soldiers from the Belarusian army, including the mortar team he was currently spotting for. He had been even more surprised when he found out they were joining them officially. The tide for the People's Army was turning, an officer from the Belarusian army had told Vincuk.

"They've been asked to leave," the officer had said. "But they seem reluctant to do so, so we've been asked to encourage them."

In the compound below, the sound of small arms fire started to echo. Vincuk smiled, knowing that somewhere down there were Yuri, Grigor, Dmitry, and Ruslan. This might be their final battle, and he hoped it would be a successful one for them.

"Forward one hundred meters, right by thirty meters!" Vincuk shouted, his attention fixed on one of the white trucks that the People's Army were using. There were several soldiers milling about at the rear, trying to unload weapons. A few seconds later, he saw the truck disappear in a cloud of smoke and, a few seconds after that, the sound of the explosion reached them.

When he had seen the World Health Organization van arriving earlier, Vincuk had been confused. The compound was obviously a military one, so there was no reason for it to be there unless it had been captured. Given what he had seen on the television in other parts of Belarus, and what he himself had witnessed in the villages, he wouldn't have put it past the People's Army to masquerade as health care workers. Then he had watched as three people had been led from the back of the van, their arms tied behind them. One of them was Mikhail who was supposed to be on his way to safety.

A hurried telephone call had ensued with his headquarters. Vincuk had pleaded for the attack on the compound to be brought forward. His senior officers hadn't been convinced and it had been the Belarusian army who had in the end sanctioned the request based on the fact there were hostages there from the World Health Organization. Vincuk had said nothing of Mikhail's role, figuring that given their earlier actions in Belarus, the army was trying to get as much public gratitude as possible. He didn't care about that. All he cared about was trying to keep Mikhail and his companions safe.

"Forward seventy-five meters, left thirty meters!" Vincuk shouted.

The mortar round, while not a direct hit, was close enough to obliterate the machine gun nest that was about to open up on the approaching soldiers.

CHAPTER 127

"**G**et into the fridges!" Caleb shouted at the top of his voice as glass fragments flew across the room. His ears were ringing from the explosion and he knew the others would be, too. He saw Phoebe staring at him, slack jawed, as she tried to comprehend what was going on. It was Mikhail who reacted first, pulling at her arm to get her to move. Stumbling, he dragged her toward the closest fridge as another explosion, this one not as close, shook the building.

That was good, in Caleb's opinion. It meant that someone was probably acting as a fire controller, zeroing in the mortar he had just heard onto its intended target. The fact the second round had been further away meant that they probably weren't the target. But he also knew it could be random fire, and that the next mortar could smash through the thin roof of their own building at any second.

Caleb gripped the scalpel Phoebe had handed him a few moments earlier when she had told Timofei she needed his advice. It was slippery from the wounded soldier's blood, and he almost dropped it as he tried to turn it round to get the blade to where he needed it to be.

The door to the building slammed open, and Stepan came running in. His eyes were wild, and he had a rivulet of blood running down the side of his face. Caleb was disappointed that the injury wasn't more serious, but perhaps he might be able to do something about that. Stepan shouted something in Russian at the two soldiers in the room who left in a hurry and then he turned his attention to Phoebe and Mikhail who were just crossing the threshold of one of the disused fridges. He didn't have his rifle anymore, but he did still have a sidearm in a holster. If Caleb could get to it, he could use it.

Caleb worked as quickly as he could, using the scalpel to saw through the zip ties. He felt the thin blade slice through his flesh as he did so, but paid it no mind. His only focus was on getting his hands free to get that weapon. Stepan shouted something else in Russian at Phoebe and Mikhail and Caleb saw that he was holding something in his hand. It was the pin of a grenade.

"Stepan!" Caleb shouted just as the zip ties securing his wrists snapped. The soldier's head whipped around and he stared as Caleb lurched across the room toward him.

Caleb knew he didn't have time to grab the pistol. As he broke into a shuffling run toward Stepan and closed the distance between the two of them, he flashed his arm out, embedding the scalpel in the soft flesh below Stepan's jaw. Caleb's other hand reached out and grabbed Stepan's shoulder as the scalpel wobbled in his throat, the blade angled slightly upward.

"Just as it is appointed for man to die once," Caleb said through gritted teeth as he pushed the blade of the scalpel toward Stepan's brain stem, "and after that comes judgment." With a final shove, Caleb embedded the scalpel fully into Stepan's neck and closed his eyes. The noise of the battle raging outside the building faded, and all Caleb could hear was the screaming of the demons that were coming to collect Stepan's soul. Then that noise too faded, and Caleb heard something else.

It was the sound of a grenade falling to the floor.

CHAPTER 128

As Stepan's body slumped to the floor, Caleb knew he had three courses of action. He could do nothing, which in this case wasn't an option. If he did nothing, the grenade would explode and kill him. It would almost certainly kill Phoebe and Mikhail as well. Although they were inside a fridge with thick walls, the fragments would enter the metal container through the open door and ricochet around inside it, indiscriminate in what they went through.

His second option was to throw himself on the grenade and absorb as much of the explosion as he could. This was a better option than the first, but he would still die and there was no assurance that Phoebe and Mikhail would survive. There would still be shrapnel, and with this option some of that shrapnel would be parts of Caleb's body. Bone splinters could be just as deadly as metal fragments. It wasn't like in the movies, where the hero saves his friends with a muffled thump as the grenade goes off harmlessly beneath him.

The third option, and the only viable option, was to kick the grenade away as far as he could and hope for the best. It wasn't much of an option, and he would probably still die. Caleb knew the lethal range of a grenade was somewhere between five and twenty meters. He might be able to kick it five meters away, but he certainly couldn't kick it twenty.

Caleb swept out his foot, glancing up at the fridge door as he did so. He needed to kick the grenade to the left as the door to the fridge opened to the right. That way, it would offer some protection to Phoebe and Mikhail. He wanted to say something to Phoebe, but there was no time, and even if there had been, he wasn't sure what to say. What should his last words to her be? His foot connected with the grenade, sending it on its way.

Almost in slow motion, the grenade rolled across the floor, bounding off some glass shards as it did so. In a few seconds, they would be more shrapnel.

Caleb closed his eyes and waited. If this was to be his final seconds on this earth, he wanted them to be peaceful ones, at least in his mind. He wasn't scared of death. Caleb knew it was an inevitability and, like sex and comedy, all about the timing. He smiled, hoping that perhaps the grenade was a dud.

As he felt the concussion wave from the grenade envelop him, and felt the white hot fragments piercing his body, he realized it wasn't.

CHAPTER 129

Phoebe knew she was screaming, but she couldn't hear anything other than a high pitched whistle in her ears. She could see Mikhail was shouting something, but she couldn't hear that either. Had the fridge door caused some of pressure wave as it had been slammed shut by the explosion? She raised her hands to her ears and pulled them away, fully expecting to see blood on her fingers from ruptured eardrums, but there was nothing.

Mikhail had his shoulder against the door of the fridge, and he was trying to open it. The whistle started to fade as she joined him, their combined weight enough to move the buckled metal enough for them to squeeze through. When she stepped through the door and saw Caleb's crumpled body lying a couple of yards away from the door, she ran to him.

"Caleb!" Phoebe screamed, this time just able to hear her own voice above the whining in her head. His clothing was tattered, with numerous ragged patches. As she looked, she could see blood starting to seep through the material. "Caleb!" she screamed again, but there was no response. He was hurt, and badly, but she could see from the rise and fall of his chest that he was alive. The question was how long would that continue?

Phoebe reached out and grabbed his top, ripping it from his chest.

"Mikhail," she shouted as she looked at the wounds on Caleb's chest and abdomen. These weren't ones he would be able to suture himself. She counted at least six, if not more, and God only knew what damage they had caused internally. "Bandages! I need bandages!"

The door to the building opened, and a soldier rushed in. Unlike Timofei and the others, he was wearing a different uniform. She saw him looking around the room until his eyes found Mikhail.

"Mikhail?" the man said. "Is that you?"

"Yuri," Mikhail said, the relief obvious in his voice. "Please, we need help." Phoebe saw the new arrival look down at Caleb's broken body. Then he turned and ran from the room.

"Mikhail, the bandages?" Phoebe said, trying to focus on what she was doing and who she was. A doctor, with a patient who needed her help. The fact the patient was Caleb was irrelevant, but at the same time had never been more important.

Phoebe worked quickly to try to stem the bleeding. She couldn't press too hard on the wounds in case there was shrapnel underneath them. But Caleb didn't need bandages. He needed a hospital.

A moment later, just as Phoebe was trying to wrap a bandage around Caleb's head where there was a jagged wound a couple of inches long, the door opened again and two soldiers ran in. Phoebe saw with relief that they both had red crosses on their arms. One of them was carrying a medical bergen, which he unzipped with practiced ease as the other snapped a pair of nitrile gloves on and started examining Caleb.

Phoebe sat back to let the medics do their work. They were good, working methodically to try to stabilize Caleb. Her bandages were replaced with proper field dressings, and one of the medics had cannulated Caleb and was pushing intravenous fluids into him. She felt a pair of hands on her shoulders and realized that Mikhail had squatted down beside her. He looked at her, his expression almost inconsolable.

"Should we pray for him?" Mikhail asked.

"I think that's probably a good idea," Phoebe replied in a whisper.

CHAPTER 130

TWO WEEKS LATER

C aleb closed the Bible one of the nurses had lent him and sat back in his hospital bed. He ached all over, which the doctors had told him was not just from his wounds but from the peritonitis that the resulting sepsis had caused. He shut his eyes and, after a quick prayer of thanks, thought back over what he had been through, which was all he seemed to be able to do.

He remembered nothing of the explosion, or the subsequent evacuation by the Belarusian army to one of their field hospitals. His first memory was being taken to the operating theater where, he had subsequently heard, he had been operated on for over eight hours, technically dying twice in the process. But it seemed the man upstairs wasn't ready for Caleb's company just yet. Caleb was faintly disappointed that he had no near death experience to report. No tunnel of light, no sense of absolute dissolution, no reunion with those who had passed before him. All he had were memories of coming round after the operation, and the pain he had been in being indescribable.

"How are you feeling today, Caleb?" a male voice said. Caleb opened his eyes to see Yefrem, the doctor who was now responsible for his care, looking down at him with a kind expression. He had a parcel in his hands.

"Not too bad, thank you Doctor Yefrem," Caleb said.

"Are you ready to be discharged?"

"I think so," Caleb replied.

"I have a parcel for you," Yefrem said, placing the package in his hand on Caleb's bedside table. "It's from England."

Caleb looked at the parcel for a few seconds.

"Do you think it's bad of me to ask her not to come" he asked Yefrem.

"No, not at all," the doctor replied. "I spoke with her this morning. She told me that she knew at some point you would ride off into the sunset."

"She said that?" Caleb said with a smile.

"Those were her exact words. She also asked me to tell you that her life is richer for having had you in it, even if only for a short time."

Caleb closed his eyes again. He felt sad, but at the same time, he felt content. When he reopened them, he was alone. He reached for the parcel and unwrapped it. Inside was a small cloth bag and a robe, freshly laundered. He unfolded the robe and a small piece of paper fluttered out. Caleb picked up the paper and read what was written on it.

Genesis, Chapter One, Verses 14-19.

Caleb smiled. The verse was referring to the fourth day of creation, according to the Old Testament. He realized there was something written on the other side, and he flipped the paper over. When he saw what was written on it, his smile broadened.

You told me He has Thursdays off.

JOIN 'TEAM PREACHER'

To receive a complementary e-copy of the companion novella to The Preacher series, you can join 'Team Preacher' now. The novella's called *First Rodeo*, and is a reader exclusive. It's not available in the stores, and never will be.

By joining the team, you'll be the first to hear about new releases, giveaways, competitions, and special bonuses.

Visit *nathanburrows.com/teampreacher* to join.

THE KEEPER

Caleb returns in Book 4 of *The Preacher* series, *The Keeper*, available in early 2024.

In the heart of Rome, an elite team of thieves hatches a daring plan to steal a priceless relic from the Vatican.

Little do they know, they're not the only ones with their sights set on this mysterious artifact.

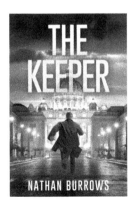

ALSO BY NATHAN BURROWS

The Preacher Series

The Preacher

The Hunter

The Keeper - *Available early 2024*

British Military Thriller Series

Man Down

Incoming Fire

Enemy Within

Man Overboard

Gareth Dawson Series

Blind Justice

Finding Milly

Single Handed

Writing as N.D. Burrows

The Butcher

The Baker

The Candlestick Maker

Milton Keynes UK
Ingram Content Group UK Ltd.
UKHW030956260824
447446UK00005B/389